DYNASTY OF STORMS

Volume I

RISING THUNDER

Book One of the Warrior's Trilogy

by

BRANDON CORNWELL

2nd Edition

Copyright © 2019 Brandon Cornwell

ISBN-13: 9781797635439

To my amazingly supportive family
Thank you for putting up with me
and my boatload of insecurities
during this lengthy (yet fulfilling) process.

This book is for you. I love you all.

<3

Table of Contents

ACKNOWLEDGMENTS

First, I would like to acknowledge my brother, Ray. He was instrumental in the development of this world and the characters in it. Without him as a sounding board, and finally as the artist of the original cover, I never would have gotten this book, the first of many, out of my head and on to paper.

Second, my grandfather Roy. He supported my decision to write when I was a child, and helped me brainstorm the original title. Though the title has changed, I'll never forget sitting in his Jeep after a fishing trip, and discussing ideas on what to name it, instead of the ripped off title I had chosen previously. Thanks, Grampa.

To my wonderfully tolerant friends, putting up with my hassling about beta reading, giving me feedback, so on and so forth while I honed my writing style, you guys were instrumental in the completion of this project. Also, sit tight, I'm going to be hitting you up again. Chris, John, Matthew, Nick, Cristian... there are seriously too many of you to list here. Thanks, guys.

And to my wife. I know I've been a bit of a bear. For stepping up and pushing as hard as you have in your own business, for picking up the slack when I dropped it, and for supporting me in my decision to write for a living, thank you. I love you forever.

THE YEAR OF ERDE

Chapter One

New Flower Moon, Year 4368

It wasn't every day that a king died.

The great hall was filled with warriors, nobles, and priests, each dressed in their finest clothing or ceremonial armor. Brightly polished steel and studded leather glinted from under thick furs. Various family crests adorned breastplates, intricate knotwork tooling steel and leather alike, setting the nobleman apart from the warrior. Each man had his finest weapon at his side, mostly swords and axes. Even the priests had their ceremonial war hammers hanging from their belts.

Elias looked out over the crowd, his eyes fixed on the door that led to his friend's chamber. He was head and shoulders taller than almost everyone in the room, so it was easy for him to see, even in the dim torchlight of the hall. A guard stood on either side of the door, and the crowd kept a respectful distance.

The stiff, embroidered cloth of his dress tunic was uncomfortable. Rolling his shoulders, he tried to move the seams to a place they didn't rub against his skin, but the garment was too well fitted. It had been made for him specifically for this occasion, but that didn't make it any more comfortable. He tugged on the hem, settling the garment against his skin, and let out a long sigh.

Despite the crowd, the hall was rather quiet. There was a feast laid out upon the long table that ran the length of the room and mead filled every cup, but there was none of the banter and rowdy merry-making that normally filled the room. Brynjar had been a noble king, good and just, and his looming passage to the next world sat upon the city of Valtheim like a wet blanket.

The door to the king's chambers opened, and a white-robed priest stepped out. He beckoned to Brynjar's eldest son, Brandt, and disappeared back into the darkened room. Brandt – a tall, richly dressed man in his forties with white streaks in his black hair – stood and followed the priest, closing the door behind them. Brandt was a good man, a strong warrior, and due to be Brynjar's successor. Elias had known him for his entire life; he would make a good king, provided the nobles accepted him as such.

Elias took a slice of roast pork and a roll from the table, and meandered around the room, conversing with some of the men gathered there. Those men that were from Valtheim spoke with him openly, while the men from the surrounding territories were curt or ignored him entirely. In this hall full of men, he was the lone elf; most of the Northerners were not used to the presence of other races in their midst. The north was a very harsh place, and the men that lived there were very harsh men.

The captain of the king's personal guard, a heavyset, gray-haired man named Wilhelm, sat on a bench near the end of one of the tables. He nodded to Elias in greeting. "Good eve to you, Elias."

Elias nodded back. "Good eve to you." He took a seat next to the old warrior. "Has there been any news from Brynjar?"

Wilhelm shook his head. "Nothing you and I haven't heard already. The sickness in his lungs has gotten worse and spread to the rest of his body. He burns now with a fever... he's not likely to see the sun rise." He took a swig from his drinking horn. "It's been a long time coming," he said with a sigh.

Elias nodded, feeling his stomach clench. "Yes... yes it has." Brynjar wasn't the first king he had seen pass. The men of Brynjar's line remained mighty until either a sickness or wound took them in their old age.

His mind turned to the past, remembering when he had been brought to the city at the foot of the great Stromgard mountain, where these Northmen had made their hold. He had been taken on as a ward of Torbjorn, the lord of one of the southern kingdoms. As that man grew old, he was succeeded by his son, who had been a grown man when Elias had arrived, with a small child of his own. That child was Brynjar, who was now on his deathbed. Elias had watched Brynjar grow, had trained with him, attended his wedding, and held his oldest son Brandt on the day of his birth.

The second chieftain, Brynjar's father, was fond of hunting elk when he wasn't busy fighting with rival tribes, uniting the North into what passed for a kingdom. No matter the season, whether they were in rut or not, he could be found hunting the noble beasts with a spear, bow, or lance wherever they traveled along the rivers and valleys.

His passion for hunting proved to be his undoing when he was gored by a particularly large buck. He lingered just long enough to pass on his legacy to Brynjar, now grown to a man with a family of his own. Elias stayed as his friend and confidant, though he was in no way an advisor. Though he was accepted in the city of Valtheim, the Northmen wouldn't have tolerated an elf on the king's council.

Elias was pulled out of his memories when two warriors, their armor covered with bearskin cloaks, pushed their chairs away from the table, leaving half-eaten plates and half drank tankards of ale. He watched them go, his stomach clenching tighter. Every time a king died, his place in the North became uncertain for a time.

Wilhelm's hand on his shoulder brought him back. "Don't worry, lad. You've been a part of the north longer than they have... we'll be sure to remind them of that if their protests become too... visceral."

Elias nodded, and ate his meal in silence, sitting near to the captain.

It seemed like an eternity before the door opened again, and the white-robed priest called Elias's name. The quiet conversation in the hall stopped abruptly as he stood and walked towards the king's chambers. He could feel every eye in the room follow him as he ducked through the door, drawing it closed and shutting out their stifling gaze.

There were a handful of people inside, standing around the great bed upon which the king lay. Eira, slender and lovely even in her old age, stood near Brynjar's hand, holding it in her own. Her silver hair was pulled back into a tight braid, woven through and through with white ribbons, just the way Brynjar liked it. Were it unbound, it would have nearly graced the floor.

On his other side was Brandt, standing next to a scribe. A table was covered in parchments, spread out to let the ink dry; likely the last decrees of the dying king. A second priest, robed in white with a red belt, stood at the foot of the bed, quietly intoning the last rites of the men of the North.

Brynjar slowly lifted his hand, waving the priest away. "There will be time for that when I'm actually dead, godsman. Trust that your time will come soon enough." He dropped his hand, breathing heavily. "Is that Elias I see? Come here, my old friend. My eyes aren't as good as yours anymore."

Elias approached the bed, sitting on the chair that was vacated by the scribe. Even on his deathbed, Brynjar had always been a large man, nearly too tall for his own bed, and even now his barrel chest was like a mountain under the white sheets. Not even the sickness that was taking his life could wither him away entirely.

Elias set his hand gently on top of Brynjar's and smiled slightly. "They never were, your Grace."

Brynjar, turned his head, looking at Elias. "Still as young as you've ever been. Every time I look at you, you make me jealous for the longevity of the elves." He chuckled, which fell away into coughing. "Tell me, is there any elf magic that can bring me back to the vigor of our youth, or cure this ailment of my lungs?"

Elias shook his head. "If there is, my lord, I do not know it."

Brynjar grunted, closing his eyes. "Just as well. Seventy years is a good long time to live in these mountains. I imagine my chair won't be getting any warmer while it waits for my ass to polish it in the afterlife."

Elias gently squeezed the old king's hand, tears suddenly biting at the corner of his eyes. "They will sing songs of your victories until the mountains are ground to dust, Brynjar."

Brynjar coughed again, harder, his large frame wracked by the spasms. Elias set a hand on his shoulder, holding him steady. As his coughing fit subsided, a priest wiped his lips, the cloth coming away stained with blood. Brynjar pushed the cloth away and sank back into the bed, his labored breathing slowing again. He grimaced, shifting his shoulders slightly.

Brandt leaned in, pushing his father's gray-streaked black hair out of his face. "Rest, father. Conserve your strength."

Brynjar scoffed. "Conserve it for what? I'll not make the dawn, you heard the priests. They don't call them last words for nothing." He shook his head. "Kings, princes, warriors, farmers... in the end, we're all ash on the wind."

He pulled his hand away from Elias and gestured towards him. "I called you in here for a reason. You were on my mind as I was putting my affairs in order. The runes had words for you... I was going to tell you on Midsummer's Day, but..." His shallow breath became labored, and he waved a hand at the priest who had called Elias into the room. "Well, you tell him. I don't have the time; I am a very busy man, after all."

The priest stepped forward, towards the foot of the king's bed. "When the runes were cast at King Brynjar's behest concerning your future with us, they spoke to our priestess of a journey. The runes Raido, to the west, and Hagalaz, to the south, with Jera falling atop Othala in the center, and Perthro just beside them."

The priest tilted his head towards Elias. "Raido signifies journeys, and as it fell to the west, this means that you must travel west. To the south is Hagalaz. This rune signifies destruction; sometimes good, sometimes bad. Avoid the south, if you can. Perhaps it is not safe for you to return to the land of your birth at this time."

Brynjar grunted again, grimacing. "Get on with it. There's a point to this mumbo-jumbo."

The priest bowed slightly. "Yes, your Grace." He looked back to Elias. "Jera represents the cycle of the year, and Othala represents our homeland, here at the foot of the great mountain. Midsummer is upon us in a fortnight;

you should start your journey before our Midsummer festival. That is when fortune favors you the most, as shown by Perthro."

Brynjar reached out and gripped Elias's hand, surprising Elias with his lingering strength. "You've spoken to me many times that you wish to find your place in this world. It can't have been easy for you, living among men... you've watched three kings grow old and die now, and you've still got the face of a boy."

Elias nodded. "You were but a boy when I came here. Everyone else has passed the veil."

Brynjar turned his head to glance at Elias, and for a moment, the old spark came back to his eye. "Seems an auspicious time then, eh? Get out before you can catch old from us."

Elias shook his head. "I'd never dream of abandoning you. You've been the best friend I could have asked for."

Brynjar laughed once, straining. "Hah! You would dream, and you have." He patted Elias's hand, then pulled away. "The truth of it is, both you and I know that if it weren't for my word, you'd have been driven out of the north long ago. There are many lords and bannermen who see you as an outsider, an intruder. There will be arguing and vying for power when I am gone, but I have faith that Brandt will take my place."

He pointed at Elias, squinting his eyes. "It's you I'm worried about. Brandt will be busy, and most of my men will be busy with him, protecting my kingdom from the vultures."

He dropped his hand onto the bed. "Go on then, make your plans. You have my blessing. After my funeral, and before midsummer, go west, Elias, and find your place, away from stupid, short-lived men who can't see past their own beards." The old man grimaced, stiffening on his bed. "Leave me now. I want to spend the last hour of my life with my wife and children, and I'm going to say things that are for them only." He weakly waved a hand at the priests. "That goes for you too. I'll be talking to the gods sooner than you will, I reckon... save your breath for my pyre."

Elias stood, bowing slightly, his eyes stinging as tears threatened to take them from him. "It has been an honor to know you, Brynjar. Give your father and grandfather my greetings."

The priests ushered Elias out of the room and closed the door behind him. He passed through the hall, his surroundings a blur. He barely noticed the crowd as he pushed through it on his way to the large double doors of the great hall. He didn't look at anyone, though a few men tried to speak to him as he pushed both doors open and stepped out into the night. He could feel their eyes upon him, he could hear their low murmurs following him as he walked down the steps that led to the courtyard.

A strong hand caught his arm, and he whirled to face whoever had stopped him.

It was Brandt. He pulled Elias in closer, speaking quietly. "Latch your door tonight, Elias. There are lords who came from hundreds of miles away, and they didn't get to see my father. That won't sit well with them. Do you still have your sword?"

Elias nodded, his tears driven back by that wrenching in his stomach. He knew that many of the lords didn't approve of him, but would they really try to kill him?

"Good. Keep it by your bed tonight. I'll have a guard posted by your door." Brandt released Elias's arm and patted him on the shoulder. "We'll get through this."

With that, Brandt turned and walked back into the great hall, leaving Elias on the steps. He hurried to his small house, which was not far from the courtyard in front of the king's hall, and latched the door shut as soon as he was inside. He lit a candle, sat down on his bed, put his head in his hands, and cried. Brynjar had been the last person who had been living when he had come to the north, and now he was gone

~   ~   ~

3rd Waxing Flower Moon, Year 4368

It had been three days since Brynjar had died. The sky was clouded over, and a summer storm threatened to overtake the valley where the city lay, at the foot of the great Stromgard mountain. The rain would be good for the rivers and streams, refilling them during a dry time of the year, but Elias hoped it would hold off until tomorrow. This was the day they held the king's funeral.

He had helped cut the grass back from the bed of gravel that the pyre had been built upon. He had lifted the fir and cedar timbers high and packed the straw into the hollows between the dry logs. He had helped saw and build the steps that led to the top of the pyramid of lumber, straw, and pitch.

And now he stood amongst the citizens of the kingdom, watching as his friend's body was carried up the steps by Brandt and several other men. It was decided that since he was not a true man of the North, it would be seen as an affront to the gods if he were to help carry Brynjar to his final resting place.

At the north end of the pyre, a priest was intoning about this or that, but Elias paid him no attention. He was here to pay his respects to the man who had been his closest friend for the last sixty years, not listen to a priest blather on about rainbow bridges and halls of mead, ice giants, and battles in the afterlife.

The priest paused in his ceremony as Eira, the queen, climbed the stairs and lay a silk-wrapped bundle next to her husband's body. Her black velvet cloak covered her from head to toe, but Elias knew what it was; she had cut off her braid, as per tradition, and was laying it to burn with the king.

One by one, various lords and warriors from around the Northern Kingdom climbed the stairs and lay their offerings next to the king until his body was entirely obscured under them. Once the lords were done, the citizens of the realm, farmers, merchants and the like, put their offerings around the base of the pyre. Elias himself had brought his wooden sparring sword, the one that he had used to practice with Brynjar when they had both been boys. It seemed fitting to Elias as a gift, and he really had nothing else to give.

Once all of those present had given their offerings, eight archers stood around the pyre with flaming arrows. A flash of lightning, followed by a distant peal of thunder, gave the whole thing a very surreal light, making the hair on the back of his neck stand up. He felt a hand on his shoulder and turned to see Brandt next to him.

"This is it, I suppose," Brandt said, his eyes on the stack of logs that held his father. "Borne to the heavens on the smoke, his body sent back to the winds and the earth."

At a signal from the priest, the archers loosed their missiles into the pyre. The flames flickered to life, devouring the straw, igniting the pitch soaked logs hungrily. The heat surged forth, almost unreal in its intensity, causing most of the villagers to step back. The fire reached to top of the pyre swiftly, twisting into a slight vortex from the updraft caused by the flames.

"Leave this very night if you can."

Elias looked at Brandt. "Is there trouble?"

Brandt shook his head. "Not yet. Not for you. But there are whispers that some of the lords are planning a coup. Nothing we can't deal with, of course, but there might be fighting. There was when my father took the throne, and there may be now."

Elias set his jaw. "I can help you fight."

"I know, and there is no other sword I'd rather have by my side. But the gods say this is not your battle. I was there when the priestess read the stones... let me make things settle down here for a time. Go west and see what is in store for you there."

He reached out and embraced Elias, whispering to him. "My sources tell me that three lords, from the north and west, plan to vie for the crown and split the kingdom amongst them. They will make their move on Midsummer's Day; you need to be well gone by then. They say that your presence here is an affront to the gods, and you *will* be targeted."

He released Elias. "One year. Give me a year, then come back if you wish. I would not see my brother slain by rebels and bigots."

Elias's head swam with this news. He reached out and clasped Brandt's hand. "I wish you luck, brother," he said, echoing Brandt's sentiment. "I will return."

Brandt nodded. "I will make offerings for your safety."

They both turned and watched the flames as they grew higher. The heat baked them both, but neither stepped back until the timbers began to sag into the middle, and the king's body was lost to the pyre.

~　　~　　~

It was near dusk when Elias left the embers of Brynjar's fire. Warm, fat rain drops fell from the gathering clouds, and thunder echoed through the mountains around the village. A thin wisp of smoke rose behind one of the nearer peaks to the west; the lightning there must have started a small fire. With any luck, the rain would put it out before it got out of control.

Brandt's words were heavy on his mind, a weight he could almost tangibly feel as he walked back to his house. He had already packed his most valuable possessions and had them sitting in a haversack near his door, next to the longsword that the elves had left with him when he had been sent to the North. He latched the door behind himself and looked them over. A folded piece of parchment on the ground in front of the door caught his eye, and he picked it up, unfolding it.

The rigid, angular script of the northern kingdoms was scrawled in a rough note.

Brandon Cornwell

Not a man of the north.
Bushwalker get out.

He stared at the note for a few moments, then crumpled it into a ball and threw it into the corner.

Brandt was right. He would leave as soon as night was deep enough.

Chapter Two

7th Waning Flower Moon, Year 4368

Midsummer's Day was about a week past, and the sun beat down on the mountains with a relentless indifference. Elias wiped the sweat from his brow, flinging the droplets to the ground, watching them evaporate almost instantly. He could feel the heat of the gravel under his feet, even through the thick leather soles of his boots.

Pulling the stopper from his waterskin, the young elf took a deep drink of the warm water and made a face. There was a creek nearby, and he'd be walking along it if it wasn't infinitely harder to traverse than the road. He hitched his pack up higher onto his shoulders, and cut off the road, into the shade of the trees.

It wasn't much cooler here, where the ground sloped downwards towards the floor of the ravine. Even the cover that the fir and pines gave wasn't enough to cut the summer heat away entirely, though it was a bit of a respite from the baking he was getting from the direct sun while he was on the road.

Stepping carefully on the moss covered boulders at the edge of the stream, Elias lowered himself to a small gravel bed that sloped into a wide pool. Pouring out the last of his warm water, he refilled it with fresh, cold water from the creek. He took another long drink and topped his waterskin off again.

The cold water was just far too inviting. He'd been on the road in the searing heat every day for nearly a fortnight and had at least another two days ahead of him before he got out of the mountains and reached the coast. He dropped his pack on the shore, leaning his sword and bow against the boulder he had climbed down, and stripped off his shirt. Kicking off his boots and undoing his trousers, he stretched as he nerved himself up before wading into the water.

Elias was not disappointed, catching his breath as the cold water reached his thighs, then his stomach. He pushed forward into the pool, causing a small wave to roll across the otherwise still surface. Ducking his head under, he completely submerged himself and pushed off of the rocky bottom, floating through the water.

His head broke the surface near the center, and he paddled across to the other side. He wasn't a strong swimmer, but he knew enough to keep himself from drowning. The deeper water was much cooler than the surface, and he shivered slightly but smiled nonetheless.

"Oh, that's good," he murmured to himself, since there was nobody else around. "I needed that." The sound of his own voice was strange; it was the only voice he'd heard since he had left Pine River two days before. His feet touched the sandy shore on the other side, and he pushed back to the middle of the pool.

He wasn't in any sort of rush. He had brought enough food to keep him fed for a fortnight if he hunted while he traveled. Deer and turkeys were plentiful in these mountains, as were game fowl. He was by no means a master archer, but he could hunt, and well. He floated on his back in the calm water, beams of sunlight breaking through the canopy of willows and dogwoods.

Nobody had followed him when he left Valtheim that night. He had traveled south at a pretty quick pace, making good headway for three days before allowing himself to slow down. His feet weren't used to the long walking, and he had given himself blisters with the pace he'd been keeping.

Elias sat up most nights, thinking about Brynjar, Brandt, and the people he knew back at the foot of Mount Stromgard. He wondered if Brandt had successfully pushed back the usurpers and if there had been a battle. He had heard no news in Pine River, but that was unsurprising. The politics of the Northmen were of little concern to the southerners, and he was likely the first traveler to come through from the north since Brynjar's death.

There had been men and elves there, and the odd dwarf, but there had been little in the way of hospitality. To the elves he was a freak, to the men he was a giant, and to the dwarves, well, he was an elf. He had made his time there very short. If this was the welcome he could expect outside of the Northlands, then he had his work cut out for him.

He hauled himself up onto the sandy shore with a sigh and froze.

There were footprints in the sand. While travelers weren't unheard of along this road, he hadn't seen any since he had left Pine River two days ago, and these were fairly fresh, maybe a day old at the oldest. The marks were large, as large as his own shoes, and deep; they weren't made by bare feet, no, these were made with steel clad boots. Steel boots meant armor. Armor meant soldiers or raiders.

Elias pushed back into the water, heading back to his clothes and pack, his mind churning over the prints in the sand. Men from the north seldom came this far south; they viewed the southerners as weak and worth little beyond trade. Would the nobles challenging Brandt really send riders after him? And if so, how had he missed them?

The only other thing that could have made a footprint that large would be an orc. The men and elves of this region were smaller than the Northmen, and so made smaller tracks, not to mention the fact that he hadn't seen a single armored human since leaving the North.

It was probably nothing, he told himself. He wasn't the only person to use this road, and the heat was oppressive to everyone. Someone else likely just needed water or a quick swim. Nothing to get worked up over... and yet he could still feel his heart pounding. Who would wear heavy armor in this heat?

Elias used his shirt to dry himself and quickly dressed, leaving his shirt to dry on top of his pack as he walked. He adjusted the leather straps that held his belongings in place, shouldered his pack, and headed back to the road. On the way, he searched for signs that someone had passed that way recently.

Now that he was looking, the landscape spoke to him, and he read its secrets like an open book. Close to the water, bracken ferns grew in the lee of stones and fallen logs, thick and lush in the shade of the forest. Near the water's edge, the fir and cedar trees were dotted with willows and dogwoods, short and gnarled, debris from last winter's floods collected and entangled at the base of their trunks. A few tall cottonwoods towered over all but the fir trees, which dominated the landscape.

Pines and spruce were scattered amongst them, while the odd manzanita bush grew in patches of sunlight left when a fallen tree tore a hole in the canopy, fighting for space with scrub oaks and dogwood. The bracken fern and dogwood lost the battle for ground as he climbed up the side of the ravine towards the road, replaced by sword ferns and small black oak trees, twisted and stunted under the overbearing evergreens.

Elias registered most of this almost subconsciously as he looked for signs of passage. Snapped twigs, scuffed moss, bent fronds, any of these could mean that someone had come through here. Beyond the occasional game trail, though, there was nothing. No more footprints, no signs that anyone other than him had come this way recently.

Once Elias made it back to the road, he paused, considering his options. He could head back to Pine River and wait for a caravan, or he could continue on to Fairhaven, at the coast, and get there in two days if he stepped out. Looking back and forth for a moment, he was still, listening to the mountains.

There was no wind at all right now, and the forest was quiet. A few birds chirped, the cicadas made their continuous buzzing, but nothing else. He shook his head. He was being foolish. There was no reason he should be wary of travelers along a road; where else were they supposed to travel? Not to mention the fact that he hadn't received the warmest of welcomes when he had passed through the last town... apparently, they were as fond of giant elves as his own people were. No need to go back there.

Nonetheless, he moved his longsword to his belt at his left hip, and stepped a little quicker, keeping watch as he traveled.

The sun was almost touching the western mountaintops when he decided to make camp for the night. He stowed his pack out of sight of the road and strung his bow. He had enough food to last him to the coast, but he wanted some fresh meat.

The grouse were fat and lazy in the summer heat, but the cool of the evening was starting to rouse them. It wasn't long before he shot one in a clearing. The grass was matted down in many spots, evidence of a deer herd that had bedded there recently, which made for an excellent, clear shot. He field dressed the bird and returned to the road.

The creek had meandered closer to the road as he traveled and was not far off. A wide patch of gravel and sand lay between the treeline and the water, perfect for a campsite. It had been used as such many a time before, as was evidenced by the existing stone rings with charred wood in the centers. It was important to keep the fire contained, lest a stray spark or ember drift into the forest; the forest was dry, and a single spark could potentially start a wildfire that would blaze out of control for weeks. Many of the larger trees bore the burns of previous such fires but stood tall and firm nonetheless.

Elias was in the midst of setting steel to flint, when he heard a footstep behind him. He startled and turned. How had someone been able to get so close to him without him hearing them?

A gigantic figure stood not ten feet away, covered head to toe in blackened plate armor. On the breastplate, there was a large insignia, an eight-pointed star set in a ring, with a red stone in the center. The figure had an enormous, two-handed sword in one hand, almost as long as he was tall. And the figure *was* tall, as tall as Elias was himself.

Elias stumbled back, upsetting his tinder pile. "Who are you?" he stammered, scrambling to his feet.

"Who I am is of no concern to you, Elias of Stromgard."

The figure's voice was young, deep, like Elias's own. He grabbed the hilt of his sword, still hanging at his left hip. "How do you know my name? Who are you, and what do you want?"

The armored figure stepped forward, causing Elias to draw his blade. "My name would bring you no comfort, nor would it change what is about to happen. I am here for you, Elias. You have something that I want, and nothing can stop me from taking it from you." The figure put his other hand on the hilt of his sword. "I want your life. Prepare yourself."

Elias held his sword in one hand, staring at the knight that was facing him. He had never seen him before in his life, and had no idea what he was talking about; frankly, he wasn't interested in finding out. He took off at a dead run, bolting towards the road. The knight stood there for a moment, then took off after him.

Elias reached the road just before something struck him in the back and knocked the wind out of him. He tumbled to the ground, his sword falling out of his grasp, the skin on his back feeling like it had been frozen and burned at the same time. He wheezed, rolling to a crouch as the knight approached.

"You run like a coward. At least stand and face me. Die fighting, like your blood deserves."

Elias scrambled over, grabbing his sword and jumping to his feet. He spun to face the knight just in time to block a hard overhand blow. The power behind the swing was enough to make his hand go numb, and he reeled from the strike. He had just enough time to parry another strike at his stomach and square off against the knight again. He gritted his teeth, his heart racing, his pulse thundering in his ears.

The armored figure circled slowly, keeping his sword between himself and Elias. "Good. Get that blood pumping. Get angry!"

Elias lunged forward, throwing a flurry of strikes at the knight, each one parried effortlessly by the enormous blade. He couldn't get close enough to strike without the tip of the greatsword seeking his flesh, and that made him keep his distance. Sweat beaded on his forehead as he drew back, his longsword ready to parry.

The knight reached up to his helmet and pushed the visor up. Pale white skin, almost ashen in its lack of color, greeted Elias, along with two silvery gray eyes, the irises like mercury around dull red pupils. They glowed like low embers, and Elias got the feeling that his assailant stared through him, into his very being.

Black flame started to spread from the knight's feet across the gravel, licking upward as if it had a mind of its own, creeping towards Elias as the knight stepped towards him again. The flame climbed up the knight's legs as he beckoned to Elias with his free hand.

"Enough of this. The time comes. Prepare yourself, little lamb, that you may fulfill my purpose."

The black flame surged towards Elias, and he scrambled back away from it, almost tripping over a stone on the road. He kept his balance, but the black fire reached him. Instead of heat, Elias felt searing cold, burning him just as surely as fire would have.

"Get away from me," he yelled, slapping and kicking at the flames. "Leave me alone! I don't have anything for you!"

The knight reached out, as if gripping something, and Elias felt something grab him by the neck. He was lifted slightly off the ground and dragged forward, his boots scraping against the gravel. He clawed at his neck, trying to make whatever held him let go, but the only purchase his fingers found was on his own skin. He was pulled slowly closer to the knight's sword, which was pointed at his navel.

Suddenly, an axe crashed down on the knight's sword, knocking it awry, and Elias was released. He slumped to the ground, coughing and choking. He looked up, his eyes bleary, to see a number of men – maybe a dozen, wearing various kinds of armor – either running up the road towards them or surrounding the knight and himself.

One of the newcomers, an older man with messy black hair and an unkempt beard, both shot through with gray, squared off with the knight. "Easy there, big boy, just put down your sword and we'll have us a chat. No reason for anyone to die now."

The armored figure let out a barely human snarl and lunged at Elias. The older man slapped his sword aside, but only just. The edge grazed Elias's shoulder as he dove out of the way. There was the sound of metal clashing, then an explosion behind him, and black flame washed over Elias, stinging his skin with the burning cold. He rolled to face where the knight had gone, bringing his sword to bear, but the armored figure was nowhere to be seen.

He staggered to his feet, stepping back away from the men who were similarly recovering from the blast. He shook his head, clearing the remaining haze from his eyes. He stood up completely just as several of the men regained their wits and turned to face him.

"By the gods, that's the biggest damn elf I've ever seen," one of the men whispered, a thick built, redheaded man in leather armor that was studded with metal rivets. He was the one who had swung the axe a moment before.

Elias kept his sword at the ready, between himself and the newcomers. "Who are you?" He felt like a fool, repeating himself over and over.

The older man stepped forward, lowering his sword "My name is Jonas. This fine fellow here is Martin, my second, and these men you see behind me are members of my crew. And you are?"

Elias kept his sword between himself and the men, still uneasy. The knight could return at any moment. "My name is Elias. Elias of Stromgard."

Jonas nodded. "Well met, Elias. Now, what say we sheathe our swords and talk, because I have *never* seen any shit like that before."

Elias sheathed his sword as Jonas did his own. "That makes two of us."

Martin lowered his axe, and the rest of the men sheathed their swords. The tension in the air noticeably lessened.

"Well then," Jonas said, sitting on a fallen log at the side of the road. "Let's get that cut looked at." He beckoned to one of his crew, a younger man with limp black hair and a slight frame. "Geoff! Bring the bandages. This fellow is in need of some attention. The rest of you lot spread out, see if you can find where that big metal bastard went."

Geoff walked over, carrying a haversack on one shoulder.

"Elias, this is my surgeon and priest, Geoff. Geoff, this is Elias. See to his shoulder, would you?"

The young man looked up at Elias, who towered over him. He raised an eyebrow. "I think it would be a bit easier if you were to sit down."

"Oh, right. My apologies." Elias sat down on the log near Jonas as the rest of the mercenary group spread out, checking the area. Jonas sat on the log, dropping his own pack to the ground in front of him. Removing a pipe from a pouch, he began scraping it out with a knife.

Geoff worked quickly and efficiently, cleaning the wound with fresh water from the creek and a fragrant oil from a vial that smelled strongly of lavender. Elias braced himself, steeling his resolve to not move or flinch. He looked up to meet Jonas's eyes as Geoff put in the first stitch.

Jonas struck a small match and held it to the freshly packed pipe. "So, Elias of Stromgard. What brings you through these woods on this fine summer's day, aside from trying to get yourself killed by a giant, magic knight?"

"Just traveling to the coast."

"Joining family in Silva Aestas?"

Elias shook his head, catching a disapproving frown from Geoff. "No. I am coming from the North." He gestured to his giant form, keeping his shoulder still. "Most elves aren't frightfully accepting of those who are as big as I am. I've lived with the Northmen since I was young."

Jonas puffed on his pipe. "Aye, you're a right big bastard, I'll give you that. Still, I didn't fancy the elves to throw one of theirs out into the world of us mere mortals."

Elias flinched as Geoff put in the second stitch. "The men of the north were kind enough to take me in, but my time with them is done. Maybe there's work on the coast. That's where I'm going."

Jonas puffed smoke out of his nostrils. "So who was that, with the armor and the bad attitude?"

Elias shook his head again, careful not to move his shoulder. "I honestly have no idea. This was the first I've ever seen of him. He kept talking about my blood, and that I had something he wanted."

Jonas looked at him oddly. "It's true, the times we are in are strange, and make strange men do strange things. Awfully fancy armor for a bandit, especially in this weather, but with trolls, orcs, ogres, and who know what else roaming about down south, I suppose nothing is impossible."

Jonas leaned back on his haunches and blew a smoke ring in the still air. "Stromgard... That's the name of the great mountain north of Rockhill, aye? I'm guessing then that's the clan you stayed with? King Brynjar's hold?"

Elias nodded. "Yes. I was his ward." The line of questioning was getting a little uncomfortable; while Jonas had, after all, saved his life, he still didn't like being interrogated.

Jonas narrowed his eyes a bit, regarding Elias. "Well, if work's what you're looking for, I've got a proposition for you. We're finishing up a job now, and set to take another in Jetty in a week or so. I need all the warm bodies I can get, since I get paid for each sword I bring to the table. Join up with us, learn the coast. There's gold in it for you, if you can carry your weight and swing a blade."

Elias thought about it as Geoff tied off the third stitch. A mercenary life would afford him a better living than a dock hand or laborer, but it would also be more likely to get him killed. It wasn't often one saw a retired mercenary. However, it would keep him moving, with less opportunity for whoever that was that attacked him to find him. It would also give him time to find out why the knight would be hunting Elias, specifically.

He stood, pipe in hand, and stretched his back. "Well, you have a few more days to think it over. Our destination is Fairhaven, then south from there. Only a day's march to the shore, then north half a day. We should be there by noon the day after tomorrow."

Geoff stood, admiring his handiwork. "Well, it'll be a week or more before you'll want to swing a sword again, but you should be good if you have to in the meantime. You can at least travel, and not bleed all over everything."

Elias flexed his arm up and down, feeling it out. The stitches Geoff had put in held nicely, and though they pulled and hurt, the pressure from the bandages helped keep the pain down a bit. "Thank you, Geoff, I owe you a favor for that."

Geoff shook his head. "No, some bandages and cleaning ointment is what you owe me. Just mend quickly... I don't want to have to try to restitch that."

Jonas dismissed Geoff. "Don't mind him. He doesn't like blood when it doesn't come out of someone he's trying to kill. Best damn medic north of the valley, though. Says he thinks he might be able to sew back on fingers and hands after they've been cut off. I greatly doubt that, but he is good."

Elias stood and looked back towards the creek, where he had left his pack. "I don't have much... a single grouse at my camp by the creek. You're welcome to it, as thanks."

Jonas chuckled. "Don't worry about that, lad. We'll supply our own feed." He turned to the side and called out. "Martin!"

The redheaded axeman walked over. "What?"

Jonas indicated the forest with a toss of his head. "See if you can bag us a deer. I think some meat is in order."

Martin grumbled and drew his bow, heading for the woods.

Jonas puffed on his pipe again, then stood, lifting his pack. "Well, rather than sit about here on the road, how about you lead us to your camp. It can't be far."

Elias led the way to the gravel bar on the creek, and the men went about setting up camp. Two small campfires were started, blankets were laid out, packs were unslung, and boots were kicked off. Several of the men went swimming, and even Jonas sat with his feet in the water.

"I can march like a young man still," he said, wincing, "but that doesn't keep my feet from reminding me of my age at the end of the day."

"So where are you marching to? You said you had work in Jetty?" Elias was feeling a little foolish for talking so much earlier and revealing where he came from. The northerners weren't generally much of a problem this far south, but they were known to be raiders, and some of the people here may have had run-ins with them.

Jonas stretched, his back and shoulders popping audibly. "Just finished a job in Pine River. Going to collect the remainder of our pay from our employer in Fairhaven, and after that, yeah, we've got a contact in Jetty. Bigger port, more to do there. Not just fishermen and fishwives." He looked askance at Elias. "You ever been to a port town?"

Elias shook his head. "I've lived my whole life in the forest or the mountains.

Jonas chuckled. "Then you've yet to really live."

Chapter Three

8ᵗʰ Waning Flower Moon, Year 4368

The mercenaries traveled fast. A march that would have taken Elias most of two days was finished by the end of the following day. Elias spent the time chatting with Jonas as they marched at a lively pace. The company made for a swift journey, as Elias listened to the men swapping tales while they walked. Most of the stories were about this or that job; it seemed that while they were all familiar with each other, they hadn't been working together exclusively for very long.

A few hours before dusk, they followed the river out of the mountains to a broad, even plain, dotted with trees here and there. In the distance, farms stood out in the fields, and herds of cattle and sheep roamed through the tall grass. The traffic on the road increased as farmers drove their carts past, giving the mercenaries a wide berth.

"They don't know the difference between soldiers and honest working men," Jonas explained, gesturing at the farmers. "Some of them probably think we're here to raid, others think we might be deserters, and others just have no idea who we are, and so give us space."

Elias frowned. "Deserters?"

"Aye. There's been word of an army forming south of Lonwick, in the southern end of the plains. Orcs, ogres, some men, trolls, and worse. We occasionally run into scouting parties south of Greatport, but rarely this far north."

Elias frowned, absorbing this new information. This must have been what the priests meant when they said to avoid going south. Castle Lonwick was the capital of the aptly named Kingdom of Lonwick, and was situated in the middle of the enormous valley that was east of the bay of Greatport. Most of the citizens of this kingdom were elves, though humans, dwarves, and others weren't unknown. Most of the human settlements were just within the northern borders, where there was more contact with the human kingdom, north of the valley, or along the coast, where shipping and fishing were viable industries.

"What happens if the Felle Army pushes north?"

Jonas shrugged. "I imagine much the same as what happened to those unlucky enough to be far enough south when they started assembling. Ogres do have a taste for the flesh of men and elves, and the Felle Army has more than just orcs and ogres in its ranks."

Elias shuddered slightly. "Is there nobody marching to their aid?"

Jonas laughed. "You have been out of Lonwick for a while, haven't you? The elven king in the south holds less sway. Men aren't fond of a monarchy that doesn't support them and still insists on taxes. No, I imagine that the only aid Lonwick will get from this region is from themselves."

Elias shook his head. "That doesn't seem right."

Looking askance at Elias, Jonas shrugged. "Right and wrong is a mutable thing to people just looking to survive."

Elias marched on in silence, mulling over the situation. He had not been in his homeland for a very long time, but just abandoning people while they were conquered by an army of man and elf eating monsters... there was no heart in that.

Jonas clapped Elias lightly on the shoulder. "You're young yet. You'll find that convincing people to go and fight and die for someone they don't know is a battle you can't win. You don't have to like it, but not liking it won't change it."

~   ~   ~

They camped that night near the beach. After being in the heat of the mountains for so long, the chill of the evening wind made Elias shiver under his blanket. The fire flickered in the breeze, mostly sheltered by the pit they had dug in the sand.

Jonas and the rest of the mercenaries didn't seem to mind the chill in the air. They lounged around the fire, drinking wine from skins and telling stories. One young man, Timothy, seemed to have a flair for telling tales, recounting several well-known stories.

One of the more popular ones, drawing laughter from the most of the mercenaries, was called The Sea Elf Maiden. It was about a beautiful young sea elf who spent all of her time flirting with suitors, varying from noblemen to the king of sea lions. She managed to stay unmarried, dallying with the richest and most handsome human men until she came across a young human priest, who asked her if she was still pure.

In a falsetto, Timothy acted out the part of the maiden. "Why yes, good sir, I have been chaste my entire life!"

Timothy turned, switching roles as he continued the narrative. "At just that moment, the priest leapt forward, casting a net over the poor elf maiden, pinning her to the ground! He threw off his robes, revealing himself to be none other than... the King of the Sea Lions!"

Timothy acted out a short struggle that ended with the maiden being married to the king of sea lions, to the cheers and applause of the mercenaries. When the king found that she wasn't a virgin, and had tricked everyone involved, he cast her into the sea to be swallowed up by a whirlpool.

"The moral of the story is if you spend your whole life being chaste, eventually you'll get caught, and as we all know..." Timothy made a stirring motion with his hand, as the mercenaries roared out the last line with him. "What goes around comes around!"

Timothy bowed amongst applause and laughter, and sat down on the sand next to Elias, who chuckled as he finished clapping. "That was well done."

Timothy tore open a loaf of bread, passing half of it to Elias. Biting into the part he kept, he spoke around a mouthful. "That's one of my favorites. Simple, easy to remember, with a funny punchline at the end."

Elias bit into the bread himself. "How long have you been a storyteller?"

Timothy shrugged, clearing his throat with a drink from his wineskin. "Oh, as long as I can remember. I wanted to be a singer, but I couldn't carry a tune if it were in a pail, so I kept to stories. Plus my da told me if he caught me singing one more time he'd put me in a dress and sell me to a sailing ship, so that was really the end of that."

Elias furrowed his brow. "Why would he do that?"

Timothy tore off another bite from the loaf of bread. "Well, when you're a woodcutter's son, you're expected to be cutting wood. I didn't exactly feel like doing that all the time, so I didn't. That didn't set too well with my da, so he gave me a choice, the axe or the road. I chose the road." He gestured to Jonas, who sat off to the side, conversing with Martin. "I started with him about three moons ago, and I've had more gold in my pocket than a woodcutter ever had."

Elias nodded, settling down into the sand, clutching his blanket around him. Despite the cold, he was content. The men around him made him feel comfortable, accepted, despite his size. He stared into the fire as, one by one, the mercenaries bedded down and went to sleep. As the camp grew quieter, his thoughts turned back to his home in the north, and the strange armored knight who had attacked him the day before.

Why would a knight be after him, especially one who could create cold fire and vanish without a trace? Elias had nothing in this world – was nothing to anyone, now that he had left the Northlands. He stared into the flames as the sound of the waves lulled him to sleep. His dreams were filled with clashing swords, the steel gray eyes of the dark knight, and an unshakable sense of dread.

~   ~   ~

The morning dawned brisk, a light dew having settled over the junipers and dune grasses. The mercenaries traveled north along the coast after breaking camp, keeping to the waveslope where possible. The firmer sand gave better purchase than the dry sand farther away from the sea, and the road itself wound around the base of the coastal hills. It was shortly before dusk when they reached the town of Fairhaven, nestled amongst the coastal cliffs between two crescent shaped bays.

Fishing boats, freight vessels, and a few privateer ships were tied to the long wooden piers that extended into the deeper, rocky southern bay, while the western bay was wide, shallow, and sandy, with nets and campfires scattered above the reach of the tide. Racks of tiny surf fish were spread out to dry near the fires, while fishermen dipped more out of the waves with wide nets on triangular wooden frames. A few taller frames sported larger fish, and there were even a few large gray sharks hanging, being cleaned and cut into steaks for preserving.

The city had a palisade wall that ran from shore to shore in a semicircle on the inland side of the city, with a broad, tall gate standing open. Jonas, Elias, and the others were stopped by two guards as they approached.

"State your business in Fairhaven!" one of them said, holding a halberd in front of himself.

"Our business *is* business. We have a contract to fulfill with the owner of the Lighthouse Tavern." Jonas produced a rolled parchment from inside his tunic, showing the guardsman.

The guardsman looked it over before handing it back. "Due to the threat from the south, only two will be allowed in the city. The rest of you can camp away from the wall. There's a clearing about fifteen minutes walk back up the road; you can set up there."

Jonas looked back at his men. "Alright, you heard him. Martin, you're with me. The rest of you, find a suitable place to pitch camp. I'll be back no later than tomorrow morning."

The guards stepped aside to allow Jonas and Martin to pass, while Elias and the rest of the men set out to the campground. Though he was loath to admit it, Elias was a bit less comfortable with Jonas being gone, as the majority of the mercenaries either ignored him or paid him little mind. He kept mostly to himself that night, chatting with Geoff when the other man wasn't busy, or resting near the small fire.

There were other groups camping nearby, mostly merchants it seemed, but they all kept to themselves. They slept in shifts that night, Elias taking the third watch with two other men. The sun was rising over the mountains before Jonas returned, bleary-eyed and smelling of ale. Five other men had joined him, and went around the camp, greeting friends

Elias raised a brow. "Business, huh?"

Jonas grinned broadly behind his unkempt beard. "The best kind of business always involves spirits."

Geoff piped up. "Did we get paid?"

Jonas tossed him a pouch that was full of coins. "Make sure everyone gets their cut."

Geoff handed out coins as the men broke camp, and by the time the morning fog had burned off, they were headed south. As soon as the shore was close enough, they cut away from the road and traveled along the sandy coastline.

"Why not take the road?" Elias asked Geoff, as he trudged through the sand, his feet sinking in whenever he stepped forward. His calves ached from the shifting ground beneath them; walking on sand was very different from walking on a packed gravel path.

"The road leads back inland, on the mountain side of the bay. If we take it, it adds ten miles to our trip. Half a day's march, at least. We're aiming for Jetty, and that town is on the northern peninsula. May as well follow the shore. Here, walk on the sand where it's wet. It doesn't move around quite so much."

Walking on the waveslope was easier, and Elias soon became accustomed to the way it shifted under his steps. Though not as easy as the packed dirt and stones of the road, it wasn't as bad as the loose sand.

Elias walked near the front, alongside Jonas. Near midday, his curiosity got the better of him.

"What was the job that you finished in Fairhaven?"

"A delivery job. Someone in Pine River wanted something sent to Fairhaven, and they didn't want to be seen delivering it."

Elias raised a brow. "That required ten men?"

Jonas chuckled. "Some things are too important to be sent with just a courier. Couriers are easy to rob or kill. Ten mercenaries, not as much."

"Wouldn't a larger group attract more attention?"

"What would you expect to see in a land under the threat of war? A group of men traveling light, fast, and armed, or a rich man in a carriage, taking his time about things? Sometimes going unnoticed isn't the same as going unseen."

Elias pondered that for a moment. "I suppose that makes sense. What did they need delivered?"

Jonas shrugged. "It was a sealed box and a sealed envelope. We didn't get paid if the seals were broken, so they were delivered intact."

Elias shook his head. "The men of the North sent single couriers on horseback to deliver notices or summons. A group of armed men would be seen as a threat."

Jonas laughed, looking up at Elias. "Then, if we want to earn coin and survive doing it, it's a good thing we're not in the North, isn't it?"

~　　~　　~

The day wore on as they moved along the coast, traveling along the road when the shore became too rocky, or during high tide. Nearing dusk, they came to the top of a hill, overlooking the wetlands and dunes that surrounded the large bay. The body of water was shaped like an exaggerated peanut, with an opening to the ocean where the bay was thinnest. The southern shore rose quickly to mountains, enormous trees covering the slopes, while the northern and eastern shores were flatter, marshier, and waited for several miles before allowing the mountains to make their claim.

A thin fog had rolled in, obscuring most of the bay in the failing light, but the lights of Jetty could be seen through the mist. They decided to make camp on the hilltop, and proceed in the morning.

Martin went hunting and brought down a deer shortly after they made camp, so the men had fresh venison for dinner. Jonas took a seat next to Elias on a large fallen log as he ate, while the rest of the men talked and laughed around the fire. Timothy kept himself busy by telling another bawdy tale to whoever would listen.

After he finished his roast, Jonas tossed the bone into the fire. "So, Redwood, you've had some time to think about it. Want to make some gold?"

Elias raised an eyebrow. "Redwood?"

Jonas chuckled. "It's what the men have nicknamed you. Rather than call you Bushwalker, they named you after the giant trees around here."

Elias frowned. "I was raised in Silva Aestas for a century. I know what redwood trees are."

Jonas leaned back, regarding Elias. "Prickly bastard, aren't you? It's not meant in malice. Trust me, there are many a nickname one could get that aren't nearly so flattering."

Elias shrugged. "Maybe so. What would I be doing?"

"Escort. There's a man who needs to travel from Jetty to Pine River. Normally not a hard trip, but a few unarmed men in a carriage are easy picking for less scrupulous folks. They want fifteen men. That's about what we've got. They'll pay thirty gold lions per man, half up front, half when we get to Pine River."

Thirty gold coins was more money than Elias had ever had at one time in his life. "Thirty? Why so much?"

Jonas shrugged. "No catch. Looks pretty straight forward. Rich men like to throw money at problems, especially when their own safety is involved. All you have to do is be there to catch it."

Elias sat, staring into the fire for a moment. "I'll need a new sword."

"What's wrong with the one you've got?"

The memory of fighting the armored man on the trail was quite fresh with Elias. "This one is far too short, far too light. I need a greatsword."

Jonas made a face. "Giant anchors, those are. Far too slow. A man who knows how can get inside their range, and make 'em worthless." He held up a hand, ticking off his points on his fingers. "You can't fight indoors, you can't fight next to your comrades, you can't be sneaky with them, and you can't draw them fast."

He gestured at the surrounding men. "Not one of these men have a greatsword."

Elias shrugged. "Nevertheless. I think I will keep my eye out for a larger blade."

Jonas scoffed. "Well, it's your money to waste if you join up. Just keep in mind you need to bring enough food to feed yourself."

"I'll keep that in mind."

They sat in silence for a moment, the sounds of the camp dying down as the men bedded down for the night.

"So does that mean you're in?"

Elias nodded with a half smile. "I'm in."

Jonas settled on the ground, leaning against the log that they were sitting on. "Good. There's strength in numbers, and you're big enough to count for two." He tossed a blanket over his lap and closed his eyes. "There's a blacksmith in Jetty. See what he has to offer if you must."

~   ~   ~

Even though it was midsummer, the morning dawned cold. The mist from the evening before had thickened overnight, and looked like an extension of the sea running on to land. It flowed around the low areas, making islands of the hills that led up to the mountains on the east side of the bay. It was nearly noon by the time the fog burned off, and they had reached the stretch of beach leading up to Jetty's gates on the narrow peninsula.

A wall of timbers and earth had been constructed from the bay to the sea, cutting off the southern end of the peninsula from the rest of the world. Near the middle of the wall, the timbers rose higher, supporting a massive log that had been sawn in half, acting as the top of the entryway. The gates, made of thick planks bolted to massive crossbeams, stood half open, several guards standing watch. One of them approached Jonas, shaking his hand warmly.

"Hello, my friend. Jetty has been quieter since you last left."

Jonas laughed, clapping the man on the shoulder. "You mean they don't still whisper my name in hushed tones behind every corner? I must be getting old!"

"Oh, your name was mentioned, but with less whispering and more snickering. Not every day a man gets thrown out through this gate."

Jonas rubbed the back of his head. "Aye... that was one hell of a night. I'm surprised you had enough wits about you to follow an order."

The guardsman laughed as well, releasing Jonas's hand. "I only matched you drink for drink for an hour or two. You didn't leave enough ale for me to keep up." He chuckled, crossing his arms in front of his chest. "So tell me. Why have you come back to Jetty?"

Jonas gestured at the gate. "Meeting a client here. A rich man needs an escort to Pine River. Set to meet his man here in four days, and if all goes well, we leave with him."

The guard shook his head. "You know that's not allowed."

Jonas spread his arms. "What am I to do? Wait outside the gate like a dog? My men have gold, and they want to spend it. You can't tell me that business has been good this past season."

The guard sighed. "I can't let you in. You cause more damage than can be repaired by the coin you spend... but you do spend coin. I will have to ask the mayor."

Jonas cringed, and turned away. The guardsman shook his head, chuckling, and walked into the town behind the gate. Elias raised a brow as Jonas returned to the group.

"What was that all about?"

Jonas rubbed the back of his head, running his fingers through his dark hair. "I... we may have gotten a little rowdy last time we were in town. A few windows were broken, a few teeth, maybe a few jaws..."

Martin chuckled. "We tore up the greater part of the hotel district that night. We'd just come off of a long job, and we all had some, uh, steam to blow off."

Elias was shocked. "You tore up the entire town by blowing off some steam?"

Jonas dropped his pack on the ground and sat down on it. "You obviously haven't seen what twenty men can do when they've been away from wine, women, and song for a season."

Elias shook his head. "No, no I haven't seen that. The Northmen are seldom away from any of those for any length of time."

Jonas chuckled. "I swear, I'm pretty sure that was the night Geoff got his first woman."

Martin clapped the younger man on the back. "To hear him tell it, it was the first night he had three!"

The men laughed as they settled in for the wait, the heat from the sun held at bay by the steady, cool breeze from the ocean. An hour went by before the guardsman came back, accompanied by several other men at arms. A tall, clean-shaven man led the way, his neatly clipped gray hair thinning slightly on top. Jonas stood as he saw them approaching, but the man waved him down.

"No. No, you stay down. This will be brief."

Jonas paused, looking the man directly in the eye, before rising to his feet anyways. The rest of the men, Elias included, joined him.

The man drew up, ten guards at his back. "You still don't like following directions, do you, Jonas?"

Jonas smiled a half smile, bowing slightly. "You have me dead to rights, sir. How can I be of assistance to you today?"

The mayor crossed his arms in front of his chest. "You want entry into my town. I don't want to let you in. I offer you a deal."

Jonas spread his arms, smiling broadly. "I am extremely fond of deals! What have you in mind?"

The mayor held up a single finger. "One. If I allow you back into my town, you leave it in the same state you entered it. No broken windows, no brawling, no shenanigans."

Jonas nodded. "I think I can agree to that."

The mayor held up a second finger. "Two. When your business here is concluded, you leave. No extended stays. No longer than a week."

Jonas thumped Geoff on the chest. "I don't think the women could handle us for longer than a week, eh boys?"

The mercenaries laughed for a moment, but it was short lived.

"Three. There is a band of scouts from the Felle Army that have been spotted in the hills across the bay. I want them gone before I let you in the gates."

Jonas stood a little straighter. "You want us to hunt a band of scouts. From the Felle Army." He took a step forward, and the guards behind the mayor stepped forward as well. Undeterred, Jonas spoke again.

"I just want to be completely clear on this. You want me and my men to do the work of regular army, and... go to war?"

The mayor shook his head. "No, I want you to do the work of sellswords and deal with a problem." He inclined his head towards Jonas slightly, raising an eyebrow. "You are still mercenaries, right? Not glorified babysitters? Or am I mistaken, and you're ready to retire now?"

Jonas scowled. "This sort of job is not what I normally do. It's not what my men normally do. This sort of job gets men killed." He looked up, and smirked, his eyes narrowing. "It doesn't come cheap."

The mayor smiled slightly. "I would imagine not. I am prepared to offer you thirty gold lions per scout."

"Make it seventy, and you've got a deal."

The mayor shook his head. "You're out of your mind with that price, and you know it. Let's just cut to the chase. You'll take fifty, or you won't get past these gates. You need this town and the business it provides."

Jonas paused, considering the offer. He looked around to his men, and was met with subtle nods. He turned back to the mayor and held out his hand. "We have a deal then."

The mayor turned away without shaking Jonas's hand. "I expect to see proof. You know the customary proof for a bounty. Right ears, no left. Reports say that there were between ten and fifteen scouts." He started towards the gates. "I will accept ten. No less."

With that, the mayor and his guards walked back through the gates, which were then drawn shut behind them, leaving Elias, Jonas and his men standing alone outside of it. He turned to them, rubbing the back of his neck, wincing a little as he faced the sun. "Well... it looks like we're going hunting. Anyone who doesn't want to go, well, you know how it works. You can cut out now, and anyone who's game can come with us and earn some lions. Consider it a bonus as to what we were going to do before." He gestured at the gate. "It beats sitting here waiting for them to open the doors, in my humble opinion."

Martin sighed. "You know me. I'm always good for it."

Geoff nodded. "And you'll need to be patched up after. I'm game."

One by one, the men gathered in front of the gate murmured their assent, Elias among them. After the last man agreed, Jonas clapped his hands once. "Alright! We've got four days to find these sons of pig-whores, kill them, get back, get paid, and let this town lick our wounds. I say we get started now. We should be able to make it to the other side of the bay by nightfall."

Jonas lifted his pack. "Let's move out!"

Chapter Four

10th Waning Flower Moon, Year 4368

As they made their way around the bay, the mercenaries questioned some the residents of the farms and houses they passed. A road ran along the bay, first going north along the peninsula, then east through the marshes on the north shore, and finally south along the eastern shore, between the bay and the fields leading up to the mountains. Nobody had seen the scouts themselves, but several farms had lost some livestock over the last fortnight – mostly young cattle or adult goats.

The tracks always led back to the hills. Most of the time, they were roughly the size of a man, just a bit deeper, as if the one making them were significantly heavier. However, at two of the farms that were closer to the edge of the forest, the tracks were different.

It was Geoff and Timothy who found the first set of tracks, at a small goat farm near the hills. Elias looked them over, analyzing and comparing them to the previous tracks. They were smaller in size, but deeply depressed into the ground, as if the one walking had been up on its toes, and enormously heavy. The tips of the tracks were split into four separate toes, each with a cleated indentation at the tip, like a claw. Jonas identified them as troll prints.

Elias had seen tracks made by trolls before, though he had never seen a troll face-to-face. The tracks he had seen were all barefoot, and he had assumed that trolls were simply very dangerous animals, like bears. He had heard that they were cunning, but not intelligent, and the men of the north occasionally hunted them. They never brought the bodies back, though, not even for trophies; the smell was far too foul. Even the spears used to kill them were burned afterward.

Martin found the second set of tracks in a cattle pasture closer to the hills. They were hard to miss, as they made a straight line of scuffed dirt through several shattered split rail fences. He called out to the rest of the men, gathering them in from their ranged out search line.

Jonas and Geoff were examining the tracks as Elias approached. They were deep in the soft soil of the pasture, and resembled large hand prints. The main part of the track was round, and deep at the heel, almost like a palm had been pressed into the ground, with short, stumpy toes leaving shallower indentations into the ground. Martin looked down at the holes in the soil, and shuddered. "Ogres."

Jonas, crouching in front of the tracks, put his face in his hands and cursed under his breath. After a moment, he looked up. "Are you sure?"

Martin nodded. "Completely. There were a few groups, herds, tribes, whatever they have, down in the southern end of the valley, south of the capitol. We couldn't leave livestock out at pasture overnight or the ogres would kill them with rocks and eat them raw right there. Sometimes, they would break into the barn and slaughter the whole herd, just to kill them. They wouldn't even eat them." He shuddered again. "I still remember the sound of the calves..."

"That's enough!" Jonas snapped. "I've never fought an ogre before. How did you kill them?"

Martin scoffed. "Kill them? We didn't kill them. Not ourselves. We burned them out. They retreated farther south, they'd come back after a few years, and we would burn them out again. It kept their numbers in check, but it never got rid of them."

Elias stood. "So. We have orcs, trolls, and ogres."

Jonas groaned. "I should have stuck with seventy lions a head."

The tracks led straight through the pastures and into the hills. Once the ground started to climb, the ogre's tracks were joined by the trolls and the booted tracks from earlier. The trees grew larger, casting a deep shade over the rising hills, while the soil itself gave way to rockier ground. It was harder to track their quarry in these conditions, but the telltale scuffed stone, broken branch, or twisted fern led them deeper into the rising hills until the sun sank below the sea.

Jonas threw down his pack and swore. "There's no sense in fumbling about in the dark. We'll camp here. No fire tonight, and keep your voices down. Orcs and trolls can smell fire for miles, and they can hear a fly fart on a windy day. Let's hope we find them tomorrow."

~　　~　　~

The trees towered above Elias, the tops mere silhouettes against the clear night sky. The waning moon was dark this night, but the stars shone brightly. A light breeze blew in from the sea to the hills, bearing a slightly salty scent.

He leaned back against an enormous tree, unable to sleep. He had volunteered for the first watch for this reason. He and another man sat silently, listening to the sounds of the forest, wary for any signs that might signal an ambush. Elias's night vision was superb; he couldn't see in the dark as well as, say, a dwarf, but elves were known for being able to hunt accurately at night. For him, the starlight was all he needed, and if there had been a full moon out, everything would have been as clear as day.

He shifted uncomfortably against the rocky ground. This was far more tension than he was used to. Even amongst the men of the north, he had never gone on raids, as he was a ward of the Northlands, not a citizen. He had spent many days and months and years training with the young men and women, but he had never actually been in a fight in the sixty-four years he had spent in the valley at the foot of Mount Stromgard.

His mind turned back to his time there, and he started to have second thoughts as to why he had left. There were no ogres in the fortified city of Valtheim. No orcs, no trolls, and no armored knights with cryptic messages trying to kill him. The only threats there were ones he knew about, ones he could see.

He sighed. Whatever happened, here he was now. Older than anyone present, yet still the youngest member of the party. Everything he owned in this world was with him in his haversack, and the sword he had been left with when the elves delivered him to the Northmen strapped to his hip, hunting orcs for gold.

The hours wore on with Elias lost in his own thoughts. His eyelids grew heavy, and he leaned his head back against the tree, fighting his weariness. The last two hours of his watch went by slowly, but eventually, the bright star in the west touched the horizon, and he was able to wake Geoff for his turn. Though the night was cold and the ground was hard, it was not long before Elias fell asleep.

~　　~　　~

The men walked single file down the road, the trees looming over them like monoliths, their tops lost in the morning mist. The forest floor was relatively clear, save for the bed of fallen needles and occasional thickets of ferns and underbrush. Though he had lived under these trees for the first century of his life, they felt foreign, judgmental, like ancient elders standing over him, looking down with disapproval.

A sound behind him made him turn. As he watched, the shadows around him coalesced, drawing up into a large humanoid form in front of him. It was the dark knight that he had met on the road to the coast, forming from the darkness of the forest. He tried to backpedal, to call out, but his legs and voice seemed frozen, unable to obey his bidding.

The shadow knight reached an arm out towards Elias, and without touching him, lifted him off the ground. A black, shadowy blade appeared in his hand, and he brought it back to strike. Elias cried out as the blade flashed forward.

~ ~ ~

11ᵗʰ Waning Flower Moon, Year 4368

Elias startled awake when Jonas kicked him lightly in the backside. "It is dawn. We move in ten minutes." He looked down at the large elf. "You sleep fitfully, for a giant."

Elias sat up, rubbing the sleep out of his eyes. "My dreams were not pleasant." His head throbbed, and his face felt heavy. Indeed, he had not rested well at all.

Jonas tossed him a dark waterskin. "Take a drink of this. It'll help you wake up, but drink it sparingly, else it will lose its potency for you. It's not hard to build up a resistance."

He pulled the stopper, sniffing the dark, strong smelling fluid. It was bitter, and he choked a bit as he took a drink. He grimaced, stoppering the skin and passing it back to Jonas. "What is that? It tastes terrible."

Jonas chuckled as he stowed the waterskin in his pack. "It's a tea made from the roasted beans of a plant that grows far south of here. The ones that grow it call it morning milk."

Elias took a swig from his own waterskin, making a face. "It tastes terrible," he repeated.

"No, it's not a wonderful taste. But neither are carrots, and those are apparently good for your eyes."

Elias hauled himself to his feet and began stowing his blanket. "Being born an elf is good for your eyes too, and that tastes significantly less bitter."

Jonas quirked a brow. "Does it?"

Elias had no response.

The morning was cold and foggy, but the trail soon became evident. The beasts they were following started walked in a mob, making it difficult to count them, but the amount of damage they did to the landscape made them easier to follow. While he was loath to admit it, Elias did feel the mental haze of the morning clear long before the fog of the bay. Maybe there was something to that drink Jonas had given him.

The tracks led a winding path up the foothill, towards a pass between two modest peaks. As they traveled, it became clear that there were two ogres, at most, and perhaps three trolls. The orc tracks all seemed to tread over themselves, but there were at most fifteen, perhaps less.

"Twenty beasts to our fifteen," Martin said in a hushed voice. "This is not going to be an easy fight."

As the sun sank towards the sea, Geoff jogged towards them from farther along the trail, where he had been scouting ahead. "Just over the next ridge, there's a cave. The tracks led inside, and the smells and sounds makes me think they are still there."

Jonas nodded. "Sleeping during the day. That would make sense for the trolls. They can't abide the sunlight."

Elias nodded. "So, we ambush them in their sleep?"

Jonas shook his head. "They are not animals. They will have left a watch." He looked around at the men who were gathering around. "We have eight bows among us, and about twenty arrows to a man."

Martin patted his quiver. "I've got thirty."

"Good. There's some dry grass behind us, and pitch from that downed pine," Jonas pointed at the deadfall. "Let's make some arrows we can set alight, and fire into the cave. Hopefully, we can kill the trolls before they get outside... I don't relish fighting them on open ground." He hiked his pack up onto his shoulder. "Come now, I want to see where we'll be fighting. This ambush will need to be quick, so there's not much time."

The band of mercenaries swiftly climbed the hill to the ridge, Elias bringing up the rear. They slowed to a walk, then a crawl as they came to the rounded, grassy top of the hillside. There was a small, bowl-shaped flat below, with a pond in the middle and a small stream leading from it to the rest of the valley. To the south was a steep cliff face made of bedrock, and amidst the boulders at its base was a deep crack in the cliff. Bones and entrails littered the ground in front of the cave, the smell of death and rotting flesh wafting up towards them.

Jonas pointed to a ravine across the clearing from the cave. "We'll approach from there. That pond is likely shallow, but it looks deep enough that crossing it would slow them down. That will force them to run around it, opening them up to our arrows. When they close with us, we fall back into the draw, letting them bottleneck in at us."

Martin turned to look at Jonas. "Are you mad? We'll be trapped in that ravine!"

Jonas shook his head. "It shouldn't come to that. Plus, look at the ridges. That ravine opens up to the valley below. We can fully retreat if we need to." He pointed to the top of the cliff, a bit higher than they were on the ridge. "I see some loose boulders up there. Elias, head up there and see if you can make some of them come down as the ogres exit the cave. Can you climb a rope?"

Elias nodded. "I can."

"Good. That means you can climb down one too. Take this." Jonas tossed Elias a large coil of rope, wrapped around the middle to keep it from tangling. "Tie it to a tree, a large one, a bit back from the cliff. After you've dropped the boulders, or the ogres are out of the cave, toss it down and come in from behind." He pointed to the three men closest to Elias, one of them being Timothy. "You lot join him, help be his eyes, and come down the rope with him."

"The rest of you, keep your swords ready, just inside the trees. As soon as they round the lake, come in with a shout, as loud as you can, and cut them down. If everything goes well, we should have them to ribbons before Redwood gets his boots on the ground."

He looked around at the men on either side of him. "Do you all know what you're doing?"

There was a muttered chorus of 'aye's, and Elias nodded, his pulse suddenly thundering in his ears.

"Then quick fucking about and get to it. You have fifteen minutes. Get where you're going."

Elias's breath caught in his throat, and he felt a little dizzy. This was real. It was really happening. He wondered if this was how the Northmen felt before a raid as he circled the valley with the three other men, climbing the slope towards the clifftop. It took maybe seven minutes before they were there, directly above the cave.

Just as Jonas had said, there were a few boulders, about the size of a man, perched on the edge of the cliff. Elias positioned himself behind one of the boulders, while Timothy tied the rope to a tree. He tested the boulder's weight. He could move it, and well. There were two other boulders nearby, and he pushed against those as well, shifting them slightly from where they perched. That gave him three large boulders... hopefully enough to crush the ogres.

He could see small flames flicker to life in the ravine, standing out in the growing darkness. Dusk was settling quickly, and the clearing was in a place that was sheltered by the ridge to the west. As soon as he noticed the flames, eight men – Jonas and Martin among them – shouted out a wordless battle cry. There was a commotion in the cave that sounded like wolves and hogs snarling, and a single long, deep rumble, and all eight arrows streaked across the pond and into the cave below. The growls and squeals turned into pained yelping; at least some of the arrows had found their marks.

The ground trembled as the rumble turned into a roar. It was like a score of demons were crying out all at once. Timothy crouched at the edge of the cliff, holding on to a sapling and looking down. He started waving his arm and pointing to the base of the cliff. "Now, Elias! Push the rock down now!"

Elias gripped the boulder, his fingertips scraping on the rough, mossy stone. It moved, but was much heavier than it had seemed the first time he had budged it. His muscles bunched as he pushed with his legs and back, ripping the boulder free from its perch. Adrenaline made his stomach flutter, and his hands and arms shook as he strained against the boulder. When it finally tipped over the edge, he almost followed it, catching himself on a small tree.

The boulder tumbled down the steep cliff, bouncing twice on the way down, before striking the ground next to an ogre and rolling over an orc, crushing its legs. It was the first time he had ever laid eyes on an ogre, and the sight made a chill run down his spine. It was at least twelve feet tall, covered in thick leather armor, and nearly half as wide as it was tall. Arms like legs sprouted from its massive torso, with thick hands gripping the haft of an axe that seemed too big to be real, rough forged and sharp only in the loosest of interpretations.

Beady red eyes glowed in the waning light, peering back at him from the shadows of a metal helmet. Elias realized he had been standing, staring with his jaw agape, as the second volley of flaming arrows streaked across the pond, thudding into the ogre and a few of the orcs.

None of them fell.

The ogre turned to face the ravine and roared again. Elias gripped another boulder and heaved against it, his adrenaline adding to his frantic strength. The boulder ripped free faster than the other one had, hurtling down the cliff, boosted by his panicked strength.

Whether the beast was too stupid to move or if it thought the boulder wouldn't hurt it, Elias couldn't tell. What he did see was the spray of blood and pinkish-gray matter that spewed from the underside of the boulder as it crushed the helmet and accompanying skull. It fell to the ground, driven by the boulder like a hammer to a nail, and Elias swore that he could feel the earth shudder as it landed.

Three creatures bolted from the cave, sprinting towards the pond, long limbs covered in dirty gray hair. They ran with a hunch, clawed hands nearly dragging on the ground, their backs and legs covered in black leather studded with metal plates. Flaming arrows struck two of them and they burst alight, stopping in their tracks to howl and beat at the flames.

Another ogre came sprinting from the cave, out of range of the boulders quicker than Elias could break another loose. "Down! Down! Down the rope!" he shouted, grabbing the thick fiber and swinging down over the edge.

The cliff face was not a completely vertical edge; it had a slight slope to it that Elias used to slide downwards. His heart beat faster than it ever had before, and his vision took on a red tinge. He swallowed his fear as he reached the pile of stones at the bottom of the rock face and his boots found purchase again. The other three men were descending rapidly, so he jumped clear, drawing his sword from its sheath.

Instantly, he was set upon by an orc. The creature beat its blade against his, the powerful blows driving Elias back as he fended them off. What the beast lacked in skill, it made up for twofold in savagery and strength. The creature clashed with him, locking blades and shoving Elias back against a boulder. Elias pushed back, bracing against the stone, knocking the orc off balance, and set upon him with the point of his blade, driving it through and into the ground. The orc screamed like a hog being gutted, and bludgeoned Elias in the face with the fist that held its sword. Elias caught the creature's wrist, forcing it back to the ground as the creature's other hand scrabbled at his throat.

The back of an axe flashed down and crushed the orc's face in front of Elias, causing him to startle and fall back. Timothy was standing over the creature, both hands on the haft.

"Are you alright?"

Elias nodded, breathless.

"Then come on! The fight is over there!"

Elias scrambled to his feet as Timothy turned and ran towards the skirmish at the opening of the ravine. Gripping his sword, he wrenched it free of the dead orc, and sprinted after the smaller man.

As he reached the battle, the second ogre swung his massive axe in a deadly arc, knocking three men down and killing another, crushing his ribs with the blunt weapon. Timothy darted in, sinking his axe into the ogre's lower back, burying it to the haft. The ogre howled and spun to face Elias and his companions, throwing the axe at them, reaching behind itself in a vain attempt to remove the weapon that was lodged there.

Elias dove to the right, dodging the axe, but the strangled scream he heard told him that one of the other men wasn't so lucky. He turned to see the axe buried into the ground, having crushed Timothy's arm at the elbow, severing it against the soil.

Suddenly, the ogre roared and fell, an arrow sticking out of its helmet, embedded in its eye. The third troll was being hacked to pieces, and Jonas was dispatching the final orc, running his sword through its chest. Kicking it off, Jonas swung hard and relieved it of its head, a final shout tearing out of older man's mouth as he did so. Raising his blackened, bloody sword over his head, he let out a wordless cry, echoed by the mercenaries that were still standing.

~   ~   ~

They made camp farther down in the valley, away from the stink of the battlefield. Most of their weapons and some of their armor were left at the scene of the battle, due to the smell. The orcs and ogres were bad enough, but the troll blood was enough to make anyone walking nearby retch.

They had a fire that night, as they had had no more reason for stealth. Two of the mercenaries checked the cave; there was almost nothing of value, and barely any air to breath. Piles of rotting meat, offal, and broken equipment were all they found, save for a single chest. They took it out with them, but could hardly stand to keep it with them, stained as it was with filth. They left it at the edge of the pond to be dealt with in the morning.

Four men had been killed outright in the battle and two more had taken wounds that they were not expected to recover from; Timothy had lost his arm and too much blood, while another man had been run through by a dirty orcish blade. They were laid out near the fire, and Geoff had given them a liquid made from poppies that dulled their pain and made them sleep.

Elias sat by Timothy, keeping the younger man company while the medicine took effect. Timothy muttered a few words, parts of stories, but mostly said nothing coherent. He kept reaching over to grab the stump of his right arm, which was wrapped in bloody bandages and had a cord tied around it to staunch the flow of blood. The other men had taken some wounds, but nothing terribly serious. Elias had helped with the basic aid, applying bandages and washing wounds, as he had only a few scratches. Jonas had gone to find a source of water that hadn't been fouled by the orcs, ogres and trolls.

Once Timothy fell asleep, Elias went to find Jonas. He was easy to follow, his passage leaving a dark path in the dew covered grass, where the light of the stars wasn't reflected back to Elias's keen eyes.

He found him about two hundred yards from the camp, standing on the bank of a small river. Elias made sure that he made enough noise that Jonas heard him approaching. Still, the older man did not turn to face him until they stood side by side.

Jonas looked up, forcing a smile across his grim features. Elias was suddenly very aware of how much older the man was, though he had seen fewer years than Elias had.

"So how was that for a first battle?

Elias furrowed his brow. "How do you know it was my first battle?"

Jonas chuckled, clapping Elias on the arm. "You were as white as a fresh bed sheet when I told everyone where to go. I wasn't sure you'd be able to fight, even as big as you are."

Elias frowned. "I'm not a coward."

Jonas frowned back at him. "I didn't say you were. You're untested, is all, and this was not an easy fight."

Elias turned to look over the shrub-dotted field. The noise of the stream running over the rocks in its bed was the only sound there. "Well... at least we won."

Jonas nodded, sighing. "Yes. Yes, we won, but at a price. Those men we lost... they were good men. Good men whose lives were spent fulfilling an errand best left for a militia or a squadron of soldiers."

Elias looked down at Jonas. "Is this not the sort of thing you do?"

Jonas kicked a stone hard enough to send it arcing into the water. "No, goddammit! We're bodyguards! We make our money off of protection! We scare men away from other men! We don't hunt packs of orcs, and we don't die on the job! You can't feed a family if you're dead!"

Elias nodded, not knowing what to say.

Jonas sighed again, and crouched down to fill the waterskins at his feet. "How many did we end up killing?"

"Two ogres, three trolls, and thirteen orcs."

Jonas was silent for a moment. "That's eighteen. Nine hundred coins split between fifteen men." He looked up at Elias. "Well, fourteen men and one elf."

"We return the shares of the fallen to their families, then?"

Jones bent down, and started filling the waterskins from the creek. "Aye. The weapon and purse of each man, with their share of this job. There's a courier station in Jetty, we should be able to contract them to take care of it."

Elias crouched down to help Jonas. "What of the men we lost?"

"They died in their homeland, so we'll bury them here, under stones. Once we burn the dead beasts, we'll bury them and mark their names. If their families want to retrieve their bones, they'll know who is who." He sighed, and tied off the last skin. "It won't be much of a funeral, but it's what we can do to honor our dead."

Elias stood, gathering the filled skins. "Then we shall honor them in the morning."

Chapter Five

12th Waning Flower Moon, Year 4368

The fog was thin that morning as the men labored. Timothy and the other wounded man had passed in their sleep, as Geoff had expected, bringing the number of their dead to six. The fallen mercenaries were washed and laid out in their armor to await their internment. The men that were able dug shallow pits into the earth and gathered stoned to cover them with. Geoff said a few words over the six graves before helping to cover them over with stones. Elias offered to carry their swords, bows, and personal belongings; the rest of their food and other supplies were divided amongst the surviving men.

After they dealt with their dead, the mercenaries began the distasteful task of collecting their bounty marks. They gathered ears from all the beasts except for the trolls; one of them had its ears burned off by the flames that had killed it. They took the right hands of all three trolls instead, to prove their kills.

They dragged the corpses of the dead beasts into two separate piles, one at each ogre, and covered them in dry brush and wood from nearby deadfalls. It took most of the morning and into the afternoon to gather enough fuel, but there was no grumbling amongst the men as they worked. Jonas said he would not have the bodies of the Felle Army scouts rotting so near to their fallen comrades. Though the task itself was distasteful, the rest of the men agreed.

As the pyres burned, they returned to their camp and started taking it down. Martin scowled. "I don't know if they smelled worse living, dead, or burning."

Jonas rolled his blanket tightly and bound it with a cord. "Dead, live, burned, the smell will soon be behind us. We leave as soon as the flames are low enough that they won't catch the rest of the forest on fire."

As they waited, two of the mercenaries hauled the chest they had found down to the campsite, doing their best to wash the filth off the outside. Once it was cleaned of most of the grime and gore that caked it, Martin took an axe to the lock, breaking it open.

Inside was a pouch of gold coins, stamped with a different mark than the lion that adorned their own currency. A folded piece of parchment turned out to be a crude map, with the northern end of the great Lonwick Valley marked out, as well as the path through the mountains the scouts had taken. The bays of Jetty and Fairhaven were circled, with a strange script jotted next to them. The roads to Pine River and Rockhill were marked in red, leading south to Castle Lonwick.

A second piece of parchment was folded around an iron medallion. The paper was covered in writing that nobody there recognized, though only Elias, Jonas and Geoff could read well. The medallion itself had no chain to it, and was blackened iron, still covered in firescale from when it had been forged. The outer edge of the piece was a raised ring, with an eight-pointed star touching it at its points. In the center of the star was a deep red stone with a crack in it, the color of fresh arterial blood.

Elias turned the medallion over in his hands. "The knight that attacked me on the road from Pine River had this on his breastplate."

Jonas nodded, considering the information. "Well, that definitely means that he was a part of the Felle Army, and they're making their way north. If this map means anything at all, it looks like they were scouting out bays. See, here, they circled Jetty and Fairhaven, though they ignored Greatport... too heavily guarded, perhaps?"

Elias drummed his fingers on his knee, pondering the indecipherable writing. "I wonder if this has clues to what it is they were looking for, and why."

Martin tossed a soiled rag into the fire. "What does it matter? We're not here to stop them, we're here to kill this lot, and this lot only, and we did. The rest of it is not our concern. Let the soldiers from Lonwick deal with them."

Geoff threw a stick at Martin, bouncing it off his leg. "What good will an elven army be for us, when they are three thousand miles away and fighting their own war?"

Martin spat and scowled. "They're not three thousand miles away, ya damn fool, they're three hundred miles away, and that's if you take the long route through Greatport and up the coast."

Geoff frowned. "May as well be three thousand for all the good it would do us. The only thing they send up here is tax collectors. I'd wager we're on our own."

Martin shook his head. "Fact remains, we're no army, and it ain't our job."

Elias sat quietly, looking into the fire, rolling the medallion in his hand. What did that knight want from him? Why travel all the way to the edge of the Northlands to attack just him, when the armies of Lonwick were still far to the south?

~   ~   ~

Once the flames had died down to a level where they no longer had to be monitored, the men made their way back over the western ridge and down towards the bay. The bodies of the Felle scouts were surprisingly flammable; there was hardly anything but bones left among the embers as they crossed back to the sea side of the ridge.

Elias paused at the top of the hill, taking one last look into the valley. The bonfires kept it well lit, though the sun was making its slow journey towards the sea. He could see the six cairns in the trampled grass, arranged in an arc at the edge of the clearing. It would not be hard for the families of the fallen men to find them.

The usual banter of the mercenaries was nonexistent, with most of them keeping to themselves. The only conversations were those of necessity as they cut through the forest towards the bay. They made camp at the treeline near the fields as the sun sank below the water. The walk was taking a bit longer than usual, as there were some men with wounds that slowed them down.

The sea breeze was a little more pronounced here, so the night was cool but clear. They sat around the fire, perched on fallen logs or on the ground. The sounds of the forest were broken only by the crackle of the flames.

One of the men started tapping out a slow rhythm on one of the pieces of firewood, the sound having a nearly musical tone to it, clear and sharp. Another man joined in, tapping the butt of his walking stick against the hollow log he was sitting on. The deep, echoing bass accompanied the other rhythm nicely. Before long, Geoff pulled a small wooden flute from his pack, and joined in, a simple melody floating out as his fingers worked over the precisely drilled holes.

At first, Elias was worried that the sound would attract anyone who happened to be near the road, perhaps more scouts, but soon, the soothing, simple music settled his nerves. Every man, himself included, was soon tapping a foot or nodding their head in rhythm. Even Martin, as dour as he could be, joined in by tapping a short, thick stick against the blade of his dagger, making a high, musical ringing.

Some of the men took turns singing songs, various tales of heroism, comedy, or loss. Elias wished that Timothy was there, to tell a story to lighten their hearts.

After a while, Jonas started humming a tune that Elias had never heard before, and the rhythm of the impromptu music changed to follow his. He started singing, his roguish accent fitting well to the tune. Elias hadn't figured Jonas to be much of a singer, but he did quite well.

Of all the gold that e'er I lost
I've spent it in good company
And all the harm that e'er was done
At least it ne'er was to me
And all I've done for want of wit
To memory now I can't recall
So fill to me the parting glass
Farewell and peace be with you all

Oh, all the comrades that e'er I had
They're sorry for my going away
And all the sweethearts that e'er I had
They'd wish me one more day to stay
But since it falls unto my lot
That I should rise and you should not
I'll gently rise and softly call
Farewell and peace be with you all

No more men sang after Jonas, but the rhythms continued for a short while afterwards. Elias fell asleep listening to them, his dreams dark, clouded by the face of the knight that had tried to kill him on the road barely a week before. Now, they had found a medallion that matched the insignia on his armor. Elias still had no idea what the knight wanted from him, but he resolved to find out. He had a feeling his life depended on it.

~   ~   ~

13ᵗʰ Waning Flower moon, Year 4368

They approached the gate of Jetty around noon. It stood open, as it had the first time, with several guards posted in front of it. Jonas stepped ahead of the rest of their group as they grew near. The same guard that had greeted him before stepped out from the shade of the gate.

"Hello, Jonas. Welcome back. I take it you've met the Mayor's terms?"

Jonas nodded, and tossed the tied bundle of ears and hands on the ground at the guard's feet. "Eighteen. Thirteen orcs, three trolls, and two ogres. Your mayor promised us fifty lions a head for them."

The guardsman stared at the bundle. "... eighteen? By the gods, Jonas."

Jonas waved the words away. "To hell with that. Just fetch him, that we may complete our business. We have wounded men that could use some rest and comfort."

The guard gestured to another man, who hurried into the town. It was nearly half an hour before the mayor arrived, flanked again by a squadron of militiamen. He stopped just short of Jonas and his crew.

"You have returned, victorious I hear?"

Jonas nodded. "The job's done. We're here for what we are owed."

The mayor looked over the group. "I seem to remember a greater number of men stood before me three days ago."

Jonas clenched a fist. "You know what you sent us into. Six of our number are buried in those hills."

The mayor nodded, his bravado faltering for a moment. "For that, you have my condolences."

Jonas spat on the ground between them. "I don't want your condolences, I want what is owed, and I want you to get out of my way."

The mayor frowned, setting his jaw. "You should remember who you're talking to, sellsword." The militiamen around him stepped forward, hands on their hilts. "You might have done this city a service, but I am still its mayor."

The mercenaries stepped forward, hands on their weapons as well. Elias stood next to Jonas, towering over everyone present, the grip of his sword feeling minuscule in his hand. After their battle on the hill, was there to be more bloodshed? He cleared his throat, drawing the attention of everyone present.

"I am sure that the mayor means no disrespect, and means only to honor our fallen comrades with his words. It would be best, I think, to conclude our dealings quickly, that we might all get out of the sun, and attend to our business." He nodded towards the mayor. "You, undoubtedly, have much ahead of you this day, running a port of this size, and we have arrangements to make for the families of our dead."

Jonas looked up at Elias strangely, as if he was debating an objection, before patting him on the arm. "The elf speaks wisdom. This heat does nobody any favors, least of all my humour."

"Agreed. He does speak with the wisdom of his kind." The mayor turned to the men behind him and gestured for them to come forward. Two men carried a small iron banded chest, setting it down in front of the mayor. Pulling a key from his finery, he unlocked it and drew out nine pouches.

"Fifty gold lions a head, as agreed. I'll leave the sorting to you, but rest assured, it's all there." He dropped them into a burlap sack and handed it to the guardsman who had greeted them. As the guardsman delivered the gold to Jonas, the mayor gestured to the ears and hands on the road. "Take those and burn them. Scatter the ashes into the sea at the south end of the city. Don't walk them through town, the smell is bad enough out here. Take a boat along the bay, and for the love of the gods, don't let the troll blood get on you. That stink never goes away."

The mayor looked up at Elias as Jonas divided the coin amongst the men. "You speak with the mind of an elf, and yet you dress like a man of the north and keep company with brigands. Praytell, where are you from?"

Jonas snorted behind Elias at being called a brigand and handed the tall elf a pouch of coins. Elias crossed his arms, dropping the pouch into the front of his tunic. "I was born in Silva Aestas but was sent to live amongst the men of the north many years ago. It was time for me to move on and make something of myself, so I set out from Valtheim three weeks ago."

The mayor nodded, regarding Elias closely. "An interesting tale, no doubt. Perhaps someday I'll invite you to my manor, and you can relay it to me."

Elias did not respond, and the mayor nodded. "Right then. Our gates are open to you now. Thank you for your services, and remember the first part of our agreement. Try not to make a mess. I'd hate for there to be a repeat of last time." He turned and waved to his armed entourage, and strode back into the town, The guardsmen stood aside, leaving the path through the gate open.

Elias watched them go, starting when Jonas patted him on the back. "A regular negotiator, are you? We should make you our ambassador." He turned back to the men. "Come on, lads, there's ale to drink and lonely women in this town in need of our company. Our brothers are overdue for their wake. Let's not disappoint them!"

~   ~   ~

The city was set up in a fairly efficient manner. A broad road led from the gate to a wide, open area where townsfolk bustled about their daily business. In the middle of the square was a low stone structure covering a raised stone ring, likely the town's well. Wooden buildings surrounded the open area, with wide streets leading off to the east, west, and south. On the east side of town, two large buildings dominated the shore of the bay. One was taller than the other, at least four stories high. Ornately carved pillars decorated the front, and there were an obscene amount of balconies on all of the faces of the building that Elias could see. It had to be the mayor's mansion, judging by the gaily colored pennant flying from a spire on the tallest part of the building.

The other was an enormous square structure, wider than the mansion, but not as tall. Regularly spaced windows broke the monotony of the darkened redwood boards that made up the exterior; this was most likely the inn.

Elias followed the road south through into the large square, townsfolk giving him a wide berth as he walked past them. Men and elves of both genders bustled about, as well as short, stocky dwarves. Elias couldn't tell the men from the women from behind; they were roughly the same size, about half as tall as he was, and dressed in fairly similar clothing. From the front, however, the primary difference was that the men sported long, thick beards, often growing down to their belts or farther.

Jonas chuckled as he walked with Elias. "Never seen a dwarf before?"

Elias looked down at Jonas. "Of course I have, but here? By the sea? I thought they only lived in the mountains."

Jonas shook his head. "Nah, they only work mines and quarries as much as they do because that's what they're told to do. Working with metal and stone is a skill their kind have in abundance, yes, but just as many work wood or grow vegetables or fruit trees." He pointed towards the docks at the bay. "Many of those ships were made by dwarven craftsmen. They do a bit more work away from the hills this far north."

Elias furrowed his brow. "What do you mean, told to do? Told by whom?"

Jonas snorted. "You have been away from your own kind for a while, haven't you? Told by the elves. Farther south, that's all there is, and the dwarves have been told to keep to themselves and dig if they know what's good for them. They apparently don't get on very well with the forest folk, and the sentiment is returned."

Jonas stood by Elias as they stopped next to the well in the center of the city square. "I've got some business to attend to... I'll need to hire couriers to deliver the weapons of the fallen to their kin, and that won't be cheap. I'll see if they will take the coins we found in the cave... if not, I'll have them melted down and re-cast into lions."

Elias looked down at Jonas, surprised. "You can do that?"

Jonas shrugged. "Not me, personally, no, but Jetty has a master of coin. The hills here and inland have gold in them, and it's fairly useless unless it's turned into coins or wares. I can't buy a courier with a necklace, so lions it is."

"What, they just melt them down and recast them right there?"

Jonas laughed. "No, that takes time and a certain amount of gold, which we don't have. They'll trade it out for an equal weight, minus their cut. Everyone is in the business of lining their pockets."

Elias nodded. "That makes sense. Business is business."

Jonas patted Elias's shoulder. He seemed to have a habit of doing that; at first, it had seemed a little patronizing, but over time Elias had come to realize it was just a part of the man's friendly nature. "It is at that." He looked up, putting a hand over his eyes to shield them from the sun. "You still set on that sword, Redwood? You handled the one you have well enough."

Elias nodded. "I am."

Jonas shrugged "Do what works for you, I guess. The blacksmith is at the south end of town. See what he has, but mind you, we don't have time to have one made. We've lost three days, and we're due to meet Lord Woodsetter here tomorrow at noon."

"Lord Woodsetter?"

Jonas nodded. "Our next customer. I'd meant to have a bit more time to rest up, but this is the way of it. We'll take our rest in Pine River, once we've escorted him to where he's going. You'll need to take some time to resupply here; your pack comes out of your pay, and you have more than enough of it to make it last." He shook one finger at Elias warningly. "Keep it close, though. These streets are known for their pickpockets. Meet us at the inn when you're done. I'll have a room for us." He lifted his pack up onto his shoulder. "One more thing; try to keep the questions to others to a minimum. There are those who would see that as an opportunity to take advantage."

With that, Jonas turned and walked away, leaving Elias to his own devices. He looked about and caught several children staring at him. They turned and ran as soon as he looked in their direction. With a sigh, he headed south along the main road.

Shops and booths lined the road, offering different products and services. One such shop was open to the air, a small forge belching smoke into the clear air. A farrier, it seemed, making horseshoes and parts for wagons. A wagon stood nearby, blocks supporting an axle that had no wheels.

Some of the townsfolk stared at him unabashedly as he walked past, others pointedly didn't notice him. The shopkeepers, however, called out to him as he passed, offering various goods. One of the merchants was a hunter, it seemed, and had stacks of jerky, pork, beef, and venison. A coin later, and he had a leather-wrapped bundle that should last him for most of the trip stowed in his pack.

At the southern end of the town, nearest to where the peninsula ended in the channel that connected the bay to the sea, there was the blacksmith's forge. On racks set out in the sun was a broad selection of tools and weapons, suits of armor on stands; chainmaille, leather breastplates studded with small iron plates, and steel helmets of varying designs. Several men were polishing and cleaning the swords, replacing them on the racks when they were oiled and sharpened.

One man held a sword that was longer than he was tall. The sun glinted off of the massive weapon's edge in a way that caught Elias's eye, instantly drawing his attention. From a distance, he couldn't tell the workmanship, of course, but it was exactly what he was looking for, in terms of size.

He approached the man polishing it. "How much for that sword?"

The man looked up, then up again. "Bloody hell!" he said, not bothering to hide his reaction to Elias's presence. "You're a great whopping elf, aren't you?"

Elias set his jaw, ignoring the man's comment. "That sword. How much."

The man looked down at the sword he was polishing, seeming like he was seeing it again for the first time. "This one? I don't know that it's for sale. You'll have to talk to Darby." The man hooked a thumb over his shoulder, indicating a short, square figure in the forge. "He can set the price, if any at all."

Elias nodded, picking his way past the racks of tools and weapons. The stout man was busy at the forge, smoke rolling about in the still air. Sparks flew from red hot steel, the dull cherry of the glow shining through the haze like a small beacon. The strikes of the hammer beat a steady rhythm against the anvil, gripped in a fist almost as large as Elias's own. Elias cleared his throat, to draw the man's attention.

"I hear ya there. What do ya need?" Darby's voice was deep and gruff, but not unfriendly.

"One of your workers was polishing a sword. I'd like to know how much it is."

Darby didn't stop working. "Longswords're three gold lions, shortswords are two. Hand and a half swords range from three t' five, dependin' on which one y' want."

Elias shook his head. "The one I want is as long as I am tall. I asked the man polishing it, and he sent me to you."

The next hammer strike didn't land. Darby paused in his work and looked up at Elias. Even though Elias was bent down to peer under the edge of the roof, the smith still had to look upwards to meet Elias's eyes.

"I see. That's a good amount o' sword. Ya sure ya want it?"

Elias nodded. "I'd like to inspect it before I decide, but I believe so, yes."

Darby squinted, wiping sweat from his brow. "I don't have time t' go over it with ya today. These blades aren't gonna forge themselves, and I have a quota t' fill." He struck the steel one more time before burying it back into the red coals of the forge. "Come back tomorrow, before noon. We'll look it over then."

Elias frowned. "Tomorrow before noon? That's a bit of a wait."

Darby scoffed as he fished out another red hot bar. "It's also the only sword like it south o' the Northlands. If you want it, yer gonna need to wait 'til tomorrow." Hammer strikes started falling again as Darby resumed his work.

Elias scowled as he turned away from the forge. He hated waiting.

Chapter Six

14th Waning Flower Moon, Year 4368

The salt air smelled fresh and cool in the morning, not fishy and stagnant like he had expected. Being on a bay had its ups and its downs, with one of the downsides being the smell. Fishing was a huge part of making a living here, and the ever present aroma of fish had confirmed this when they arrived. Not this day. This day, the air was clean and clear, with a slight breeze coming from the sea, making short work of the morning fog.

Running a hand through his short hair, Elias faced the rising sun, just now clearing the low mountains to the east. The triangular sails of the fishing boats darted to and fro over the shallow bay. Occasionally, one of the boats would pause long enough to haul in a net full of wriggling silver fish, or a cage full of crabs or other underwater critters.

Elias sighed. By the gods, he hated fish.

He turned and ducked through the door to the inn room he had shared with several of the mercenaries and Jonas the night before. They had mostly left him alone, deciding instead to lose themselves in food, drink, and women, dealing with the aftermath of their mission in their own ways. The rest of the patrons of the tavern had been mostly focused on themselves, and the rest of the time they were too oblivious to notice anything else. There had been a marked lack of elves, though the dwarves had been out in force. He was unused to this level of racial mixing.

Stretching, he grunted slightly as he felt the tight muscles in his shoulders and lower back protest. The beds here were far too small for him, so he had ended up on the floor in front of the small hearth. Even with all the blankets and furs laid down, the floor was as hard as one would have expected, being made out of wood. Even the dirt on the side of a road had been softer.

He kicked the footboard of one of the four occupied beds, causing Jonas to snort and stir. Bleary-eyed, the older man sat up, scratching his unkempt scruff.

"Eight hells, Elias, what is it? What the bollocks do you want?"

Elias slipped on his tunic, turning away. "It's well past dawn. You sleep like the dead, old man. We're due to meet our employer in less than two hours." He strapped his sword belt around his waist, weaving and tying the leather through the iron rings, adjusting the sheath of his longsword so that it rode comfortably at his left hip.

Jonas flopped back down on the bed, groaning a little before rolling over and swinging his feet to the ground. "Be a good lad and fetch me some ale."

Elias scoffed. "I've four times as many years as you, old man, and I think you drank all the ale last night. The last thing you need is more."

Jonas growled a little, more of a grunt and a groan rolled into one. "You might have seen more years, elf, but you're younger in life, and you know it. I'll decide when I've had enough." He rose shakily to his feet and rubbed his face. Squinting into the sun, he stumbled towards the open window, chamber pot in hand.

Elias turned away, still put off a bit by the brazen attitude of the mercenaries. Jonas chuckled as he emptied his bladder into the pot while looking out into the bay. "On the road or in an inn room, a man still needs to piss. Can't always traipse off into the woods to water the grass." The man hitched his trousers back up and dumped the pot out the window onto the rocks below. "If orcs or bandits raid a caravan you're guarding while you're off making streams, it's mighty hard to get paid."

Elias shrugged. He could feel a surge of pride and irritation rise up inside of him despite his cool exterior, but he pushed it down, as he had done for years. His own kind had shunned him for his abnormal size in his youth, and while they were more subtle, that just made their words cut that much deeper. At least what humans lacked in subtlety, they also lacked in wit. "I'm going to get some food and pick up my sword. I'll meet you at the square in an hour and a half."

"Your sword? You've already been to see the blacksmith?"

"It was the first place I went." While he had drank a mug of ale with the rest of the men, to honor the memory of the fallen, he had kept it to one. He knew well the effects of alcohol, as the Northerners were master brewers.

He shouldered his pack and ducked through the door frame into the low hallway. It was dim and smoky, lit by flickering candles in dirty lanterns. The smells here were strong and none too pleasant, with an ever present odor of feet, of all things. Feet and dirty bodies.

He did his best not to curl his nose in disgust as he made his way to the entrance of the tavern. Several people jostled into him, likely just to make a point, but they bounced off of him more than he off of them. Most people gave him a wide enough berth.

As he stepped outside, he smelled the fish. On the second floor balcony, it hadn't been evident, but here in the streets, the smell was pervasive. He huffed a sigh. The sooner they moved out from this smelly town the better. Life on the road was far preferable to the noises, smells, and stares of city living.

Keeping a hand on his belt pouch to ward off cutpurses, he made his way through the streets to the south end of the peninsula that separated the bay from the sea itself. The loud, raucous voices of the hawkers rang out over the crowds, selling cheap baubles and wares from across the water for far more than they were worth. The bone beads and pearls from the islands were popular here, as were the bracelets and bands touted as gold from this or that lost kingdom or far away land… little more than polished brass. He let his attention wander over the booths as he passed them on his way to the blacksmith. This was a different road than he had taken the day before and had different booths, closer to the docks.

"Come, come, see the treasures from the lost islands of Greenreef! The greatest craftsmanship ever seen on these shores, from the hands of the sea-elves!" The pieces on display were attractive; polished stone and coral beads, bracelets and necklaces, pearls set in silver, and volcanic glass from the mountains of fire rising out of the sea, which the islands themselves were made from. He'd never been there, of course, but there were many tales about them, even in the Northlands. Maybe one day he'd see them himself, he mused as he moved through the crowds and stalls.

"Beads and silks from the oases of the burning sands! No finer gems or bones will you find! Ivory, rubies, emeralds and diamonds!" Elias had no desire to ever go to the eastern desert beyond the plains and mountains, but he had to admit that the gems and stones that came from the walled cities around the oases were captivatingly beautiful. They seemed to retain the fire of the sands that birthed them, and sparkled like coals in the early sunlight. He lifted one to the light and looked through it toward the sun.

"Buy it or leave it on the table!" snapped the man who stood next to the cart, snatching it out of his hand when he went to put it back. "I don't need any bushwalkers getting their greedy elven hands on these precious stones!" The slur stung a bit, and he walked away from the cart. Just as well, there were small bubbles inside the stone, almost too small for even Elias to see. That 'gemstone' was glass.

"Fish and crab! Lobster and clams! Fresh caught, ready to cook fillets! Bacon and beef, pork and venison! Halves, quarters, or jerky!" Ah, now this is what he was looking for. He didn't want to take from the supplies he had purchased for the trip, since he had the coin to feed himself now. Drawing a few copper lions out of his belt pouch, he bought a thick, tender slab of jerky, and a small loaf of bread from a vendor nearby. Slicing it in half with the small dagger he kept sheathed at his left hip, he made an impromptu sandwich and ate it as he headed towards the armory.

As he approached the building, he took the time to study it, having been somewhat preoccupied the day before. The armory was shorter than almost every other building in the town, its low stone walls supporting the broad, ceramic tiled roof. The twin smokestacks pumped black coal smoke inland over the building, pushed by the sea breeze, leaving a perpetual black grime coating most surfaces directly downwind of the forge. The sandy gravel of the street was covered with a thin black layer of soot, with footprints breaking through it, leaving gray tracks.

The forges and furnaces were already roaring, almost drowning out the ocean, while the ring of hammers against steel pierced the mid-morning air with a satisfying rhythm. The racks that had been scattered in front of the forge the day before were mostly bare, a few men carrying tools and weapons out for the day's display. It seemed that they took them in and put them away every night, which made sense, to deter theft.

He had never worked steel himself, but it was always a craft that fascinated him. To draw metal from stone and form it into objects that had a use, to know how to cool it and quench it, to know how to heat it and strike it to make it resilient; it was a craft skill he had great respect for. He had spent much time with the iron workers in the Northlands, and their love of iron, steel, and copper had been instilled in him.

Darby saw him coming, and paused in his work. The man was almost as wide as he was short, shorter even than most elves, but more massive by far. He wasn't a dwarf, necessarily, unless he was afflicted by the same curse that made Elias himself a giant amongst his kind, but he was by no means just a man, either. Perhaps bloodlines had crossed, and the metalworker drew his skills and his appearances from mankind's subterranean cousins.

"You're back again, lad?"

"I am, Darby. I've decided I would like to purchase the greatsword."

The blacksmith quirked an abnormally bushy eyebrow. "I know it's none o' me business, really, but do ya know how to use a sword like the one ya got yer eye on?"

Elias shrugged, grinning. "Hit the other man with it really, really hard." Despite his gruff and slightly abrasive attitude, the blacksmith was warm, friendly, and Elias liked him. He looked at the weapons that were in various stages of manufacture. Blade blanks sat off to the side, ready to be ground down and smoothed, various lengths, widths, and shapes. Several assistants were working on those parts, grinding the edges smooth on a large stone wheel attached to the windmill, fitting crossguards and handles to the tangs, pinning the pommels and handles into place, and wrapping the handles with wet, stretched leather. One older man sat with a rack of swords next to him, honing the blades on a wide, flat whetstone before putting them on a final rack for inspection.

Darby flipped the blade he had been working on, inspected it, and struck it a few more times with his hammer. Sparks flashed in the shade of the stone roof as the hammer struck red steel, which was rapidly cooling to the dark, burned gray of the rest of the blanks. "I've got a moment, now, to pull it out. D'ya have the coin for it, lad?"

"I've got some coin. I was hoping you'd be interested in a trade."

"A trade? For what?"

Elias removed the longsword and sheath from his belt, and held it out to the smith. Darby raised an eyebrow at him again, and buried the blade he was working on back into the coals of the forge. "I'm not sure if you've noticed, lad, " he said, in a conspiratory tone, "but I'm not exactly experiencing a shortage of blades. I've got more than I can shake my tongs at."

"Yes, but this is elven steel, and already made, so you can sell it without having to smelt the iron, hammer it into steel, or make the fittings. Ready to go with no extra effort, as it were."

The blacksmith laughed. "What do I look like, a trader from the burning sands? And 'elven steel'? My steel would cut it like it was copper!" The blacksmith picked up an axe head that had yet to be fitted to a handle, and struck it against a steel rod that was sitting on a workbench, cutting half a foot off the end. "Can yer elven steel do that?"

Elias drew the blade, not at all sure it could. Holding the steel rod against the workbench, he swung the longsword down hard. With a ring, several inches of the steel rod skipped across the floor. He held the blade up, inspecting it. Where the sword had struck the bar, there was a deep scratch, a bit of a nick, but no real damage. None that would make it unfit for service, at least.

Darby took the blade and inspected it himself. "It's hard steel, there's no doubt. Good balance, straight edge…" He shook it a bit, listening for any sounds, then sheathed it. "No rattles in the hilt, tight sheath. Why d'ya want to get rid of this one, then? It's a good blade." All earlier bravado aside, the blacksmith was appreciative of good craftsmanship.

"It's far too small. A sword like this should have a blade as long as the wielder's leg, but the pommel comes to just under my belt. My hand barely fits between the guard and the pommel, so using it with two hands is not an option. I definitely need a bigger weapon, and I'm not fond of axes." It was true; the sword was made for an elf of normal proportions, and as such was far too small for him.

"Ye've got a point, at that. Unfortunately, I have no use for it." The smith turned to face him again, holding up a single thick finger. "Fifteen gold lions. That's half of what its worth, and I'll not take a single coin less. I hope you've got it still, and haven't spent it all on wine and women."

Elias nodded, ignoring the playful jab. "I want to hold it first, to make sure it's exactly what I want."

"Trust me, lad, if a greatsword is what ye want, yer gonna want it." Darby turned to the side, leading the way out the back of the building. On his way out, he shouted at his assistant. "Thomas! Lay off the bellows for a moment. Keep the steel hot, but don't y' dare melt my swords unless you want me t' replace them with yer bones!"

Even though he hadn't been in the armory for long, the bright sunlight made Elias squint as he stepped out the back, between the windmill and the smelter. The heat from the forge had become stifling, and he welcomed the ocean breeze that cooled the sweat on his brow. There was another stone building, this one with a wood shingled roof, about ten yards away from the forge. Since the workers had been moving weapons out of the armory to put them on display, the heavy iron-clad door was already open, the thick lock hanging from the hasp. Stepping inside the building, Darby gestured for Elias to follow.

Inside, dust motes hung in the air, swirling as they were disturbed by the passage of the smith. The smell of honing oil, leather, and steel was thick in his nose, and on every wall of the room were racks for holding weapons. Most of the spaces were empty, but a number of swords, spears, axes, halberds, and pikes were stored. Some helmets, breastplates, gauntlets, and greaves were here and there, strapped to rudimentary armor stands, and several barrels held handle blanks for polearms.

Darby headed towards a rack that held the absolutely massive sword, and Elias got a good, up-close look at it. The handle made up about a foot and a half of the total length, and the blade at the hilt was nearly as wide as

Elias's palm, narrowing until about six inches from the point, where it swept into a wickedly sharp tip. The blade was thick, almost half as thick as a finger in the middle, with a fuller running two-thirds the length of the blade. The handle was wide and oval shaped, wrapped in shiny black leather, with steel rings locking the wrap into place every few inches, to aid with the grip. A round brass pommel was at the bottom, with steel bands running around it for reinforcement.

Darby lifted the sword off of the wall, grunting under the weight of it. Gripping it on the handle, against the guard, with the flat of the blade against his left palm, he held it out to Elias.

Elias took the blade firmly, supporting the blade with his other hand as the smith let go. The sword was heavy, but not too much for him to hold. He moved his grip so that he had both hands on the handle and held it out in front of him. The long handle and heavy pommel helped with the balance, but it was obvious that this was not a blade made for fencing. It was made for cutting through a man in one swing, and for someone who was very used to swinging heavy things. "This sword has to weigh at least twenty pounds!"

Darby nodded. "At least. I used enough steel and brass in that monster for five other swords."

Elias took it out into the sun. The blade was perfectly polished, and while the edge was no razor, it would definitely cut a man if it hit one. "How did you come by making this?"

Darby rubbed the back of his neck. "Well... it was requested by someone else, but I don't think he'll be wanting it anymore."

Elias paused in his examination of the sword. "Why is that? What sort of man would need a sword like this? Not that I'm complaining, not at all..." He swung the sword in a few arcs, the edge cutting the air with a satisfying hiss.

"He never gave me his name, but I was pretty sure to remember him. Big man, bigger even than you. Ugly as a bag of sinners. Had to have some ogre's blood in him somewhere. Huge hands, he could barely fit them on the handle, even as big I made it, skin kinda green or yellow, I couldn't tell. Provided half of the iron and the leather too... that iron was wicked hard to melt. Had t' fire the forge hotter than I ever have since." Darby shook his head. "The day he was to come give me what he owed on it, he was lynched and hung. They said he killed and ate a man raw with his bare hands." The blacksmith shuddered. "If he'd have had this sword, I don't know that they would have gotten him. As it were, he put two men in their graves and another dozen to the healers."

Elias paused. "Darby, this sword is worth more than you're charging me for it. I can't take it knowing that I'm not paying for it."

Darby scoffed. "D'ya think I'm in the charity business? That sword was all but paid for, all but fifteen lions. Those fifteen coins in your purse will finish that off. Besides… who else am I going to sell it to? It's yours, lad. All ya gotta do is buy it." He held the sheath upright like a walking stick, the top of it well over the short man's head.

"What d'ya say? Do we have a deal?"

Elias took the scabbard and sheathed the enormous blade. "How much for a harness to wear this on my back while I'm traveling? I don't think my belt will work for this."

Darby offered his meaty, calloused hand. "Throw in an extra silver, and I've got one that'll work for it well enough."

Elias took the smith's hand. "Then we have a deal."

Chapter Seven

14th Waning Flower Moon, Year 4368

Elias stood near the well in the town square, leaning against one of the hewn wooden beams that supported the roof of the structure that covered it. He was used to feeling like he stood out but now, with a shiny new gigantic sword strapped to his back, it felt even more pronounced. For a moment, he regretted his decision, but that was fleeting. The weight of it on his back was reassuring, even if he knew he'd need to become accustomed to it. He pushed his reticence away; it was almost time to meet his employer.

Jonas was thankfully present, even if he still looked a bit rough and smelled of beer. He was sitting on a crate in the shade of the well house, having a lively chat with Martin. It seemed strange to Elias that a single night of celebration could work to erase so much of the melancholy that had haunted the group after the loss of six of their members, but almost everyone was in better spirits.

Jonas looked up at Elias, grinning from behind his unkempt whiskers. "So you bought it then? Just had to have the great huge sword, eh?"

Elias frowned slightly. "After being attacked on the road, then battling the orcs, it proved to me that a longsword isn't nearly long enough."

There was a slight snickering from some of the gathered sellswords. Jonas grinned again, mischief in his eyes. "Boy, it's not about the size of your weapon, it's all in how you use it!" The men about laughed openly now, with a few whistles and catcalls. "Though I can understand wanting to know what it's like to be able to fit both hands around something at the same time. Never lacked for that knowledge, myself."

Amidst the peals of laughter from the more seasoned men, Elias felt himself getting irritated. During his time with the Northmen, he was never openly picked on, though he had been excluded often enough. Quiet discrimination he was used to, even from his own kind, but this was more than most people had dared to do since he was a child.

"Maybe I should wrap both of my hands around your neck, old man, " he said, pushing off of the beam and taking a step towards Jonas. "Perhaps that's a satisfaction I should discover."

Jonas laughed again, reaching up to clap Elias on the shoulder. "Oh come on, you moody shit, I'm just tuggin' your rope. If I didn't prick you every now and again, you'd think I didn't like you. Besides, you can't kill me yet, I haven't gotten your pay from our esteemed employer. It'd be a shame to have to try to stay fed on the wages you've had as yet, especially for a big bastard like yourself."

Elias's irritation evaporated, leaving him feeling foolish. This was just how Jonas was around his men, teasing and joshing them. There were no tongues held here, and the crew seemed to be more or less loyal to each other and to him, especially since their battle in the hills. He was new, low in the pecking order, and subject to hazing, now that he was formally a member of the group.

He set his jaw. Nowhere was it written that he had to like it.

Jonas glanced down the road from the south, and snapped his gloved fingers to the rest of his men. "Form up. Our gilded benefactor approaches." He stepped out of the shade of the well house and into the already hot sun as a carriage came up the road from the south.

On either side of the carriage were two mounted riders, while one wizened old man sat in the driver's seat, the reins in hand. The carriage was pulled by oxen, while the riders were on rather unremarkable horses. Elias himself hadn't ridden a horse since the elves had taken him north; there was no reason for it when he lived mostly within the walls of the city, and he had quickly outgrown most of the steeds the Northmen raised.

The carriage drew up to the well house and one of the riders dismounted, opening the door on the near side. A small, thin, bald head stuck out of the opening, from behind a black velvet curtain. Elias tried not to stare, but he swore that the man's nose was so long he could probably smell Elias from across the square.

Jonas went into an elaborate, flourishing bow. "At your service, m'lord Woodsetter. I've assembled the finest caravan guardsmen on this side of the Gray Sea"

Beady, birdlike eyes darted about. "This is all of your men?" The man didn't even bother to greet Jonas. "I count nine, yourself included. Your message said fifteen."

Jonas stood, looking around at the assembled men. "It did? Aye, it did, well, eh, these nine swords more than make up for the difference! Each man here has half again the strength of your standard escort, and twice the skill!"

"I still only count nine. This will damage your pay, Master Jonas."

Jonas stiffened slightly. "If the cargo arrives unharmed, what is the difference if I do it with nine men, or ninety? Some of the lads had purses bigger than what was offered." He took a step back, turning slightly away as

Elias quirked a brow at him, wondering about the mistruth. "If they aren't to your liking, m'lord, we could always allow you to go on your way unsullied by our presence." He gestured with his chin towards the chained and locked cargo on the back of the carriage. "I'm sure whoever is waiting for that will understand the delay needed to find a new escort."

The scrawny man made a sour face and snarled. "Fine! So be it! If one hair on my head or one sliver of wood from those chests is harmed, you'll get not one gold lion from me!"

Jonas turned back, a wide grin on his face. "Excellent! When do we depart?"

"As soon as my manservant arrives with the supplies I sent him out for. I expect him to be at the front gate within an hour, and I will expect you there as well." With no further ceremony, the old man pulled his head back behind the velvet curtain, and the rider shut and bolted the door.

Jonas turned back to the assembled mercenaries. "You heard the man, to the city gates! If he's waiting, we're waiting. The job starts now! If a brigand or churl so much as lays a finger on that cart, I'll take my wrath out on your hide!"

The men fell in around the cart, ranging out to give a decent perimeter, Jonas near the door and Elias taking up the rear. Martin and Geoff took the front flanks, near Jonas. The more he saw of them, the more he understood the hierarchy of the mercenaries. While they had traveled quite informally to this point, it made sense that there would be a stricter structure once they were on the job, as it were.

The townsfolk made way for them as they proceeded along the sandy cobblestone road towards the tall, sturdy palisade and earth wall that marked the north boundary. As he passed through the opening, Elias noted the construction of the gate. An enormous redwood log had been sawn in half, and laid with the flat side on the bottom, supported by the earth and palisades on either side. The edges, near the outside of the log, were a dirty white, but the heartwood was a deep, rich red color, hence the name the trees were given.

The cart moved to the left side of the road, just past the gate, and pulled up. The oxen were fed, and the horses were tied while they waited for Lord Woodsetter's manservant. Before too long, a stooped, hurried, anxious looking man jogged into sight, carrying a few burlap wrapped satchels that were bound with twine. They smelled strongly of lavender, mint, and other, headier scents. He clambered to the top of the pile of chests, knocked twice, and held on to the ropes there. Elias wondered what kind of man their employer was that his men were so anxious and quiet, when compared to the boisterousness of the mercenaries. He was somewhat uneasy with the sharpness of the man's tone when speaking to Jonas, but the pay sounded good, and the road was short.

It was just three days journey back to Pine River. Just about a week on the road, assuming no delays, and they would be back in Jetty. Maybe their employer was just an especially cranky healer, which would explain the herbs and the rush.

Elias fell into the rhythm of the march, keeping a solid pace, feeling lucky that he was tall enough to miss most of the dust coming from behind the cart. Some of the men were laughing and joking as they marched, marking the miles with the stories and boasts he had become used to. While he didn't have many stories to tell himself, he enjoyed hearing the tales of the others, even if he had heard some of them more than once over a fire on the roadside.

There was the time that Jonas had been a young man tracking a pair of escaped orc fugitives, following them through the trees and mountains to the east, to the edge of the burning sands. When he found them, they had run themselves near to death, and their green skin was so blistered and sunburned that it had turned blue.

"What did you do when you caught them?" one of the men asked.

"The bounty was to be proven by bringing back the right ear of each orc. I made a deal with 'em. They give me the gold they stole and their right ears, and I give them their lives. It took a little bit of convincing, but they agreed to it, though the bigger one had to be convinced by the smaller one and myself."

"Why didn't you kill 'em?"

"Because all I needed was their ears. Besides, they had plenty of life in them to earn another bounty, and it's a lot easier to ask about for a one-eared orc than it is to ask about an orc that looks like every other orc. Better to claim two bounties off of one head than just one."

"But they were orcs! Best to just stick 'em good and fast when you come across 'em."

Jonas shook his head. "Orcs are orcs, elves are elves, dwarves are dwarves, and men are men. I've got nothing against them just for being what they were born to be. You don't kick a dog when he licks his balls, do ya? No, you wait until he humps your leg, then you kick the hell out of him."

That elicited a number of laughs from around the cart, and the stories resumed for the rest of the day's march. As the sun settled towards the sea, they struck camp on a clearing surrounded by brush oaks, juniper, and eucalyptus. The lingering scent of juniper berries hot from the sun filled the grassy space, carried with the slightly fishy breeze of low tide. This stopped the vast majority of the wind, and kept them out of sight of the road. Three of Jonas's men took the first watch, while the rest gathered firewood, pitched tents, and sat about the fire, cooking their dinner and settling in for the night. Woodsetter's men were to take the second watch, so they set up their master's tent and retired early.

Elias sat on the ground, his legs crossed, with his sleeping roll and pack against the small of his back, and the giant sword on the ground next to him. Hard, dry bread and jerky were his meal for the evening, washed down with water from a nearby spring. He wondered how water so close to the sea could be fresh, when sea water ran through sand so easily. He resolved to figure it out some day.

The sun was sinking below the waves behind the trees, and darkness was setting in, shrouding the trees in their blue-black curtain. Even his eyes couldn't pierce that veil, but the only sounds coming from the darkness were rustling birds and small animals.

Martin returned from a hunt, having killed a rabbit, and roasted it over the fire. The rest of Jonas's men were sitting about in various other positions, chatting or rolling over to sleep. Some of the men were sharing stories of this battle or that fight or this adventure or that job, a continuation of their conversations during the day. Geoff turned to Jonas, and asked around a mouthful of jerky, "Hey Jonas, how old were you when you killed your first man?"

Jonas swallowed a mouthful of salted mutton. "Mmm. Fifteen. And he was more of a boy than a man, as I was. Took a job guarding a priest from brigands on the road from Lonwick to Fairhaven. Weren't many bandits on the roads those days, so I figured it'd be easy money. Bastard crept up on us in the night, kicked me in the head while I was sleeping. Guess he thought he'd knocked me out. He was in the middle of beating the friar's gold out of him when I put my sword through his back." He scoffed slightly. "Was too nervous, too scared. I stabbed too hard and stuck the friar in the shoulder. He died of an infection a week later."

Geoff nodded. "I was seventeen."

Martin spoke up, interrupting. "You mean last month?"

Geoff threw a boot at the other man, amidst laughter from the mercenaries that were still away. "Piss off, Martin. It was four years ago. He tried to break into a store room I was guarding in Rockhill. Wasn't quiet about it either, the idiot. Kept scraping and prying with a crowbar right up to when my axe split his shoulders in half. Guess he thought the gold was worth his life." He turned towards Elias. "What about you, Redwood? When did you first kill a man?"

Elias shook his head. "I've never killed a man."

Martin scoffed, his thick frame shaking from the motion. "Never killed a man? Are you saying the orc was the first thing you've ever killed? I didn't know you were completely unblooded."

Elias tossed a branch onto the small campfire. "I didn't say I was unblooded. I said I'd never killed a man."

Jonas gnawed on a mutton bone. "Come on then, share with us. How big was the lass, and did you at least bed her first, you murderous dog?" The rest of the men laughed as Elias took a bite of his jerky, and stared into the fire for a moment.

"I was one hundred and four. I lived in Silva Aestas, and it was customary for all the boys to learn how to fight with a longsword. Training started after your first century, and carried through for eighty years. There was a boy, an elf, fifty years my senior, and he was to train me on the basics. For four years he did as little as he could to get by… he resented having to teach the 'monstrous oaf', as he called me. During a training accident, I put a waster though his chest."

Martin looked up from his meal, quirking one reddish eyebrow, his chubby mouth following suit. "You accidentally put a waster though his chest, " he repeated, the doubt evident on his face.

Elias stirred the fire with a branch, sparks and cinders floating lazily into the night sky. "I didn't just pop up to this size overnight, I've always been very large, very strong. While we were training, my sword broke and I didn't notice, because I had lost my temper and I wasn't paying as close attention as I should have been. I took a solid blow to the head just as it happened."

Jonas spoke up from around a mouthful of mutton. "So you don't remember killing the boy?"

Elias shook his head. "When I regained my senses, Ayluin was dead. When my waster shattered, it had broken to a sharp point, and, not knowing my own strength, I had driven it clean through him."

Geoff whistled. "Damn, that's rough. Is that why you were living in the north?"

Elias nodded. "The magistrates convened, found me to be a danger to the city, and so they banished me to live amongst the northern tribes of men." Elias frowned, tossing the branch onto the coals. "It was thought that their culture, barbaric and warlike, would better suit me than the finesse and skill of my own kind."

The men around him were silent. Martin tossed a branch onto the fire as well, stirring the flames up again. "You said you were a hundred years old? I mean, I know elves live a lot longer than normal people do... how does that compare to us?"

Elias bristled slightly at the 'normal people' comment. After all, the nearest organized kingdom was ruled by his people, and there were at least as many elves in this area as there were men. "I was one hundred and four. Every ten years for us is as one year for you. Roughly. That's why we don't often mix with your kind. Your lives are barely a blink to us."

Martin spoke up from his bedroll. "How old are you now?"

Elias frowned and settled back, adjusting his pack to act as a pillow. He was getting uncomfortable with this line of questioning about himself and his past. "One hundred and sixty-eight."

Jonas quirked a brow. "You spent sixty-four years with the barbarian lords of the Northlands, and you only just got yourself a greatsword this morning?"

Elias shrugged. "They didn't want an elf fighting how they fought, so they gave me no formal training, and had their women teach me how to handle a longsword so that I wouldn't be useless in a fight. They never took me on raids, since I didn't have their blood in my veins... Aside from the people who lived in Valtheim, the nobles didn't trust me to have their backs when steel was drawn."

He shifted against his pack, settling down into a more comfortable position. "The king's sons, however, would spar with me when they had time or will to do so. I'm not completely ignorant in the use of a greatsword."

Jonas yawned and lay back. "Well, as fascinating as your yarn may be, at this point I'm gonna tell you all to shut your gobs and get some sleep. Our shift for watch comes sooner than you think, so close your eyes while you can."

Elias and the rest of the men drew out their blankets and lay about the fire, the cool ocean breeze held at bay by the low flames and the warm summer air from the mountains. The stars twinkled lightly, occasionally obscured by the passage of clouds coming off the sea. Elias wondered at how the wind was blowing out towards the water, as gentle as it might be, but the clouds were moving inland. He watched the slow, dark masses moving until sleep took him amidst the growing snores and breathing of rest of the men, thankfully free of the specter of the dark knight.

~   ~   ~

Smoke. Elias woke to the smell of smoke invading his nose. It wasn't wood smoke, either, it was more cloying, clinging to his throat and making him choke. He kicked back and pushed himself away from the fire, thinking that maybe he'd rolled in his sleep and thrown his blanket into the fire, but no, he wasn't close enough for that. His eyes stung and he could barely see. He heard men coughing, cursing, and boots stomping around the campfire.

He tried to rise to his feet, but strong hands grabbed him by the shoulders and bore him back to the ground. A bundle of smoldering herbs was thrust into his face, the smoke making his head spin, embers burning his skin while the dried stalks scratched him. Squeezing his eyes shut, Elias tried to hold his breath, but he hadn't been prepared and couldn't hold it for long. Swinging his arms wildly about himself, he struck at his assailants in the dark.

Grabbing the figure that was holding the herbs over his face, he shoved it away. He drew in a deep breath, but found that the rest of the air was no cleaner, and almost collapsed in a coughing fit. There was more activity now – yelling, cursing, and the sound of steel clashing. He cracked his eyes open just enough to see some shapes through the burning and watering, though he couldn't make out anything but vague figures, and was unable to tell friend from foe.

The campfire was a glowing column of smoke, the coals freshly lit by flames that were starting to crackle on new material that had been thrown on it. In the haze, he couldn't tell who was attacking who, what with the smoke obscuring most everything in the wan moonlight.

Panic gripped Elias as he crouched to grab his sword and was bowled over by the figure he had thrown away. His wind was knocked out of him from the impact. As he gasped for another breath, the bundle of herbs was thrust back over his face, and he breathed deeply of the smoke coming from it. His vision seemed to explode into a million pieces, and the last thing he recognized before everything went too blurry to see was a hooded face, seemingly made of cloth with two shiny disks where eyes should have been. He struggled to swing his arms at the figure but his limbs refused to obey him. A numbness settled over his face, and consciousness was gone.

Chapter Eight

10th Waxing Sap Moon, Year 4304

Elias stood in the circle of stones, awkward and too tall, even as young as he was. He was already as large as a fully grown soldier, and more muscular than most of the elven men in the city. Today, the young elf training him was to show the council what Elias had learned over the last four years, to see if he had progressed enough to move on to a more advanced trainer, and take on a first year student himself. Every year for the last three years, he'd been denied and sent back to learn the first year material again, his ineptitude blamed on his freakish size.

His trainer, a young, skilled elf named Ayluin, stood across the ring, scowling. He made no secret of the fact that he hated Elias, and while his actions were always subtle, he went out of his way to make Elias's life miserable. Such bullying was subtly ignored by the elders of his city, though whether through apathy or shared prejudice was unclear. Elias could not figure why… he looked up to Ayluin, and did his best to learn the drills and forms, despite his large size and general lack of agility. Now it was time to show what he had learned during the last four years of drilling.

These exercises were done with wasters, to protect the students from injury while training. Three magistrates stood around the circle to observe the bout. One of them turned to Elias. "Are you ready?"

Elias nodded, and the magistrate turned to Ayluin. "Are you ready?"

Ayluin's eyes never left Elias. "Yes."

"Then fight. We will be the judge of whether the student has learned sufficiently to advance."

The two boys stepped towards each other, Elias's steps measured and even, Ayluin striding forward as if this were a task that he simply wanted to finish as soon as possible. The space between them rapidly closed, and Ayluin struck first, hard and high, to the left. Elias blocked it with his blade, barely recovering in time to cover his head from the swipe from the right. Ayluin pressed Elias back until Elias misjudged a swing, and took a solid strike to the stomach.

"Ayluin wins the first round." The magistrate turned to Ayluin, who was smirking slightly. "Remember that the failure of the student is the failure of the teacher. Return to your sides."

Ayluin's smirk was replaced by a scowl, and a murderous glare at Elias.

The boys returned to their respective sides, Elias doing his best not to hunch over. Ayluin was swinging hard, harder than usual. He always did on these tests. Elias was aware that older boy was trying to make him fail, and didn't know why. Discouraged, he steeled himself to just make it through the test.

The magistrate's voice called out over the ring. "Proceed."

Peripherally, Elias could see other young elves, male and female, taking their tests in adjacent rings, flurries of activity almost distracting him. Ayluin closed on him swiftly, and Elias focused more on defending himself, blocking the strikes that the other boy was throwing at him. Ayluin set his jaw and redoubled his efforts. Splinters flew from the wasters from his onslaught, Elias blocking most of the strikes, his larger size giving him a bit more reach than the other boy had. However, he wasn't as skilled, and over-reached again, putting himself in harm's way. Ayluin's waster found its mark on the back of Elias's hand, making him almost drop his weapon. Instinctively, Elias grabbed hold of Ayluin's other hand with his own, and struck back while the older boy was surprised, catching him under the arm with a solid blow to the ribs, driving the breath from him.

Ayluin jerked his hand free and staggered back, holding on to his ribs, staring at Elias in anger and surprise. The magistrate's voice rang out over the ring. "Elias wins the second round. Return to your sides." Ayluin narrowed his eyes, and stalked back to his side, pacing in the dirt inside the ring, waiting for the next round to begin.

Elias was angry now. Ayluin didn't need to hurt him. He didn't need to swing this hard, he just needed to spar, to let Elias show if he knew what he needed to know to advance in his training. He didn't need to humiliate Elias in front of the elders. Elias stood firm, narrowing his eyes himself, glaring across the ring. The corners of his mouth turned down. Ayluin was smaller than he was, despite being almost fifty years older. The leather wrapping the handle creaked under his grip as he gritted his teeth.

The magistrate looked between the boys, and, after a slight pause, looked to Ayluin and nodded. "Proceed."

Ayluin started across the ring, stalking towards Elias. Elias gripped his waster in his aching right hand, and broke out into a sprint. Ayluin sidestepped, swinging hard for Elias's head, but his weapon found only wood as Elias blocked hard, sending the other boy's sword rebounding wide. Elias pressed his advantage, using his strength to push the other boy back step by step, forcing him to block instead of attack. The anger and spite in Ayluin's eyes started to evaporate, being replaced by doubt.

Elias felt something rise up inside of himself, a white hot fury, born from his years of abuse at the hands of the bully before him, and he pressed harder. He was vaguely aware of someone calling his name, but the red haze that clouded his vision and the thundering in his ears left absolutely no room for anything else in his perception beyond Ayluin. With both hands gripping the handle of his waster, he drove his advantage home.

The other boy swung hard for Elias's head, and Elias blocked the strike savagely. The sound of cracking wood barely filtered through his haze just as he saw Ayluin raise his waster above his head for a hard two-handed downward strike. Elias took the moment and drove the point of his waster into the boy's sternum just Ayluin brought his weapon down on Elias's skull. There was an explosion of light and pain, then darkness.

~   ~   ~

New Summer Moon, Year 4368

Elias's head ached. He tried unsuccessfully to open his eyes, stirring slightly as the world heaved and swayed underneath him. His hands and feet hurt, his muscles cramped and starved for blood. His legs tingled from the knees down, and as he gradually regained his wits, he realized he was laying on his side. His arms were behind his back, and his knees were pulled up nearly to his chest. He tried to correct his position, but his arms wouldn't move forward. He realized he was bound.

His eyes snapped open, and were greeted with more darkness. He turned his head, and felt rough burlap scratch against his nose and cheeks. He had a hood over his head, tied about his neck with a rope. The rope wasn't tight enough to choke him but definitely restricted motion and breathing. He strained against his bonds, the rope cutting into his flesh and holding firm. Whoever tied it knew how to tie knots that wouldn't loosen at a simple tug. He didn't think he'd be able to break the ropes... they were far too thick.

Something struck him in the chest, just under his sternum, driving the air out of his lungs. "Quit your straining. You'll be untied soon enough." A man's voice that he didn't recognize.

"Where am I?" he demanded. The answer was another strike to the chest, making his head spin again. Elias's breath was coming fast, stifling in the heavy burlap. The world kept bobbing and rocking about, and he became aware of the sound of wood beams creaking and groaning. In the distance, he heard could hear the sounds of waves rushing. He was on a boat.

Footsteps came from behind him, sounding like they were descending stairs. Another man's voice that he did not recognize spoke. "How long until they wake?"

The first man answered. "This one is already awake. The rest should rouse within the hour. Maybe three hours before they're able to take their places at the oars."

"The giant is awake? Take off his hood."

Hands grabbed him by the shoulders and hauled him into a kneeling position. As he moved, he became aware that his hands and feet were connected by another rope that effectively hobbled him. The rope about his throat momentarily tightened, cutting off his breath and causing a surge of panic. However, the knot was swiftly undone and the hood was pulled off, the light from the room blasting into his eyes as he coughed.

He looked around, his eyes bleary, getting his bearings. Eight other figures were scattered throughout the dusty room, lying among the crates, all of them bound and hooded like he had been. The man who had removed his hood was standing to his left, and another man was standing at the foot of a flight of stairs, the bright sun behind him all but blinding Elias.

The man from the stairs, a well-built man in somewhat finer clothing, stepped forward. Grabbing Elias by the jaw, he turned his head to the side. "An elf? I've never seen an elf this big." He turned Elias's head the other way, inspecting him like one would inspect a goat before purchase.

Elias jerked his chin out of the man's grip. Before Elias could brace himself, the man struck him across the cheek, almost bowling him over. He bent down next to Elias, gold glinting off of his rings. "Feisty bastard, aren't you? What do you think, giant? Should we slit you from sternum to stem and use you to bait sharks, or would you be of better use to us on the oars?"

"Don't they waste away at sea? I heard that if they get too far out of their forests, they just die." The man to his left frowned, kicking Elias onto his side. He was dressed considerably shabbier, his clothing dirty and worn, threadbare in a few places. A scraggly, mangy beard sat lopsided on his chin. "I think Woodsetter tried to get one over on us. He looks strong enough, but if he keels over in a few months, we wasted too much gold on him."

Elias kept his mouth shut, blood running from the corner of his lips. Though he didn't speak, he held the eyes of the well-dressed man who hit him, not looking away. The man laughed and stood. "He's got plenty of life in him. Besides, there's another elf in the hold, scrawny old bastard, and that one hasn't died yet. Make sure this one finds his way to an oar when the rest of these meat-bags wake up."

Elias lay still, watching the two men as they made their way up the stairs. A hatch slammed shut, and he could hear chains being dragged over the top. What sounded like a padlock clicked into place, then dropped loudly upon the hatch. The timbers continued to creak around him, and even though he was getting used to it, he could still feel the rolling and swaying of the room around him.

He had been unaware of his heart pounding like an insane marching drummer, but as he lay there, it became quite obvious. Slowing his breath, he closed his eyes and attempted to regain control over himself. Closing his eyes did nothing to help his equilibrium, and he vomited, retching against the rough wooden planks.

He rolled to his back, away from the mess he'd made, and examined the facts. He was on a ship of some sort, that much was obvious from the short conversation, the rolling, and the noises around him. How large of a ship, Elias couldn't tell. Large enough to have a storage hold, obviously, and large enough to have oarslaves. He strained against his ropes again, then relaxed, rolling into a slightly more comfortable position. Whoever had tied him must have had experience. The ropes that bound him didn't budge.

Woodsetter had betrayed them, that much was obvious. It was no wonder he hadn't been too worried about the cost of the protection, just in the number of men that had joined the expedition. If he had plans of stealing back the gold he'd paid out, and then selling the mercenaries as slaves, then the initial investment would matter a bit less.

There was a thumping behind him, as one of the other men started to regain consciousness. Elias rolled awkwardly to face his fellow captive. He wasn't entirely sure, due to the hood over the man's face and the dim light, but he thought it was Martin. The bound man's thick, chunky build looked familiar enough. He shuffled across the dusty floor, keeping his eyes shut to protect them. "Martin!" he whispered, keeping his voice down to avoid drawing attention. "Martin, is that you?"

The bound figured stopped struggling. "Elias? Where am I? Why am I tied up?"

"We were betrayed. Woodsetter sold us to sailors, and we're on a ship."

Martin thumped again, struggling against his ropes. "No shit we were betrayed! Why are we on a ship?"

"Oarslaves, from what they said. Two of them were here. They took off my hood, talked about chaining us to oars when we woke up, then left."

Martin paused for a moment. "Oarslaves? I'm not a goddamn oarslave! I can't be an oarslave!" He started struggling harder, banging and thumping around. Some of the other figures started stirring at the clamor Martin was making. "Let me out of here! Let me go!"

Something struck the trap door at the top of the stairs. "Stop that racket now!" a gruff voice bawled out from behind the hatch. Martin continued thumping and shouting, and before long, several of the other mercenaries joined in as they gradually came to. Elias struggled out of the path of the stairs as the chains started rattling. He could hear them being drawn through metal rings, then the hatch opened. Four men rushed down the stairs, cutlasses drawn. Elias didn't recognize any of the men; neither of the first two was with this group.

Most of the rest of the mercenaries had the good sense to quiet down, but not Martin. He kept thrashing about, his breath coming in ragged gasps between his ever more frantic screams. "Let me out of here! Get this goddamned hood off of my-!"

Martin's rant was interrupted by a kick to the throat from the first man down the stairs. The other three men stood around Martin and kicked him in the ribs, the back of the head, the stomach and the legs. Martin's gagging was replaced by coughing and retching as the blows rained upon him.

After a few moments, they stopped kicking the bound man. The hood was stained with blood in front, where Martin's mouth would be, and in the back, where he'd been kicked. His breath came in ragged coughs and gags as he tried to curl up and shield himself from any more blows. The man who led the way down the stairs leaned down close to Martin's ear, who started at the sound of his voice.

The man, who Elias assumed was a pirate of some sort, started speaking quietly, but his voice rose to screaming as he continued. "The next time I tell you to shut yer goddamn mouth, you shut your maggot filled, dirt munching mouth or I swear to every god of every sea I will stuff your guts full of crabs and use you for shark bait! Now have I made myself clear or do I need to kick another load of shit into yer worthless carcass?!"

His response was more ragged sobbing from under the rough burlap of the hood. Elias watched this all from his position against a support timber. The man who seemed to be calling the shots was short, broad shouldered, and hairy. He wore no shirt, a leather kilt, and black boots that went to his knees, strapped tight with tan leather sinews tied at the ankle. A threadbare bandanna covered the top of his head, with a thin, ragged beard underneath.

Elias memorized the look of his face. None of the finer details were visible in the dusty light, but his large nose and prominent forehead were hard to miss. A fat, square jaw with a slight hanging extra chin, and lips that stuck out. Recognizable, to say the least.

The man turned to look at Elias. Narrowing his eyes, he moved towards the giant elf. "So you're the giant everyone's been talking about. I'll bet you can get an oar moving right quick. But don't think you get any extra food on account of your size." He drove his boot into Elias's stomach. Elias saw it coming and was able to brace for the blow, but it still knocked most of the wind out of him. "We'll get the piss out of those eyes soon enough." He turned to one of the other men. "You and Durk, take this tree-monkey and find him a seat. He's strong enough now."

The two men he pointed at grabbed Elias by the arms and lifted him upright. One of them slashed the rope binding his ankles, which allowed him to finally stretch out his legs. He rose to his feet, but had to stay hunched over due to the low ceiling. The two men pulled him roughly up the stairs and onto the main deck, into the bright sunlight, causing him to wince and stumble. The two men holding him had to hold onto his elbows, which were nearly as high as their shoulders. Half guiding, half dragging, they moved him across the crowded deck while his eyes adjusted to the light.

He was moving towards the rear, or stern of the ship, which had a large cabin with a closed door. On the left side of the door was another hatch that sat open, leading to more stairs going down. He looked around, searching for an escape route, and saw nothing but the sea. They had already left land far behind, and the wind was carrying them swiftly westward.

One of the men pulled a curved sword out of a sheath, and held it at his back, while the other man held the rope hanging from his hands and led him like a dog on a leash down a flight of stairs that was about half as long as the one he had come up, occasionally tugging, almost causing him to trip. He was still a bit woozy, and the rocking of the ship didn't do any favors when it came to him keeping his balance. He had been unconscious for what looked like half a day, judging by the sun.

As his eyes readjusted to the darkness, the sights and smells that assaulted his senses were almost enough to make him retch again. At least forty prisoners sat on benches, their ankles chained to the floor and their hands shackled to large oar handles. The oars were about as thick as his wrists, protruding eight feet into the hold from either side; most of them had two prisoners chained to the handles, while some benches were vacant. The benches had oval holes cut in them that led to the bilges down below, and the smells that came from them betrayed their purpose.

He was dragged to one of the benches, and sat down close to the aisle that ran down the middle of the room. The other occupant of the bench was a slender, frail-looking older elf, his skin a very pale, almost blue color. The oars were not currently in use, and the ends were tucked under metal hooks on the floor, keeping the paddles clear of the water. The room itself was dank, damp feeling, and smelled horrific; just being on the oar deck filled Elias with a sense of dread and panic.

The prisoners either stared at the handle of the oar in front of them or watched him with vacant, expressionless faces as his hands were clamped with manacles. The chain that connected them ran through a metal eye that was bolted to the oar, securing him in place, while his ankles were shackled to the floor in a similar fashion. Only then were the ropes that bound his wrists cut off, and he could feel the blood return to his hands.

The two men left him without any further ceremony, and beyond a few furtive glances, most of the oarslaves ignored him as well. His benchmate, however, kept turning his head to stare at Elias. He examined his surroundings and his situation. If he spread his hands as far as the chain of his manacles allowed him to, he could get them as far apart as his shoulders were wide. His feet, on the other hand, could barely stretch out past the oar. He could tuck them under his bench on either side of the tube that the hole he sat over led down, but not much more than that. He was quite effectively anchored in place.

Elias moved his attention to the rest of the room. It looked as though the room he was in took up the vast majority of this level of the ship. There were fifteen oars on either side of the room, each about eight feet apart. His oar was near the stern of the ship, on the port side, third from the back. The deck was bout thirty feet wide, from port to starboard, eight feet of which were taken up on either side with the benches for the oarslaves. There were hinged grates in their deck, leading to the hold below, and above those were solid wooden doors leading to the upper deck.

Wooden beams rose from the floor to the low ceiling at the end of each bench, supporting a heavy wooden framework that the deck sat upon. At the front of the room was a single large drum with a stool on the bow side. Two leather wrapped sticks were hanging from a nail driven into a nearby support. Elias assumed that this was for keeping rhythm when the slaves were actively rowing.

"Greetings," said the older elf that he was sitting next to. "My name is Marl."

Elias continued examining the room, looking for any way he could break free. "I am Elias."

"Now is not a very good time to try to free yourself."

Elias turned to look back at Marl. "What?"

Marl shook his head. "Not right now. The men aboard this ship are always more vigilant, more ready to kill right after they've taken new slaves onto the ship. It keeps the rest of us in line."

"I've got to get out of here!"

Marl nodded slowly. "Absolutely. We all do. But we can get out of here alive, or we can get thrown overboard with a knife in our throats. I, for one, want to go home."

Their short conversation was interrupted by Elias's companions being dragged in, one at a time, and chained to oars. Most of them looked somewhat battered, as if they had struggled. Martin looked the worst for wear, his face and hair covered in blood, and his left earlobe torn and puffy. He had apparently put up more of a fight after Elias had been escorted out. Shortly, all of the empty spaces were filled, save two. An elderly man three oars up from him, and an emaciated young woman across the aisle were both alone at their oars.

The last man to be brought in was Jonas. He walked more than he was dragged or pushed, leading the two men that were escorting him. He started to sit by the old man, but before he could even take a seat, one of his escorts, a skinny man in faded, multicolored clothes, hauled on the rope his wrists were tied to, almost bowling him over. Jonas recovered his feet, glaring at the man who almost knocked him down. "Alright, alright, princess, where would ya have me sit, then?"

The pirate glared, baring his teeth. "You mouthy son of a whore!" he spat, punching Jonas square in the stomach, doubling the mercenary over. Jonas coughed and struggled to keep his feet as he was hauled to his bench. As he was being shackled to the oar, he turned to look at the man who had punched him, a cheeky grin on his face.

"A son of a whore, am I? I didn't know you and I were brothers!"

The pirate looked at him for a moment, confused.

Jonas sighed. "I mean your mother's a whore too."

It took a moment for the flicker of understanding to cross the pirate's face, and when it did, it was quickly replaced by anger. He seized the front of Jonas's shirt and struck him three times before Jonas tried to hold up his hands to protect himself.

"Alright, alright! I take it back! Your mother is a fine woman from a noble household!"

The pirate grabbed Jonas by the neck, his long, dirty fingernails digging in. "You're not sorry yet, you mincy, nancy little fairy! But you will be." He lifted Jonas slightly from his seat, his gapped teeth bared in Jonas's face. Jonas tried to turn away, presumably from the smell of the pirate's breath.

Elias pulled hard on his wrist chains, but they held firm. He had never felt so helpless before, watching his comrades get beaten and abused. They were part of a band, a group, and he wasn't able to come to their aid. A slender hand gripped his wrist, and Marl whispered to him.

"Now is not the time. Don't give them an excuse to kill him."

"That's enough." The voice of the well-dressed man rose over the sounds of struggle. He stood not far from the pirate attacking Jonas; Elias recognized him from the room where he had regained his senses. He had entered the deck so quietly that Elias hadn't seen or heard him until he spoke.

"Turn him loose. If you injure him too badly, he won't be fit to row, and we will need all the backs we can get. Woodsetter failed to fill his promise this time around." The man looked over at Elias for a moment, narrowing his eyes, then walked back towards the stairs. "Gab, you're needed on deck. Get up there now. We're four weeks from Greenreef, and we weren't able to replace some of the weaker slaves. If we want to make any sort of good time, we'll need every inch of sail we've got."

Gab, the pirate who had been beating Jonas, turned back to him, glaring daggers. The foul breathed man spat into Jonas's face and dropped him, storming up the stairs. As the hatch slammed down over the stairs, Jonas hunched over, doing his best to wipe his eyes off on the sleeve of his tunic.

Turning his head, he saw Elias watching the exchange. With a lopsided grin, he chuckled quietly. "Well now. Isn't this a pretty pickle we're in. Looks like we're going to Greenreef."

Chapter Nine

? Summer Moon, Year 4368

The days passed slowly for Elias and the oarslaves. If the winds were strong, their oars were hooked on the floor to keep them suspended above the water, allowing the wind to bear them across the waves. If the seas were calm, then they rowed. The drum at the front of the oar deck beat a steady rhythm, every stroke falling on the fourth beat. If they were moving too slowly, the beats fell faster, and they rowed faster. Never did the beat slow; it only stopped when they were allowed to sleep.

The slaves were fed once a day, at dawn. Leftovers from the pirates' meal the night before was common for them, thrown into a pot with water, slurried up and served as a mush in wooden bowls. At first, Elias and some of the mercenaries refused to eat the revolting concoction, but by the third day, most of them had relented.

Most conversation was squelched by the two guards that sat at a table in the front of the room no matter what hour of the day it was. If they were rowing, the guards paced up and down the aisles, berating or whipping any rower who didn't keep rhythm with the drums.

The new slaves seemed to be the most punished, which was not surprising. They yelled out at their captors from time to time with bursts of anger and resistance. These were met with cudgels and short whips. Martin, as beaten and bloodied as he was, seemed to put up the most consistent fight, while Geoff, who was chained on the bench next to him, more or less kept his head down and rowed.

Jonas was more conservative, keeping mostly to himself. He had been chained next to the one female oarslave, a slender, lanky woman with dusky skin and thick, curly black locks. She kept her head bowed at all times, her face hidden behind the tangled curtain of her long hair. The only sounds she ever made was a slight humming while she slept, leaning against the back of her bench. It was a song without any real tune or melody, repeating at random.

All the slaves in the hold were human, except for Elias and Marl. The older elf was slender and lanky, struggling to move the oar, but Elias's greater size and strength more than made up the difference. As they rowed, they were able to communicate in short, broken conversations. Marl was from Greenreef, the main island of the chain they were sailing to. He had been captured and pressed into service six months prior, while traveling along the coast north of Greatport.

"Why did you come to the mainland?" Elias found that conversation, inasmuch as they could manage, kept him from despairing at their situation.

"I was searching for someone," Marl spoke between gasps and grunts, straining against the oar as they rowed. "Our prophecies speak of a savior from across the sea, a great warrior who will lead us against the men who have stolen our islands and lives from us."

Elias heaved against the oar, propelling it along with the rhythm of the drummer. "Did you find the warrior?"

Marl shook his head, resting a moment with his hands on the oar as Elias rowed. "No. There were many great warriors, but none of them cared for our plight, and the gods led me to nobody while I was there." He shook his head, perspiration dripping from his brow. "All I want to do now is go home, with or without finding the one who will fulfill the prophecy. I miss my family, I miss my gods, and I miss my islands."

Elias related the story of how he left Brynjar's stronghold at the foot of the Stromgard mountain, and his travels with the mercenaries. He told Marl of the greatness of King Brynjar, the challenges facing Brandt, and his flight from the land of the Northmen. Marl seemed particularly interested in the dark knight that attacked Elias on the road.

"So you have no idea who this figure is, or what he wanted?"

Elias shook his head. "The only idea I have is that he wore the same symbol on his armor that the Felle Army scouts had on their coins, and an iron medallion. That makes me believe he is with them."

Marl pondered for a moment as they worked. "What did the symbol look like?"

Elias grunted, hauling on the oar handle. "It was a black star with eight points, like the one that represents the gods, set in a circle with a red stone at the center. The sign was stamped on the coins, and embossed into the knight's breastplate."

Marl nodded his head. "I've seen that shape before. It is worn by certain men from the mainland. Not all of the men wear them, only some of them. I think they are soldiers or mercenaries that travel with the pirates."

A cane struck a beam near Elias. One of the pirates walking up and down the aisle barked out, "Less yakking, more rowing, or next time my rod finds flesh!"

~　　~　　~

13th Waning Summer Moon, Year 4368

Four weeks went by, with almost no change to their surroundings or their situation. Elias was intimately familiar with the pattern of the wood grain on his oar. His hands were growing even more calloused than they had been before, though he had gained a number of blisters and sores from the shackles around his wrists and ankles.

Some other unfortunate soul had etched marks into the seat next to him, though the tally marks came without a legend. Days? Weeks? Months? Certainly not years. Most of the marks had been worn away by subsequent slaves and their backsides. About a week in, he decided to revive the practice, even if only to salvage a part of his sanity by marking the passage of time. There was a link on the chain that bound his left wrist to the oar that had a metal bur on it. If he moved his right hand as close as he could to the eye that the chain ran through, he could scratch the bench with the bur.

Always his mind churned on how to escape. He was keeping his wits about him, but just barely. The cramped quarters were the most miserable he had ever been in, and he found himself longing for the open shade of the coastal forests near the bay or the majestic mountains of the Northlands. Fresh air would be a gift in the murky dank of the oar deck.

He needed to unlock these chains, if he was to get loose. His hands were shackled to the oar and couldn't reach any of the guards as they walked up and down the aisle between the benches, so snatching the keys or throttling a guard was not an option, even if doing so wouldn't bring the entire ship worth of pirates down on the oar deck.

The days that he rowed were grueling, but surprisingly bearable with the broken conversations he was able to have with Marl. He hadn't lost his will to break free. The sight of his comrades losing their hope broke his heart, but it didn't break his spirit. Every time he looked over and saw Martin's beaten and bloody back, he steeled his resolve.

The days he wasn't rowing, however, were torture. Hour after hour of just sitting on his bench, staring forward. Too much movement would attract the attention of the guards, which resulted in beatings. He was trapped in his head, on this boat. He needed something to keep his mind busy.

He constantly studied his surroundings, searching for something he could use to break loose, but there were many other factors to consider. The fact that he was not a sailor and had absolutely no idea how to sail a ship once he broke loose was a major one, as well as no way to coordinate with the other captives while the guards were present, which was always.

His oar was anchored to the hull of the ship by eye bolts driven through both the oar and the hull. A short length of chain, about a foot long, connected the two with a lock, so the oar could not be pushed through and lost overboard. However, the years of rowing had taken their toll on the thick handle of the oar. It had been worn down from the constant rubbing against the iron-clad rim of the hole that acted as the pivot point of the oar. It was still thick at the point where it had worn the most, but only about half as thick as the rest of the handle.

There were few times that the slaves were unsupervised. When the guards changed, there was usually a four or five minute gap, sometimes longer, as the replacements would arrive to relieve the current shift. These shift changes seemed to happen fairly consistently, around feeding time, shortly after noon, and a few hours after dark. This made Elias wonder if there was a dwarven clock somewhere on board. There were few other devices that were as accurate for telling time,

It was an hour or two past dusk on the first day of the fifth week since they had been captured, according to Elias's marks. He leaned back, his hands in his lap, while Marl slumped forward, resting his head on his arms, and his arms on the oar. The oars were currently held in place by the steel catch in the floor between the ends of the benches that kept the paddles suspended above the waves.

Elias could hear the pounding of feet on the deck above him. That was not an uncommon sound, though it was normally a bit less active at this time of night. He stared forward, listening to the waves lapping against the sides of the ship and the muffled voices overhead. A man bearing a lantern came down the stairs, and hollered at the guard in the front of the room.

"Oi! Cap'n broke out the rum! We'll make Greenreef by dawn! Come up on deck, we've got roast pig and lemon biscuits, and Durk has his fiddle."

The pirate looked over the slaves, and pointed to the woman sitting next to Jonas. "Bring her, too. The Cap'n wants 'er cleaned up for him."

None of the other oarslaves reacted, not even the woman who was pointed at. Nobody, that is, except for Jonas. Elias could see the tension building in the man's shoulders and the sudden sharpness of his gaze. Apprehension filled Elias as he watched and waited.

As the guard drew near, keys in hand, Jonas lashed out, grabbing the key ring with a precision Elias didn't know the man had. The pirate grunted in surprise, then swore as Jonas bit him, trying to wrest the key ring out of his hand. The pirate let go.

And like that, Jonas had the keys. Freedom was within their grasp! Scrambling with the keys, Jonas frantically tried to unlock his manacles. He got the key in, gave it a twist, and the manacle fell away with a solid thud to the deck.

That was when the sap came crashing into the back of Jonas's skull. He lurched forward as the pirate struck him again and again on the head, neck, shoulders, and back. Jonas tried to shield his head with his hands, but after the third blow, Elias saw his arms go limp, and he slumped against the bench in front of him, over the chains that kept his right hand bound to the oar.

The pirate growled, tossing the sap towards the aisle. "Sunnuvabitch!" He grasped his wrist, where Jonas had bitten him, and kicked the mercenary in the ribs. Jonas's prone body didn't react.

Elias gripped the chains binding his ankles, pulling on them as he watched, helpless as the pirate made sure Jonas wasn't any more of a threat. The pirate unlocked Jonas's other wrist and ankles, then dragged him to the front of the room. There, he chained Jonas to the post that the drumsticks hung from, in full view of the rest of the slaves. He turned again, blood dripping from his hand to the floor... Elias wasn't sure if it was Jonas's blood, or the pirates.

"Let that be a lesson to the lot of you! We'll be feeding this one to the boars on Greenreef, and if any of you so much as *dream* of pulling any shit like him, " he kicked Jonas in the stomach for emphasis, "you'll be joining him!"

The pirate stormed back to Jonas's benchmate. Roughly, he unlocked her chains, grabbed her by the hair, and dragged her towards the stairs. Hooking the key ring to his belt, he switched his grip to the woman's wrists and pushed her up the stairs. Elias could hear the chorus of cheers as the pirates caught view of the woman. Jonas slumped, sitting mostly upright, his wrists chained together behind his back, around the post. Blood ran down his face, and his breathing was shallow.

Hands shaking, Elias gripped the chains that held his ankles to the deck. He pulled hard, but the links bit into his hands, not letting him put his full strength behind it. Nevertheless, he heard the plank the chains were anchored to crack.

So did some of the other oarslaves. Suddenly, every eye in the room was on him. Nobody had said a word since the pirate left, but now there was a flurry of murmurs.

"Elias. What are you doing?" Marl's voice was soft but urgent. Elias ignored him, and cast about for anything that could help him break loose. His eyes fell on the oar in front of him, and his heart jumped into his throat as he got an idea. Pulling it free from the bar anchoring it in place, he moved it close enough that he could put his feet over it.

He exhaled deeply, and pulled his feet up and over the chain that bound his wrists to the oar, setting them down on the other side of the handle. Now, the oar was between his feet and the anchor that kept his shackled ankles bound to the deck. He lifted the oar handle, and felt the manacles at his ankles bite into his flesh. It was painful, but not as bad as the chains bit into his hands.

The murmurs turned slightly louder now. "Shh!" Elias hissed, getting into a squatting position, holding on to the oar handle behind his legs. Resting his forehead on the back of the bench in front of him, Elias gripped the oar handle and braced himself. He had done this style of lift before, when working with the men of the North. They would have frequent tests of strength as part of their celebrations, and his unnatural size made him a constant participant. This was how the Northmen would brace themselves to lift the tongue of a wagon that had been loaded down with stone.

He started to pull up, keeping his back straight, and pushing with his legs as Marl scrambled back onto the bench. The plank under Elias groaned, cracking a bit more. He relaxed for a moment, adjusting his grip, and stepped back slightly. Again, he lifted, pushing with his legs and pulling up with his shoulders and back. The plank creaked and cracked a bit more, then, with a snap, the bolt tore free, trailing splintered wood.

Elias quickly sat back down, stepping back over the oar, so that it was in front of him again. Standing up, he jerked the oar towards the aisle. The short chain caught, keeping Elias from pulling it all the way in, and though he pulled on it, he could not break it loose from the hull. His escape would be of no use if he could not free himself from the oar.

"Out! Push it out!"

The old man who sat a few benches in front of him was watching him. He pointed at the oar. "Push it back out! The bolt is rusty, you can snap it against the hull! But be swift, it'll sound like a drum!"

Elias paused, looking at the hole the oar went through. It had room for the oar to move, but not enough to let the bolt out, driven through the wood as it was. He steadied himself, stood as upright as possible, and drove the oar out through the hole as hard as he could. With a loud thud and a sharp ping, the bolt snapped off, dropping the chain against the hull.

Marl was on his feet now, his hands on the oar. "Again!" he hissed, pointing at the bolt that connected his manacles to the oar. The older elf pulled his chains taut, making sure his hands were well out of the way. Elias drove the oar against the hull again, snapping off the second bolt.

Acting swiftly, Elias pulled the oar back in until the thinner, worn down section was sitting on the iron-rimmed port in the hull. Pushing the oar back, he wedged it in place until it couldn't move anymore. He could hear feet on the stairs, no doubt someone coming to check on the noise of the oar slamming against the hull. Bracing against his bench, he shoved against the handle with everything he had, muscles bunching against the strain.

Begrudgingly, the oar began to splinter, then gave way under the punishment, snapping off and dropping the paddle into the ocean. Thinking fast, he propped the oar back into place, the splintered end at the hole in the hull it once protruded from, and quickly resumed his seat as the guard stormed into the room.

"What the hells was that noise?"

The slaves murmured slightly, shifting in their seats and staring very intently at the oars in front of them. Elias prayed none of them would give him away before he had his moment to strike. He had to find a way to get the keys from the pirate, so he could free the rest of the slaves and mercenaries. He tightened his grip on the oar handle and steeled himself for the strike.

The pirate glared out over the benches, searching for a culprit. His eyes fixed on Martin.

"You. It was you, wasn't it? You goddamn troublemaker!"

Stomping down the aisle, the pirate closed on Martin, sap in hand. Elias had to do something, and fast, or Martin would get a beating much like Jonas had.

Almost as if on cue, the pirate started issuing threats and insults as he walked down the aisle. "I'm gonna break your fuckin' feet, you miserable son of a fisherman's whore!"

"You're a coward."

The pirate froze, his eyes wide at the sound of Elias's voice. Elias lifted his head so the man could see him clearly, even in the dim light of the oar deck. The pirate took a step closer, clenching his fist around the handle of his sap.

"What did you-"

Elias cut him off with a snarl. "I said you're a coward! A milk-fed babe has more courage than you do, you sallow-skinned weakling."

The pirate seemed to be struck dumb by the reality of a slave speaking to him like that. He stared back at Elias, his cheeks quivering with rage. Elias swore he could even see a tic forming at the corner of one eye. He started towards Elias, raising the sap high to deliver a heavy blow.

A blow that never landed. As soon as the pirate was in range, Elias lunged forward, swinging the oar handle as hard as he could. It slammed into the side of the pirate's head with the sound of a potato falling on a table. Before the pirate even hit the ground, Elias was on him, baring his teeth as a low growl, punctuated by his exertion, rumbled out of his chest. He grabbed the stunned pirate by the feet – the only part that he could reach – and dragged him closer. As soon as he was close enough, he struck the pirate three times with the butt of the handle, feeling the crunch of his skull as it gave way to his onslaught like fragile pottery.

The stunned silence that filled the room quickly gave way to murmurs from the slaves. Every head was turned, watching as Elias tore the key ring from the dead man's belt and unlocked the shackles around his ankles and wrists. With a clatter, the chains connecting him to the oar fell loose, still bolted to the wooden handle.

And that abruptly, he was free; free and armed. The section of the oar handle he held was about six feet long and shaped very much like a war club. From the sounds up on deck, not much notice had been taken of the noises from down below.

He moved immediately to Jonas, checking on the wounded man. He was bleeding from some cuts around his eyebrows, and his eye was swollen shut, but he was breathing. He unlocked the shackles that held him to the post, and lay the wounded man down on his side.

Elias's mind raced. He had to figure out a way to fight off the pirates, kill them all. He only had himself and eight trained fighters to go up against who knew how many cutthroat pirates.

He kept the oar handle nearby as he moved back towards the front row of slaves. "Can you sail? Can any of you sail?"

There was a slight chorus of 'aye's, and a few nods and raised hands. "Can any of you fight?"

Silence greeted him this time.

"We need to fight to get loose. I don't want to live out the rest of my days rowing this rickety bucket across the ocean while pirates whip me!"

Some of the slaves were nodding in assent, looking back and forth between each other. The quiet murmur started rising among them before a single voice spoke out over them.

"The pirates keep their swords in the armory so they can pose as sailors until they decide to board another ship. It's at the back of the hold." It was the old man again, speaking from his bench. "There is a key on that ring."

Elias looked back to him. "How do you know this?"

The elderly man spread his hands. "This is my ship. They took it from me, and stuck me and my crew down here."

Martin whispered urgently, "Elias! For the love of all things sacred, hurry up!"

Elias started unlocking the manacles attached to the oarslaves, his heart beating hard in his chest. After four weeks of captivity, the prospect of freedom was enough to make him giddy. Starting with his fellow mercenaries, he moved down the middle aisle until he reached the captain.

"Which key opens the armory?" Elias asked as he removed the old man's chains.

"The one with a brass handle, looks like an anchor." The captain rubbed his wrists. "Thank you, master elf."

Elias removed the brass key from the ring, handing keys to the shackles off to Martin. "Call me Elias."

"And you can call me Delain. Let's get my ship back."

Elias and Delain crept towards the grate farthest aft, towards the rear of the ship. Though Elias hardly needed the help, Delain lifted one side of the large metal grate that covered the access to the hold. "Martin! Once you get everyone freed, help them down here. Marl, see to Jonas. We're going to arm up and take this ship!"

Marl moved towards Jonas silently as Martin cursed, causing the slave he was working on to cringe. "Are you out of your mind?"

"Do you have a better idea?"

Martin finished removing the man's chains, and sighed. "Dammit. No. I don't."

"Alright then."

Delain held a finger to his lips. "The crew quarters are in the forecastle, but some of the men will sleep in the hold. The rocking of the ship is less severe down there. They might not all be topside." Elias nodded and lowered himself down into the hold, reaching up to help the old man down. He crept among the crates and sacks, looking for any threats. He paused in his tracks, looking up at ceiling for a moment. Blood dripped between the planks underneath where he had killed the guard, forming a small puddle on the floor in front of him.

A snort and grumble caught his attention, and he dropped to a crouch. On a pile of burlap sacks, one of the pirates lay on his back, spread-eagled. Elias crept up on the man, his bare feet silent against the deck boards, until a loose plank groaned loudly under his weight. The pirate sat up, blinking, looking directly at Elias.

Elias pounced on the man, one massive hand clamping over the pirate's mouth, the other one gripping the man's neck in a stranglehold. The pirate's arms started flailing about before balling his hands into fists and bludgeoning Elias. Elias ducked his chin down, taking most of the blows on his shoulders and the back of his head. Adrenaline made his breath come fast and hard, while the struggling man gagged against his hand. Elias gritted his teeth, his pulse thundering in his ears as he clenched his eyes shut, pressing his forehead against the panicking man's brow.

It seemed like an eternity before the pirate stopped fighting back, his blows becoming weaker until his arms dropped to his sides. Elias held him there for a few moments longer, until he could feel the man's pulse stop under his grip. Elias let go, leaning back on his haunches, staring at the bug-eyed countenance of the pirate in front of him. There was blood all over his teeth where they had cut into his lips from the force Elias had been putting on him, and his neck was discolored where Elias has crushed it with his other hand.

Elias looked down at his hands. They too were covered in blood and saliva. He wiped them off on the dead man's shirt and headed back towards the rear of the ship.

Delain had the door to the armory unlocked when Elias got there. Inside were about twenty cutlasses, ten bows with quivers, and around fifteen short-handled axes. Enough to arm a bit more than half of the slaves.

Elias was a little disappointed to not find his sword amongst the weaponry. The oar handle he had would serve him well, but he wanted a cutting edge. He started handing weapons to the slaves who were showing up behind him.

Once all the weapons were handed out, he directed the rest of the would-be warriors to the belaying pins – which were between a foot and a half to two feet long and shaped roughly like clubs – and gaff hooks scattered about the hold in small piles here and there. After everyone was armed, Elias addressed the crowd.

"Half of you go to the front of the ship, the other half of you stay here with me at the stern. Now, when I give the signal, I want you to charge up the stairs and kill every single pirate you see."

One of the slaves spoke up. "But they're better armed, and we're starved! They're pirates, and we're just slaves!"

Elias stood fully, his head among the beams that supported the deck above him. "Do you want to stay a slave? Do you not have a family to go home to? Do not hesitate, because they won't. If you don't kill the pirate in front of you, he will kill you. It's not a maybe, there is no guessing here. You will die if you do not fight, and so I intend to fight."

There was a murmur of assent through the crowd.

Elias pointed to the mercenaries that had been captured with him. "Half of you should lead the charge to the deck, soften the pirates up for the slaves. We're stronger, we've been below deck for less time. The other half will stay with me and lead the way up this staircase. We'll catch them from both sides and meet in the middle."

Four of the mercenaries, including Martin and Geoff, led half of the slaves to the staircase at the bow. Elias and the other three mercenaries stayed at the stern, huddling on either side of the staircase, out of view of the deck.

Topside, the celebration continued unabated. Elias could hear raucous laughter, shouting, and fiddle music mixing with the sounds of the sea. When Martin signaled they were in place, Elias turned to his men. "Is everyone ready?" Without waiting for a response, he roared out the signal.

"Now!"

Chapter Ten

13th Waning Summer Moon, Year 4368

Using the railing of the stairs to propel himself forward, Elias charged up the stairs, wielding the broken oar like a giant club, the chains still dangling from the middle. He took the stairs two at a time, outpacing the mercenaries who were right behind him. He could hear shouting from the bow of the ship as he broke into the torchlight. The fresh air hit him like a breath of heaven, but he couldn't stop to enjoy it. The fiddling pirate was turning towards him, a shocked expression on his face.

Elias swung the handle with everything he had and destroyed the man's skull. Blood and flesh sprayed forward, splashing across several other shocked pirates who were yelling and screaming in surprise. Not slowing down his charge, Elias was upon them before they could get their swords drawn, swinging the oar handle with frantic, devastating force. As he struck the pirates, his fellow mercenaries led the slaves into their quarry behind and around him.

The clashing of steel and the smell of blood filled his senses, and his vision tinged red. He had felt this before when he fought, and this time he reveled in it. His blood rose hot in his veins and he let out a battle cry, wordless, just sound and fury tearing itself out of him as he ripped into the stunned pirates with his improvised war club. Where the battle with the orcs had kept him anxious, the month he had spent chained to an oar had bestowed a furious rage.

Elias brought the handle down on another pirate, crushing his skull and slamming him to the deck in one strike. Adrenaline coursed through the blood that thundered in his ears. He grabbed one of the pirates by his shirt and tried to throw him, but the cloth gave way, tearing under his grasp. The pirate staggered back, sword in hand, then lunged forward, swinging at Elias.

Elias's oar handle struck the basket hilt of the cutlass so hard that the brass was crushed against the pirate's now very broken hand. A second strike liberated the man from pain by breaking his neck.

Chaos reigned on the deck as slave and pirate clashed, many pirates falling before they had a chance to grab weaponry. Only a few of the pirates carried their swords with them, and it was these that the mercenaries targeted first. In the fray, one could see the difference between the frantic, terrified slaves, and the aggressive fury of the mercenaries.

Something heavy landed on Elias from behind. A rope wrapped around his neck, cutting off his air. There was a shout, and suddenly, the rope tightened, and Elias felt himself being lifted off his feet. The weight started slipping off his back, but Elias grabbed it and dragged it around in front of himself as he was lifted off the deck.

It was the pirate that had beaten Martin in the hold when Elias first woke up. Bald head, long nose, square jaw – definitely him. Elias had a hold of him by the upper arm. The pirate was yelling and reaching for a knife he had sheathed under the arm Elias held.

He knew he didn't have much time left. Already his vision was starting to go dark as he hung by his neck. He grabbed the knife out of the pirate's belt and stabbed at his face with it, striking him in the eye. The man screamed as Elias let him go, dropping him to the deck. Reaching up, Elias grabbed the rope with his left hand and hauled on it, trying to lessen the weight he was putting on the noose. He sawed frantically at the rope with the knife, struggling to breathe

Without warning, he dropped, rope and all. He fell maybe six feet, the rope still tight around his neck. Hands grabbed at him, and he started flailing about with his arms. His vision was almost black by the time someone grabbed the rope around his neck and loosened it.

Looking up, he gasped for breath as his watering eyes met Delain's.

"Are you alright? Can you breathe?"

"Yes, " he croaked. A pirate was rushing towards them, cutlass raised, screaming from behind the old man. Elias shoved him out of the way, and lunged forward, catching the pirate by the wrist and the neck. The pirate beat at Elias with his other hand as the giant lifted him off the ground. Hoisting him high, Elias brought him down with as much force as he could muster, striking his head on the edge of a barrel that was lashed to the deck. The pirate's movements ceased, and Elias threw him overboard, stripping him of his sword.

"Elias! Elias, the captain is not here!" Delain's voice called out to him from not far away. The old man had a gaff hook and a belaying pin and was holding back a pirate armed with a long wooden pole.

Rushing in from the pirate's side, Elias swung the cutlass hard, trying to break the pole in a single swing. Unfortunately, the pirate saw him coming and sidestepped him, using the pole to parry Elias's strike. The end of the pole came back with blinding speed, catching Elias in the stomach. If it had been a spear, Elias would have been impaled. As it was, he had the air driven out of him and staggered back. He and the pirate faced off, each at the ready, each waiting to strike.

A belaying pin struck the pirate directly in the eye, causing him to stagger and curse, letting go of the pole with one hand. Clapping a hand over his eye, he tried to cover himself from the new threat as well as Elias. He failed when Delain's gaff hook sunk into his arm, and Elias ran him through with the cutlass.

Delain grabbed Elias's wrist. "You have to find the captain! If you can kill him, the rest of the pirates might surrender!"

Forcing a surrender was one of the last things on Elias's mind at the moment, but the old man made sense. Elias nodded assent; he fight had been fast but was not over yet. They had the element of surprise, but the pirates were starting to regroup.

There was a clear path to the aftcastle, and Elias took it. Charging forward, he struck the door with his whole body weight, holding the cutlass clear. The weathered wooden door cracked and splintered, bursting inwards and slamming against the wall, opening to a small entry room with another door directly in front of him. Elias braced against the door frame and kicked the door near the handle, splintering wood and knocking it open.

The smell of lavender and jasmine filled the warm, moist air that greeted him. A large copper tub of steaming water was to the right, and clothes were strewn about the room. The woman who had been dragged up from the oar deck set on the bed, naked, her knees drawn up as she recoiled from the commotion at the door.

As Elias burst into the room, he parried a strike from the left just in time to protect himself. The captain was swinging a longsword at him, naked from the waist up, his breeches untied. He struck a few more times, with Elias repelling each swing, then backed off to readdress. He moved back and forth while Elias stood his ground, keeping the cutlass between himself and the captain.

The man started stalking towards him. "I should have cut you into ribbons the moment I saw you, you giant shit!" he spat, menacing Elias with the tip of his sword. Elias suddenly realized that the longsword the captain was using was Elias's own, taken from him when he had been captured.

Elias held the cutlass ready to parry, trying to keep an eye on the captain and the battle behind him as well. He couldn't tell by the shouting who was winning, and he didn't need to get caught between the captain and any pirates behind him.

The captain must have realized what Elias was watching for, and yelled out. "Someone get in here and kill this fucking elf-"

His shout was cut off mid-sentence by a flash of steel from behind him. His eyes snapped open and his swordpoint dropped. He staggered forward a single step, then his throat was slashed out. Blood poured down his chest as he dropped the sword and grabbed at his neck with both hands, frantically trying to stem the flow of blood as he fell to his knees. The woman from the bed stood behind him, holding a dagger, her right arm covered in dark arterial blood.

She stood without moving, still naked, water droplets glistening on her skin, looking down as the captain gurgled his last breath. Lean though she was, she was still very much a woman, and not as skinny as Elias had thought. Her skin was much darker than his, but not black – more a light, leather-like brown, but much smoother. White and pink scars marked her shoulders, arms, stomach and thighs, a few disappearing into the dark hair between her legs.

He averted his eyes when he realized he had been staring. "Are... uh... are you..."

"Get down!"

He spun around to see a pirate charging him with a small harpoon. He raised the cutlass to parry the charge, but before the pirate could close the distance, her dagger flashed past Elias, embedding itself in the man's eye. Elias turned back to see the woman picking up Elias's sword. "Watch yourself! Stay alive!" Her thick, sharp accent added force to her words.

"Thank you. Do you need-"

"I can handle myself right now. You handle them." She pointed out the door as she started rifling through the clothes on the floor.

Elias looked down at the dying captain on the floor, gurgling in his death throes. Grabbing the body by the wrist, he dragged it out through the battered doors, and with a mighty heave, threw the corpse onto the deck, striking a few clustered pirates with it.

"Your captain is dead! Throw down your weapons and your lives will be spared!"

Most of the pirates had grouped up, surrounded by the mercenaries and remaining slaves. One of the pirates cursed and slapped a mercenary's blade to the side with his own. Before he could throw another strike, an arrow embedded itself into his throat. He fell to the deck, gurgling blood and grasping at the arrow. Martin stood on the forecastle, nocking another arrow into the bow he held with his bloody hands. He nodded to Elias, then pulled back, taking aim at the pirates again.

"I swear to you now, drop your weapons and you won't be harmed. However, if you want to die, keep them in your hands."

The pirates looked between each other, then lowered their weapons. At the sound of metal and wood landing on the deck, the slaves raised a cheer. The ship was won.

~   ~   ~

Elias heaved the last pirate body over the edge of the deck. Of the thirty pirates that had been on board when the battle started, eight remained. However, of the fifty-five slaves that had broken free, twenty-eight survived. Even with the help of Elias and his companions, the pirates had killed as many as they lost, including two of the mercenaries. Martin had lost a finger to a cutlass, and Jonas was still unconscious. Elias was bruised, somewhat battered, but for the most part without serious injury.

The bodies of the fallen oarslaves were laid out on deck, with the two mercenaries laid separate from them. The remaining slaves and Delain all agreed that a burial at sea was the best option for those who had fallen. Delain, having retaken his position as captain, oversaw the funeral.

The bodies were wrapped in cloth, of which there was an abundance in the cargo hold, weighted with ropes, and lowered over the side of the ship. The two mercenaries were kept in the hold, for cremation upon landfall; Martin had said that it was customary for men from the mainland who died while away from their homeland. The surviving pirates, however, were chained to the benches on the oar deck. Geoff and another man took up station to guard them, ensuring no escape attempts.

Elias threw a bucket attached to a rope over the edge of the ship and pulled it back up. He used the seawater to wash the blood and grime from his hands and arms, then poured it over the rail and back into the sea. As soon as they made landfall, the entire deck would need to be washed... there was blood everywhere.

Delain was in the process of assigning jobs to the freed slaves according to their abilities and keeping the vessel sailing smoothly. Some of the rigging had been damaged in the fight, and the first order of business was to get it repaired enough to limp into port at Greenreef, which was visible in the growing light of dawn.

Marl had stayed with Jonas for the entirety of the fight, and was still with him now that he had been moved to a bed in the crew's quarters. The older elf was trained in the ways of a healer, and had more experience than Geoff. He was able to stabilize Jonas, cleaning and bandaging his wounds after the battle.

Elias looked out over the bow of the ship, to the west. The sky was still nearly black on the eastern horizon, but it was lightening just enough to reveal the rising islands. Each island had a tall mountain rising near the center of it, one of which had a plume of smoke rising from the peak. Elias had heard of the mountains of fire that rose out of the sea, but he had never entirely believed the stories... how could fire rise out of water? And yet here it was.

The woman from the captain's chambers stood at the bow as well. She had dressed in plain trousers and a tunic, belted about the waist with a red sash, Elias's sword in its scabbard hanging from her left hip. Her hair was pulled back in a blue ribbon, the ends of which were woven into the rest of her black locks. She had said very little since the end of the battle, and the new crew had mostly left her alone.

They stood in silence for a while, watching the waves roll past as the ship moved steadily towards the island. Elias wanted to talk to the woman, ask her name, but had absolutely no idea how to do so. He was used to living and interacting with men, or women who acted as mother figures to him. This was a woman completely unknown to him, and though he had no inclinations towards her, he felt awkward initiating conversation.

"My name is Jenna."

He turned towards her, surprised. "Excuse me?"

She turned as well, putting her back to the railing, and leaning back slightly. "You've been standing over there trying to figure out what to say to me for at least ten minutes. I figure you ought to at least know my name. It's Jenna."

Elias cleared his throat. "Ah. I'm Elias. Pleased to meet you."

Jenna quirked a brow. "Are you?"

Elias had no idea how to respond. "Should I not be?"

Jenna smirked and looked back towards the approaching islands. "You never know. I could be one of the most insufferable bitches you've ever met."

Elias shrugged. "Maybe. I haven't seen that yet, so for now, I'm going to assume you're not. I did spend my youth around elves, and they can be pretty insufferable."

Jenna smiled then, still looking out towards the islands. At first, she didn't say anything, and the silence stretched out for a time. Elias started feeling somewhat uncomfortable, like he should say something. "Is there, uh, anything I can do?"

Jenna pushed off of the rail. She walked up to him, her shorter stature dwarfed by Elias's massive frame. "Don't treat me like I'm broken. Yes, I have a past, no I do not want to talk about it. Yes, things have happened, no there's nothing you can do for it. Treat me like the person that I am, not the one you think I am."

Elias held her deep, almost black eyes with his own and nodded once. "Yes, ma'am."

Jenna smiled, reaching up and patting his chest. "Excellent." She started down the steps that led to the main deck. "We should make landfall in about four hours, if not sooner, I think. I'm going to see what these bastards have lurking in the mess hall, and maybe we can get these men fed."

Elias watched her go, unsure of what to make of the enigmatic woman. One thing he did know was that she still had his sword, and he wasn't exactly sure how to ask for it back. He leaned against the rail, looking towards the approaching islands.

This was not what he had had in mind when he left the Northlands. Not at all. There was one upside to this unexpected trip, though... it would be very difficult for the Felle Army knight to track him here, unless the others from the Felle had a way to communicate faster than sending a ship.

Marl stepped to the rail beside him. "The air smells like home here. It's been far too long since I left. Well over a year." He pointed to the largest of the landmasses on the horizon. "That island there is the one you mainlanders call Greenreef. His true name is Rapa Matomato, the Green Giant. Behind him is Rapa Wahine, the Giant's Wife. Their children stretch out to the west, forming the rest of our islands."

Elias looked down at Marl. "Which one is your home?"

"Rapa Matomato. It is where the largest village of my people is, and I am the leader of that village. My wife has been leading in my place." He smiled slightly, closing his eyes and breathing deeply through his nose. "Every night I dreamed of coming home to my wife and my daughter. She is about your age, but every bit as formidable as her mother." He glanced up at Elias. "You should come with me to my village once we dock at the port. I daresay it's more comfortable than any accommodations on this boat."

Elias nodded. "I'd like that. I haven't been to an elven village since I was barely a century old."

Marl smiled again, broader this time. "Then it's settled. Once the men at port are done with us, we'll head out." He pushed back from the railing. "I'm going to go check on our patient. Try to find some sleep if you can. You'll need it."

Elias smiled. "I will when it comes to me. Thank you, Marl."

He turned back to the west, listening to the waves lapping at the hull of the ship as it sailed towards the island, the sky growing lighter as dawn approached.

~　　~　　~

14th Waning Summer Moon, Year 4368

Elias stood at the gangplank, watching the mercenaries escort the captured pirates off the ship. Delain stood on the pier with a group of officials from the port that was named after the island chain, Greenreef. They had docked at the largest of the islands, as it was the most well known as friendly and safe to non-pirate vessels. Some of the smaller islands at the western end of the chain had been commandeered by pirates and turned into fortified refuges, almost like a sort of anti-government society.

The settlement here had been founded by men and elves from the mainland, and as such retained much of the culture and practices of the lands of origin, however, the tropical climate and the presence of natives on the island made for an interesting mixture of cultures. The administrative buildings were made of stone to withstand the occasional tropical storm, but most dwellings were made of wood and thatch, both of which were abundant on the island.

Dock workers were busy upon the piers and the shore, moving cargo to and from several other ships. However, there was a bit of a crowd at the foot of the pier they were docked at. Apparently, the ship they had retaken was well known as a pirate vessel, and there had been a bounty on the heads of the pirates who sailed it. The port authority was trying to decide exactly how to pay the bounties, since all of the dead had been thrown overboard. Delain had produced the captain's log, which numbered the pirates at 30, eight of which remained alive. Those eight had already been paid for, twenty gold coins a head. The other twenty-two were what was being debated.

Elias left the haggling to Delain. He would take his share, of course, but the ship needed repairs and supplies for the return to the mainland, as well as a crew of able bodied sailors capable of making the voyage. Much of the cargo could be sold off, as the owners were presumably no longer alive to claim it, which would help with the costs immensely.

As the last pirate was transferred to the custody of the port authorities, Elias turned back to the forecastle and went to go check on Jonas. The man had been unconscious for a long time, which was dangerous.

As Elias entered the cabin, he could hear Jonas grumbling. Marl was sitting on a stool next to him and looked up as Elias approached.

"He's not conscious yet, but he is making noises, and has been for a few minutes now. He will likely wake up soon."

Elias sat down on the bed next to Jonas. "Not soon enough. He's the reason we're free."

Marl looked at Elias quizzically. "I remember it a bit differently."

Elias shrugged. "I wouldn't have had the motivation to try if he hadn't first. I just followed his lead." He looked down at Jonas's face, the top of his head wrapped in bloodstained bandages, a patch over his swollen eye. "He was the leader of the group I was captured with, and he fittingly led the way to freedom... if not in person, then in spirit."

"You need to take credit for your own achievements, Elias."

Jenna's voice cut through the ambient sound of the port bustle. She sat down across from Elias and Marl. "It was you who broke your bonds, and you who took the keys. You led the charge, and you killed the captain."

Elias was taken aback."But I didn't! You did!"

Jenna shook her head. "Not according to the men. You burst through his door, caught him in an act of villainy, and cut his throat. That's what they believe, and that is the story they will tell from this day forward. Elias, the Iron Oarsman. Liberator of slaves, crusher of pirates."

Elias shook his head, chuckling slightly. "That is a reputation I neither want nor need."

Jenna leaned back, studying him. "Be that as it may, you have it. So now, it begs the question; what are you going to do with that reputation? What are your plans now that you're no longer bound to the sea?"

Elias looked down at his hands. "I honestly have absolutely no idea."

Jonas coughed next to Elias. "I know what I am going to do, you giant lummox."

Elias startled and knelt on the ground next to Jonas. "You're awake! Welcome back, old man!"

Jonas groaned. "Save your welcomes and fetch me a bucket."

Elias slid a bucket containing clean water over just as Jonas rolled to his side and retched into it. There was precious little for him to lose, but he lost it nonetheless. He held the man up by his shoulders, supporting him while he was sick, then helped him lay back. Marl readjusted Jonas's bandages as Jenna watched the whole thing fairly passively.

"The vomiting is normal," she remarked. "He was struck hard enough to bruise his brain. You can see the bruising by his eyes-"

Jonas grimaced. "I can assure you, my dear, the bruises aren't limited to my eyes."

She smirked slightly at the older man's sass. "I think you'll be right as the tide after you rest and heal. You may lose some vision in that eye, but you'll live."

Jones closed his good eye. "So tell me the good news then?"

Jenna chuckled at that, setting a hand on Jonas's. "The good news is that your man freed us. After your valiant effort, Elias broke his bonds and led the battle to retake the ship." Her eyes met Elias's and held them as she continued. "He slew the guardsman and took his keys, then freed us all. His victory over the captain caused the pirates who survived to surrender." Her gaze almost seemed to challenge him to correct her.

Jonas glanced at Elias. "Really? Elias? Well now." He settled his head back against the pillow, closing his eye again. "You'll have to tell me how that happened."

Elias excused himself as Marl emptied the bucket out a window, and Jenna started recounting the story to Jonas. "I wasn't there, myself, but as the men tell it, after the guardsman dragged me to the deck..."

Chapter Eleven

14th Waning Summer Moon, Year 4368

Elias stood on land for the first time in over four weeks. The absence of the wave motion was disconcerting at first, making his legs feel rubbery, but it only took a few moments to get used to the difference. Now he understood why sailors referred to sea legs and land legs.

The air was crisp and clean. It was the smell of the ocean, not stagnant or fishy like Jetty had been. The port here was in a wide, deep crescent shaped bay, shielded from the winds of the east, but open to the ocean to the south. Two long arms of the mountain behind the city extended into the waves, white sandy beaches running from the sea up to the green jungle that covered much of the island. Tropical birds shouted at the intruders, their song mixing with the sounds of men, elves, and gulls.

Marl stepped up beside him. "What are you looking for?"

Elias shrugged. "I don't know. Just looking, mostly." He pointed at the white plume rising from the top of the mountain. "Is that really smoke?"

Marl laughed. "No, that is not smoke. There is a hot lake in the crater on top of the mountain. It is a sacred place, where the seers of my people can speak to the gods. It is actually where I am going now."

Elias looked down at Marl, furrowing his brow. "You're not going home immediately?"

Marl shook his head. "No. I have questions for my gods, and I have been away from them for far too long. I will speak to them, and then I will go to my village. Each is about half a day's walk from here. I suggest you stay here for the night; I will come back for you when I am done on the mountain. Is that acceptable to you?"

Elias nodded. "It does."

Marl gently patted Elias on the shoulder, then, without another word, set off through the busy dock. As he passed, he was mostly ignored by the men, but the elves stepped out of his way and let him pass as they went about their work.

Once off of the docks, Elias wandered through the town for a while, getting to know the layout. There were several other ships at port, and sailors bustled here and there, purchasing fruits and meats from the vendors that were scattered through the stone paved streets. Most of what was for sale was seafood, followed closely by pork and fowl. There was very little beef and no venison. Baked goods were very different from what was on the mainland, using potato flour instead of wheat. The texture was different, but not bad.

The primary buildings near the long stone piers were stone as well – interlocking bricks carved from gray limestone. Some of the buildings had archways made of blocks of black volcanic glass, which stood out in stark contrast to the lighter stone of the walls.

The weather was exceedingly mild. Even though the sun was bright and hot, the constant sea breeze kept it from being overwhelming. Despite the breeze, though, Elias found himself stripping off his shirt to let the air cool him. Most of the men here were naked from the waist up, and some of the women as well, their skins tanned dark.

The elves, however, were divided into two types, it seemed. Some of them walked around like the men, shirtless and tanned, while others wore long, loose shirts and wide-brimmed hats to cover them from the sun, their fair skin almost unnaturally white, even for elves.

These were Marl's people, the sea elves, as they were called by the people from the mainland. They spent much of their time in the water of the coves and rivers of the island. Most of what they were working with in town was from the sea. Fish, shellfish, dried seaweed, pearls, and shells were all among their wares.

The city was built into the rising slope of the mountain, so by the time Elias wandered to the northern side of the town, he was above the rest of the city. Here, the stone buildings gave way to wood and thatch, and the streets were made of packed dirt, sand, and gravel.

Small children ran around playing while older children chased them, their mothers calling out to them while they bustled about. One such woman, a comely human of mainland descent, stopped and stared at him as he walked past, her jaw dropping open. Men paused in their work to watch him pass.

It wasn't long before he had attracted a small and none too subtle group of children following him. They mostly spoke a language he couldn't understand, though he could occasionally make out some words of the common tongue. Giant, they were calling him. It made sense, really, but it didn't put him at ease.

Just past the northern edge of the town, there was a road and a fence. Nothing too impressive, the split rails nevertheless seemed to hold the jungle at bay, the undergrowth pushing all the way to within arm's reach of the road. Brightly colored flowers and dense foliage made seeing through the wall of the jungle impossible. Elias stopped at the fence, resting his hands on it as he studied the plants. There was nothing here he recognized... it was entirely different from what he knew on the mainland.

"That one grows the papaya. Hard to find a place on the island that you can't reach out and pick one. "

Elias turned to see a child standing next to him. His broad-brimmed hat and poncho identified him as a sea elf, as did his nearly bluish white skin. His electric green eyes regarded Elias with a quiet curiosity as he leaned against the rail.

"Is that so?" Elias asked. "Which one is the papaya?"

The child pointed to a tree with fruits all over it, about the size of Elias's fist. "That one there. We slice it up and dry it. Tastes like candy, and wards off sickness for those who stay at sea too long. "

Elias had seen the red fruit for sale at the pier but hadn't tried any. "Is it good to eat when raw?"

"Oh, yes. A little messy, but nothing a swim can't fix. Same with the mangoes. They are the yellow fruits you would find dried in round slices. " The elf pointed again to some low hanging fruits on another tree. "Nobody has ever starved to death on Greenreef. "

Elias leaned against the rail as well, looking over the fruiting trees. "I would imagine not." After being stuck in the hold of the ship for so long, it was nice to have a conversation with someone new, even if that conversation was with a child.

The child hopped up on the railing. He appeared to be maybe a century old, give or take. "You're from the mainland, aren't you? From the ship that came in this morning."

Elias nodded, leaning against the fence himself, causing the timbers to creak slightly. "I am."

"Were you a pirate or a slave?"

Elias laughed. "If I were a pirate, I would be in chains right now."

"So you were a slave then."

Elias shook his head, bemused at the brazen questions the child was asking. "Not exactly. I was a mercenary that was captured and made to row the ship. When we broke free, we stopped being slaves."

The child frowned. "What is a mercenary? Is that like a warrior?"

"Kind of like a warrior. We fight for and protect the people who pay us our wages."

The young elf nodded thoughtfully. "So you fight for gold."

Elias nodded too. "I did."

A woman's voice called out from the village. "Kauri! Come over here, it is time to go!" She was a thickly built, not unattractive elf with a basket tied to her back like a backpack. She wore the same broad-brimmed hat and poncho of the sea elves, and stood at the head of a trail.

The boy hopped down immediately. "Coming mama," he shouted, sprinting towards her. They headed down the trail, along with several other women and children. Elias watched them go, leaning against the fence. It was the first time he could recall a member of his own race not treating him like a sideshow freak. He closed his eyes and raised his face to the sun, a smile growing on his lips.

Yes, he was going to like it here.

Elias found his way back to the busy seaside district of the town, which was much larger than it had appeared when they had first arrived. There was a tavern near the dock that Delain's ship was tied off at, which had a good number of rooms and was made of stone, and so was nice and cool. There, he took his meal and rented his room with his share of the bounty from the pirates. The port authority had decided to pay out a quarter bounty for each pirate listed in the captain's log, since they couldn't verify that Elias and the crew had killed them. This still left Elias with a decent sum, enough to outfit himself, if his belongings weren't found when the contents of the ship were fully cataloged.

Elias ate his meal with Martin and Geoff, as Jonas was still on the ship, and Jenna was tending to him. After he ate, he went to his room, barred the door, and was asleep almost immediately, despite the fact that his feet hung over the edge of the bed. The soft, hay-filled mattress and thick wool blanket were heavenly after spending so much time chained to a bench.

~   ~   ~

New Grain Moon, Year 4368

Elias startled awake at a knock on his door. Sunlight peeked through the gaps in the shutters on the windows, leaving long, bright splashes of sunlight on the floor of his chamber. Marl's voice came from outside his room.

"Elias! It's nearly noon! If we are to make it to Seagate by dusk, we will have to leave soon!"

Bleary eyed, he opened the door, letting Marl in as he gathered his few belongings. "Did you already make it to the top of the mountain and back?"

Marl nodded, leaning against a freshly cut stave. "I did. The trails were familiar to me still, so I made good time."

"What did the gods have to say?" Elias did not consider himself to be a religious elf; he wasn't particularly spiritual and put little stock in what he couldn't see and feel with his own two hands.

Marl smirked a little. "The gods are fond of their secrets and told me only what I needed to hear. All will be revealed when it is time... after all, the tide neither stops nor changes for anyone."

The path to the village was long and winding, cresting a tall ridge that lay between the port where they had docked and Marl's village. As they walked, Marl pointed out the landscape and told the legend of how it was formed. Long ago, before the men or elves walked the land, there was nothing but sea. According to the sea elves, the goddess of the winds and the goddess of the ocean lived there, exploring their realms endlessly. The sun shone down upon them, warming them by day, and when he slept, so did they.

As the centuries crawled by, they grew bored with their featureless kingdom and longed for a change. The gods of the mainland wanted nothing to do with them, and so they were alone in the great expanse of the ocean, counting waves, until a young mountain god of the coast took pity on them. He asked them to take him to their realm, so he could see it for himself.

They carried him to the center of their realm, where the water was deepest, and he saw the vast empty expanse. Under the sea, however, the mountain god could see the hot earth, buried under miles of water. He dove under the waves, swimming to the very bottom, and caused the earth to crack asunder. The very lifeblood of Erde spewed forth, flowing across the ocean floor where it cooled, building up layer after layer. The layers rose higher and higher until, with smoke and steam, it broke through the surface of the sea and reached for the sun.

Ocean and Wind were overjoyed. Ocean pulled all manner of life from the coasts – fish and clams and sharks – and brought them to the island. Wind carried seeds and birds to the islands, and together, they turned the hard, hot rock into a lush green jungle paradise, full of life and beauty. When the mountain god saw what they were doing, he was pleased, and created more islands from the bottom of the sea, leading a trail to the west, which the fish and trees and flowers grew and covered. The goddess of the ocean brought coral and planted it near the islands, to protect the islands from her waves, preserving them for the ages.

As they crested the ridge, Marl was wrapping up his story. "When the goddess of the ocean saw what the mountain god had grown from out of her waters, she embraced the mountain, and kissed him, to show him her love for his creations. Where he wrapped his arms around her, the land still juts out to sea, and that forms what the men from the mainland call the Seagate. Where she kissed him, a sweet, fresh spring pours out of the mountain, and into the sea. And this is where we built our village."

Stretching out before them was the southwestern coast of the island. Built directly on the sand in a sheltered lagoon cove, lean-to shelters constructed of bamboo and palm fronds made up the bulk of the village. Throughout the beach, there were tall palm trees planted at regular intervals, providing shade to the villagers.

The mountain rose to the north of the village as it had in Port Greenreef, but here, arms of black stone reached out and wrapped around the beach, meeting at the far end of the lagoon. The rock was porous, somewhat jagged in places, but worn down where travel made it expedient to do so.

A passage had been pounded by the waves where the two arms met, leaving an archway that led from the lagoon out to sea. Larger ships, like the one Elias had arrived on, would have their masts snapped off if they tried to pass under the arch, but the carved canoes of the sea elves that Elias had seen at Port Greenreef could pass through three at a time.

There was one building that was more permanent, perhaps three stories tall, built of wooden planks that seem to have been salvaged from boats. The roof was made of sail cloth, covered over with palm fronds that were lashed into place with rigging. The building was set farther back from the water than the rest of the buildings, where the sand transitioned to sturdier ground.

As they drew closer to the building, he could see the tar covered timbers that were sunk into the ground were at one point masts, whereas much of the siding was old hull planks. The light skinned elves moved in and out of it, going between the building and the water or various other shades.

In front of the building, there was a large ring of stones in the sand with ash and charcoal in the middle. It was surrounded by logs that had been chiseled into benches and torches that were set into the top of bamboo poles driven into the ground. None of the flames were lit, since it was the middle of the day.

Elias was extremely conscious of the fact that almost none of the elves wore anything above the waist. Their skin ranged in color from pearly white to a very light blue, and a few individuals had skin as blue as sapphires. A group of elves about Elias's age came running across the sand towards him and Marl.

One of them was a lively, full figured young woman with skin a shade of blue almost as dark as the sky, bright green eyes, and jet black hair that shone in the sunlight. She was naked save for a white leather loincloth tied about her waist with a woven red string, just above her hips. Her stomach was a slightly lighter shade of blue, and an emerald set in silver hung from a piercing in the bottom of her navel.

Her breasts bounced as she ran, not large enough to be ponderous, but substantial for a girl of her age, which seemed to be slightly younger than he was. Jumping as she reached Marl, she wrapped her arms around his neck and kissed him on the cheek.

He caught her, though he was almost bowled off his feet, and laughed.

"Welcome home, father! It has been so long! The messenger told us you had come home yesterday, but went to commune with the gods! What did they say?"

He set her down, chuckling. "Patience, my dear, patience. All will be told this evening, I promise. "

She pouted, glancing over at Elias. Slipping to the side, she peeked at him from behind Marl. "You didn't tell me the gods were going to send you back with a giant red elf, " she said, batting her emerald eyes at Elias.

Elias could feel the blood rushing to his face even more, and knew he was blushing. He turned his face away, suddenly speechless, not knowing what to say.

Marl laughed again. "Go, my daughter, your beauty surpasses your modesty. This is Elias, from the mainland. His people are from a land much colder than ours, and must always cover themselves; they are not used to the freedom our islands bless us with. Fetch your feather shawl for the time being. "

"Yes, father!" She gave him another kiss on the cheek, and stole a glance at Elias before running away to the village, the group of boys and girls following. Elias watched her go, struck by her beauty. She moved with a lithe grace, her hair flowing behind her as she sprinted over the low dunes. She disappeared into the large wooden building, hardly even slowing. Elias glanced to the side to see Marl watching him. He flushed again.

"I'm... I'm sorry. I did not mean to stare. "

Marl chuckled, clapping Elias on the shoulder. "If I were to be upset at someone for appreciating her beauty, then I would be doing my daughter a disservice. She is beautiful, and you are young. The gods do not frown on us for recognizing the beauty they bless us with." He gestured towards the wooden building. "Come. I wish to introduce you to the members of our tribe. "

Elias walked across the sand, irritated with himself. He hated feeling like he had done something to embarrass himself, and he felt that way now. Blushing always made him embarrassed, which caused him to blush more, which made him more embarrassed. A vicious cycle, to be sure.

Inside the building, the floor was covered with bamboo and reed mats, with woven chairs here and there that were padded with sheepskin. The front doors were left wide open, as well as the doors on the inland side of the building, allowing a pleasant breeze to flow through – enough to keep the air fresh and cool. Rope and bamboo ladders hung on either side of the room, giving access to the levels above. Thankfully, the ceiling in this room was tall enough for Elias to stand fully upright; not many rooms outside of the Northlands had given him that luxury.

Most of the elves in the room stopped talking and looked at him as he entered behind Marl. He stood awkwardly in the door frame for a moment before half a dozen young children pushed past him, playing some game or other. Marl was talking to a few other older elves, his arm wrapped around a woman who was slightly shorter than he was. He waved to Elias with his free hand and beckoned for him to come over.

As he approached, Marl held a hand out to him. "This is Elias. I met him on my way back from the mainland. "

The woman Marl had his arm wrapped around looked him up and down. "This one is Elias? He is bigger than I had heard."

Elias nodded. "I am. How is it that you know of me? I only landed on Greenreef yesterday morning. "

The woman smirked. "It is not every day one can rally slaves into fighters and overthrow a pirate ship. Though I must say, the account I heard sold you short. "

Elias frowned slightly at the reference to his height. "How do you mean?"

"They said you were tall. You're also the size of three of our warriors. That wasn't mentioned at all. "

Marl interrupted the exchange with introductions. "Elias, this is my wife, Jayd. She manages the tribe while I am away. While I am here, she oversees hunting and fishing parties for the tribe. "

Jayd took Elias's hand when he offered it. "The pleasure is all mine, I am sure. " There seemed to be a smile or a laugh just behind her eyes.

Marl set his hand on the shoulder of another elf, a lean, scarred figure with white streaks through his black hair. "This is Tao. He trains all of the warriors here and leads them to battle if and when they are needed."

Tao shook Elias's hand firmly, not saying a word. His eyes were an almost white blue, contrasting with his darker, tattooed blue skin. He held Elias's eyes the entire time, and Elias could see the fierceness in them. This was definitely not an elf to be trifled with. Black and red spirals and patterns covered his arms and shoulders, but his chest was decorated with what looked like the claws of some beast. There were dozens across his upper chest and more on his stomach. His cheeks were decorated with dots arranged in groups of three, forming small triangles.

Marl's daughter came jogging towards them, a woven shawl of white feathers covering her shoulders and chest. "Father! Shall I start the preparations for the celebration tonight?"

Marl nodded. "Yes, Coral. Draw wood from the salvage pile, get your friends to help you. Do we have any salted pork?"

"No, but there are several hogs fit to slaughter. "

"Good. Have the herdsmen prepare one for this evening. We'll start the fire an hour before sunset. Our guest prefers pork over fish. "

~   ~   ~

The sun was setting to the west, framed on one side by the islands, freed on the other by the sea. The flames crackled and roared at the slight breeze that was able to make its way into the protected cove, dancing through the pile of timbers that filled the firepit high enough that Elias had to stand to see over it.

The members of the tribe of sea elves danced around the fire, singing songs, beating drums, playing flutes, and making merry. Elias sat on a low bench, several large abalone shells in his lap, each piled with different delicacies; pork, dried and fresh fruit, and toasted grains each took their places in various shells. Bread studded with fruits and drizzled with different juices or wines sat on wide, sanded wooden platters, sliced and arranged in a way that pleased the eye.

It seemed that the only real utensils that were used by the tribe were the ceramic cups and goblets that were passed around. Shells were used in place of bowls, and flat, smooth pieces of wood were used as plates and platters.

The food and dancing lasted until well past sundown, when the villagers started taking their places on the benches around the fire, many sitting in the sand that was still warm from the day's sun. Elias had drunk his share of wine and was feeling relaxed, laughing and talking with many of the tribe members, learning about their islands and people. Coral, in particular, paid him a lot of attention, laughing at his jokes, bringing him food and keeping his cup full of wine. She answered every question he asked her enthusiastically, delighting in his curiosity.

He did not mind the attention at all; he found himself more and more comfortable with her as the festivities went on. As the night wound down, he found her at his side, sitting close to him, sharing the heat of the fire and their bodies. She had changed to a white leather halter and a skirt made of braided grass. The strands of beads and shells around her neck sparkled in the firelight, the polished surfaces reflecting the flames with iridescent flashes.

The whole tribe hushed suddenly as a figure approached the fire. It was covered in furs and had a large bear's head. In one hand, it held a long staff with a curving, hooked end, and in the other, it held a plain short sword, similar in design to weapons on the mainland.

When the figure drew close enough to the fire, it pulled back the bear's head, revealing Marl. He held his arms wide, signaling for quiet, though the people gathered around the fire were already silently watching him. The flames illuminated his face eerily as he looked around the gathered elves. When he spoke, his voice echoed powerfully off of the walls of the cove, the gentle, calm tone that he had always spoken with before replaced by a deep intonation.

"I have been across the sea, searching the breadth and length of foreign shores. I have returned, and been to the meeting place of the gods. I have asked for their guidance, and I have received an answer."

Coral's hand found Elias's, squeezing it tightly as Marl addressed his village as a whole for the first time since he had returned. Elias gently returned the squeeze, his attention locked on Marl. What had the gods told him?

Chapter Twelve

New Grain Moon, Year 4368

Elias watched, riveted, as Marl reached into the furs and cast a handful of powder into the flames. With a green flash and a sharp, metallic scent, the fire roared back to life, sending blue, red, orange and purple tendrils licking towards the stars overhead.

Marl stretched his hand out, as if he was gathering the attention of the crowd before him. "Long I searched for the one of prophecy, for the warrior from across the sea who would bring the fury of the gods to the vile intruders that lurk in our islands. I was set upon by the kin of those that have stolen the Hollow Island, and keep our loved ones prisoner on Kanga Motu!"

He cast another fistful of powder into the fire, making the flames reach up again. Elias's head swam with wine, mesmerized by the many colored flames.

Marl clenched his staff like the handle of an oar. "For six months, I was chained in the belly of the pirate ship, being forced to row them from place to place. I watched as my fellow slaves were beaten and starved and whipped, and I too was subjected to the cruelty of these monsters in human flesh."

He stalked around the fire, recounting his tale to the crowd. Elias was impressed with his storytelling abilities; he was both informative and interesting to watch. Every set of eyes was locked on Marl as he spoke. "As we grew nearer to Rapa Matomato, our guest, Elias, broke free and led us in overthrowing our oppressors, killing or capturing them all! We sailed into Port Greenreef victorious and free! As soon as I was ashore, I went to commune with the gods atop our great island."

Marl extended his hand to the mountain behind him. "As I lay under the holy water of the caldera, I received a vision from the sea. A vision of Greenreef, free of the oppressors that steal our lives from us! Free from fear, from loss! That our brothers and sisters in other villages can live in peace, not fearing that their children will never be able to count their years as we have!"

The murmur that ran through the crowd went all but unnoticed. Somewhere, the rhythm of a drum had started keeping time with Marl's words and gestures. "In this vision, a great ship, carved from the bones of slaves, sailed across the sea. As I watched, a red light passed over it, and it was changed from blackened bones into a ship carved from trees that touch the sky, flying a standard with a red field with a rainbow star in the center. The sails shone silver in the sunlight, blinding her enemies. "

The drumbeat quickened as Marl moved around the fire, recounting his vision to the assembled villagers. "This ship devoured or destroyed those of the pirates that plague us, growing larger and more powerful with every ship it consumed. It sailed to the Hollow Island, and flushed out the pirates there, cleansing the island and pushing it back beneath the waves. The sails unleashed a cyclone that stripped away the buildings, and the ship let out a cry that shattered stone."

Elias was fascinated. A ship carved from a single redwood tree would not be the largest ship ever made, by any means, but it would be enormous. Did the vision mean that the ship would be made of redwood, because then it could definitely be larger than any ship he had ever seen, since a ship could be as large as it was built. Or did the vision mean that someone would carve a ship out of a redwood in the same way the sea elves carved their canoes out of smaller logs? In that case, the ship would be much smaller, but it would be the largest canoe ever made.

Elias's scattered musings were interrupted as Marl continued.

"This vision is not without calamity. As I watched the great Red Ship cleanse the Hollow Island, I saw Greenreef burning. I heard the cries of our people as they held their young in their arms, as they buried their elders. The gods demand a price for our freedom, retribution for allowing the Mainlanders to defile their paradise. We have grown soft, complacent, and this angers the gods of the storms and the mountain's fire. It saddens the goddesses of the sea and the jungle."

Marl cast a hand towards the fire again, causing it to roar and rise up, forming a mushroom of flame rolling into the sky. The heat caused Elias to put up an arm, shielding his face. As the flames subsided, he was somewhat surprised to find his left arm wrapped around Coral's slender waist as she all but sat in his lap. She was just as riveted by her father's words as he was.

"There is one among us who will lead us into redemption. He is of the sea, but not of Greenreef. He was born amongst strangers and born again amongst blood. I was told I would meet him across the sea, and it has been so."

Uh oh.

All eyes were on Elias now, and the murmuring had come to a complete stop. Despite the haze of the wine, he suddenly understood that Marl was talking about him. It should have been obvious, but he'd been far too caught up in the story, the wine, and the warm beauty pressed against his side.

Marl gestured at Elias, confirming his thoughts. "Elias, the gods have brought you to us to cleanse their islands of the plague of men that has infested them. Will you help us?"

Before Elias could answer, Coral slipped a leg over his lap, facing him. She draped her arms around his neck, her emerald eyes glittering in the light of the torches, her back to the fire. He could feel her breasts pressing against his chest as she breathed, gazing into his eyes, into his soul. "You cannot refuse the will of the gods, Elias, " she breathed, running her hands down his shoulders, to his massive chest. "You were brought here for this time. "

The feel of her stomach against his skin was electric. Though he did not know what he was supposed to do, at this moment, he had no will to resist. Any objections he had felt melted under her gaze. "I will. I will do what I can. Nobody deserves to live under the whip. "

The villagers cheered as Coral threw her arms around his neck, her lips finding his in the flickering light. He had no idea what he had gotten himself into, but at this moment, all that mattered was that he was not only needed, he was wanted. His hands wrapped around Coral's waist, and he lost himself in the passion of her kiss.

After all, who was he to deny the will of the gods?

~   ~   ~

Elias lay on his back on a mat of woven reeds, sheepskins padding the ground under him. His head swam with wine and the events of the evening. He could see the stars twinkling at him through the gaps in the thatch, and a very slight breeze penetrated the woven bamboo walls. Was he really some kind of ordained, chosen liberator? He didn't feel like a hero, but at the same time, the thought of these people being attacked and harassed by pirates made his blood boil.

He laced his fingers behind his head, closing his eyes. If Delain agreed, they could resupply and retrofit the ship, and use it to hunt pirates. If they happened to capture any alive, they could turn them in at Port Greenreef for a bounty. Jonas would likely be on board enough for that, as would most of the rest of the mercenaries. That would finance their mission, along with the aid they would get from the sea elves.

A noise at the open end of the lean-to caused him to halfway sit up.

"Who's there?"

"I am." It was Coral.

He sat up all the way, concerned. "Is something wrong?"

She moved in the darkness, a barely visible shadow crossing the distance between them. "Nothing is wrong. I came to keep you warm this night. The sea breeze can be chilling to those not accustomed to our islands."

"Oh, that's alright, I'm not cold-"

Coral's lips cut him off, her tongue playing against the tip of his. Her soft hand caressed his chest, fingertips running from his sternum to circle his navel, causing him to jump slightly at the sensation.

She broke the kiss, and he could hear the smile in her voice. "Is something wrong?"

He shook his head. "No, nothing's wrong. I'm just a little ticklish. "

Coral giggled. "Is that so?" Her left hand found his cheek as her lips moved to his neck, kissing and running the tip of her tongue over the pulsing vein under his jaw, her fingertips tracing circles against his cheek. Her kisses moved down, tracing a path from his neck to his chest.

He felt frozen in place, unable to do much but lay back and witness what she was doing. His quickening pulse thundered in his veins as he set his right hand on her thigh, running it across to her lower back. She was back in her loincloth; he could feel the woven cord holding it in place over her hips.

As his fingertips ran over the dimples at the base of her spine, her lips found his left nipple at the same time her hand found his right. He gasped as she pinched and suckled at the same time, sitting back up. "Coral-"

She sat up with him. "Is something wrong?" she asked again, her low voice seductive in the darkness.

"Coral, I don't think... uh... you don't have to do this."

She sat back. "Do you not want me? Do you wish me to leave?"

Elias shook his head emphatically. "No, that is not it at all."

"Then why do you stop me?"

Elias was torn. In the one hand, his body was responding, and responding in full force. On the other hand, should he really be doing this with a girl he'd just met? "I don't know if this is right to do."

She moved to straddle him, sitting on his lap, her hands on his chest again. "My father is not the only one who receives visions from the gods. All of those from our line are gifted in that way. My father, his father, and his father's mother. I am no different."

She caressed his shoulders, running her fingers along his collarbones. "It was foretold that my promised would be the one to free the tribes, and I would bear his son." Gently, she kissed him again. "That would be you, Rapa Whero."

Elias quirked a brow, puzzled. "Rapa Whero?"

She giggled again, wrapping her arms around his neck. "It means Red Giant."

Elias could feel her bare chest pressing against his and his objections crumbled even faster. He set both hands on her hips, pushing her back slightly. "I don't want you to do anything you don't want to do."

She moved her hands to his cheeks, turning his head to face her eye to eye, despite the darkness.

"Then I won't," she said, pushing him back down against the sheepskin.

~   ~   ~

1ˢᵗ Waxing Grain Moon, Year 4368

Elias's eyes snapped open, which he immediately regretted. It seemed as if the drummers from the night before had spent the evening pounding on his skull instead of their instruments.

He had rolled to his back in the night, and the morning sun filtered through the thatch walls of the three sided structure. He sat up, looking about. Coral was nowhere to be found. Had he been dreaming? He shook his head, which he also immediately regretted. He had certainly drunk far more wine than he should have last night. He may have been raised in the Northlands, but he hadn't inherited their ability to drink without ill effect.

It was maybe halfway between dawn and noon, the sun low over the eastern arm of the mountain, but already it was warm on the beach. He could hear the villagers bustling about, a few of them visible from the open side of the shelter, which faced the south, towards the sea. He caught a familiar flash of blue skin and raven hair, and saw Coral swimming. He stood then, abruptly conscious of the fact that he was still naked. He cast about for his trousers, then drew them on. He felt like he needed a swim as well.

The sand was still cool against his bare feet as he approached the gentle waves of the waterline. The firmness of the wave slope felt good against his feet, and the lapping waves against his ankles were soothing.

Coral caught a glimpse of him, and waved, treading water for a moment. She slipped under the water, and surfaced much closer than Elias thought she would. She was apparently a superb swimmer. He waded into the water of the cove, catching his breath as the cold water surged around him with the waves. He waded in until the water was up around his chest by the time Coral reached him. She swam up to him, treading water in the flowing tide.

"Good morning, Elias! Did you sleep well?"

He nodded, shivering slightly. "I did. And you?"

Coral grinned, her teeth as white as pearls. "I slept like the dead!"

The waves rolled about him, lifting him up for a moment before his feet touched the ground again."You were gone when I woke, I wasn't sure what happened."

She floated up to him, wrapping her arms around his shoulders and her legs around his waist, holding herself against him in the gentle waves of the lagoon. "I woke up a little early and felt like swimming. Are you hungry? There is meat and fruit, bread and water in the lodge."

He nodded, using his arms to tread water for both of them."Breakfast sounds good."

They left the water together, walking across the warming sand towards the lodge. Coral was wearing her halter and loincloth again, but on the beach, she had a woven grass skirt laying on the sand.

Pausing for just a moment to tie the skirt in place, she took his hand, and though she couldn't twine her fingers with his, she wrapped her hand around his and held it all the way into the lodge. A few of the tribe members watched them enter the building, a few of them chuckling and pointing. Elias blushed a bit, his ears burning, but Coral was smiling.

"Ignore them. You're just new to them, a novelty. Your purpose will be proven in the weeks and months to come."

Marl approached them from the side. "This is true. Most of our people here don't fully understand what you represent to us."

Elias frowned. "And what exactly is that? I am only one mercenary."

Marl smiled. "Look not at what you were, or what you are. Think instead of what you can be, and what you will be."

Elias opened his mouth to say more, but Marl held up a hand. "We will speak more of this later. Now, you should eat and enjoy the morning. You must go and speak with your companions from the ship. They will be of great assistance in the coming times."

Elias was quiet as they filled shells with slices of roast pork and fruit bread from the night before, mulling over what had happened. Coral noticed his mood and stayed close, but quiet. After they had gotten their food, she led the way back to the lean-to that they had used the night before.

When they got there, Elias saw that someone had taken the sheepskins and mat, replacing them with a larger mat and more skins. Bouquets of wildflowers hung from woven cords, lightly scenting the mid-morning air, while baskets of fresh fruit were arranged by the opening of the structure.

Bananas, passion fruits, and pomegranates were all in the same basket, with various citrus and grapefruit taking up another. A wooden bowl held a mixture of berries, of which Elias recognized strawberries, blackberries, and raspberries. A few jugs of water with some ceramic cups finished the small banquet.

They sat in the sand in front of the shelter, chatting as they ate. Coral told him about life on the island, and Elias told her about life on the mainland. She was especially interested in the mountains and forests.

"So, your mountains do not breathe smoke and fire like ours?"

Elias shook his head. "Not in thousands of years. They are much taller, but I think their fire has gone out. All but a few are quiet. I have heard that there are mountains in the far north where the ice never retreats, that still shake and pour fire, but I have never seen them."

She nodded, chewing a bite of fruit bread. "The islands to the west of us have given up their fire, too. The farthest west is the Hollow Island. Legends say that it was once a great island, like this one, but there was a cataclysm that pulled everything but the volcano under the waves. Over the years, the mountain collapsed into itself, letting the sea into her. It was considered a cursed place. Now even more, since the pirates have claimed it as their own."

Elias pondered as he ate. "What do the pirates do? I mean, I know they need oarslaves, but they didn't seem to like elves as such. They talked about elves wasting away, not having the longevity that humans did."

Coral furrowed her brow. "They hunt us for capture. There is an island close to their stronghold where all of the trees have been cut down. They make our people farm food for them, raise their animals. They leave no boats on the island, so they cannot escape. At least half of our people are held there."

Elias lifted a jug of water by one of the handles and poured two cups. "How many other villages are there?"

Coral sipped the cool water. "There are three on this island, which we call Matomato Rapa. It means Green Giant. There is at least one village on each of the five others that are not held by the pirates. Our largest village is on Taonga Tama, the farthest west of the islands still under the control of my people. The name of the island means 'Rich Son.' It is this village where most of our warriors and craftsmen reside."

Elias nodded, pondering as he finished his meal. "I think it is time for me to go back to my companions in Port Greenreef."

She stood then, smiling. "Very good! I will prepare immediately!"

Elias caught her by the hand. "I think, Coral, I should go alone. I need to convince several people to help us, and I think it would be easier to do if they didn't know about... us."

Coral frowned then, a sharp look on her face. "Are you ashamed of me?"

Elias released her hand as she pulled it back. "No! Why would I be ashamed?"

She crossed her arms under her breasts. "Then why do you not want me to come with you? Why are you hiding me from them?"

Elias was bewildered at her sudden turn of mood. "I'm not hiding you from them!"

"Then I am coming with you."

Elias blinked. "It's not that I do not want them to know about you. Not at all. It's that if they think I am being influenced by a pretty girl, then they might not take me seriously."

Coral did not relax her stance. "And why not?"

Elias squirmed a little under her scrutiny. The scene must be comical, he thought, a giant being cowed by a tiny elf maiden. "It was... known that I had no experience with women. Now I will be coming back with a beautiful elven girl, asking my crew to risk their lives for her benefit? I doubt they will see my request as unbiased."

Coral's look softened for a moment. "Hm. This may be true. Perhaps if I accompany you as a liaison from the tribe?"

Elias shifted in the sand uneasily. "I know these men. They would say I was doing it to try to find a way into your skirt."

"Then I won't wear a skirt."

Elias dropped his face into his palm. "That's not what I meant."

"Then speak plainly!"

Elias looked up at Coral. Despite their intimacy the night before, he really did not know her well at all. He leaned back on his elbows and exhaled sharply.

Coral's emerald eyes met his, and her stance softened a bit more. She stepped over him, and sat on his lap, straddling him. She rested her arms on his shoulders, clasping her hands behind his head, looking down. "I am worried that you won't come back."

Elias sat up, setting his hands on her slender waist. "No. No, I wouldn't do that."

"But how can I know?"

He lifted her chin, bringing her eyes to his. "I promise you that I will return. I have nothing else to offer but my word. But I will return."

"He speaks the truth."

Both Elias and Coral turned to see Marl leaning against a walking staff, watching them from under his wide-brimmed hat. Elias was suddenly very conscious of the fact that the seer's daughter was straddling his lap.

Marl held up his hand. "Don't be shy. I wasn't born yesterday. However, the sun is high already. If we want to make it to Port Greenreef before the heat strikes, we need to get walking. You should stay here, my daughter."

Coral scowled at him, rising to her feet. "As you wish, father." The last word was spat with as much attitude as could be respectfully thrown at an elder. She turned on her heel and walked away, towards the lodge.

Elias rose to his feet as Marl chuckled. "I'll be in trouble when we return. I imagine you will be as well."

Elias had no response. He just watched her go, ruefully rubbing a hand through his hair. "I truly do not understand her."

Marl laughed, patting the giant's arm. "Elias, I have lived for four and a half centuries, and I do not understand her, or her mother. There are some mysteries that are not meant to be known." He gestured to the east. "Let us go."

Chapter Thirteen

1ˢᵗ Waxing Grain Moon, Year 4368

Elias trod along the path to Port Greenreef, the sun beating down on his bare shoulders. He was glad that his skin had retained its tan during the time he spent in the oar deck, else he'd be burning to a crisp now. Marl seemed comfortable enough under his hat and poncho, though Elias couldn't fathom why. Any cloth on his shoulders now would be stifling.

The usual sea breeze was completely absent as they walked. The sky was clear and cloudless, but the weight of humidity had settled over the island, obscuring the distance in a bluish-white haze. Sweat poured from Elias as he climbed the ridge between the Seagate and Port Greenreef.

Marl handed Elias a water skin. "Drink. You need it much more than I do."

Elias paused under the canopy of a mango tree. "Are you sure? I don't want to take from what you brought for yourself."

Marl waved the objection away. "I am fine. I've lived in these islands long enough to become accustomed to the heat. You will acclimate too, in time."

Elias unbound the stopper and took a long drink. Resting his back against the tree, he looked towards the port, then back towards the village. They were roughly halfway between the two, about three hours of walking ahead of them. He passed the skin back to Marl, who took a short drink then stoppered the container, binding it with the leather thong.

They rested for a moment in silence, the hilltop eerily silent. Elias leaned against the tree, while Marl sat on a rock, looking out over the sea. Even the songbirds were quiet in this heat.

It was Elias that broke the silence. "Do you really believe that I am the one who will deliver you from the pirates?"

"Yes," said Marl without hesitation.

After a moment, Elias asked, "Why? Why me?"

Marl turned to face the young giant. "Why did the gods pick you, or why do I believe that you will be the force that frees us?"

Elias pondered that for a moment. "Both, really."

Marl nodded, collecting his thoughts. He drummed his fingers on his walking stick – a long, simple white pole of polished wood – then said, "When I went to the summit of the mountain, I lay in the waters until the gods spoke to me. I did not know how long I floated there. As I meditated, the gods granted me visions that showed a giant figure standing on a pirate ship made of bones."

Marl frowned for a moment. "This figure held a great sword and rode on a ship piled high with the corpses of pirates. Blood trailed in his wake."

Elias interrupted him. "This is not the vision you told your tribe about around the fire last night."

Marl smiled slightly. "The members of my tribe are a simple people. They don't often have the ability to be discerning about that which they hear, as some of them have never left the island they were born on. There are those who live in my village who have never even been to the port of men. They only know humans from the pirates that attack us, and fear them all as devils with short lives.

"In this way, I can interpret the visions that the gods give me in a way that they can understand. It is not only my privilege to receive the visions, but it is my duty to bring them to my people in such a way that they can grasp them." He glanced at Elias, quirking a brow. "Which is now what I am trying to do for you."

Elias looked down, chagrined. Marl laughed, flicking a pebble at Elias. "You're so serious, all of the time! You need some joy in your life. I hope that is what Coral will be for you."

Elias shifted uncomfortably. "I... she is a very fine girl. Woman. I look forward to getting to know her better."

"As does she, I am sure. Would you like to know the rest of what I saw?"

"Yes, of course. Sorry for the interruption, please continue."

Marl raised his eyebrow at Elias again. "So serious. Anyhow. As the ship rode into the harbor with the giant figure at its bow, the black, skeletal form of the ship was transformed into a great red vessel, carved out of the wood that grows on your shores, the great redwood trees of the mainland. The figure disembarked, and moved through the city, waiting at the far side, on the mountain. I saw myself walking beside this figure, whose shadow billowed behind him like a torn sail.

"This figure walked with me, and his ship kept pace with him along the shore. As it traveled, pirates fled from its path. Each ship that did not flee was cleansed red and devoured by the shadow figure's vessel, causing it to swell in size until it was the largest ship I have ever seen."

Marl paused, furrowing his brow. "I could see all of the islands, and they all burned. Port Greenreef was burned and riddled with cannon fire. The pirates destroyed my village, even shattering the Seagate with their attacks." He twirled the pole against the ground. "When the figure and I reached the cove, there were so many dead that I could not go on. The figure took his ship and sailed west. When he reached the Hollow Island, he brought it down with fire and cannons.

"It was at this time that the figure's shadow left him, and flew east, back to the mainland. The figure's ship chased it to the west, and that is when the vision ended. I awoke with great sorrow, but as I headed down the mountain, I could see the ship we arrived on, and it all made sense to me. You are the warrior from across the sea that I prophesied, and the gods showed me thus in the vision they granted me."

Elias pondered as he leaned against the tree. Marl's vision seemed to be accurate, at least in a metaphorical sense. He wasn't sure how much he believed in gods and visions, but if Marl's visions were true, then it would seem that his coming was indeed foretold.

"Coral said that her promised would be the one to battle the pirates, and that since I was the one foretold, that person was me."

"Do you have an issue with this?"

Elias pushed off of the tree. "Not precisely. I like her, very much, but I don't know her, and she doesn't know me. What if she doesn't like me?"

"That is a decision that is hers to make."

Elias frowned. "Not if she feels that it's been made for her by a prophecy or a vision."

Marl laughed again. "Methinks you underestimate my daughter. She is much like her mother. Jayd was given a prophecy that her husband would be the seer, who was an older member of our tribe at the time. He fancied her quite a bit, but she did not love him, so pursued her heart instead." Marl shrugged. "I became the seer of our tribe on my two hundred and eightieth year, and married Jayd that spring."

Elias nodded. "As you say. I suppose we'll see what happens, won't we?"

"We definitely will," said Marl, pushing himself away from the tree. "Come, the heat of the day is nearly upon us. We'll want to get this walk done as soon as we can."

There was a slight breeze in the port, for which Elias whispered a thankful word to the sea. Even Marl seemed relieved that the walk ended with a reprieve from the heat. They filled their water skin from a small fountain near the western edge of the city and drank their fill. When their thirst was sated, they went to the beach to cool off in the waves and Elias could see the pier.

The ship was still at port, of course. The tall masts dwarfed the fishing boats that were docked all around it. Dock workers bustled to and fro, transporting supplies to the boats and cargo to the shore. There was significant activity on Delain's ship, as well as a scaffold hanging over the starboard side, and the word "Iron" painted in white lettering. It seems the repairs for the vessel were well underway – Delain was wasting no time in restoring his ship

After Elias and Marl rinsed the dust and sweat of the walk off of themselves, they made their way along the shore towards the docks. Falling in with the flow of men, elves, and sea elves carrying crates to and from the deck, they boarded the ship.

Delain stood at the door of the aftcastle while workers bustled about, a large roll of parchment in his hands. He waved to Elias when he caught sight of him, setting the roll on a crate and beckoned him over. It seemed as though he was regaining his vigor by being able to oversee his ship again.

"Elias! It is excellent to see you! Are you well?"

Elias shook the old man's hand. "Yes, I am. What is all this?" Elias gestured to the workers bustling about.

"My ship has been poorly kept by the bastards that took it from me... they may have been passable sailors, but they weren't shipwrights, by any means. She was barely seaworthy when we docked here, and I aim to remedy that." Delain frowned, unrolling the parchment. "The hull needed new pitch to seal the cracks, and the deck was in dire need of repair. Luckily the mast is still sound... there's nary a tree on this island that could replace it."

Elias shook his head. "How can we afford all of this? The bounty on the pirates that we captured wouldn't pay for it all, would it?"

Delain grinned wide. "The pirates had a significant stash of loot in the hold, more than enough coin to retrofit the ship and resupply! We've divided the excess amongst the survivors, and we're working on selling the remaining cargo that we don't need. Each man has gotten his share of the coin, and will from the profits as well. Yours is in a chest in my chambers."

Elias was taken aback. He hadn't expected to return to this, but was pleased nonetheless. He opened his mouth to speak, but Jonas's voice cut him off from the other side of the ship.

"Redwood! You giant bastard! Where have you been?"

Elias turned to see Jonas leaning on a cane in the doorway of the forecastle, his head wrapped in fresh bandages, a patch covering his left eye. Turning back to Delain, he said, "I actually need to speak with you and Jonas. Any of the other mercenaries that were captured with us as well, if they're present."

Delain squinted at Elias, looking askance at Marl, who had remained silent to this point. "What's on your mind, son?"

"I'll tell you when we're all together."

Delain sighed. "A flair for the dramatic, eh? Well, I suppose you've earned it. These blokes can work unsupervised for a moment."

Jenna stepped through the doorway behind Delain. "Am I invited to this conspiratory meeting?" she asked, hands on her hips.

Elias could almost feel the challenge in her words. "I wouldn't dare exclude you! Of course!"

Delain laughed. "Wise beyond your years! Except that you've got a bloody great deal more of them than any of us." He turned to Jenna. "How exactly would that work then?"

Jenna sniffed. "You're all men. It's a wonder no matter what age you are."

~   ~   ~

Most of the men that had been freed from the oar deck were still on shore, reveling in their freedom – however, Martin and Geoff were present, as well as Jonas, Jenna, Delain, and Marl. Elias closed the door and sat on one of the beds.

Jonas interrupted Elias before he could start. "Alright, boyo, before you spill the beans, I've got something for you." He gestured to Geoff and pointed to a long, tall, cloth wrapped bundle propped against the hull. Geoff brought it over, grunting under the weight of it, and handed it to Elias.

He knew exactly what it was before he even unwrapped it. It was the sword he had purchased in Jetty, just before their capture. The blade and hilt were still polished, reflecting the light of the sun from the open window. "Where did you find it?"

Delain smiled. "I had a feeling it was yours when I was cataloging the items left in my quarters, so I showed it to Jonas. He said you'd be rather perturbed if we sold it."

"No I didn't, I said you'd be a right pissy old elf."

Elias laughed, leaning the sword against the hull. "Indeed I would be. Thank you for returning it to me."

Jonas reclined on one of the beds, closing his good eye. "Right, no need for hugs and tears then, get on with it. What have you to tell us?"

Elias cleared his throat, suddenly anxious. He didn't know how exactly to go about pitching the idea to his companions. "Right. So. As we all know, pirates are a problem here. I don't think any of us here would argue that point. In the day that I have spent with Marl and his tribe, I have been told and shown how much of a problem they are for him and his people. From what I have heard, over half of their people are imprisoned on an island and forced to grow food for the pirates and their stronghold. They repair their ships, grow their crops, and raise livestock for them."

Delain nodded. "Seems likely enough. There's been an embargo against selling or buying anything from known pirates for as long as there has been a port here. Doesn't stop everyone, but it does mean they need to come up with their supplies elsewhere."

Elias nodded as well. "Right. They also harry and attack merchant vessels throughout the islands, which is why there's a bounty on the heads of any pirate captured or killed."

Jonas chuckled. "Aye. Twenty coins a head if brought back alive, fifteen if not. Not a bad take."

Geoff and Martin nodded. The money was definitely talking, for them.

Elias took a deep breath. "I propose that we retrofit the ship as a privateer, and hunt these pirates. In this way, we can collect bounties that make it worth our time, and we can help Marl and his people. We are well paid, and we do a good deed in the meantime." He spread his hands. "It makes our trip over not a complete loss, and we can return home rich men, just by doing what it is we do."

Jonas scoffed. "We're a security group, not a private army, lad. This is a job for soldiers, mariners with the navy. We're more there as a presence to scare off any highwaymen what might come for a wagon of loot."

Martin snorted. "That worked out so well last time, didn't it?"

Jonas frowned. "You weren't complaining when I was counting out your coin, ya shit."

Geoff shook his head, looking at his hands. "No, we weren't complaining, but we didn't expect the job you found to be for a slave trader in disguise."

Jonas threw his hands up in disgust. "Bloody hell, neither did I! It was supposed to be easy money, just a quick trip to the mountains and back! You've both done that run a dozen times!"

Martin held up his bandaged hand, displaying his missing finger. "Aye, and none of those times ended like this one began. I'm considering buying a farm for all the trouble this has been!"

Jonas narrowed his eye, glaring at Martin. "That's funny. I never pegged you for a coward. I suppose looks can be deceiving."

Martin growled. "Call me a coward again, and you'll be sporting another eye patch, old man. You're the one who thinks hunting pirates is too dangerous."

Jonas sat up. "Said those words, did I? I don't think I did, you impudent shit!"

Martin stood, clenching his fists. "This impudent shit killed pirates and lost a finger while you were out cold."

Elias stood now, hammering a fist against the hull, the blow like a drum beat. "For the love of the gods, that's enough!" he boomed, his deep voice resonating in the room. All eyes were on him. "Fighting amongst ourselves gives nobody any blessings! If you don't want to hunt the pirates, then don't! Go home, go back to what you were doing before this. I will stay and fight, even if I have to take a ship by myself and steer it to the edge of the world and back! It will be done, with or without you. What I offer is a piece of the bounty and the chance to kill the same kind of ilk that put us where we are now!"

Everyone else had sat back down and was staring at Elias. His outburst spent, he felt silly standing while everyone else looked up at him. He retook his seat, putting his hands on his knees. "Like I said. If you're in, you're in. You get a share of every bounty. Any ships we capture, we return the cargo to the owner if we can. If we can't, we sell it and divide the profit."

Delain held up his hand. "The Port Authority would be the ones issuing the letter of marque. They may demand a share."

Elias shrugged. "Then their cut comes off the top. No matter what, we still profit, pirates still hang, and Marl's people are freed."

Jenna paced in front of the door. "I don't know, I don't like it. What if we fail in taking a ship? I don't know about the lot of you, but I've spent enough of my life chained to an oar." She glanced at Marl. "What do the sea elves plan to do to help us?"

Marl stood. Leaning on his walking stick, he addressed those present. "My people will furnish food, water, and repairs to vessels, just as our enslaved brethren do. We've been a seafaring people for thousands of years; we know how to waterproof a ship, even those of men. We can repair any damage that occurs, and tend to any wounded. Your overhead costs would not exist."

Delain raised his eyebrows. "You have a dock deep enough to accommodate a proper vessel?"

Marl looked straight at Delain. "Who do you suppose owns most of Port Greenreef?"

Delain was silent, thinking about what Marl said. "Fair enough. I'm in."

Jonas sat up, blustering. "What? You've got almost no life left to you! You want to spend it getting killed by pirates?"

Delain shrugged. "I don't have much life left to me," he repeated back to Jonas. "Seems like a good enough way to go. Besides... my life was stolen from me. May as well try to steal some back."

Martin nodded. "I'm in. The bastard that took my finger might be dead, but all of his buddies still breath. That doesn't sit right with me."

Geoff sighed. "I'm in as well. I don't think I could not join up in good conscience. Besides, the money sounds pretty good, and if we have the element of surprise, then we have the advantage."

Jonas lay back. "I don't believe it. You've all gone mad. I wasn't aware that I was signed up with a bunch of damn paladins."

Suddenly, Jenna whipped the door open, grabbing a figure from the other side and throwing it into the room. The figure, dressed in a broad-brimmed, woven grass hat and poncho sprawled on the deck, rolling to its back. As they all jumped to their feet, the figure threw back its hat, revealing long, raven black hair and sky blue skin. Emerald eyes flashed up at Jenna, then over at Elias.

Elias swore, and Marl shook his head. Jenna looked up at them, raising an eyebrow. "I suppose you two know this one?"

Marl sighed and nodded. "Yes. That is my young, impetuous, disobedient, and headstrong daughter. She means well, but is sometimes more willful than she is intelligent. Her name is Coral."

The young elf rose to her feet, adjusting her poncho accordingly. "I had no desire to stay behind while the 'menfolk' went ahead and secured our futures for us," she said, angrily.

Jenna scowled. "You told her to stay behind? Why?"

At this point, Elias was completely at a loss for words. Marl shook his head and opened his mouth to speak, but Coral cut him off.

"It was thought that I would discredit Elias, that his request would not be taken seriously if it was known that he was involved with a woman of the tribe."

She crossed her arms, facing off against the seven others. "My presence discredits no man. I am not a distraction, nor am I just some silly girl to wait behind at camp."

Elias dropped his hands. "That is definitely not what I meant to say."

"But it is what you said! Speak plainly!"

Jonas glanced between Coral and Elias. "So. You're doing this for a girl?"

Elias pointed vehemently at Jonas. "See!? See!? Didn't I tell you he was going to say that?"

Jonas snorted back a laugh. "Of course I would! It's the truth!"

Jenna set a hand on Coral's shoulder. "His opinion doesn't matter. He's not even going to help anyways. Come with me. I want you to tell me about your people and the pirates." She turned to Delain. "We're going to use your quarters."

It wasn't a request, but Delain waved it off anyways. "By all means."

The two women left the forecastle, and the men sat and stood in silence for a moment. Then Martin looked up at Elias and grinned. "Damn, son. I'd murder a fleet of pirates for that one too. You work fast! Good catch."

Elias dropped his head in his hands amidst the laughter and shoulder-slapping of the other men while Marl stood to the side and chuckled.

~　　~　　~

Elias stood on the stern of the ship, his back to the port, looking out to sea. He wore new clothing, purchased with his share of the spoils. The brown leather tunic that he wore over a white cotton shirt was tooled with the intricate geometric designs favored by the Northerners back on the mainland. By comparison, his plain leather trousers were quite simple, but they had been made with double reinforced knees, which made them quite functional. The tooling returned on his boots, the thick, rough leather still not fitting him quite right. They would break in, but until then, they would rub uncomfortably.

He had his sword harness on over his tunic, the weight of the huge weapon oddly comforting. He was unable to draw it in this position, but the harness was for transportation, not combat.

He felt good in new clothes, clean and well fed. His hair had grown out a bit during his time at the oars, so he had gotten it clipped short again. Now, a slight evening breeze cooled him, a welcome respite from the stifling heat of the day.

"I wonder how many slaves died this day, rowing under the whips of their masters."

Elias turned to see Jenna reaching the top of the stairs. "I don't know. Too many, no doubt."

She stood next to him at the railing. "Do you aim to change that?"

Elias nodded, still looking out to sea. "I do."

"And the girl? What role does Coral play in that?"

"She is a fine woman. I am lucky that she finds me acceptable."

Jenna looked up at him. "Really? Is that what you have to say?"

Elias looked down. "Look, I don't know what I have to say. I just met her yesterday. I got drunk, she says I'm her promised, Marl says I'm the ordained liberator of his people, and here I am. What am I supposed to think? Do I like her? Yes, I like her very much. I have no idea who she is. I know that she likes swimming, she loves pearls, and her favorite feeling is laying on the sand in the morning sun. She like mangoes and oysters, and her tongue is sharper than this sword."

Jenna smirked. "She does have a way with words."

Elias nodded, staring intently at the railing. "She does at that." He turned, leaning against the rail, crossing his arms over his chest. "Everyone is so concerned over whether or not I like her. Yes, I like her. Do I love her? By all the gods, I don't know. I don't know what love is. My mother died when I was very young, and I never knew my father. I don't know that I have ever loved anyone, so I don't know if I can say that I do love her, or will love her. I don't know that I am worth her love, but her prophecy says I'm supposed to father her children." He shook his head. "That's a lot to put on someone."

Jenna was quiet for a moment. She sighed and turned to face Elias. "I understand."

Elias looked down at her, his crystal blue eyes bright in the last light of the setting sun. "Do you? Because I sure don't."

"That is to be expected."

Elias chuckled mirthlessly. "I suppose it is."

"Not for the reasons you think. You're still young, for your kind, as is she. These sorts of things happen. Just make sure that you're doing this for what's in your heart, not what's between her legs."

Elias frowned. "Quite the subtle one, aren't you?" he said sarcastically.

She shook her head. "Life has not afforded me subtlety."

They stood side by side, watching the sun vanish into the waves. Jenna reached out, setting her hand on Elias's elbow.

"Tomorrow, as per Delain's orders, we will start fitting the ship for war. He and Jonas are already negotiating the marque with the bounty commission here in Port Greenreef. We're all on board. Marl has pledged fifty warriors for every vessel we capture, to fully crew our armada. He says his kind are adept mariners, and can learn to sail our ships quickly. I believe him."

Elias raised an eyebrow. "Jonas is negotiating as well?"

Jenna smirked a bit. "We've built an understanding, he and I. When I told him I was going to help, his tune changed dramatically."

Elias pushed off the rail, pacing the deck. "Well now. I did not expect that, I'll admit."

Jenna smiled at him. "That too is to be expected."

Chapter Fourteen

10th Waning Grain Moon, Year 4368

The sea spray flew behind the ship as it raced across the waves. Elias hadn't dreamed that a ship could move as fast as this, but Delain was more than a competent captain – he was a master. Even the years he spent under the deck rowing hadn't dulled his skill. With a full complement of sea elves crewing the vessel, the water rushed under the bow like a roaring river, the slow bob of the waves completely muted by the speed at which they traveled.

In the distance, growing ever closer, was a ship identified by the Port Authority as guilty of piracy. Smaller than the Iron Oar, as Delain had rechristened her, the ship was barely two-thirds the length, and half the width. She had only two masts to the Iron Oar's three, but should have been faster, due to how shallow she was.

Delain roared orders to the sailors as he manned the helm, keeping the Iron Oar's bearing true. Every scrap of sail was unfurled, and the wind was at their back. Men and elves rushed about, hauling ropes, tying them off, untying them, and all sorts of tasks that Elias had no inkling what they were.

Knowing how to crew a sailing ship wasn't his job; he was heading up the boarding crew. Elias stood ready, rope and hook in hand, next to a dozen other elves, each armed to the teeth. Each rope was attached to an anchor on the starboard side. The ropes ran through a pulley on either side of the ship, bolted to the thick timbers of the deck.

The plan was to hook the other ship, kick the anchors overboard, and let the ropes pull the pirate vessel into the Oar. She had been reinforced beneath the decks for this purpose, and large rolls of sailcloth were ready to be slung over the side to pad the impact of the other ship colliding with them.

Before long, the other ship drew close. Elias could see the men rushing about on deck, brandishing cutlasses and boarding axes, shouting at them. He could not hear them over the rush of the water, but it didn't matter. These were the enemy, and they were about to be conquered.

The sails slacked as they drew alongside the enemy ship, and the Iron Oar slowed.

"Aim over the ship!" Elias shouted, standing with one foot on the rail and whirling his hook above his head. He let it fly, overshooting the enemy ship by a solid twenty feet. He hauled on the rope, dragging in the slack until he felt the three-pronged grappler catch firm. On either side of him, other sailors were doing the same.

"Now!"

The anchors were thrown overboard, their ropes hissing across the deck like insane snakes. Both vessels shuddered as the anchors hit the end of the ropes, hauling the two ships together. A few of the ropes had hooked the railing of the other ship, rather than anything sturdy, and ripped it off, sending it hurtling through the gathered pirates, bowling some of them over.

Elias drew his sword, tossing the sheath aside. He didn't have the harness on this time, as trying to draw his weapon would have been impossible, opting instead to carry it in his hands. Several crew members heaved the rolled sailcloth over the side as the distance between the ships closed.

Ten feet.

Six feet.

Four.

Elias got a running start and leapt over the railings, swinging his sword in a powerful downward arc. The cutlass in his path didn't stand a chance, nor did the man wielding it. The giant blade shattered the cutlass, driving itself into the man's shoulder and down into his guts. Bracing a boot against the man's shoulder, Elias kicked him off his blade. Around him, elves and men clashed, hooks and swords beating against spears and axes. The shouts of battle drowned out even the rush of the sea as Elias carved a path through the pirates towards the helm.

A man brandished an axe at him, howling and swinging like a madman. Elias caught the swing with his blade, turning it aside and following it with a powerful backhanded blow with his right hand. The man's head snapped to the side, impacting the mast before he fell to the ground, unconscious or dead.

Another pirate shoved past him, a panicked look on his face. Elias's boot caught him in the stomach, doubling him over. A warrior from Elias's ship clubbed the man on the back of the head, and he stopped moving. Elias stepped over him as he mounted the stairs to the small aftcastle.

Before he even reached to top, the man at the helm threw up his hands, and screamed, "I yield! I yield! Don't kill me!"

Elias grabbed the short, fat man by the front of the shirt and dragged him towards the main deck. "Command your men to surrender! Do it now!"

The captain started waving his arms above his head. "Throw down your weapons or they'll kill us all! Hurry! Throw down your weapons!"

In the chaos, not everyone heard the order, and a few kept fighting. Those were either killed outright or subdued in short order. After the last man dropped his weapon, Elias released the captain.

"On the deck, with your men. Now. Fight back, and I'll cut you in half. Reach for a weapon, and I'll cut you in half. Make a single move I do not like, and...?"

The captain nodded his understanding. "I get it, I get it. You'll cut me in half."

Elias pushed him towards the stairs. "You're not as stupid as you look."

The elves on both ships raised a cheer. The battle had been brief, but was won.

~   ~   ~

Jonas walked amongst the corpses that were laid out on the captured ship. He eyeballed the one that Elias had struck with his first blow, shattered cutlass still in hand. He looked up at Elias and raised an eyebrow. "What, were you trying to make two out of him? I don't think the bounty works that way."

Elias shrugged, wiping the blood off of his blade onto the shirt of a dead pirate. "Twenty-seven captured, twelve killed. What does that come to?"

Jonas did some quick figuring in his head. "Seven hundred and twenty. Not a bad take."

"Not to mention the cargo. What's the Port's cut?"

Jonas sighed. "A solid fourth of whatever is on board. Absolute robbery, if you ask me. They're worse than the pirates who stole it in the first place." He snorted. "We're paying for the privilege of saving their necks from this scum."

Elias chuckled. "No, we're paying a fee to be able to have the rest of the property be declared spoils of war. Otherwise, we'd be obligated to track down whoever they took this from."

Jonas grumbled as he inspected the ship. "Say it however you want to, the fact is they're taking money from us against our will. Hide it behind a parchment, it's still robbery."

Martin called to Elias from the other side of the deck. "Redwood! You should come see this."

Elias and Jonas stepped over the bodies between them and Martin. Laid out separately from the rest of the pirates were four men clad in black leather armor. On their chests were eight-pointed stars, embossed into the black leather, with a red patch in the middle.

Jonas frowned. "What do you make of this?"

Elias pondered for a moment. "Felle Army, obviously. Marl said they were working with the pirates. These must have been on board for travel or oversight or something. Are they carrying anything? Notes, orders, anything?"

Martin rifled through their pockets, tossing the contents onto the deck. "Just some gold, jerky, trash... that's it."

Elias shook his head. "They'll fetch a bounty just as well as the pirates. We'll turn them in with the rest." He left Martin and the elves to the cleanup and climbed up a rope back onto the Iron Oar. Their ship was significantly taller than the one they had just taken, so there was a bit of difference between the heights of the decks.

Delain was directing the crew on where to stow the prisoners for the voyage back to port. The oar deck had been left as an impromptu holding cell, while the blacksmiths back at port fashioned the iron grates needed for proper containment. For now, though, the shackles and benches that were already in place worked well enough.

Martin stayed behind on the enemy ship, preparing it for the return to Port Greenreef, with twenty warriors to help him sail it. There didn't seem to be any major structural damage, and the rail that was torn off in the battle could be easily replaced. The only troublesome thing about it was that the section of rail was generally used with belaying pins to anchor ropes to. After surveying the damage, Delain instructed the elves how to repair it well enough to limp the ship home, and returned to his position at the helm of the Oar.

When everything was said and done, Elias was surprised at how easy it had been. He had expected a lot more resistance, a whole lot more combat, and a whole lot more blood. They had taken the other ship so completely, so quickly, he almost felt like it was a setup, like there was something that was going to go wrong. Was the ship going to sink? Was it bait? Had they been lured away so that another pirate vessel could attack the port or one of the villages on the island?

It wasn't until he saw Coral waving to him from the end of the pier that he let himself relax. It really had gone that smooth. Maybe this wasn't going to be as hard as he thought. After all, they hadn't even lost one member of their crew. A few wounds, some of them serious, but nobody was dead. Even Jonas – as sour as he was about the Port Authority's fee – had to admit how well it had gone. Everyone seemed to be in good spirits.

Before they had even had a chance to tie off, there was a representative of the Port Authority waiting on the pier, parchment and quill in hand. He and two assistants went through the captured vessel, writing down every item aboard. Delain had two deckhands helping the auditor, both to speed up the process and to protect their interests.

The whole process took a day, keeping both ships moored to the pier, so Elias took this opportunity to spend some time with Coral. There was a small papaya grove on the western side of town that provided shade, and a spring that gave them clean water. They walked through the trees, enjoying the mild weather, chatting about this and that. Elias found the small talk comforting, though he often didn't know what to say. Coral was talkative enough for both of them, though, and that kept the conversation flowing easily.

Elias reclined against a mango tree, Coral laying on her back, pillowing her head on his lap, He ran his fingers through her hair as he gazed out to sea.

"What was your mother like?" she asked, looking up at him.

Elias frowned, pondering. "I don't really remember. She died when I was barely thirty. She had black hair and very pale skin, I think. I was told that she had violet eyes. She had a reputation for being very kind, very loving... the people of Silva Aestas missed her."

"How did she die?"

Elias shrugged. "I honestly don't know for certain. Nobody would tell me about it, and I left Lonwick before I knew which questions to ask. All they would tell me was that I was the firstborn twin, but my brother didn't live. It was suggested that she died of a broken heart."

"And your father? Was he a giant like you?"

Elias laughed. "No, not as far as I know. He died before I was born. He was a scout for the king, and was out on patrol when he was killed. A band of orcs, I think they said it was. He was blonde, with blue eyes like mine. I was told that I took more after him than my mother, at least as far as my looks."

Coral smiled up at him, her eyes twinkling. "Then I would have to say that your mother was a very lucky woman if your father looked like you."

Elias blushed at the compliment and smiled. "Thank you, Coral. You're not half bad yourself."

She rolled over, giggling and shoving him. "Not half bad? So only half of me is not bad? Which half would that be?"

He grinned, catching her wrists. "That would probably be the half starting below your neck and above your knees."

She feigned shock. "Augh! You monster! I knew it! You sailed to Greenreef just to despoil our maidens with your rapacious ways!" She threw a leg over his lap, straddling his waist. "I shall battle you for my honor!"

Elias released her wrists and wrapped his hands around her slender waist. "Never have I faced such a terrifying foe! I shall have to redouble my efforts!"

Coral wrapped her arms around his shoulders, kissing him passionately. "It shall be of no avail! I've already got you surrounded!"

He spread his hands meekly. "I admit it! You are better than I am! Mercy, I surrender!"

Coral's hands worked their way down his chest and to his trousers, undoing the tie there. "Twas a battle too easy to win. I expect a ruse! No, best to finish the deed!" Her hands found him, and he immediately responded.

She narrowed her eyes at him. "Hidden weaponry! What treachery is this?"

He reached down, gripping her backside. "Ah! You've discovered my flanking maneuver!"

She lifted up on her knees, settling onto his lap. "I think we'd better disarm this foe, just to be certain." She positioned him underneath her, and lowered herself. He caught his breath a little, his hands moving to gently rest on her waist.

She settled her hands back on his shoulders. She lifted herself back up again, then settled further, lower than the first time, causing him to release his breath. "I think we have them on the run."

He slid his hands up her sides, pushing her halter up and passing over her breasts. "Truly, I am no match for you."

She leaned forward, kissing him again as she rocked her hips up and down. "Yes you are," she purred, nipping at his lower lip as she increased her rhythm. "You're the perfect match for me." She rested her full weight on him, wincing only slightly at the end. She stopped, her eyes closed as she rested her forehead against his.

Elias lifted her chin to look into her eyes. "Are you alright?" he asked her, concern showing on his face.

She opened her eyes, the crystal green seeming to drink him in as she looked at him. "I am perfect," she said, leaning into him, resting her head on his right shoulder. Her right arm came up, and she ran her fingers through the short-cropped hair on the back of his head. Arching her back, she slowly resumed her motions.

Setting his hands on her hips again, he started lifting with her motions, thrusting with his hips to meet her. She let out her breath in a long, low moan of pleasure, and it was over for him. She gasped, clutching his chest as her tremors subsided, and he leaned back against the tree, wrapping his arms around her.

She rested her head against his shoulder, her eyes closed, as her breathing slowed. Elias stroked her hair, looking out to sea, the afterglow of their passion almost palpable in the afternoon air.

"You have bested me, sir." she murmured into his shirt. "The spoils must go to the victor."

He reached down to kiss the top of her head. "Then you shall take all."

~   ~   ~

Elias and Coral walked side by side along the path, hand in hand. There was a secluded beach near the papaya grove, Coral felt like going for a swim, and Elias felt like joining her. The path descended steeply, but was wide enough for them to walk side by side. High brush surrounded the path, making for a very private location. Not that Coral cared, but Elias was more self-conscious.

The sand was hot under their bare feet, so they sprinted to the wave slope. Coral got a head start, but Elias quickly caught up with his longer stride. He scooped her up in his arms as he caught her, and kept running, dodging around the rocky sections, staying on the sand. She wrapped her arms around his neck and laughed, holding on for dear life.

He slowed when his feet touched cooler sand, setting her down. They both stripped, leaving their clothes draped over a large stone outcropping near some tide pools, and waded into the warm, shallow water. It swirled around them as the waves surged, lifting them with the swells. Coral floated effortlessly next to Elias, who was actively treading water to stay afloat.

Coral giggled as he swam next to her. "You paddle! Why do you swim that way?"

"What do you mean?"

"You paddle like a hound! Do you know how to swim like elves do?"

Elias scowled at her. "I'm an elf! I swim like this! That means this is how elves swim!"

Coral laughed as she swam around him. "Come on, I'll teach you. It would be easier at the Seagate, but this will do for now."

They spent the rest of their time in the water swimming, Coral teaching him how to make longer, measures strokes, how to control his breathing to increase his buoyancy, and how to ride the surf. The sun was moving lower in the sky as they stepped out of the waves, tired from swimming for so long. They sat on the rock that they had left they clothes on, drying in the sun before they dressed to return to Port Greenreef.

As they were warmed by the sun, Elias looked over at Coral, who was laying on a section of smooth volcanic glass, her blue skin covered in tiny goosebumps. Her skin was quite a few shades darker blue than the rest the sea elf tribe, and Elias was curious why.

"Were you born with skin darker than the rest of your people? Neither your father nor mother have skin like yours."

She looked back over her stomach. "It's how our skin reacts to the sun. You and your human friends get tanned, your skin darkening that way, while ours turns darker blue."

Elias turned towards her, tracing circles on her stomach around her navel. "Why are the rest of your people so much more pale? You all live here on the same island, shouldn't you all be blue?" He tickled her abruptly before going back to running his fingers over her skin.

Coral squirmed under his tickling fingers. "Stop that!" she giggled. "Most of us wear hats and covers to shield our skin while on land. It's considered beautiful to maintain your fair skin, like a sign of not having to work in the sun. I don't find such a thing shameful." She turned her arms back and forth, looking them over. "I like this shade, and I like the sun."

A rustle in the bushes behind them drew Elias's attention. Three men dressed in green and tan – two armed with cutlasses, one with a boarding axe – came out of the brush. One of them pointed at Elias. "He's the one. Kill him, and take his head. We'll share her when we're done."

Elias stepped in front of Coral. "You go! I'll hold them off!"

"With what!? You're naked!"

"I don't know! Just go!"

"They'll kill you!"

The men advanced down the path as Elias stepped to the edge of their perch. "If you don't go they'll kill both of us!"

The pirate who had spoken before laughed. "No, we're not going to kill her. She's got other uses. Sea elf quim starts out tight and stays wet!"

Elias leapt down to the hot sand as Coral crept backwards towards the sea. The three men spread out, blocking off the trail. Coral might be able to swim to safety, but Elias wasn't strong enough of a swimmer yet. He cast about for a piece of driftwood, anything he could use as a weapon.

"Elias! Here!"

A rock the size of a large cannonball flipped through the air towards him. He caught it easily in one hand, and faced off against the three men. They looked amongst each other and laughed.

Elias hurled the stone as hard as he could at the man closest to Coral, the one with the axe. It collided with him above the sternum with a sickening crunch, deflecting upwards into his jaw, shattering it. He fell to the ground with a strangled cry.

The other two men rushed Elias, brandishing their cutlasses like machetes. Elias jumped and dodged them as best he could, staying out of striking range while frantically looking for something to defend himself with.

Another stone, about the size of his fist, struck one of the pirates in the shoulder, making him flinch and curse, turning towards Coral.

Elias seized the moment, rushing the other pirate, catching his hilt mid-swing. The momentum of the blade carried it into his shoulder, though most of the force was spent. The edge sliced into his skin, making a shallow wound while his other hand caught the pirate about the neck and squeezed, cutting off his air.

He kept the flailing man between him and the remaining attacker, who backed away, looking between Elias and Coral. Elias advanced on him, using the pirate he held as a human shield. The other man looked again at Coral, and rushed towards her.

Shoving the man he held to his knees, Elias stripped him of his sword, and charged after the third man, who was scaling the rock Coral perched on. As she turned to leap off of the rock, he caught her by the hair and dragged her back, causing her to scream.

Elias's vision turned red. He scaled the rock as the pirate whipped Coral around to stand between himself and Elias. He started to bring his sword around towards Coral's chest. "One more step and I swear to the gods I'll-"

He caught the blade of the cutlass in his left hand, and hooked a punch around Coral, striking the pirate in the head with the brass basket hilt of the cutlass he had taken from the second man. The pirate dropped, releasing Coral, who scrambled out of the way. Elias's blade flashed down, slashing through the man's neck, striking sparks against the stone as it severed his head.

Elias whirled, jumping off the stone as the second man scrambled towards the first man's axe. Elias threw his cutlass, striking the man in the ribs with the hilt. The blow was formidable enough to slow him, letting Elias reach the axe at the same time the pirate did.

He stepped on the axe handle just as the pirate grabbed it, pinning his hand to the ground, and proceeded to stomp on the man's face until he rolled to his back. Stooping down, Elias grabbed the axe from the stunned pirate's grip and let sunlight into the rib cages of both men with two heavy downward swings.

Elias stood, covered in blood, most of it not his own. His shoulder throbbed, but didn't really hurt at the moment. He started searching the bodies.

"Elias! Elias, you're hurt!"

He turned to see Coral climbing down from the rock. She had blood splashed across her chest, and her hair was disheveled. He rose from the corpse in front of him. "You're covered in blood! Did he hurt you?"

She shook her head. "No, just pulled my hair a little, maybe bruised me. But you're cut! We need to get that cleaned and dressed! And your hand!"

Elias shrugged it off. "We need to get back to port, immediately. Who knows if there are any others out there. Quickly, let's get this blood off of us."

They rinsed off in the surf, taking stock of Elias's wounds. The cut on his shoulder, while long, was not deep or especially serious. The cut on his hand, however, would need to be looked at by Geoff. He could flex it, but it hurt, and needed bandaging.

They dressed while still wet. Elias searched the bodies, looking for any note, orders on parchment, anything that might give a hint as to who sent these assassins, but found nothing. They grabbed the weapons and hurried along the path, Coral carrying both cutlasses, while Elias wielded the axe. They couldn't afford to stay there any longer if there were more pirates in the bushes, and Elias had to let his companions know that they were being targeted.

Chapter Fifteen

10th Waning Grain Moon, Year 4368

Elias sat at a table in a tavern, his left hand outstretched and resting on the tabletop. Jenna was applying a dressing to the cut on his palm, while Geoff applied a sticky paste over the wound on his shoulder. Coral was seated to his right, while Delain and Jonas were sitting across from him. Martin sat between Coral and Jonas, a mug of ale in his hand.

Martin scowled. "We need to strike back, hard and fast, before they know that the assassins failed."

Delain shook his head. "Who do we attack? The pirates or the Felle Army?" He tossed a pendant on the table. It was a black iron eight-pointed star on a steel chain. "They all wore one of these. I sent one to the temple with one of Marl's warriors, and one to the Port Authority. Hopefully, one of them can tell us more. Until then, I'd advise caution."

Elias scowled. "The four soldiers on the ship we took today, and now these three. What on earth are the Felle Army doing here in Greenreef?"

Delain shook his head. "I don't know. Like attracts like, perhaps the pirates have struck a deal with them. Perhaps they were defectors. We can't question dead men, unfortunately, so we'll likely never know."

Geoff spread more of the warm, sticky mixture over the cut on Elias's arm. It stung a little but the mixture seemed to have some sort of anesthetic in it, so the sensation was short lived. "So we're just going to let them try to kill one of ours, and not retaliate?"

Jenna put another turn of linen around Elias's palm, tucking the ends the wrap where it extended to his wrist. "Our retaliation will be to survive, and cleanse their ilk from these islands until they are nothing but a bad memory."

Coral had said very little since returning to town, mostly just answering the general questions of if she was okay, was she hurt, so on and so forth. Most of her answers were short, one or two word sentences. She stayed very near to Elias at all times, which worried him. He had never seen her this subdued before.

Delain had noticed too, making sure that the young elf maiden had water and fresh bread rolls nearby while Elias was being tended to. He reached out and patted her hand. "Don't you fret, young miss. Elias will be right as rain in a few days. He's a great stout lad... those scratches won't even slow him down."

Jenna nodded. "The callouses he had from rowing protected his tendons... none of them were even nicked. It was just a cut through the skin. It'll leave a deep scar, no doubt, but he'll heal up to be just as good as he was before."

Coral nodded, but withdrew her hand from Delain, wrapping her hands around the ceramic cup in front of her. Delain furrowed his brow. "What troubles you?"

"It's nothing."

Jonas and Delain exchanged looks. Delain stood, stretching. "Well, I think I'm going to go look over the repairs to the ship we captured. Martin, Geoff, I'll need some help moving some of those crates."

Martin grumbled. "I'm not done with my ale. Get one of the deckhands to help you."

Jonas kicked Martin's chair, nearly causing it to topple. "Get off your ass, boyo. Make yourself scarce."

Taking the hint, Martin hastily drained his cup and left. Geoff tied off the bandages around Elias's shoulder, and took his leave as well, following Delain out the door. Once they had left, Jonas patted Elias on his good shoulder. "Mend swiftly, you great prick. We need you well."

Jonas exited, leaving Jenna, Coral and Elias alone in the tavern, save for the barkeep, who was busily polishing glasses. Coral didn't look up from her cup of water. Jenna moved to sit next to her. "Is there anything I can do?"

Coral shook her head again. "No. Unless you can guarantee this won't ever happen again, no."

Jenna set her hand gently on Coral's wrist. "This is the way of battle. People get wounded, people die."

"I know that."

"It's unavoidable."

"I know that too."

Jenna was silent for a moment, at a loss for words. Elias wanted desperately to say something to set Coral at ease, but didn't know the words to say. Jenna perked up suddenly, a smile on her face. "Do you believe in your prophecies?"

She looked up at her quizzically. "Yes, of course. That's why we're doing all of this."

Jenna shrugged. "Then it's settled. Until Elias fathers a son, he can't be killed. Practically immortal."

Coral furrowed her brow. "What do you mean?"

Jenna spread her hands. "Your prophecy says that he is your promised, and you will bear his son, right?"

Coral nodded, catching on. "And according to my father's prophecy, he will shatter the Hollow Island."

Jenna nodded again. "So, if those prophecies are true, then he can't be killed until those things happen. If anyone in this war has a guarantee to survive, it's Elias, and you as well. I don't see you cradling a son in your arms yet."

Coral smiled. "That makes sense. I like that thought."

Elias chuckled slightly. "I'll admit, I'm fond of it myself."

Coral shoved him affectionately with her shoulder, frowning. "Still. The prophecy says nothing about you remaining intact. Men can still be horribly wounded, and father children."

Elias grinned at her. "But can they destroy islands and capture pirates?"

Coral rose from her seat, standing behind him. Draping her arms over his shoulders, she leaned over and kissed him on the cheek. "Tempt not the gods, my love. Prophecies are not things to be taken lightly, nor spoken of lightly."

He was taken aback. Never had she used the word love with him before. They had been together for a few weeks now, as the work on the Iron Oar had taken some time. He had spent much of his time with her, when he wasn't busy with other tasks, and had grown very fond of her. However, he had never told her he loved her, and neither had she said it to him. He didn't want to lead her along, nor push her too fast, and he honestly didn't know how he felt. He knew he liked her, very much, but he didn't know if what he felt could be called love.

He turned his head to look into her expectant green eyes. "I'm sorry, Coral. I will be careful."

She smiled, a disappointed look crossing her face for a moment. "I know you will." She kissed him again, a quick peck on the lips. "I'm going to bed. The sun rises early. Don't be too long?"

"I won't."

After Coral left, Elias and Jenna sat in silence for a moment before Jenna rose, and brought two cups of ale. She set one gently on the table next to Elias, then took a seat across from him. She leveled a look at him that told him he was in trouble.

"I agree with her. Be careful."

He took a drink from his cup. "I already said I would," he replied, defensively.

"I don't mean in battle. Apparently, you can handle that well enough, even if you get yourself cut to ribbons. I mean with her."

He spread his hands. "What am I supposed to do, lie to her to make her feel better?"

"It would be the manly thing to do. Maybe you should man up."

He set the cup down, frowning. "That would be immoral. I'm not going to lie to her. I like her too much to do that to her."

"Do you? You like her too much to lie to her, but not enough to spare her heart?"

Angrily, Elias drained the cup of ale, and slammed it down, shaking the table. Jenna had to grab her cup to keep it from tipping.

"Then you tell me what to do! What to say! How I can make her know how I feel without lying to her, without leading her to believe something I don't know that I believe myself?"

She narrowed her eyes. "Figure your shit out."

Elias clenched his fists. "That's easy, then. It's settled. I'll just say what I need to say and absolutely no care whatsoever about the truth. Is that what's expected of me? Is that what I should do? Just damn the unsurety, and go ahead and tell her what she wants to hear, no matter whether or not it crushes her if the truth turns out differently?"

Jenna leaned back, crossing one leg over the other, setting her ankle on her knee, a very unladylike posture, save for the fact that she was wearing trousers. She regarded him levelly, draining her own mug of ale.

"No. That's not what you should do. I'm not going to tell you what to think or say, but I am going to repeat this; figure yourself out. If not for her, then for yourself."

She rose from her chair, and left the tavern, leaving Elias alone at the table. He sat for a while, brooding into his cup. He was angry with Jenna, angry that she seemed to accuse him of daring to feel how he felt... or didn't feel. He had no idea what it felt like to be in love, so how could he say that this was or wasn't it?

He took his mug back to the bartender and left a few silver coins on the counter before climbing the stairs to the room that he and Coral shared when she was in Port Greenreef. It was on the third floor of the tall stone structure, on the seaward face, with a breathtaking view of the bay.

He opened the door gently, the hinges creaking in the wan candle light.

Coral sat on the edge of the bed, naked, brushing her hair with large, coarse teasel. She looked up as he entered, and smiled. "That wasn't long at all."

He smiled back. "I am tired. It has definitely been a day."

She went back to brushing her hair. "It has."

The sight of her made his heart ache. He wanted so badly not to hurt her, no matter what he decided he felt. The pale white light made her blue skin look even lighter and her black hair even darker, with the red light of the small fire from the hearth adding a certain warmth to the otherwise cool glow. Her full breasts cast perfect shadows across her chest and onto the bed, her skin smooth and alabaster. He wished he had been taught in the art of painting, so that he could save this image forever onto a canvas.

She paused what she was doing to look up at him again. "What is it?"

He crossed the room, kneeling on the ground in front of her, setting his hands on her knees and running them up her thighs to her back, not gripping her, just caressing her skin. Even as he sat on his knees, he dwarfed her. She looked up at him, slightly confused. "Is something wrong?"

He shook his head. "No. Not right now." He leaned forward, pushing her back onto the bed. She let him, spreading her legs to make room for him between them. He kissed her on the forehead, then gently on the lips. Pushing himself back on his hands, taking care not to disturb the wrapping on his hand, he looked down at her and sighed. "You make me feel so lucky."

She laughed, running her fingertips over his chest, her knees rubbing lightly against his sides. "You say strange things at strange times, Elias. I don't understand you, but you make me smile."

He smiled and kissed her again. "That makes two of us." He leaned back, taking her hand and lifting her upright again, then sat on the bed behind her. He took the teasel from her and brushed out her hair while she sat on the edge of the bed. They chatted more, about the port, their companions, the forests of the mainland, each other, so on and so forth, as he brushed and braided her hair. When he reached the end, he took a red ribbon from on the bed and tied it in place. She patted it down, then examined the end.

"Elias, this is excellent! Where did you learn to braid this tight?"

He reclined on the bed, resting his head on the pillows. "The men in the north braid the hair of their women, in the same way they braid their bowstrings. It was presumed that even if none of the women would wed me, it was something I should know."

She lay down next to him, playing with the end of her braid and pillowing her head on his arm. "Were the women of the north fair?"

He wrapped his arm around her shoulders, pulling her close. She rolled to her side to accommodate him, drawing one knee up to rest on his stomach. He chuckled. "There were some women who were beautiful in the manner of the men of the north, tall, strong, and fair skinned, golden of hair and blue of eye. But their lives are very short in the north. Their beauty fades in the blink of an eye, and the years line their faces with the hardship of winters, wolves, trolls and other beasts of the mountains."

She played her fingers through his hair as she snuggled against him. "Did you ever love any of them?"

He was quiet for a moment. "No. I never loved any of them. I don't know if I know what it is to love. I don't know what it feels like, so I can't say yes. I was fond of many of them, but in a very distant way."

She nuzzled against his chest, her breath warm against his skin. "Then I shall show you what it is to be loved, so that you can learn. My poor giant, nobody ever taught you how to be a person, they just made you be a man."

He reached over and pulled the linen quilt over the top of them, and soon her breathing became long and deep, her arm heavy against his chest as she slept. He closed his eyes, feeling every inch of her against his skin, her warmth comforting, her touch soothing. If this is what it was like to have someone, he could get used to this.

~   ~   ~

11th Waning Grain Moon, Year 4368

He woke to Coral crying out and leaping away. He sat up as she fell off the bed, scrambling. Immediately he rolled to her, catching her flailing arms.

"Coral! Coral, what's wrong?"

She gasped, looking directly at him, her eyes wide and terrified. As soon as her eyes met his, she burst into tears and collapsed into his arms. He held her close, rubbing her shoulder as she cried. He had absolutely no idea what to do, so he just held her, confused and dismayed.

Through her sobs, she tried to explain what happened, but she was stammering so much that he couldn't understand her well enough. He lifted her back onto the bed, and poured her a cup of water from the pitcher on the table in the corner.

After she got a drink and calmed down, she tried again to explain what happened. She had woken from a nightmare, in which she was back on the beach, and the three men were attacking them again. Every time they swung their weapons at Elias, they cut him more and more, until they had cut him entirely to pieces, then they turned on her. She had woken up screaming as the second man was taking his turn.

Elias rubbed her back. "That will never happen, I promise you."

She wrapped her arms around him. "I know. It was just a dream. But it was so real... I think I'm going to be up for a while."

He sat next to her on the edge of the bed. "Would you like me to stay up with you?"

"No, you get some rest. You need it."

He nodded, then kissed his fingers, and pressed them to her cheek. "Please come back to sleep when you can? I'll keep the blankets warm for you."

She smiled, and set her hand on top of his, pressing it against her cheek. "I will."

He lay back down, on his side, and covered up. It took him a while to get back to sleep, but he did end up drifting off.

~   ~   ~

When Elias woke in the morning, Coral was snuggled under his arm, her smooth skin warm against his front. Early sunlight filtered through the window shutters, which she had closed in the night, tracing paths through the dust motes hanging in the air. Gently, he moved out from under her and sat up. She murmured in her sleep, shifting to lay on her stomach, hugging her pillow to her chest. He smiled, watching her for a moment, then covered her up with the blanket. As much as he enjoyed the view, he didn't want her to be cold, and the stone walls of the tall building held off the heat of the day for a long time.

He got up to revive the fire, stirring the coals and adding kindling. Soon, he was able to coax flame out of the slumbering embers, warmth pushing out into the room. He slipped on his trousers, boots and tunic, and headed down to the commons room to fetch food for breakfast.

When he returned, he set the platter of sliced meats and cheeses on the table, with a fresh, still warm loaf of bread next to a small serrated knife, and a small plate with a dollop of butter. Coral stirred, sitting up as she rubbed the sleep out of her eyes.

"Good morning, Elias."

He smiled, slicing the bread. "Good morning. Did you sleep better?"

She stretched, the blanket falling to her waist. "In your arms, I slept like I was floating on the ocean."

He smiled, bringing her a sandwich and cup of water. "Good, I'm glad for that. You didn't eat much last night, you're probably hungry."

She set it aside. "Let me wake up first, silly!" she teased. She took a drink of water, then flopped back down on the bed., burying herself under the blankets. "These stone houses are always so cold!"

"Then come sit by the fire!" he said, tickling her through the blankets, making her squeal and flail about. She threw off the blanket and leapt at him, bowling him over onto the bed. She hauled the blanket over the top of them.

"I've got a better idea. Why don't you warm me up?" She planted a long kiss on his lips as she ran her hands down to his waistband, tugging at the tie holding it in place.

~   ~   ~

They sat naked on a sheepskin rug in front of the crackling fire, the platter of meats and cheeses in front of them, the quilt across their shoulders protecting them from any lingering cold in the room. They broke their fast in front of the hearth, roast ham and cheese between slices of still warm buttered bread.

They chatted about this and that, enjoying their time with each other. As they finished their meal, Coral grew quiet.

"Is something the matter?" Elias asked, spreading butter on a slice of bread.

She shook her head. "Not precisely. I have made a decision, though, and I don't know how you're going to like it."

He paused, glancing back at her. "Okay? I'm sure whatever it is, it won't be that bad. What is it?"

She turned her cup in her hands, fidgeting, not looking back at him. "I'm going to go back to my village at the cove."

He nodded, layering cheese and meat on the bread. "I totally understand. We can head out as soon as you're ready."

She shifted uncomfortably. "There's a bit more. I don't think we should lie with each other anymore."

He paused, a sudden twist in the pit of his stomach. "Did... did I do something I shouldn't have?"

"No, that's not it at all!"

He sat down, his back to the fire, nodding slowly. "That is, of course, your choice."

She moved forward, setting her hands on his shoulders, kissing his cheek. "Oh, Elias, don't be upset! I still want to be with you, but I fear that if you put a son in me, then you won't have the protection of the prophecy that Jenna mentioned last night! I don't want anything to happen to you, and I know you have many more battles to face!"

He nodded, his stomach unclenching. "I understand. It makes perfect sense, really."

She clung to him then, wrapping her arms around him. "Oh, please don't be upset! It's not that I don't want to, I just don't want you to get hurt!"

He wrapped his hands around her waist and set her on his lap. He was sitting cross-legged, and she wrapped her legs around his waist. "I am not upset at you, not at all. I totally and completely understand, I really do. If I said I wasn't a bit disappointed, then I'd be lying to you, and I'm not going to do that. But you are right. If we keep this up, it won't be long before you carry my child, and then all guarantees are gone." He honestly wasn't sure if he believed the prophecies, but at this point, he was dedicated, and she very obviously did.

She looked up at him. "You're not upset?"

He huffed a sigh and rolled his eyes to the side. "Well, I might be. Crushed, even. Heartbroken. I don't know if I can get through the day without the promise of your body to slake my thirst. After all, an elf lives not off of bread alone..."

She shoved him, giggling. "You just had your 'drink,' you great glutton!"

He wrapped his arms around her, burying his face in her neck, growling and nipping her neck while she squealed and struggled. They wrestled for a moment before they disengaged. Having lightened the mood, they got dressed and packed their few belongings, quickly straightening up the room before they left, locking the door behind them.

Elias returned the key to the innkeeper and stepped out into the city streets with Coral. The day was already warming up, and people bustled here and there, pushing carts, carrying baskets, and going about their business.

They made their way to the pier where the Iron Oar was docked.

As usual, Delain was already up, directing repairs and modifications, transfer of cargo, and the general goings-on. Elias waved as he saw them, and he waved back. "Good morning, m'boy!" the old man called out. "What are you up to this morning?"

Elias shouldered a small pack, closing the distance between the two of them. "Good morning! I'm here to get my sword. I don't want to make the walk to the cove without it, this time. Coral would like to go back to her village."

Delain nodded. "Seems wise! The repairs should be done by tomorrow night, so we'd need you back by then to go over our next plan of attack, but you're free until then."

Elias nodded. "I'll stay there tonight, then come back tomorrow morning."

Delain looked about. "Do you want to take some of Marl's warriors with you? It's better to travel in force, if you're worried about an ambush."

Elias started to decline, but Coral's hand on his arm made him reconsider. "While I think I could handle anything that came my way, I'd rather be safe than sorry. I'll take five warriors with me."

Delain gestured at a group of elves that were transferring goods from crates into barrels, beckoning them over. "Take ten. Marl sent a detachment of fifty more over last night, to crew the new ship. They arrived by canoe this morning, and I've had trouble figuring out what to do with them all." He spread his hands. "I only have enough work for half of what I've got already, and a pack of war-hungry sea elves wandering through Port Greenreef won't really set anyone's nerves at rest."

Coral grinned, and Elias chuckled. "I'd imagine not. Alright then, I'll take these fine warriors with me. I'm going to get my sword from the hold."

Delain set his hand on Elias's shoulder. "It might not be a bad idea to keep that weapon with you, son. If there was one ambush, there's almost sure to be another. Stay wary."

Elias nodded and descended the stairs. The weapon locker was unlocked, and full of spears, bows, and hundreds of arrows. The flights were mostly white, but every arrow had a distinctly colored feather. He had asked about this once, and Coral had explained that it was for distinguishing which arrow belonged to which warrior, so they could tally up their victories appropriately.

As he came back on deck, he saw Jenna and Coral embracing, smiling and bidding each other farewell. The women had grown close in the weeks since Coral had come to the port to stay with Elias, and the parting would be melancholy for them both. As Elias approached, Jenna broke away from Coral and turned to face him.

"Travel safely, Elias. Take care of this young woman until she is safely back with her own people."

Elias nodded, still somewhat irritated with her for their conversation last night. "Of course. I will return tomorrow afternoon."

She nodded and clapped him on the shoulder. "See that you do. I will see you then. I've got some ideas that Delain and Jonas are fond of, and I'd like to share them with you."

The two elves left the ship, heading toward the western side of town, ten warriors ranging about them, chatting and telling stories as the sun rose higher in the sky behind them.

Chapter Sixteen

11[h] Waxing Flower Moon, Year 4369

Elias stood at the bow of the single decked war galley as it sped over the waves. It was small, shallow, and easy to handle, which made it perfect for attacking larger, slower vessels. He had personally led the party to capture it, and had renamed it the Slingstone. As per Elias's instructions, the bow of the ship had been outfitted with a heavy bronze cap, fashioned into a short, blunt spike. While it wasn't perfect when facing some of the larger, more heavily crewed ships they attacked, it made for an excellent support vessel.

That is what they were doing right now. Three ships had been spotted off of the coast of Wahine Rapa, the closest of the islands controlled by the sea elves, and had been identified as pirate raiding parties. Elias and his companions had harried the pirates with exceptional vigor for the last six months, and had them on the defensive. Rarely did single ships venture forth from the westernmost islands, and when they did, they were armed to the teeth.

The armada that had formed from captured vessels was getting much larger. Around one out of three ships they attacked were sunk during the battle, but the sea elves were getting better at capturing ships rather than destroying them; there were almost a score of ships anchored offshore at Port Greenreef, more than the port was equipped to handle at the harbor.

This voyage, though, was almost entirely for the strike. The target was an over-sized galleon, larger even than the Iron Oar, with three rowing decks, four masts, and ports for dwarven cannons between every few oars. The ship, along with two or three galleys, had sailed around Wahine Rapa, attacking coastal villages and driving the tribes inland, away from their livelihoods and food sources. Hundreds of villagers, maybe even thousands, had been displaced into the mountains.

They had received word from the largest village on the island, situated on the north coast of the narrowest section of land, between two mountains, that the small pirate fleet had been spotted sailing west along the coast towards one of the other islands. Elias had immediately outfitted this ship and the two fastest in the fleet, and set sail. Accompanying him was the Iron Oar, captained by Delain, and the first ship they had captured, which Jonas had renamed 'Papaya's Vengeance' when he took command.

These two ships were close to Elias's stern, but the Slingstone was smaller, faster, and shallower, so skimmed across the waves, making little wake as they fairly flew along the southern coast of Rapa Matomato, the island that Port Greenreef was on, otherwise known as the Green Giant.

They had passed Marl's village earlier in the mid-morning, the Seagate easily visible during low tide. The villagers had hung ropes of tropical flowers from the rock barrier, perhaps during some festival or other, perhaps as an encouragement to the warriors who were aboard the ships. He was too far out to be sure, be he could have almost sworn that he saw a blue-skinned figure waving from the top of the archway.

It had been almost a year since he had first landed on the tropical island, and he was getting used to being here. As often as he could, he spent his days at the village with Coral, and she came to visit him at Port Greenreef as well. However, since the night after they had been ambushed, they had not lain together. While he was definitely feeling the effects of their physical separation, he didn't bring it up, which was exceedingly difficult with how flirtatious Coral was whenever they were together.

Instead, he focused his energy and aggression on the task at hand. They were getting ready to cross a stretch of open sea, much deeper than the waters around the island, with fast and rough currents that could sneak up on an unsuspecting ship and throw it off course. He stepped down off the bow, wet with sea spray, and took a seat next to one of the warriors. Grabbing the oar, he lent his considerable strength to rowing, which was being used in tandem with the sails for additional speed.

The chop of the water in the channel slowed them ever so slightly, and the oarsmen redoubled their efforts. Before long, the westernmost tip of the big island faded behind them, and Wahine Rapa grew larger, its eastern mountain rising green in the afternoon sun.

The Iron Oar overtook them, cruising past at a comfortable speed. He could see the warriors standing on the deck, laughing and pointing as they sailed past. Elias doggedly kept rowing, his bronzed skin glistening from sweat and sea spray.

He kept his eyes on the helmsman, who was at the rudder, steering the ship straight and true. The Papaya's Vengeance lagged behind, its green hull and orange sails standing out against the blue sky and gray water. Jonas had paid for the ship to be painted and the sails dyed – at great personal expense to himself – but as he put it, there was little else to do with the coin on the island, and there would be plenty more gold to replace what he'd spent.

Presently, they finished the crossing, and the oarsmen were able to rest, riding the wind over the shallower, calmer water. They drew up even with the Iron Oar, the Papaya on their other side, closest to the shore.

Almost on cue, from behind the shell of a volcanic remnant of an island, a massive ship sailed into sight. On either side were two galleys – small, open-decked ships with one sail and a bank of oars on either side, much like the Slingstone. They were perhaps a mile distant when they hove into view, their sails tightly furled and rowing towards Elias's ships. They were not moving swiftly, but were gaining speed.

Elias ordered the men on the oars to start rowing again as he untied his sword from the mast, where he had lashed it to get it out of the way. They pulled ahead of the other two ships, and hurtled towards the giant war vessel ahead of them.

As they drew closer, an arrow struck the deck next to him. He looked up to see a volley in the air. "Archers!" he yelled. "Shields up!"

Everyone on deck grabbed their shield, which was hung on the bench in front of them, and crouched behind it, momentarily stopping in their rowing. Arrows struck the deck and shields, penetrating through at times to strike the warriors behind them. The cries of the wounded caused him to grit his teeth. He knew that this was just a part of the battle, but he hated being unable to strike back.

Archers on the decks of the Iron Oar and the Papaya loosed their own volleys, targeting the smaller ships on either side of the great galleon.

The Slingstone rushed forward, closing with the giant ship. "Brace yourselves!" Elias shouted, grabbing onto a rope that he had tied to the mast.

When the Slingstone slammed into the hull on the starboard bow of the ship, the bronze ram tore a hole below the waterline. The impact would have thrown Elias to the deck if he hadn't been holding onto the rope. The oarsmen had braced themselves against the back of the bench in front of them, riding out the impact. Seawater rushed into the bilges of the massive pirate ship as arrows struck the deck around Elias and his warriors. He could hear the pirates on the deck of the galleon shouting and cursing above him.

The Iron Oar drew up alongside the galleon, between it and one of the smaller ships, casting hooks and lines between both of them. Like tattooed blue locusts, the sea elves swung from one ship to the other, scaling rigging and leaping over the rails to attack the pirates.

"Row back! Pull free of the hull, or she'll drag us down with her!" Elias cried, attaching the scabbard of his sword to the harness he wore. He grabbed a grappling line, whirling the three-pronged hook over his head, and cast it up to the railing of the forecastle of the great ship. It didn't catch on the first try, so he hauled it in and cast again. The arrows had stopped raining down as the deck above him became consumed with melee combat.

The hook caught on the second cast. He gave it three solid tugs to make sure it was set, and started his ascent. He made short work of the climb, and hauled himself over the railing to the deck, ducking down behind some crates. He pulled his sword off of the harness, just as the Slingstone wrenched free of the hull of the larger ship. He could hear water gushing into the hold, and knew that their time here was limited. He threw the scabbard back over the railing, landing it on the deck between the oarsmen of the retreating galley, then turned back to the battle.

There were easily a hundred pirates on the deck, fighting fiercely with the warriors, mostly sea elves, who were boarding the ship in waves. Most of Elias's warriors were concentrated in a fighting line on either side of the ship as they were trained to do, pushing the pirates into an unruly mass in the middle of the deck.

Elias, on the other hand, was not in a position to just clip away at the edges of the mob. The upper deck of the forecastle was almost deserted, with ten archers standing along the rail, firing at the warriors below. He charged up from behind, swinging his massive sword like a scythe. His first swing cut through two men and into a third. The adrenaline was surging through his veins, giving him the familiar red tunnel vision. It used to scare him when he lost control, but over the last year, he'd grow accustomed to it, even reveling in it from time to time.

The remaining archers turned to face him in surprise as he rushed into them, swinging his greatsword at their necks. The first archer still had the shocked look on his face as his head was unburdened of the rest of him, falling to the deck below. The second man ducked, dodging the swing, but caught a solid kick to the face. By this time, the other five were nocking their arrows and drawing their bows.

Elias grabbed the body of the headless man, ducking behind it. It did a poor job of covering his extremities, but it caught three arrows that would have struck his torso. An arrow skimmed his chest, cutting him, but not badly. He threw the body at the standing men, scattering them as they dodged the makeshift projectile and reaching for the swords sheathed at their waists. This is what he was waiting for.

Even as they drew their swords and formed up in front of him, he crouched, supporting his sword across his shoulders. The five remaining men kept their distance, glancing between each other, before rushing him all at once.

He stepped to the right, swinging his sword as hard as he could. His blow shattered the blade of one pirate and severed his arm, driving the blade into his ribcage. Elias wrenched it free as he reversed his swing, coming in to hack through the leg of a pirate coming in from the other side. He jumped back as the now one-legged pirate fell to the deck, screaming. His blade dripping red with blood, Elias faced off against the last three.

He stood at his full height, his powerful muscles flexing in the sunlight. The three men looked up at him, panic overtaking them. One turned to run, and the other two held their swords out in front of them.

Like a striking snake, Elias's sword flashed down at the man to the left, who dodged back out of the way as the man on the right leapt in with an overhanded swing. Elias jerked his blade free of the deck in time to catch the strike on the hilt, reaching for the pirate's hand. The pirate was too fast, though, and dodged clear.

Again, Elias swung in hard from the side, and the pirate was too close to dodge entirely out of the way. The tip of Elias's blade caught his stomach, disemboweling him. The final man turned and fled onto the deck below.

Elias leapt over the rail, vaulting onto the deck amidst the pitched battle, his long blade flashing into the mob as he landed, cleaving into two pirates and dropping them where they stood. Swinging his sword back and forth, he cleared a path of enemies who either fell where they stood or clambered out of the way of his deadly scything. He could hear the pirates moving in behind him, so he started striking all about himself, his enormous sword flashing about him like a deadly, whirling dancer, leaving blood and screams in his wake. Despite the danger, the horde of pirates pressed in against him.

A broken oar handle caught his blade, knocking it down, stopping the momentum. The crowd surged forth, blades and hooks seeking his flesh, yet Elias did not know fear. All he knew was the battle, his vision tinged entirely red, no haze this time. His muscles bulged as he gripped the handle of his weapon in two hands and surged back against his assailants, smashing weapons and the limbs that wielded them.

Something hard struck him in the back, and he spun, cleaving through an oar handle and into the head of the man who tried to block his strike. Suddenly, blue-skinned warriors surrounded him, battling the pirates, driving them back away from him. Something grabbed his arm, and he pulled back to strike his enemy with the pommel of his sword.

It was Jonas. He stayed his blow, glowering down at the man from the height of his frenzy. He turned back to the battle, but Jonas held fast.

"Elias! Dammit, Elias look at me!"

Elias whirled back, baring his teeth in a snarl. "What do you want!" It wasn't a question as much as it was an accusation, a challenge for the one who would dare interrupt his carnage.

"Elias, you're wounded!"

"So are they! They're on the run!" He wrenched his arm free, and stepped towards the line of elves that were clashing with the pirates. Bodies littered the deck, both men and elves, and he stepped over them, closing with a group of pirates just as the elves that were facing them fell. He dove into their midst, cleaving and hacking with his sword until there was no opposition left. Vaguely, he could hear Jonas shouting, and warriors answering him, but the words were well beyond his caring at that point.

An explosion threw him to the deck. He looked up, his vision clearing, to see the sails of the Papaya on fire, flaming bits of wood and debris raining down around him. He looked around, dazed. Almost everyone on the deck of the giant galleon had been knocked to the ground or overboard. The sails of the Papaya listed away from the galleon; she was sinking, and sinking fast. Elias struggled to his feet, the ship heaving on the waves from whatever had caused the blast.

Through the smoke and debris, he could see that the galley that had been on the other side of the Papaya had been obliterated. Fragments of the bow and stern were rapidly sinking under the waves, as the masts of the Papaya fell to the water where the enemy ship had once been.

The elves on the deck leapt to their feet as the pirates rallied. Pockets of fighting broke out again as combatants regained their senses. Elias took a step and slipped in blood and sea spray, almost falling to his knees again. The warriors on the deck outnumbered the pirates by an easy three to one. It would not be long until this battle was over.

Sea water washed over the side of the great warship as it listed forward. Elves were jumping back from the pirate vessel to the Iron Oar, and pirates were floundering on the deck. The second galley had been captured by Delain and his warriors – Elias could hear the victory cries from across the ship.

He stepped up on the sinking rail of the warship and grabbed a rope, hauling himself upwards. The ropes that held the great ship tied to the Iron Oar were being cut, so as not to let the smaller ship be dragged down with her. As the ship sank, his right hand slipped on the rope, leaving a long, bloody smear. He readjusted his grip, and climbed over the railing.

The great warship sank until only the top of her masts were visible above the waves, settling on the bed of the shallow water. Pirates floundered in the floating wreckage, the elves fishing them out and tying their hands behind their backs. Prisoners were worth more than bodies, after all.

Elias could feel the red fading from his vision, the thundering of his heartbeat in his ears calming as he witnessed their victory. They had lost a ship, but had gained another. The largest ship they had seen in the pirate fleet had been scuttled, and another had been destroyed entirely. The fighting was done, except for a few straggling pirates who refused to stop resisting. Short work was made of their struggles, and they soon joined the ranks of the captured.

Swaying, Elias gripped the rail of the Iron Oar. He could feel the wind cold against wetness on his trousers. He had assumed it was from sea spray but when he brushed at it, his hand came away red with blood. His vision darkened as his head swam.

He could feel his balance leaving as he pushed himself back from the railing, away from the sea. "Jonas!" he shouted, as the deck came up to meet him, and all went black.

~   ~   ~

14th Waxing Flower Moon, Year 4369

He could hear again before he could see. The cries of seagulls were distant, but not terribly so – the sound of the waves almost drowned them out. The padding under his chest was firm, but not hard. Elias was laying on his front, his head pillowed on his right arm, his left arm stretch out to the side. While not uncomfortable, the position did restrict circulation to his hands, and his fingertips tingled a bit.

He stretched, rolling to his side. Pain shot up his back and down his left arm, causing him to hiss his breath out and grit his teeth. He opened his eyes, his vision bleary, and wiped the grits away.

Small, gentle hands caught his shoulder. "Slowly! Slowly, my love. You do not want the stitches to tear." He focused on Coral, her emerald green eyes lined with worry.

"What happened? Where am I?"

Coral pushed him back down onto the furs. "You're in the village, at Seagate. Jonas brought you here. You had a fever, and were shaking." She wrung out a cloth, and set the cool pad on the back of his neck. "The weapon that struck you was poisoned. That battle had been a trap."

Elias grunted, his head pounding. "Poison? Did I survive?"

Coral snorted, chuckling slightly. "No, you died. This is heaven."

Elias shook his fists lightly in feigned exuberance. "Yes!"

She lightly slapped him on the backside. "No, you silly thing, my father was able to identify the poison and administer an antidote. You were out for a few days, but you should mend."

Elias carefully stretched again. The pain and stiffness in his back radiated all the way across and down to his tailbone, and his left arm felt like dead weight. He felt like his spine needed to pop, but tensing in such a way would cause far too much pain. He pushed himself up with his right arm, easing his way into a sitting position, Coral steadying him as he moved.

Once he was upright, Coral stood. "My father and Jonas wished to speak with you as soon as you woke. I will fetch them now." She leaned down and kissed him, lingering for a moment before she departed. It was not long before man and elf arrived, Coral returning with them.

Marl stepped in, and moved to check Elias's wounds. "How are you feeling, my boy?"

"My head hurts, my back hurts, I can't move my left arm very well, and I am hungry enough to eat a horse."

He flinched as Marl pushed lightly on the skin around the stitches. Apparently, he had three shallow puncture wounds, much like the wounds a bladed mace would deliver. Marl reached around Elias, putting his hands on either side of his chest, and squeezed. "Did that hurt?"

Elias shrugged, wincing slightly. "Only a little."

"Good. No broken ribs, then. Lift your arms over your head."

Elias tried to raise his arms. His right arm was fine, but lifting it caused waves of pain to surge down his back, and into his left arm. His left arm, however, was only able to lift partway before the pain made Elias drop it.

Marl shook his head. "That is what I was worried about."

Elias felt his stomach clench up. "What were you worried about?"

Marl looked over Elias's back some more. "The weapon that hit you was not only poisoned, but it destroyed a lot of the muscle that it struck. It very nearly broke your shoulder blade. It definitely pulverized a lot of the meat under your skin. You're lucky it didn't do more damage, or you would have lost your arm. As it is..." Marl trailed off.

Elias frowned. "Go on."

Marl was quiet for a moment before he spoke. "As it is, the damage to your muscles is deep. I did everything I could, stitching you back together, but the oil they put on the blade burned through you fast, and destroyed some of your tendons. You'll be very, very lucky if you regain even half the use of that arm. I don't think it will ever swing a sword again."

Elias was stunned. "That... that's not acceptable. I have to get back out there. We have to finish this. We have them on the run!"

Jonas scoffed. "Did you miss the part where you were baited and ambushed, boy? They're targeting you, and they almost killed you. Who's to say that they're not going to lay down another trap?"

"Absolutely nobody." Elias pushed himself to his feet, gritting his teeth and forcing himself to stand despite the pain, gripping his left arm with his right hand. "That is almost assured. Once they know that they failed, I expect them to redouble their efforts."

Coral tried to push him back down. "All the more reason for you to regain your strength before you face it!"

Elias braced himself, taking her hands gently in his, wincing as his left arm dropped. "If they know that I am weakened, and they know where I am, then they could attack here and there is nothing I could do. No, better that it be seen as though I am unhurt by their attempt."

She narrowed her eyes, frowning. "Elias, you are hurt. I know you're strong. We all know you're strong. You're the most powerful person I've ever met. You should be dead, but you're standing here in front of me. You don't have to prove anything to us!"

He straightened up to his full height. Normally he slouched or hunched very slightly, to not tower over everyone else around him, but now he stood up straight. "Coral, I'm not proving anything to you. Nor your father, Jonas, Delain, or Martin, or Geoff, or Jenna. I am proving something to the people who are watching me. The pirates, the villagers here, on the other islands, the sailors and merchants at Port Greenreef, I am proving something to them."

He released her arms, and caressed her cheek with the back of his hand. "I am proving that the pirates can't win. That they can't kill us, they can't even slow us down. I am proving that this battle is already won, we just have to take it. Isn't that what your prophecy says?"

Coral turned away angrily, facing the sea, her back to Elias. A crack of thunder sounded ominously, almost too perfectly in time with her motions. Jonas and Marl were silent.

He looked down at them where they were standing, outside on the sand in front of the platform. "Well? You wanted to speak to me?"

Jonas looked at him for a moment, before shaking his head.

"What?"

"You're a damn foolish fuck, Elias. But you're a brave foolish fuck, and brave foolish fucks get themselves killed. She's wise enough to know that."

Elias looked at Marl. "Isn't there a prophecy that she will bear my son? We haven't lain together for nearly a year now. According to her, and your prophecy, she has nothing to worry about."

Marl looked at his daughter. "You're right, Elias. According to that prophecy, we've nothing to worry about." His tone and expression made Elias feel as if there was something more.

Elias opened his mouth to speak, but Marl held up a hand without looking at him. "Do you want to fight again, Elias? Do you want to immediately depart and go off to wage more war against the scourge of our islands?"

Elias set his jaw. "Yes."

"Then we have a hike ahead of us. We're going to the caldera, the summit of our mountain. I hope you're powerful enough to make this climb."

Coral whirled to face Marl, her eyes wide. "Father, no!"

Marl held up his hand. "Be quiet, Coral."

"But father-"

Marl snapped at her. "I said be quiet. I am still the speaker for the gods, and I am still the chieftain of this village. You will do as I say."

Elias had never heard Marl speak as harshly as this before. It felt as if the older elf knew something he wasn't telling. Elias turned to Jonas, who stepped back, holding his hands up.

"This is your show now, Redwood. You make the decisions here. I'll be at Port Greenreef, awaiting further orders."

Elias was confused at the sudden turn of tone. Coral was upset with him, Marl seemed angry, and now Jonas was leaving. He suddenly had no idea what was going on, or what the right choice was. He felt very alone.

Marl was looking at him now. "Well, Elias?"

He squared his shoulders, winced, and nodded. "We'd better get walking then. That storm sounds close."

Marl nodded gravely. "Indeed it does. Coral, Jayd, and a few others will be joining us. I need to gather a few things before we go." He paused, looking Elias in the eye. "If you do this, there is no turning back, no turning away. You will be a part of the prophecy of the gods, whether you want it or not."

Before Elias had a chance to respond, Marl disappeared around the side of the shelter. Elias looked over at Coral, her green eyes wide, her blue skin a shade more pale than usual. A cool wind blew from the mountain, and ran a chill up Elias's spine.

Chapter Seventeen

14th Waxing Flower Moon, Year 4369

The small procession wound its way up the mountain trail. Marl led the way, followed by Jayd, Coral, then Elias. Six more sea elves – whom Elias had never seen or met before – followed behind him, dressed in simple, one piece, white leather sarongs. Stitched with bright red patterns, there was a ceremonial look to the garments. Marl explained that they were acolytes of the priesthood, and lived in a village separate from the rest of the tribe. Occasional deliveries of supplies kept them fed, and workers from the tribe performed the upkeep on their buildings, so that they could devote their time entirely to learning.

Everyone in the party, Elias included, carried bundles of sticks, firewood, tinder and kindling, slung on their backs with strips of white cloth. While not overly heavy, Elias had to walk gingerly to keep the straps from rubbing his wounds. His left arm was in a sling, keeping it supported, so that while he was still sore, the trek didn't cause him too much undue pain.

This mountain was taller than he had guessed it to be now that Elias was halfway to the summit. Even here, well below the peak, the entirety of the southern slope of the island was spread out below. From this height, he could see the stone buildings of Port Greenreef, resembling tiny model houses from this distance. His view out to sea was greatly extended as well, and he could see the black storm clouds closing in, flashing brightly with lightning, the sound of thunder muffled at this height

The village at Seagate was mostly invisible in the slight haze from the humidity, but he could see the lodge, the lagoon, and the Seagate itself. There was a small sparkling light, barely visible from behind the lodge, where the remaining villagers were holding a small feast. There definitely wasn't any shortage of resources on the biggest of the islands.

Steps were carved into the side of the mountain, broad and shallow, about two of his paces deep. They had started just north of Seagate, and wrapped around the southern face of the volcano. The trees were beginning to thin somewhat as they proceeded eastward and upward, being replaced by stunted versions of the jungle flora, filled in with shrubs and berry bushes.

His back hurt. Walking took a lot more of his back muscles than he had figured it would, especially since it was mostly stairs and inclined paths. He was sure his stitches had pulled a little, but he refused to reach back and check, partially because that would hurt a whole lot more, partially because he didn't want to show weakness to those around him.

The sun was dipping into the sea to the west, the southern clouds rolling across its face as they reached the edge of the crater. The caldera was between them and the setting sun, so seemed to be entirely shrouded in darkness. The rim of the crater had been carved out into an archway long ago, to allow for passage into the volcanic crater, but the stonework had fallen long ago and been moved to the side of the path. The intricate designs that had once decorated it were all but worn smooth by the passage of time and weather.

Elias, Marl, Jayd and Coral all paused at the edge of the crater, as the other six members of their party proceeded ahead of them, lighting torches and setting them into holes carved into the rock on the stairs down. Ancient wooden rails ran on either side of the broad, steep path that led down to the steam-shrouded base of the caldera.

He had never seen anything like this before. Even in Silva Aestas, where ancient stone and wood carvings abounded, it didn't feel this old. The storm clouds rolled around the base of the mountain, obscuring the view of Port Greenreef below.

After the acolytes had descended into the mist, Marl led the way down, Jayd at his side. Coral had not spoken a single word during the trip. She walked next to him, staring forward, her usual bubbly, happy demeanor replaced by silence. She paused for a moment at the abrupt edge of the mist. Elias stopped too, looking down at her. Her green eyes were barely visible in the flickering torchlight.

"You don't have to do this, Elias. Even now, we can turn around and walk away. You can wait and heal and return to the fight when you're better. The gods never grant any favors. Nothing is free."

Elias frowned. "What are you saying?"

She stepped forward to embrace him, her cold exterior melting away. "I'm just scared, my love. I don't know what they will ask of you. I am afraid the price will be too high."

He bent down to kiss her. "I don't know either. But if they can renew my strength and let me fight again, I have to pay their price. I can't lose the use of my arm. I can't stop now."

She pressed her lips against his again, then threw herself into it passionately, wrapping her arms around his neck. Breaking away, she whispered, "Please, please don't do this."

He pulled back, and wiped a tear from her cheek. "Why are you so scared?"

Coral looked down, her black hair falling forward to hide her face. "I am afraid they will take you from me."

Elias lifted her chin up, looking into her emerald eyes. "Nothing in this world could keep me from you. Besides... your own gods say we'll be together. So there's that."

Coral didn't say anything else, she just bowed her head and nodded.

They completed the trip down the path, her hand dwarfed in his. Their companions waited for them at the edge of a body of water, the fading light of the setting sun completely blotted out by the thick steam rising from the glassy, smooth surface. Elias could not tell how large the lake was, but the eerie silence made it seem enormous, the mist muffling any echoes.

Marl stood to the left, Jayd to the right, and the acolytes were on either side of them, forming a semi-circle, their backs to the water. A small bonfire was starting in front of a carved stone cauldron that was filled with steaming water.

As they approached, the acolytes stepped towards them, white cloths in their hands. Marl stepped towards the cauldron, tossing a handful of powder into the water.

"These elves will wash you before you enter the sacred waters of the caldera. Nothing but your body must enter the water, so you will leave your clothes here. Someone will be with you, to keep you from drowning; the trance can be debilitating to someone who has not experienced it before."

Jayd stepped forward. "I will be with you while you float. It is important that you be able to focus on what the gods will be telling you. There should be no distractions, and I know that my daughter would distract you."

He set down his bundle of firewood, and three of the acolytes removed his shirt and sling, dipping their cloths into the cauldron and washing him. The water smelled of herbs and minerals, almost like cedar and lavender. As he knelt so they could reach his shoulders and head, the other three elves undressed Jayd and started washing her as well. Her body was very similar to Coral's, slender and lithe, but with wider hips and fuller breasts. If she was any indication as to what Coral would be when she was older, then she would maintain her beauty indeed.

He averted his eyes, looking at the ground in front of him. Jayd was beautiful, no doubt, but he didn't want to stare. Especially not in front of her husband and daughter. He rose to his feet as the elves washing him loosened his trousers, and stepped out of them. As self-conscious as he felt, the solemnity of the situation helped him stand still as the acolytes washed him from the waist down.

Jayd didn't bother averting her eyes. They were locked with his, reflecting the firelight much like her daughter's did. That, in and of itself, was more disconcerting than the fact he was having his nether regions washed by three strangers, in front of his lover and her parents, while standing in a steam filled volcano crater on an island in the middle of the ocean. The thought made him chuckle to himself.

Marl quirked a brow, barely visible in the fog. "Does something amuse you, Elias?"

Elias smiled slightly. "I can honestly say that this is not something I ever pictured myself doing."

Marl chuckled as well. "I can see that."

The acolytes stepped away, finished with their task, and took their places back in the semicircle. Elias noticed that where they stood was marked out with white stones that had been set into the smooth black volcanic glass that they stood on, as were where Marl and Jayd had stood. The stone had been carved away into stairs at the edge, running the entire circumference of the round area where they stood. His eyes had been adjusting to the low light, and he could now make out stone pillars around the water's edge, some of them cracked and broken off at various heights, others reaching perhaps ten feet upwards into the mist.

Marl stepped forward, holding a large stone carafe in his hands. "Drink this. The herbs in this mixture will induce a trance. During that trance, the gods will speak to you. What they will say, what they will demand, I do not know. But once you enter that water, you accept their terms."

Elias took the stone vessel in his hands and nodded. "I understand."

"Then drink as much as you can, and enter the lake."

The fluid in the carafe smelled spicy, herbal, and not entirely pleasant, but not revolting. He held it up to his lips, steadied his breathing, and tipped it back. He was able to drink perhaps two-thirds of the mixture before he had to stop to breathe again. Marl took it from him and handed it off to Coral, who stood nearby. Elias stepped towards the pool where Jayd stood, the water, up to her waist.

Just before he took the first step, a small hand caught his, and he turned just in time to catch Coral. She leapt up against him, wrapping her arms around his neck, pressing her lips against his passionately. After a moment, she broke away, and whispered in his ear.

"Come back to me. Remember that I wait for you, and come back to me!"

Marl grabbed Coral by the shoulder and pulled her away, almost knocking her down.

"Step back, child. This one goes to meet the gods now."

Elias let go of her, half turning to the water. "There is nothing here that could stop me. I promise I'll return." He truly did not know what she was so afraid of, but he wanted her to be at ease. He stepped down into the water.

As soon as his foot touched the lake, his pulse rose to a crescendo in his ears. The mist around him seemed to shift in color, going from white to blue to green then red. Jayd stood waist deep in the water, reaching out to him, beckoning for him to come deeper.

His perceptions abandoned reason. The mists exploded outward, clearing away from him, a rainbow of swirling colors forming vortexes and thunderclouds, flashing light and sound all throughout the crater. He could see it all – the crater, the platform, the entirety of the massive lake, the nine other elves, and even himself, stepping deeper into the water, though he was not willing himself to do so. He could feel the heat giving him frostbite as he went through the frozen surface of the steaming water... wait. That made no sense. The water tasted like the purple of clouds against his skin... no, that wasn't right either.

Elias looked around, rising above the rim of the crater, viewing the entire island around him. The volcano they were in was the most massive of the island chain, but not the tallest. To the north was a snow-capped mountain which rose somewhat higher, and then to the west, the other islands each had their own mountain. Though they were far beyond the horizon, here he could see them all – the trees, the bushes, the leaves, even the animals – but not the elves.

He could see no sea elves on any of the islands. Humans, elves from the mainland, they were present in Port Greenreef and a few isolated fishing villages here and there, but none of the sea elves. Panicked, he looked down, and only saw himself floating, alone in the steaming waters of the caldera.

He tried to will himself downwards, but he could not move, except for up. The storm clouds circled the great island now, wrapping about the mountain and flowing between it and its sibling to the north, obscuring the jungle below. To the south, the clouds swirled, rotating about a burning red ember the size of a small island or an enormous ship. Waves of blackness surged out from it, breaking upon the islands like the sea, wearing them down before his eyes.

Then, one by one, the mountains on each island lit up, starting with the one he was above, then spreading west, to the next five islands that were controlled by the sea elves. At their peaks grew great balls of fire, each burning like a sun. The light broke the waves of darkness, and pushed the storm clouds back.

The ember at the center of the storm grew brighter, and lashed out at the large island again, but was repelled. Suddenly, the ember plunged into darkness, the shadows bursting forth like arrows, pelting the islands. Wherever the arrows struck, there was an explosion of shadow and a great cry of pain.

From each island, the balls of light lashed back, casting beams between them, uniting the islands in a chain of fire that drove back the darkness once more. The darkness was cast away, spinning to the east over the ocean, and the islands were finally left in peace.

Now, Elias could move again. He had watched the preceding battle with a sense of awe and panic, but now that it was over, a strange calm settled over him, a melancholy stillness. He moved downwards towards his body.

He looked himself over, seeing himself from the outside for the first time. He was absolutely enormous compared to the elves gathered around the bonfire and cauldron. Coral sat as close as she could to the water without touching it, while Marl and the acolytes sat in various states of repose, some laying down, others leaning against a pillar. Marl himself leaned against his long staff, staring into the flames.

He suddenly realized that he could see the sea elves, whereas he couldn't during the storm. The mists seemed to be clear in the area immediately surrounding the platform, revealing the surface of the water where he floated with Jayd's help, and the open ritual platform. He was partially spreadeagled, laying on his back, while Jayd held his head above the surface. Her eyes were closed, as if she were meditating herself.

As he was looking over the volcanic temple, the water rippled, like from a small earthquake. The elves on the platform didn't react to it at all, nor when it happened again, stronger this time. Under the surface of the lake, two lights, blue and green, appeared and grew brighter, rising to the surface. Above the mists, two more lights, these ones gold and white, descended, until the entire region was bathed in an otherworldly glow. Elias shielded his face from the near blinding illumination as they all gathered. There was a flash, and the lights were gone.

In their place were four great elves made of light, as tall as he, but of different statures, seated on thrones that rested on the surface of the lake. On the farthest left was a woman of blue light, buxom and broad hipped, maybe a bit on the heavy side, but still beautiful. Wrapped around her waist was a skirt that flowed like the waves, fringed with sea foam. Her eyes flashed white like pearls, and she sat on a throne of coral.

Next to her was a figure of green light, muscular and powerful, with tendrils of red seeming to crack through his skin. Slightly shorter than the woman, he was much more massive, his broad shoulders angular and topped with what appeared to be a miniature jungle. He wore stone armor, gray and black, that covered his upper body, as well as his thighs and shins, but left his great, thick arms bare. He was seated on a massive stool of obsidian, and his eyes were like dark, deep rubies that burned with their own light.

To the right of that figure was a tall, slender being of gold, with long, flowing blonde hair, and clothing that seemed to be made of sparkling dust motes. His skin was flawlessly smooth, and a very slight smirk sat easily on his lips. Seated on a fine golden throne, he leaned against a long, shining golden spear, his diamond eyes fixed on Elias.

The last figure was seated farthest to the right, her skin as clear as ice, glowing with a white light from within. Her clothes resembled an over-sized parka, hanging well below her knees. She was slender, skinny even, and very old, a contrast to the youthful figures to the left of her. Her long white hair flowed down her back, forming the throne upon which she reclined, and coiled about her feet, the color and texture of winter frost on glass. Of all the figures present, she had eyes most like those of an elf, not resembling any gems, but as white as the clouds, maybe tinged very slightly blue.

Elias felt himself touch down on the water, the surface of it firm underneath him. He lowered himself to one knee, and bowed his head. "I am honored to be in your presence," he said, knowing that these beings must be the gods of these islands. "My name is-"

"We know who you are," the blue figure said, cutting him off, "as well as what you want. But what we haven't decided is why we should give it to you."

"Oh, for the love of life, curb your tongue." the green figure scoffed at the blue one. "With you, it's always so dramatic. He came to us for assistance to help our people, and we're going to interrogate him on whether he is worthy?"

The blue woman glared at the green figure. "I have not the luxury of sitting on the seabed for untold eons, while I make up my mind on every possibility that could be." She turned back to Elias, still frowning. "We are, as you have guessed, the spirits that control these islands. Call us gods, deities, incarnations, it makes no difference. These lands are under our control. I embody the sea and all of her wrath and bounty. To my left is the god of the Mountains, who has graciously allowed us to use his volcano as our auditorium this day."

The green figure grumbled again. "Gracious is putting it in terms other than I would use. There were no other suitable places."

Sea ignored him. "Next is Sun, the embodiment of the warmth and life that comes with each day. He is the light that drives away the darkness." Sun nodded, almost imperceptibly, and waved the fingers of the hand that held the spear, seeming quite bored with the whole thing.

"And I am the goddess of wind," said the old woman at the end of the row. "I bring the rains and the storms, and I bear sailors to and fro with my breath."

Mountain spoke next. "You are here to request that we heal you swiftly, returning your strength, so that you can continue your fight against the foreign invaders that kill our people and despoil our lands. Even though you are foreign yourself."

Sun leaned forward, regarding Elias critically. "Yes... it does seem a bit out of character for a foreigner to want to help a native population, instead of conquering it. Why would you attack and kill your countrymen, for the benefit of people who are not yours?"

Elias stayed kneeling, his head bowed. "Nobody deserves to live and die under the whip. The people of these islands are noble, good people, and the atrocities that are put upon them need to end."

Sea chuckled mirthlessly. "Good and noble? Do you really think that the elves are without fault? Do you think that they were the first beings to inhabit this island? They've been here for a long time, yes, but their ancestors took this land from the ones who were here before. These islands have been inhabited for longer than you can fathom, and the sea elves are not the first to come, nor will they be the last."

"And besides, have you not put many a pirate to the sword?" Sun twirled his spear on the surface of the water, causing ripples to radiate out from him. "Have not they been flogged through the streets of Port Greenreef before being hung? What makes your treatment of them better than their treatment of those they capture?"

Elias looked up then, meeting the eyes of the Sun god. "There is a difference, my lord, between retribution and atrocity."

Mountain leaned over and slapped Sun's throne, causing it and the entire caldera to shudder as Sun caught his balance. "We've had this discussion before, Sun. You may not care what it is you shine upon, but when it's crawling all over you, it makes a difference!"

Sun sniffed, regaining his composure. "Perhaps that is the difference between descending from on high, and living in the... bowels of this land. One takes a different point of view."

Sea held up a hand to shush the other two. "I will agree with Mountain. The invaders, these pirates, they do not venerate us or our domains. They do not keep to the festivals, they do not give us the offerings we demand. They blight our land and insult us with their presence. They must be dealt with."

Wind spoke up, having been watching the discussion through sharp, white eyes. "There is still the matter of the shadow. It did not come here until this freak tree elf did."

Elias bristled slightly at being called a freak. Since reaching the islands, he had grown used to being mostly accepted. However, decades of practice helped him keep his cool. "I know nothing of this shadow of which you speak, my lady."

Wind snorted derisively. "I'm not your lady any more than you are my vassal, mainlander, and you know more than you know that you know. You've encountered this shadow before, and it followed you across the sea. You both defied the winds and rowed your way here, your shadow chasing you."

Elias frowned, furrowing his brow. "You mean the demon that attacked me on the road to Fairhaven? I promise you, I did not bring him with me."

Sea shook her head. "You may not have brought him, but for you, he would not be here. He is here for you and because of you, and he will not leave until you do."

Elias stood, squaring his shoulders. "Then I shall slay him, and burn his body to ashes!"

The four gods in front of him erupted into laughter, causing Elias to take a half step back as the mountain trembled again. He could hear the acolytes behind him murmuring, and Marl calling out to calm them. It was as if they were behind a wall, their voices muffled and faint.

Wind leaned forward, slapping her knee as she laughed at him. "Oh you will, will you? Tell me how well that went last time? You'll just conquer this enemy that bested you once, and that will be that?" She shook her head. "I think not. Not alone. He has grown immeasurably since you last met."

Elias set his jaw. "I am not alone. I have an armada of ships and an army of sea elves and men that fight with me. Together we will defeat this shadow-demon, and return the islands to the tribes that live here now."

Sun tapped the butt of his spear against the surface of the water. "No, you aren't alone. You have indeed inspired loyalty and valor from our worshipers, and that is to be commended. However, this is not a foe you can defeat here. The pirates, yes, but not this shadow."

Elias was growing frustrated. All these gods were doing was telling him how impossible his task was, how unworthy he was, how he was at fault for coming to Greenreef, when it was he that had been captured and brought here against his will. He clenched his fists. "I was told that you would heal me, that you would allow me to return to the fight to liberate your lands from a scourge that was here long before I was."

Each god sat up a little straighter, frowning down at Elias.

"Indeed we will," Sea said, narrowing her pearly eyes. "That much is already decided, and you will indeed rid our islands of pirates. But our price is that you must also rid it of the shadow you brought with you, and you cannot defeat it here. Even trying to will bring unimaginable ruin upon the sea elves, our followers, and that is unacceptable."

"That means," said Sun as he leaned forward, a slight curl to his lip, "That once you destroy the pirate stronghold, as foretold by our speaker, you must leave, and leave forever. You must never return to these islands again, as it is your presence here that has brought the conflict to a peak. That is the cost of your arm, and of your pride."

Mountain drummed his fingers on the black stone of his seat. "Many have died that would have otherwise lived, and many more will die in the coming battles. You may have the strength to bring liberation, but you also have the strength to rob us of our followers. For this, we cannot allow you to stay."

Wind reclined on her white throne. "Defeat the pirates, sever your ties, and lead your shadow away. Take it back to your own lands, and defeat or be defeated by it there. That part is of no concern to us. We do not want it in our domain."

Elias looked behind him at the elves gathered near the water behind him. "But what of Coral? Is there not a prophecy that she and I are to be together?"

Sea leaned back on her throne. "The seers say that she is to be promised to the one who destroys the pirates. They say that she is to bear his son. That is, indeed, the prophecy that the seers have spoken."

Elias turned back, shaking his head. "I do not understand."

Wind smiled, her expression softening. "You are mortal. That is the way of things."

Elias was not at all at ease, but he had his answers. Kneeling, he bowed his head again. "As you say. I will destroy the pirates and return to my homeland."

Mountain nodded. "Yes, yes you will. Now, go back to yourself, and depart my mountain. I grow weary of the company."

Sea started to turn to Mountain, her irritated expression cut off by Mountain waving a hand at Elias as if swatting a fly. An invisible force struck him in the chest, hurling him backward as the mist thundered towards him, obscuring the gods from his vision.

Chapter Eighteen

2ⁿᵈ Waning Flower Moon, Year 4369

Water flooded into his mouth and ears as he slammed downwards. He could hear the water rushing about him as he plunged below the surface of the lake, struggling to regain his bearings and get his feet under him. Small but strong hands hauled upwards on his shoulders, pulling him to the surface. He broke into the air, gasping for breath, his feet finding purchase on the smooth stone steps. Reaching out instinctively, his right hand found purchase, which he used to steady himself. Wiping the water from his bleary eyes, he looked around.

The fog was much closer than he had remembered it during his vision with the gods of the islands, obscuring his vision. The only light that came was from the torches and bonfire on the platform, which made the fog seem thicker and brighter. There were eight figures gathered at the edge of the platform, and Jayd to his right, his hand having found her shoulder.

"Come now, Elias, we need to get you out of the water." Jayd's voice came from in front of him, causing him to double take.

He blinked, clearing his eyes, and saw that she was crouching at the edge of the steps, holding a hand out to him. He looked to his right, and saw Marl there, holding his arm. "But... when I..."

Marl chuckled, guiding him up the steps. "You were in the water for three days, Elias. You may have been in a trance, but we weren't. We took turns keeping you above the water."

Elias stepped onto the smooth black stone of the platform, and immediately caught Coral as she threw herself into his arms.

"I was afraid for you. When the volcano shook two days ago, we were worried that it would erupt again, but we couldn't wake you."

Elias embraced her tightly. So the earthquakes he had seen in his vision as the gods ascended from the lake... that had really happened. "Don't worry, Coral. I promised you I would come back, and I did." He had no idea how he was going to tell her that he had to leave the island after he rid them of the pirates. That was a conversation he was not looking forward to. His stomach knotted up at the thought of leaving her.

He released her, and the acolytes began drying him off with broad, thick white linen cloths. He looked at his hands, expecting to see them wrinkled from the prolonged submersion, but was surprised to find them smooth, as if he had been in the water for no more than fifteen minutes.

"I don't understand. My hands look as if I have only just gotten them wet."

"You won't, yet. Give it a day. Once you've had a meal to offset the drink, then it will become clearer."

Elias shook his head, his stomach growling. "I have many questions."

The acolytes all nodded, chuckling to each other. Marl outright laughed. "That too is to be expected. In this, I must insist upon patience. Rushing would do nobody any good. Your first time in the waters of the caldera will always raise many questions. Your wounds seem to have healed, though, so I think whatever happened, it was a success."

Elias reached back, feeling the skin on his shoulder. It was true – where there had been stitches before was now hardened scar tissue. His left arm felt no pain, and he could move it as if it had never been wounded. No stiffness, no pain, no muscle damage from the cutting wounds, it was as if it had never happened, save for the scar. The rest of his minor wounds were healed as well; the cuts and scrapes and bruises that had covered his arms and chest were gone, thin pink scars left in their places, standing out against his tan.

He collected his clothes and dressed. They were damp from having set in the steam for three days, but it wasn't long after they left the caldera that the warmth of the sun dried them. Coral stayed attached to his arm, clinging to him tightly, while the rest of the group ranged out at their own paces along the path. The walk down was a much less solemn thing, as the bright sun warmed their spirits as well as their bodies.

The storm that had been building as the climbed the mountain had passed, and the island gleamed as though it were covered in tiny gems, the droplets of water on the trees and bushes reflecting the sunlight. There were a few scattered leaves and twigs across the path, and Elias had to move a few small fallen trees, but for the most part, everything seemed greener and more lush than ever before. The sun rose from the east, bright and cheery, and a slight breeze from the south drove the humidity away.

It was midday by the time they reached the beach at Seagate. The villagers gathered, cheering their return, while Marl led the way through them, directly to the lodge. They climbed ladders to the highest floor, where a long table and chairs awaited them. Marl had several young elves bring up loaves of bread, sliced fruit, and pitchers of water.

Coral, Marl, and Jayd all listened as Elias recounted his vision, from the apocalyptic storm battle between the darkness and the islands, to his conversation with the gods. Coral listened in silence, her expression dark, while Marl asked questions about specific details. It was well after dark by the time he finished, the room lit by several lanterns with candles on the table.

After Marl finished asking his questions, they sat in the loft, the rush and pull of the waves audible even inside the upper floor of the building. It was Coral who finally spoke, breaking her silence for the first time since they had arrived back at the village.

"So you're leaving."

Elias shifted in his seat. "Not immediately. We still have much work to do."

"But you're still leaving."

Elias spread his hands. "Your gods demanded it."

"And you couldn't have waited a few weeks. You couldn't have just let nature take its course, and see if you could heal naturally, working your arm better." She stood up, her tiny hands clenched into fists. "This is exactly what I was worried about." Without another word, she turned on her heel and stormed out, hardly seeming to touch the ladder on the way down.

Jayd stood, her expression as dark as her daughter's. "This is what comes from the impatience of men!"

Marl started to speak, but was cut off when Jayd threw the water from her cup in his face. "I told you this was not the right path to follow!" She turned on Elias. "And she begged you not to go! She *begged* you! I hope that when you're holding that sword in your hands, it's a suitable substitute for holding my daughter. Perhaps you'll find love in the blood of your enemies!" Throwing her cup to the ground, she stormed out of the room after Coral.

Elias put his head in his hands. "I didn't know that is what they would demand."

Marl wiped the water from his face and sighed. He stood and walked to a small cabinet, and removed a stoppered jug. Pulling the cork, he poured two cups of a strong smelling, sweet wine. Setting one down in front of Elias, he left the jug on the table and took his seat again. "There's something more. Something I haven't figured out, and something the women aren't telling us. I have found that when they walk away, it is a bad, bad idea to follow them." He brought his cup to his lips, taking a long drink. "So. You sleep alone tonight. I doubt you'll find her in your hut."

Elias lifted the cup to his lips, draining it in one draught. Setting it back down, he sighed. "I don't want to leave her. Maybe she could come with me."

Marl shook his head, and took another sip from his cup. "Her place is here. She is to become the seer when I am too old to perform the task. If she were to leave the islands, the most suitable person to fill that role would be gone, leaving us without a speaker for the gods."

Elias stared at the cup in his hands. "There must be a way."

Marl stood and drained his cup. "If there is, I do not know it. The gods chose not to reveal that information to me." He set the cup down, his hand on the jug. "In fact, they never chose to reveal themselves to me, either. Only ever visions." He paused for a moment longer and refilled both cups.

Elias looked up at him. "Never?"

Marl looked into his cup. "Never."

Elias watched the seer for a moment, before looking back to his cup. They seemed to make excellent focal points when looking anywhere else seemed awkward. "I'm sorry."

Marl sighed. "It's not your fault, Elias. You've got some very difficult things to do ahead of you, and the gods know this. I do not envy you the path you are upon. You should finish your wine and get some sleep. Tomorrow comes early this time of year."

Elias nodded and drained his cup again. The sweet wine of the sea elf was a drink he had become accustomed to over the last year. "What about you?"

"I'll sleep when I am ready."

Standing, Elias pushed his chair in under the table. "I will leave for Port Greenreef tomorrow. I trust we still have a force of warriors here?"

Marl nodded. "Well over a hundred."

"Excellent. I'll take fifteen with me. Is the Slingstone at port there?"

"She is." Marl poured himself another cup of wine. "I almost forgot to mention... Delain and I have come up with an idea. In fact, the preparations are under way."

Elias quirked a brow. "Oh? And what is that?"

Marl smiled slightly. "We're going to float that behemoth you sank. Maybe something of worth will come of this."

~ ~ ~

4th Waning Flower Moon, Year 4369

The Slingstone flew over the waves again, the wind strong at her back, bearing her east across the open water between the islands. There was no need for the oars this time around, as the wind was more than sufficient to carry them to where they were going. A full complement of sea elves crewed her again, but this time, they were artisans, not warriors.

Elias stood at the bow, as he tended to. His enormous blade was strapped to his back, though he didn't expect to have to use it. It was a symbol he carried with him at all times these days, and he knew that the warriors appreciated it.

On the deck of the ship lay hundreds upon hundreds of burlap and other fiber bags that had been treated with a type of glue that made them waterproof. Two large leaves on the inside kept the two sides of the container from being stuck together, and added to their resiliency. Each was almost large enough for one of the sea elves to climb inside of, but when they were empty, they lay quite flat. Nonetheless, the stacks were piled high on the deck, between the oar benches. Each stack was taller than most of the elves on board, and they ran from one end of the ship to the other.

It wasn't yet noon by the time they reached the site of the battle, the masts of the enormous galleon still visible over the water. She had settled almost flat on the bottom of the shallow water, the masts listing very slightly towards the open sea. Four other ships were anchored nearby, with multiple smaller craft rowing back and forth from the larger vessels to the wreckage.

The Iron Oar was there, the largest of the ships, which meant Delain would be present. As they drew close, they slacked their sails and dropped their oars into the water, hauling on them to create drag. Soon, they were able to drop their anchor, and Elias boarded a rowboat to the Iron Oar.

When he boarded, Delain greeted him warmly. "I am glad to see you, my boy! I knew you were strong, but to see you standing before me it is like you were never wounded!"

Elias shook his hand, smiling broadly. Despite the discussion last night and Coral storming away, being back out lifted his spirits. "It is good to see you as well, my friend! So tell me, what is your plan here? How will we bring this beast back to life?"

Delain was positively giddy, acting decades younger than he was. "I've had this idea for years and years, but no way to ever try it! The hole we put in the ship was relatively small, but large enough for the sea elf divers to get through. We have attached a pulley and a rope to the bow near the damage, and attached the ends to floats."

He held up a finger. "Here's where it gets interesting!"

The old man led Elias to the main deck, where several large bellows – like those used on forges – were set up. One elf would hold the open end of one of the burlap sacks over the bellows, while another would work the handle, inflating the sack until it was tight. A third elf took a thick plug dipped in pitch, stuffed it into the end of the bag, and tied it tightly with woven cord. The result was a sack filled with air that was almost the size of the elves making it.

"We load these on to the rowboats, and then, with the rope and pulley, we draw them down to the hole in the hull of the ship, and inside. The elves inside push them into the upper decks, and come back for another." He shook his head. "I really don't know how they can stay underwater for so long. Maybe they do have gills..."

Some of the elves overheard the last comment and laughed heartily.

"No, old man, we just hold more of the wind in our chests than any mainlander ever could!"

Delain snapped back, "Then is that why you're such blowhards? Those sacks aren't inflated with bragging!"

Even Elias had to laugh at the feigned sternness from the elderly captain. Lending his considerable strength to the task, he worked the bellows two at a time while the sea elves scrambled to keep up with him. Once they had enough to fill a boat, they loaded them up, and Elias accompanied it to the buoy over the sunken bow of the ship.

They tied one end of the rope to an inflated sack, and two sea elves worked in tandem to haul on the other end, bringing it down slowly but surely. They were aided by workers that were down by the pulley, bracing themselves and hauling downward on the rope as well.

The sea was thankfully calm that day, but the work was grueling nonetheless. By the time the sun was setting, they had managed to get the masts standing straight up again, but the ship still lay on the bottom of the sea.

"Another day should do it," Delain reported over dinner. "The swimmers have filled the upper deck and half of the second deck. All that's left is to fill the second deck entirely, then the third. The bilges should be able to remain empty. With that, we should have enough of these waterproof sacks to bring her back to the surface."

Delain was making notes on the sides of some drawings he had made of the front of the sunken ship. "Once we get her floating, we can patch her well enough to get her to dock at Wahine Rapa. There is a channel just deep enough for her at high tide, and if we moor her there, low tide will leave her beached enough to let us patch her proper. Then she'll be ours." He looked up at Elias. "Have you given any thought as to her name?"

Elias shook his head as he ate, a mountain of ham and fruit biscuits on a platter next to him. "No, no I haven't. I want something suitably terrifying for our foes, but not dark, nothing that would be seen as a bad omen by the sea elves or the men at port."

Delain pointed his feather pen at him. "I know just the name. Call her the Leviathan. The fury of the Sea. That will bring fear to the hearts of the superstitious pirates, and reassure the sea elves, who venerate the sea."

Elias mulled that thought over. "What of the men at port?"

Delain scoffed. "You can do no wrong by them. They'll be impressed that you managed to raise her."

Elias shook his head. "I can't be the one to take all the credit. You are the one bringing her back up, not me."

Delain dropped his hands, looking hard at Elias. "Have you not yet grasped your position? You are a figurehead. You're the one everyone looks to. You get all of the credit and all of the blame. If it goes well, it's because you were there. If I do well, it's because you brought me here. If we are triumphant in battle, then it's because you planned it perfectly."

"But the planning is done by all of us! You, me, Jonas, Jenna, Marl, all of us."

Delain pointed at him. "And -you- brought us together. We work for -you-."

Elias shook his head, taking a bite out of a thick slice of ham. Washing it down with water from a carafe, he grunted. "I'm not sure that I deserve the position."

"Deserve it or not, you have it, and you're well on your way to earning it. All we have to do is get the Leviathan above water and put back together."

"What about the Papaya?"

Delain shook his head, waving his pen back and forth dismissively. "She came apart, two pieces as she fell, and lay on her side. There's no bringing her back, much to Jonas's regret." Delain chuckled for a moment. "I seriously think he mourns her like a woman lost."

Elias laughed. "Where is Jonas, anyway? Normally he's present for things such as this."

Delain shook his head again. "Bah, he's found a woman and a drink to drown his sorrows, no doubt. He hasn't been back on a ship since you woke up. He said he was waiting for his esteemed, glorious leader to tell him what to do."

Elias slumped a bit. "I don't know what I've said that has him upset with me. When we last parted, he seemed to disapprove."

Delain nodded slowly. "He does, lad. He doesn't like taking orders, and he doesn't like taking them from someone who seems as young as you do. But he does, because he knows it's the right thing to do, and you're the right one to follow. He'll keep doing so, but rest assured he'll make his voice heard."

Elias thumped his fist on the table. "Good! And you make sure you do the same! I'm not the only one spearheading this, and I can't do it without your help!"

Delain reached across the table and clapped him on the shoulder. "Be assured of that too. I plan on living my last years making a lot of noise, you can count on that!"

He looked over his sketches, and nodded. "I think that'll do it. Tomorrow we'll have her floating again, and then we'll put her back together. Until then, this old man needs some sleep. You should get some rest too."

Elias stood, holding out a hand to help the old man to his feet. "I will. I'm just going to get some air first, then I'll bed down for the night."

Delain grunted, stretching his back. "See that you do. You young folk need more sleep than we elders."

After Delain took his leave, Elias climbed to the aft castle, on the eastern side of the ship, and looked out to sea. Each of the five boats had lookouts stationed, and he could see their torches in the clear night. Several miles to the north, he could see light from the coastal village there, on Wahine Rapa, where they would be bringing Leviathan.

He had to admit, the name was growing on him, the more he thought about it.

~   ~   ~

5th Waning Flower Moon, Year 4369

By noon, the hull started to pull free of the sand. The workers redoubled their efforts, and Elias himself manned the rope that hauled the airbags down to the ship. By the time the last load of airbags had been inflated, the top of the deck had broken the surface. Her lower decks still remained underwater, but the Leviathan had risen from the depths. A resounding cheer came from all present at the momentous task they had achieved. The remaining airbags were loaded into her hull, and the damage was covered with thick sailcloth to keep them in. She rode low in the water, but she floated.

Every boat with oars was tied to the giant warship, and they began the arduous task of towing the behemoth towards land. A skeleton crew boarded and unfurled what sails they could, which were in surprisingly good shape. The rudder needed some repairs, as settling to the seabed had jammed it slightly to the left of straight, but beyond that, the vessel was mostly intact.

By the time they reached the mainland, the tide was high, which was perfect. They floated the Leviathan into the channel until she ran aground, and used great timbers to prop her up, so she wouldn't lay on her side when the tide receded.

The supplies to repair the ship were already present, as were shipwrights, both men and elves from the mainland, and a small army of sea elves. Planks were already being prepared to replace the shattered ones on near the bow, and cauldrons of pitch were being warmed over low fires. As soon as the water was low enough, and the Leviathan was settled in the sand, the workers started stripping off the parts of the hull that needed to be replaced.

"Thank the gods you didn't hit her keel. I don't think that we'd have been able to replace that without a proper dry dock. But this... this will work for repairing her hull." Delain seemed to be in his prime here, directing groups of workers in their tasks.

"How did you learn so much about building ships?" Elias asked, marveling at the older man's knowledge. "I've met plenty of sailors who couldn't do this as well as you do."

Delain was studying a chart, and looked up. "Oh, I was raised down in Greatport, a stone's throw from the shipyards. My father built cargo ships for the merchants there, and war galleys for the king. I learned to read so that I could read the schematics to him."

"Why didn't you build ships for a living then? Why not follow in your father's steps?"

Delain waved his hand. "My father was an abusive man. As soon as I was old enough to sail away, I did, but my experience at the shipyards made me more valuable for repairs than for scrubbing decks. Once I got a ship of my own, I took care of her well enough that she didn't need repairs."

Elias nodded. "That makes sense, I suppose."

Delain shouted to a group of elves who were sitting around a cauldron chatting. "Hoi there! Don't let that fire die down too low, or that pitch will go hard! Don't build it up too high, or it'll catch fire!"

Almost as if on cue, one of the cauldrons closer to the water burst into flames, causing the men and elves nearby to back away, shouting. One of the men raked the coals away and threw a thick, burned leather hide over the top of it, smothering the flames. Delain shook his head, cursing under his breath.

"Damn amateurs... what did you say? Oh, yes. Yes, everything makes sense in the proper context. Just like it makes sense that a low-born old man is sitting next to a giant on a pirate infested beach in Greenreef, teaching sea elves how to fix a giant sunken ship. Makes perfect sense."

~　~　~

7ᵗʰ Waning Flower Moon, Year 4369

Elias stood on the deck of the Leviathan as she sailed across the open water. The waves crashed on either side of the behemoth, but she didn't buck and roll like the smaller ships did. No, she pushed through the waves like a juggernaut, bending the tide to her will. Even though he had watched her sink, watched her come back to life, and aided in her repair, he still marveled at the sheer massive size of the vessel.

As wide as the Slingstone was long, she stretched twice the length of the Iron Oar. She had a total of four decks, with a two storied forecastle, three storied aft castle, and four masts. The sheer amount of rigging was staggering, and she used enough sails for three other vessels. The amount of cargo she could hold was staggering, as well as the amount of crew she required. This vessel truly was a wonder. The pirates must have been confident indeed if they were gambling this ship in an outright fight with Elias and his armada.

Though she was only on the sea floor for a week or so, she needed extensive repairs to her rigging, so they were limping her to anchor offshore at Port Greenreef, where more permanent repairs could be made. The work of the men and elves in repairing the hull was complete, but the ropes would be better repaired nearer to port.

Though Delain was fond of the Iron Oar, Elias could see the excitement in his eyes when he suggested that the old man captain the Leviathan. He had said that he needed to think about it, but by the next morning, he had moved his quarters from the Iron Oar to the Leviathan.

Elias stood on the forecastle, watching Rapa Matomato grow in the distance. When they arrived at the port, his first plan was to go from there to the Seagate... he and Coral had many things to discuss, not the least of which being his inevitable departure from the islands. It would give him the opportunity to hunt down the demonic black knight, but he still didn't want to go. However, as the gods had foreseen, if he didn't leave, neither would the shadow, and great calamity would befall the island, and thus, Coral.

His stomach knotted. The very idea was enough to make him feel sick. Maybe she would come with him when he left, despite what Marl had said... he could, at this point, only hope.

Chapter Nineteen

8th Waning Flower Moon, Year 4369

Elias and Coral sat on the edge of the platform of his small hut, his feet in the sand, hers dangling over the edge. His boots and sword sat on the planks behind him, next to his tunic. She was wearing her white leather skirt, though if it was a new one or not Elias was unsure. If it was the old one, it had been dressed up with new bead work. Her halter top was made of the same material, with a similar design in stitched beads.

She had come to the lean-to shortly after he had arrived, and sat next to him without speaking. Neither of them had said anything yet; they just sat together, watching the waves come through the Seagate.

"I don't want to leave," he said, finally.

"I know."

"I don't want you to be angry with me, either."

"I know. I'm not."

He looked down at her, her black tresses hiding her face from him. "Are you sure? It feels like you are."

She shook her head, looking down. "No. I'm not angry. Just very sad."

He reached out, setting his hand over the top of hers between them. "You could come with me."

She didn't say anything for a while. Eventually, she turned to look up at him, her green eyes striking in the setting sun, as they always were. "Elias, I'm pregnant."

He froze, looking down at her. "But... how? I mean, it's been almost three seasons since we... have been together."

She leaned against him, looking down at their hands. "It happened before. Perhaps the time under the mango tree, perhaps later that night. I didn't know I was fertile at that time, but the gods have chosen to bless us with a child."

He looked her over. She didn't show at all. She was still slender, with no sign of a tummy. "But... after nine months, why do you not show the signs?"

She sighed. "I forget that you were not raised with our people. Just as we live much longer than men do, it takes us much longer to create a life as well. Our child won't be born for another seven summers, at least."

Elias nodded, still somewhat in shock. "This... this is good news!"

She looked up at him, her eyes wide. "Good news? Now the prophecies give you no protection! You could be maimed, or killed in the process of striking the final blow!"

Elias shook his head. "Damn the prophecies! We will win this because we have to. We don't need any gods or spirits or prophecies to guarantee our victory. The fact that you and I are going to have a child makes me happy!"

Reaching over, he picked her up and set her on his lap. "Besides. Who's to say it is a boy? We may have a daughter."

She leaned against him, wrapping an arm behind his neck. "Elias, it is not wise to defy the gods or their words." She ran her fingers down his chest, from his collarbone to his sternum. "Those who ignore the gods do so at their own certain peril."

"Then we shall go where the gods can't reach us. Your gods are the gods of the islands, not of the whole world. On the mainland, they hold no power."

She shook her head. "You know I am to be the speaker for the gods here when my father can no longer do it. I cannot abandon my people."

Elias ran his fingers through her raven hair. "And I cannot abandon you."

She pressed her face against his chest. "My love, I don't know what the answer is."

They sat for a moment, the sun dipping lower in the sky.

It was Coral who broke the silence. "There is more you should know."

Elias kissed her on top of her head. "And what is that?"

Coral hesitated for a moment, then gently climbed off of his lap. She leaned against the wall of the shelter, and pulled her knees up to her chest. "There... there was only one prophecy from the gods. The prophecy that a warrior from over the sea would come to our aid."

Elias sat up. "What do you mean? Didn't your gods say that you would bear the son of the one who would rid the islands of the pirates?"

Coral shook her head. "Not exactly. The first part of the prophecy is true, spoken from the gods to my father, their speaker. The second part was spoken by the speaker, that the warrior was to get a prize for being our savior. I was to be that prize."

Elias's pulse rose in his ears. He could feel his stomach twist, and he suddenly felt sick. "So, the whole proof that I was the savior because you felt it. That was a lie." It wasn't a question, it was a statement.

Coral nodded. "Yes. We chose you to fulfill the prophecy. My father and I thought that if we could find a warrior, and I could bear him a son, then we would be able to rid our land of the invaders."

Elias sat on the edge of the shelter, staring into Coral's eyes in the flickering torchlight. "So you're telling me that all of this over the last year, our spending time together, your affection, our whole relationship, it was all just a lie to keep me hooked? To keep me baited and fighting?"

She nodded again. "That's how it started."

Elias turned, looking out toward the sea. "I see."

Coral moved over to him. Setting a hand on his shoulder, she said, "oh, Elias, I never meant to hurt you."

"No, you just meant to deceive me. I should have known it was too good to be true."

Coral shook her head, a tear rolling down her cheek. "No, no it was true!"

Elias stood, brushing her hand off of his shoulder. "No matter. We'll be wrapping up our campaign here shortly." His pulse thundered in his ears, and his stomach felt like it was trying to claw it's way out through his throat. "I'll be gone when we're done, and you won't have to cater to a freak anymore."

"No, Elias, it isn't like that!"

"No need to keep up pretenses anymore. I'll fight your war without them." Elias took his boots and tunic off of the floor of the shelter and picked up his sword by the harness. "I have an attack to plan. Goodbye, Coral."

As he walked away from the hut, he could hear Coral sobbing over the sound of the waves.

~   ~   ~

Marl was seated at the table, a cup of wine in his hand, when Elias entered through the trapdoor. The seer looked up at Elias as he approached the table. When he saw Elias's face, he sat up straighter. He set the cup down and clasped his hands in front of him. "I see."

Elias growled. "Do you now. So do I."

Marl sat still, looking at Elias. "You must understand our position. We had no way of knowing if the reign of the slavers would end in our lives."

Elias clenched his fist, his vision tingeing red. "So you whore your daughter out to lure in someone who could do your dirty work for you."

Marl stood swiftly, knocking his chair over. "Measure your words carefully, Elias," the older elf snapped.

"I have measured them as carefully as you have measured yours."

Marl froze and glanced down. "And what is it that you are planning to do with that?"

Elias looked down and saw that his sword was in his hands. He didn't remember drawing it, but there it was, the tip leveled at Marl's chest. He was still about ten feet away, but the message was clear. His breath came heavy and fast, and his vision was clouded even more by the red tinge of fury. Raising the sword above his head, he brought it down on the table, shattering the thick timber, cleaving it in half with one blow. He wrenched his sword free, kicking debris away from himself.

Marl had dodged away from the strike and landed on his backside, his back against a wall. Elias pointed the sword at him. "I am going to Greenreef tonight. I expect to see you there in the morning. You and I will see this war to the end, and then I will leave your islands."

Marl just stared back at him, not saying a word. Elias turned and descended through the trap door and down the ladder. As he exited the lodge, there was a crowd gathering outside. Coral was sprinting towards him, but Jayd caught her by the arm, pulling her in and wrapping her arms around her.

Elias strode through the crowd, feeling the eyes on him as he made for the path to Greenreef. The moon was still bright enough in the sky that he could see very well. He swiftly left the torchlight of the village behind and forged into the dark. When he was too far away to hear the commotion in the village anymore, he fell to his knees, buried his face in his hands, and cried.

~   ~   ~

It was still dark when Elias reached Port Greenreef, but the streets were lively nonetheless. This city never entirely slept, and the crew at the dock worked all hours to keep the warships stocked and in good repair. The campaign against the pirates had been good for the port's economy, and every man or elf skilled with a hammer or chisel had all the work they could do. He could see the lights on the ships that were anchored farther out in the bay to make room for those in greater need of repair.

His temper had waned by the time he reached the city, and he was exhausted. He made for the tavern where he and Coral had stayed during the early part of their relationship. Inside, the tavern was filled with patrons eating and drinking. Jonas sat on a chair, his boots up on the table, and Jenna sat in his lap, smiling and laughing. They both looked up, startled when he came in, and a hush settled over the room.

Jenna hopped out of Jonas's lap. "Elias, what's wrong?"

His face must have betrayed him. "I am tired."

Jenna rushed over to him. "Come with me, this way. Jonas, bring bread, meat, something to drink." She turned back and pointed at him. "*Not* whiskey or ale. Water."

She led Elias up the stairs while Jonas headed for the bar. Elias could hear the chatter begin again in earnest as they left the room.

Once Jenna got him into a room, she sat him down on the bed. "What's wrong? What happened?"

"She played me. The entire time, she was just playing me. Using me for her father's war."

Jenna's eyes popped wide with shock. "What? Coral? How do you know this?"

Elias dropped his sword on the floor with a resounding clank. "She told me so. She told me that she is pregnant, then she told me that the prophecy about me fathering a son with her was complete bullshit. They made it up, used her like a tool to hook me in." He put his face into his hands. "And I took the bait. I took the bait and now men and elves have died at my word."

Jenna moved to sit next to him, putting a hand on his shoulder. "She said that the prophecy was a lie? She told you that she didn't love you?"

Elias shook his head. "No. She said the prophecy about a warrior from over the sea was true, but she and Marl decided that they needed a prize, something to use entice the warrior to stay. That's why Marl was so keen to introduce her to me. That's why she was so close to me, so fast. I was being seduced, like a fool. Like an animal being baited."

Jenna patted him gently on his shoulder. "What did you do?"

Elias spread his hands. "I left. I told her goodbye and left. I confronted Marl, and I lost my temper, then I came straight here."

She stood, embracing him, pressing his head to her chest. "Oh, you man. You poor, stupid, stupid man."

He looked up at her. "What do you mean?"

She held him at arm's length. "It was obvious that's how it started. Any fool could have seen that. But what developed after it was real. Any *other* fool could have seen that. She opened herself to you, bared her heart, told you the truth, and you pushed her away."

Elias shook his head, wiping his eyes. "Our relationship was built on a lie! What can grow from a lie?

Jenna pushed him away, walking back to her chair. "I am becoming more and more convinced that all of you warrior types don't know a thing beyond how to swing a sword and headbutt your way through life with only your principles to guide you." She sighed. "She may not have loved you at first. You can't even admit to yourself that you love her, so what's the problem with that?"

She shook her head. "But it was obvious that she wasn't feigning it. Do you think a girl who just got attacked, like she was at that beach, wants anything to do with just some guy after that? That she would lie with a man unless she felt comforted by him?" She scoffed slightly. "Hell, I wouldn't lie with a man at *all*."

"But... she lied to me. From the very start, she lied to me. She hid from me the fact that she was pregnant. She even played into the prophecy, saying it protected me when it obviously didn't."

Jenna raised a brow. "Have you never been caught up in something, and had to go along with it because you didn't know what else to do?"

Elias's mind immediately went to that first night at the Seagate, when he was drunk. He agreed pretty readily, despite his doubts. "... I can see that."

There was a knock at the door. Jenna opened it, and Jonas stepped in, bearing a tray of sliced meats, bread, and cheese, as well as two carafes. "This stuff gets heavy while eavesdropping." He set the tray on a small table, and stretched his back, wincing.

Elias slumped. He felt horrible. He felt used, manipulated, and angry, but he also felt torn. He didn't want to pursue a relationship with someone who made him feel that way, but...

He missed Coral already.

"What do I do now?"

Jonas sat down next to him. "Now, you plan out our next attack."

Jenna handed Elias a slice of bread with pork and cheese on it. "And when the time comes, you talk to her." She sniffed one of the carafes. "I said no ale..."

~　　~　　~

They sat around a wide, round table in the captain's quarters of the

Leviathan. Delain, Jenna, Jonas, Martin, Geoff, Marl, and Elias all sat around a map of the islands, dotted with markers, knives, and stones. A small fleet of wooden ships sat gathered around Greenreef, while more sat gathered around both the Hollow Island and the Cursed Island.

Elias stood, pushing half of the fleet from Greenreef towards the Cursed Island. "We take our forces, and put them all on the Iron Oar and the Leviathan. Those ships will make landfall here," he pushed two ships to the middle of the eastern shore, "while the others will make landfall on the northern and southern ends, where we can have them ready to receive as many freed elves as they can. The rest will meet us at the Leviathan. Once we have torched the stores and freed the sea elves, we will sail back to Rapa Matomato, here." He set his finger on the north end of the largest island of the Greenreef chain, where they were now.

Jonas nodded. "How many men will make landfall with the Leviathan?"

Marl stood. "We have fifteen hundred warriors ready to sail, right now, each with fifty arrows and a steel spear. Four hundred of them carry swords, another two hundred carry axes. They will make landfall with the Oar and the Leviathan. On each end of the island, two hundred and fifty warriors will take to land, and aid in the fight. That will put a full army on the ground."

Jonas sat back, regarding the map. "Our spies say there are five hundred pirates on that island, with three ships ready to sail to the Cursed Island. These ships are moored on the docks of the west shore. Hollow Island is three hours away. Why so many warriors?"

Elias pointed at a triangle near the center of the island. "There is a network of caves here. Just because we counted pirates above ground, does not mean that they don't have a stronghold underground." He tapped the map at the Hollow Island. "If they have their ships here to resupply at the time we land, there will be many more pirates ashore. We need to be ready for them."

Martin sat back, his arms crossed over his chest. "They still have twice as many ships as we do, and we have heard of a great weapon they have hidden in the caves. It has been said that if the weapon was used against us, it could destroy us all."

Delain frowned. "Do we know what this weapon is?"

Marl shook his head. "All we know is that it was delivered there about two hundred years ago, and has not been removed since. The pirates themselves are afraid of it. The lead pigs into the mouth of the cave, but they never come back out."

Jonas and Delain exchanged glances. Jonas drummed his fingers on the table. "I'm betting it's a dragon."

Elias leaned forward, tapping the table. "If the pirates are afraid of it, then I am willing to assume that it's not under their control yet. And if it hasn't come out in the last two hundred years, then it most likely can't break free."

Martin shook his head again. "Even if they don't have a dragon, and if they do and it's tied up good and tight, there's still the fact that they have forty ships to our eighteen."

Geoff gestured at the map, waving his hand. "Half of them are away, raiding the mainland, or farther west. Now is the right time to hit them."

Delain nodded. "The passage west will take about a month to get there, and a month back. The ships that sailed west left about three weeks ago... so we have more than a month before they return." He pushed ten ships to the western edge of the map. "The same for the ships sailing east to the mainland." He pushed ten more to the eastern edge. "That leaves our forces roughly equal. With the blow we'll deliver to the Cursed Island, we will weaken them further, and give us the edge. With any luck, the loss of their supplies will cause more of them to desert. We wait a month, then attack their stronghold."

Delain pushed all of the ships towards the hollow island, surrounding it. "We can sail a ship loaded with blasting powder into their gates, breaking through it. Once it's through, we fire flaming arrows into it. With any luck at all, the explosion will destroy every ship and structure they've got. The ones that don't fall will be cleaned up by our men on the ships."

Jenna had remained silent, watching the plans evolve. At this point, she sat forward, pointing at the islands closest to Rapa Matomato. "What of the rest of the islands? With all of the warriors on the western ends of the chain, the eastern islands will be wide open."

Jonas stood and arranged the remaining ships around the map. "We'll only take half of our forces west. There are eight more ships, each carrying a complement of at least a hundred warriors. Three will be here at Greenreef, at the north point, the port, and at the Seagate." He tapped the map at all three points, indicating their positions.

"One more at each island, near the largest village on it, where the sea elves will gather during the raid." he tapped them each in turn, "And the last three at Taonga Tama, in case we are pursued." He set three fingers on the map on the eastern most island controlled by the sea elves. "These will be our backup in case anything goes wrong."

Jenna scowled. "For when something goes wrong."

Delain sat back. "Now, now, Jenna, this is a good plan."

She nodded, arms still crossed over her chest, "Oh, yes, it's a good plan. If everyone plays their parts, follows the plan exactly. Including the pirates." She stood, leaning over the map. "It's four days sailing to Kanga Motu. Four days. If they see you coming, it's only three hours to the Hollow Island. Three hours back."

She drew a dagger from her waistband. Tapping the tip against the map, over the Cursed Island. "You have, at most, six hours to take an entire island. To get in, kill every pirate there, and load all of the slaves onto the ships." She stuck the knife into the table, in the center of the Hollow Island. "And that is if they do not see you coming, and send for reinforcements first. We could be going into a battle that we can't win."

Elias sat back, looking over the map. "We've taken all of the islands back, and pushed the pirates out of their waters. At this point, the pirates sail wide around us before they make their way to the mainland. They sail mostly west now, which means that we've pushed our problem off on other islands, other peoples." He leaned forward, moving the ships back to the Cursed Island. "By taking the battle to them here, we gain resources at their expense, and in doing so we more than double our numbers."

Jenna leveled a gaze at him. "So you're freeing soldiers."

Jonas sat back down in his seat. "Not exactly, but I would imagine that there would be some of them keen on fighting the men that held them for so long."

Geoff looked up from the map. "How long have they been held there?"

Marl sighed. "The island was renamed the Cursed Island after it was taken by the pirates over four centuries ago. I was a child then. They took the island, burned all the trees so that we would have no wood for boats, and added to our number when they would capture us on the other islands."

Jenna turned her gaze to Marl. "You were there."

The rest of the inhabitants of the chamber turned to look at Marl, who steadfastly stared at the map. He was quiet for a moment. "I was."

"Is that why you're so keen on taking the island back? Vengeance for what was done to you and your family?"

Jonas swore. "By the gods, Jenna, lay off the man."

Marl held up a hand. "Yes. Yes, I want retribution for what was done. My mother was slain in front of my eyes, as were my brothers. My sisters were allowed to live, though they remained behind." He lowered his hand.

"They were pretty, and I am no fool. I know what happened to them. Them and every other lass they have taken from us over the last four hundred years."

He looked up at Jenna, his normally kind eyes almost glowing in the dim light. "I do want vengeance. And I want to make sure that it never happens again, to any of our women. To my beautiful wife or my beautiful daughter. To the priestesses that are training in their mountain shrine. To the innocent youth that knows not the whip nor the plow nor the heavy hand of the slaver." With each point he made, he struck the butt of his staff against the deck.

"If I could personally slay every single man that set foot on these islands from the deck of a pirate ship, I would be able to cast my last breath just after the last of theirs and die fulfilled!" He struck the deck one more time, and a flash of green burst out with a gust of wind from the bottom of his staff. Crackling green lightning crawled up the staff and along his arm, dissipating into his shoulder.

Martin and Geoff were pressed back against the walls of the room, while Jonas stood in front of Jenna, his hand on his hilt, having pushed her back from the table. Only Delain and Elias stayed at the map, eyes locked on Marl.

Marl slowly lowered his staff, and leaned it against a wall. Gradually, deliberately, he drew his chair back to the table and sat down. "I cannot drive off the scourge of Greenreef by myself. My people have been unable to do so for four centuries. And now... now, we are as close as we were the day after they took our people. We have a chance of pushing them away. Except that now, we are warriors, not dancers. Fighters, not hunters. Mariners, not fishermen."

Marl locked eyes with Elias. They had not spoken directly to each other since Elias stormed out of Seagate. "I would tell a thousand more false prophecies. I would live for a thousand times longer rowing oars. I would slay a thousand dragons. I would do everything I have done in a heartbeat again if I knew it would give me a chance." He pointed at Elias. "And you made us this way. By the will of the gods, you made us this way."

Delain leaned back in his chair. "I think, then, that Master Marl has answered all of your questions, to your satisfaction, Lady Jenna?"

She didn't immediately respond, instead just staring forward at Marl, her jaw set. Finally, she stood and bowed slightly to Marl. "I defer to your experience, Marl. I agree that this island needs to fall. But there is blood in our future. Blood and pain." She shook her head. "It won't be as easy as all this. I have a very, very bad feeling about what lay on that island."

~   ~   ~

8ᵗʰ Waxing Summer Moon, 4369

Eighteen ships lay anchored outside the harbor, boats rowing back and forth between them and the docks. The port swarmed with men and elves, buzzing with activity. The smiths had been working day and night for three days, making spears and arrows. Swords and axes took far too much steel, and as it was, the sea elves were lending their knappers to the effort, making razor-sharp obsidian arrowheads out of the surprisingly rare volcanic glass, the sole source of which was the fiery mountain on the eastern coast of Rapa Matomato.

The small, black chunks of glass were mined out of the layers of pumice, most of which were barely a foot in diameter. But even that small amount of black volcanic glass was enough to make thousands of arrowheads. And they would need thousands.

Elias stood on the forecastle of the Leviathan, looking back at the port. A large stone outcropping protected it from the sea to the east, and the ridge that separated it from Marl's village protected it from the west. From the south it was wide open, save for a few bald, steep islands where scant vegetation grew. The ship that would be the port's defense was already armed to the teeth and waiting to take its station, plus a full contingent of warriors that would be staying on land.

As each of the seven other ships that were to act as the defense were stocked, they set sail west, around the island and up the chain. He had seen to the preparations of the vessel that was to guard the Seagate himself, picking a ship that was thick hulled and strong. It carried a full two hundred warriors, and a further fifty crew, plus another seventy-five warriors who were in the village itself. He was certain that it was defended, but he worried still.

Huffing a sigh, he turned to oversee the most recent load of weaponry and supplies that was arriving at his ship. A thousand elven warriors were already aboard, and they took up far less room than he had thought they would. True, below decks, there was hardly room to walk, but there were four decks, two more on the forecastle and three more aft.

The Iron Oar, captained by Delain, was nearby. On board were another five hundred warriors, their weapons, and supplies. These were the elves that would make landfall with them, fifteen hundred of the best archers, spearmen, and swordsmen in the islands. In four days time, these warriors would be fighting and dying under his command.

He stepped down the ladder that led to the second floor of the forecastle, and into his quarters. The map still sat on the table, covered in their battle plans, wooden ships, and figurines of soldiers here and there, daggers stuck into strategic points on the islands. He looked over the map, rehearsing the plan in his head again. Land, attack the two settlements on either side of the island and funnel the captive sea elves to the waiting ships on the eastern shore, with the mountain between them and the western docks.

He set his hands on the table. It was a solid plan, but he was still nervous. He had led dozens of raids, sank many ships, and killed many pirates in the last four seasons, but this was entirely different. This would be a land battle. He had only ever fought in one of those, against the Felle scouts, and that was a very small force, in a very short time.

He turned, looking towards the great windows. A great suit of armor, forged of steel, loomed from the stand near his bed. He had commissioned it from the best armorsmith on the island when he had brought the Leviathan into port. It had taken some time, but it was done and done well. Simple, solid, and strong. Jonas, Martin, and Geoff approved, but Marl and Jenna felt it would make him sink if he fell in the water.

He chuckled to himself as he walked over, admiring the simple lines of it. He would not wear it on the ship, but it would serve him well on the island. Jonas had shown him the basics of wearing armor, which was more of a skill than Elias had figured it to be. The chain shirt was easy enough to move in, but the breastplate, vambraces, and pauldrons were a bit more restrictive than he had imagined. However, with his great blade, he would be a force to be reckoned with in the open field.

A horn sounded from outside, and Elias could feel the butterflies rise in his stomach. That was the last of the ships being loaded. It was time for his armada to move. He hadn't been back to Seagate since the night he left Coral... he resolved for it to be his first stop when he returned from this raid. He and Coral needed to talk, but right now, he needed his mind to be focused on the upcoming battle.

He huffed another long sigh and lifted his greatsword. Attaching it to its harness, he stepped out onto the deck. It was time to be a leader again.

Chapter Twenty

12ᵗʰ Waxing Summer Moon. Year 4369

The shadow of the Cursed Island loomed ahead of them, blotting out the stars closest to the horizon. They had approached from behind the largest island nearby, Ahi Maunga, the Fire Mountain, and waited until dusk before beginning the last leg of the journey towards the slave villages. They doused all of the lights on their ships, and sailed in the gathering darkness, with as much stealth as they could manage with as large of a force as they were, and the moon nearing full.

They had been sailing for four days nonstop along the island chain, farther west than Elias had ever been. Once they passed Taonga Tama, the Rich Son, they were in the open sea. Though he was technically the captain of the Leviathan, he could neither navigate by the stars nor chart the course through other means, so he had a helmsman and a navigator on board.

The warriors had hardly put a dent in the food and water stores that they had brought with them, which was enough to feed all of the warriors as well as the refugees they would be bringing back. The sea elves were getting restless, anxious to start the battle they were sailing towards. The last day at sea had been spent wrestling, sparring, and performing various war dances and chants. Elias had very little understanding of the meaning behind the rituals, but Marl assured him it was necessary to appease the gods and gain their favor.

But now, as they grew closer to the broad, low island, every elf aboard each ship was as taut as a bowstring. A thousand warriors filled the decks of the Leviathan alone, watching the dark mass approach against the backdrops of stars. They had covered their pale skin with red, white, and black war paint, the intricate designs making them look like every bit the terrifying force, silent and deadly in the moonlight.

Delain's ship led the way, several boat lengths ahead. A lantern flashed on the deck, alerting the rest of the armada. It was time to anchor and board the landing boats, while the eight other ships would sail to the opposite sides of the island and wait for dawn. Trying to bring thousands of refugees to safety in darkness was impossible; the light of the rising sun was a necessity.

Elias went into his chamber and started putting on his armor with the help of an elf trained to squire for him. He could feel the weight on his shoulders and arms, more comforting than hindering. His mind turned again to the dark knight on the road, back on the mainland, what seemed an eternity before. Is this how he felt, impenetrable and powerful? He shook his head at the thought. Even his knife had found a chink in that armor; best not trust it too much. There could be more agents of the Felle on this island.

The last things he strapped on were his greaves – metal plates covering his legs from his knees to his boots. He lifted his greatsword off of the hooks he had mounted on the wall, and proceeded to board a landing boat. His armor was heavy, but he could march in it.

The trip to shore was uneventful, save for at the beach itself. It was a narrow stretch of sand at the foot of some cliffs. Dozens of boats were landing and being dragged farther ashore, out of the reach of the tide, and moored with long stakes and ropes. Once on land, the warriors broke into two groups of seven hundred warriors each; fifty warriors had stayed behind to defend each ship, and the rest had been assigned to either the northern or southern raiding party. There was no communication here, as everyone already knew what they were going to do. Shouting over the waves would have alerted any lookouts.

Elias led the party headed north, accompanied by Geoff, while Jonas and Martin headed the party going south, and Delain stayed aboard the Iron Oar. Each was a few hours away from the village they were targeting, and should reach their destination a bit before dawn. Elias expected the battles to be short and brutal; hit the pirates before they knew what was happening, and finish them off fast.

As they traveled north, the cliff face slowly dropped until it was even with the beach, and they were able to move onto firmer footing. Walking in the sand was especially difficult for Elias, who was quite heavy even without the armor. There was a bit of noise as he walked, but it wasn't enough to worry him. Not yet, at least.

Presently, they drew up at the base of a low hill. Elias had sent a few scouts ahead, and they returned with news of a watchtower, manned by three lookouts. A few well-placed arrows closed their eyes permanently.

The sky to the east was lightening ever so slightly, so the time to act was upon them. With the hill between them and the village to hide his voice, he addressed the small army in front of him. Stepping up on a weathered stone, he drew his blade from its sheath, holding it in one hand.

"Many of you were not born when this island fell to the pirate invaders, but have heard the tale told and retold by your elders. How the men from the mainland fell upon you like wolves, destroying the lives of your ancestors and driving them from their land. They burned your villages and raped your women! Babies were torn from the arms of mothers, and dashed against stones! Elders were cut down in their beds!"

He swung his enormous blade in an arc, hacking through a small tree in one strike. "Now is the time when we repay them for the atrocities visited upon your people! Our people! Now is the time for us to take back the land they stole from you, that they stole from the gods themselves! We push them back and liberate our people, and we show them that nobody, man or elf, will live under the whip of a pirate while the wind breathes life into our chests!"

He pointed his word up the hill. "When we cross that hill, we visit death upon them, and all of the fear that comes with it! Slay any man that stands against you! This time, we fight not for a bounty. Take no prisoners, and cut down every pirate where he stands!"

In near perfect unison, the assembled elves let out a great battle cry, and seven hundred warriors surged past Elias. They ran as if they hadn't just marched for three hours after being kept on a ship for four days, screaming and howling like demons. Elias charged up the hill with them, the faster elves flowing about him like leaves on the wind. As he started down the hill, he gained momentum, his longer strides outpacing even the fastest unencumbered warrior. He let out a savage roar, holding his sword aloft as he smashed into the gate of the shoddy wall that stood around the ramshackle village.

The thin boards, baked by the sun as they were, exploded around him as he bulldogged his way through. Several pirates stood in front of him with their swords drawn, eyes wide and mouths hanging open. Wielding his greatsword like a club, he slashed through one of them in a single strike, spraying blood and entrails all over the pirate's companions, who turned and fled in terror. Elven arrows thudded into their backs, dropping them mid-stride.

The shrieking blue, red, black, and white warriors flooded into the town, moving from bonfire to bonfire, slaughtering every pirate who stood before them. Arrows started pelting down on them from watchtowers around the perimeter. Some of the warriors tried scaling the towers but were shot down by the archers above them.

"Towers! Take down the towers!" Elias bellowed, and like a living thing, his army obeyed, surging forward with axes and chopping at the stout timbers that held the archers aloft. Archers on the ground kept the pirates' heads down as the elves hacked at the wood, quickly making the first tower topple over. A dozen pirates fell with it, some of them crushed by the weight of the platform they stood on, the others set upon with spears and knives as soon as they hit the ground.

On either side of him towers were being scaled or cut down, his warriors chasing pirates into the village proper. Shouts and screams could be heard as the slaves came out of their in the commotion.

Elias charged into the slum – a massive collection of muddy streets and decrepit stray and palm thatched huts, some having been set ablaze by the pirates – five spear-wielding warriors at his flanks. He came upon a cluster of pirates surrounded by fallen elves, some painted, some dressed in rags or entirely naked. He never even slowed down, his vision red in the flickering firelight. He swung his blade hard, gripping the hilt with both hands, nearly cleaving his target in twain. His blade mired in the thick, muddy clay, and was stuck for a moment, and two men were on him, their blades beating at his pauldrons and vambraces. He let go of his sword, which stayed stuck in the mud, and grabbed one of the men, swinging him into the other before crushing his face with a gauntleted fist. He dropped the jerking pirate and grabbed the handle of his sword, only to have his hand slip off from the blood that now coated it.

A saber swung in from his right, and he held up his arm, catching it on the steel, the blow numbing his wrist. The man wielding the sword pulled back for a thrust, but was caught by a spear in the chest, and then another as two warriors ran him through. Elias turned back to his sword and, gripping it in both hands, wrenched it free and brought it down on a pirate who was pulling his cutlass out of the stomach of a falling elf, splitting his skull wide open.

Something struck his back and skittered off to his left, and he turned to see an archer standing on a hut, aiming at him with another nocked arrow. Elias hurled his sword in an overhanded throw just before the pirate released it, sending his arrow wide. Elias's weapon struck him with the flat of the blade hard enough to knock him off the roof. When he hit the ground, two elves set upon him with knives, shrieking and howling in their war paint.

Elias ran over to retrieve his sword, temporarily clear of anyone trying to kill him. He picked it up, shaking off the mud as he looked around the warzone.

The pirates that had been guarding the village had been horrendously outnumbered and were beating a retreat out the western gates. He ran towards them, vaguely aware of the fact that his legs were protesting the exertion. His breath ragged in his throat, he called out to his warriors.

"They are escaping! Run them down! Do not let a single man escape to their ships!"

As he ran through the battle, warriors broke away from the fray to follow him, chasing the pirates through the ramshackle village. As they approached the western gate, the fleeing pirates shut and barred it from the outside. This didn't slow down the elves at all, who climbed over the fence like grasshoppers, several pausing at the top to loose arrows at their fleeing quarry. Elias did not have the momentum to crash through the wall again, so he turned back to the battle inside.

There were not many pirates left. Those few were putting their hands up to surrender, only to be cut down by the fury of the sea elves; they definitely knew how to take no prisoners. As the last pirate fell, there was a great victory cry from the warriors. Though they had lost many, the village had been taken.

Elias turned to the east as the elves sang their victory to the night. Four sails stood out against the growing light of morning, heralding the arrival of the ships that would carry these elves back to the safe islands of Greenreef.

~   ~   ~

There had been over three thousand elves in the walled village, surrounded by three hundred pirate guards. They hadn't stood a chance against the overwhelming force of the sea elves.

Elias's forces had fallen by roughly a hundred elves, but overall, they had fared quite well in the battle. Not a single pirate had survived; the party Elias had sent after the escapees had returned, decorated with ears and scalps, proof of their quarry's demise.

Landing boats were already ferrying the refugees to the ships. The process was going to take much longer than Elias had figured it to, and time was of the essence. The sun had already broken over the horizon, just south of the Fire Mountain, and the pirate supply ships would be due to set sail soon, according to the scouts who had watched the Cursed Island in the week before their raid. That meant they had at most six hours of guaranteed time before reinforcements arrived. They needed to be gone before noon.

A runner came up to where he, Geoff, and the leaders of the war parties stood to oversee the evacuation, breathless and sweating in the cool morning air. Elias offered him a water skin, letting him catch his breath before speaking. The runner took a deep draught and handed the skin back.

"Jonas sends word. He and the warriors with him were victorious. Four hundred pirates were slain, give or take a score. We lost one hundred and fifty warriors and rescued almost four thousand slaves. The ships are unable to carry them all."

Elias patted him on the shoulder. "Good. Very good. What Is Jonas planning for the rest of the slaves we have liberated?"

"They are marching along the eastern coast to where we landed. Half of Jonas' warriors are accompanying them."

Elias frowned, lifting an eyebrow. "And the other half?"

The runner sat down, still breathing heavily. "Jonas is leading them to capture the supply ships. They are docked on the west coast. He plans to sail them south, and back to Port Greenreef."

Elias nodded. He called over Tao, who had come along as the leader of one of the warbands. The tall, lean, muscular elf was painted almost entirely white, with black swirls from head to toe. He jogged over and sat down next to Elias. "Yes, Kaiwhakaora?" It was a name he had been given by the warriors under his command. It meant 'savior.' He was uncomfortable with it at first, but by this point, it just accepted it as his name.

"Take two hundred and fifty warriors, and head southwest as fast as you can. Join with Jonas and his forces, do as he tells you to. Help him take the ships, and sail them south."

The warrior nodded and stood. "Yes, Kaiwhakaora. As you command." He jogged back to his warriors and started issuing directions. It was not long before a large detachment of elves left through the western gate at a full run.

Elias stood as well. "One hundred elves will stay here and assist the rest of the slaves in boarding our ships, before boarding them themselves. Sail directly for Greenreef. The rest of us will march back to the Leviathan."

As the warriors went about fulfilling their orders, one of the slaves – an old woman – approached, hanging back. Elias sat down, knowing that his size was intimidating to the elves who did not know him. "Come here, grandmother. You have nothing to fear from me. How can I be of service to you?"

Slowly, she walked up to him, dropping to her knees a short distance away. "My lord, thank you! We cannot possibly tell you how grateful we are that you finally came for us, as the prophecies foretold!"

So the slaves here had the same prophecy as the elves of the main island. "What matters is that you will be safe again, very soon. Once you board one of the ships, it will take you back to Greenreef."

She nodded, bowing low. "Yes, my lord. Thank you, my lord. But there is something you should know."

He leaned forward, his elbow resting on his knee. "What is it?"

She sat back up, her watery blue eyes meeting his. "In the mountain on the eastern coast, there is a cave. The pirates spoke of a great power there, one that they were unable to tame. They spoke of great chains, the chains they used to carry the greatest anchors up from the deeps, used to hold it down."

Elias nodded. "We know of the weapon. Have any of the pirates spoken of what it is?"

She shook her head. "They never named it, my lord, they just spoke of it, and of keeping it fed. Once a month, an entire herd of swine was brought to the cave. Our rations were dropped to feed it when it arrived, nearly two hundred summers hence."

Elias nodded. "Thank you, grandmother. Can you lead us to this cave?"

"Not I, my lord. My grandson knows where it is; he tended the herds that were fed to the cave, though he was never allowed inside."

"Has he boarded a ship yet?"

She shook her head again. "No, my lord. He has stayed to be sure that his family boards your great ships first."

Elias nodded, standing up and offering a hand to help her to her feet. "Thank you, my lady. If you could have your grandson come to me, I would visit this cave."

She took his hand and struggled to her feet. "I am not a lady, my lord!"

"And I am not a lord, my lady. Call me Elias." He smiled and gestured to the shore. "Take a boat from this place. Go where your people are, where you can be safe. Your grandson will be joining you soon. He will ride with me on my ship, once we have seen this cave and what it holds."

She bowed again. "Thank you, my... Elias. Thank you, Elias.

Elias bowed to her. "I am at your service. We will meet again, madam. Go and be safe."

As Elias prepared for the march south, a young elf with skin as blue as the deepest sapphires jogged up.

"My lord, my grandmother sent me to you."

Elias held up his hand. "Please, just call me Elias. Your name is...?"

The young elf bowed. "Yandis, sir."

Elias sighed. No matter what he said, it seemed he was bound to these grand terms. "You know the way to this cave your grandmother spoke of?"

"Yes, my lor... yes, sir."

Elias nodded and held out his hand. Yandis paused, then slowly took his hand, and shook it. Elias smiled and shook it back. "Good! We set out very shortly. You will lead us."

~   ~   ~

Elias jogged along with two hundred elves, straining under the weight of his armor. It had seemed like a wonderful idea when battle was in the future, but it did not lend itself well to moving quickly with many unfettered warriors who traveled light. However, their swift pace made for a swift passage, and the small army was on the beach within an hour and a half. They stood at the top of the ridge overlooking the beach where they had landed.

Anchored out to sea were the Iron Oar and the Leviathan. From the south, they could see a mass of approaching elves. Their dark blue skins stood out against the stark gray and white of the beaches.

They were at least a mile off, but they were moving fast. To the north, four ships sailed east, and to the south, four more. The rescue had been successful, it would seem, and they still had time.

Almost as if reading his mind, Geoff stepped forward, panting for breath. "Not much time, Elias. Maybe three hours before the pirates at Hollow Island know that we've been here... we best be swift."

Elias stretched his aching muscles and grunted his response. "Agreed. Get these elves onto the Leviathan, leave a single boat for us. I'll take ten warriors with me."

Geoff paused, and seemed like he was going to argue, but nodded. Reaching up, he set a hand on Elias's pauldron. "Be safe, Redwood. I don't want to set sail without you, and we've done enough fighting pirates for this voyage."

Elias set his hand on Geoff's shoulder. "I will come out of that cave, I promise you. We'll dine on the Leviathan this afternoon."

Geoff led the elves down the cliff, around to the beach. Elias called for ten volunteers, and before long, he had half a score of painted warriors standing behind him, with Yandis by his side.

"It's not far, my lord," the young elf said as he led the way up the mountain. "There's a wide trail where we would run the hogs into the cavern."

The walk took less than twenty minutes, and they stood in front of the mouth of the cave. The opening was smooth, as if it had been charred and melted, the rock having run down the wall like water and pooling on the ground. Smooth and glassy, obsidian covered the floor as it had in the caldera atop the mountain on Greenreef. The tunnel sloped down, round and deep, swallowed by darkness past the intrusion of the sun's growing light.

A small pile of dried torches lay to the side of the entrance, and it was the work of a moment to light six of them. Holding a torch aloft himself, he stepped into the cave.

Immediately, he was greeted with a blast of hot, dry air. A rumbling sound rolled from the depths of the cave, causing the elves gathered at the entrance to step back a pace.

"My lord..."

Elias turned to see Yandis hiding behind the edge of the cave entrance. He nodded to the boy. "Go, Yandis. You've fulfilled your task; go and join the others in the boats."

Yandis bowed again. "Thank you, my lord!" With that, he took off at a sprint towards the beach.

Elias turned to the warriors gathered behind him. "Let's see what the pirates have hidden down below." He turned back to the cavern and started walking slowly into the depths.

Chapter Twenty-One

12th Waxing Summer Moon, Year 4369

The torchlight reflected eerily off of the smooth glass walls. No cavern he had ever been in looked like this one – there were no stalactites, no pools of water on the ground. The walls were not granite nor limestone nor pumice, they were melted obsidian. Even the ceiling reflected the flames off of its polished black surface.

The tunnel proceeded at a gentle downward slope, curving to the right, a steady warm breeze pulsing from the deeps. The line of elves walked down it single file, Elias leading the way, the sound of his armor clinking echoing off of the walls of the cavern.

Another deep rumble came from the depths, accompanied by a hot blast of air. It felt almost like an earthquake, the rumbling in the air and their chests. As they moved deeper into the cave, the air grew hotter and drier. Elias knew that these mountains held fire and molten rock at one point, and Ahi Maunga was not far away... could the Cursed Island be sitting on a lake of fire as well?

The tunnel curved sharply to the left, and a smell of burned meat grew. Elias drew up short, holding up a fist to signal a stop. The elves behind him drew up close, clustering around him. He turned to face them, unslinging his greatsword and drawing it out of the sheath. Jonas's prediction was sitting at the foremost of his mind.

"Whatever lies beyond the turn of this tunnel, we must be ready for it. If it is hostile, be prepared to fight. If it is too much, be prepared to run. There is no shame in retreating if we must. If we can turn it to our cause, then that is what we shall do."

The warriors behind him murmured assent, still nervous and agitated. He turned back to the depths, and took a step forward.

"If you're going to come in here, then you should just hurry up and do it. I take it by the fact that you're not running and grunting and squealing that you're not food, so come inside and be quick about it."

The voice was powerful, loud, and reverberated off of the walls around them. Elias gripped his sword, holding it in front of him.

"There's only a need for that if you make a need for that. Come now, I haven't got all day, I'm a very busy person."

Elias looked back at the warriors clustered behind him. They hung back, gripping spears and torches, looking between Elias and each other. Elias nodded to them, and gestured down the tunnel with his head.

As he rounded the corner, a deep red and orange glow came from farther into the cave, and the heat intensified dramatically. The cavern grew wider, until it was a great chamber, larger than Elias had thought possible. The ground sloped downward, dropping off into a wide pit of molten stone. The lake of lava was large, but not as large as the caldera atop Greenreef. The ceiling of the chamber arched high overhead, with myriad tunnels leading upwards through it.

Several small, dull black islands of stone peeked out of the lava, and one long, shining one, seemingly made of small mirrors, reflecting the light of the lava around the room in small bright patches. It was as if small candles were scattered about the room, flickering on the walls, but there were none – the heat would have melted instantly.

The temperature of the room was stifling, and Elias broke out in a sweat under his armor. He looked around the room, finding no source for the voice. "I have come in, as you requested. Show yourself before I bake like a turkey!"

The silver island shuddered, and began to move. It dipped down, lower into the lava, then rose again before submerging entirely. From the edge of the pool, a bulge formed on the surface of the lake of molten stone. It rose above the edge of the pit, then higher, the lava running down like streams of thick syrup. As it broke open across the top, it rolled down like a curtain, revealing a flash of silver.

As the lava peeled away, the features behind it were revealed. Dozens of small silver horns ran along the reptilian snout, the scales reflective in the burning red light. Tightly closed eyes were bordered by ridges of spikes where eyebrows could have otherwise been.

The enormous head that rose out of the lava was at least the size of a horse and attached to a neck like a small redwood tree. The scales covering it grew larger the farther down they went, until they were the size of his hand before they disappeared back into the molten stone. On either side, about five yards back, large, flat wings rose out of the fiery pit, the leathery skin taut and mirror-like, casting shadows across the ceiling of the great chamber.

The creature's eyes slowly opened, focusing on Elias in the dull red glow of the chamber. They shone with their own light, bright blue casting a contrasting shade with the red. It was a dragon, silver-scaled and huge beyond reckoning. It had a dark black collar clamped around its neck, and an iron, eight-pointed star chained to its forehead, much like one would put decorative barding on a horse.

Elias took a step back, tightening his grip on his sword. "I've seen that symbol before, and each time, it was accompanied by someone trying to kill me."

The dragon chuckled, the noise almost deafening in the chamber. "Then you and I have something in common. Every time I see one of your type wearing it, they seem to be trying to kill me too. Though, to be fair, the sentiment is generally mutual."

Narrowing his eyes for a moment, the dragon regarded Elias. "No... you're not a man. You're an elf. A rather large one, but an elf nonetheless. You have a different smell than this lot, but I haven't forgotten the scent of mountain elves."

Elias lowered his sword. "You come from the mainland?"

Slowly, the dragon climbed halfway out of the lava, his scales still shockingly clean for being submerged in molten rock. his arms were oddly humanoid in proportion, with shoulders and elbows similar to a man's, and large, five-fingered hands, covered in fine silver scales and tipped with talons the size of short swords. Black iron manacles were attached to his wrists, just as the collar around its neck.

Leaning on its elbows, the dragon crossed his arms at the wrist, chains dragging across the black glass floor. "Yes. Yes, I was hatched on the mainland, but histories are not why you are here. What brings you into my very dangerous home, little giant?"

Elias stepped forward again. "We heard that the pirates who are terrorizing these islands were hiding a great and terrible power here, trying to bend it to their will. I wanted to come and see for myself."

The dragon spread his arms. "Well, now you have seen it. What do you plan to do?"

Elias unslung his sheath and put his sword away. "What will you do if I set you free?"

The dragon lifted a hand, and rested his chin on it. Behind him, a great tail swished back and forth in the molten stone, causing it to splash on the walls on the far side of the chamber. "I imagine I would leave this cave and try to return to the mainland. There's nothing for me here on these islands, not even vengeance. The ones who captured me have long since died, and the ones who hold me do so out of fear and ignorance. No reason to kill them for that."

Elias lifted a brow. "I thought that dragons were creatures of wanton destruction, endless greed, and a lust for gold and blood that had no rivals."

The dragon shook his head. "No... you're thinking of humans. And, well, perhaps some of my more... brash cousins."

Elias crossed his arms, regarding the dragon. "My name is Elias Stromgard. Do you have a name?"

The dragon grinned, a somewhat terrifying sight. "We do indeed have names, but they are, as would be expected from a mammal, impossible for you to pronounce. Call me Sargoth."

Elias marveled at the dragon before him. He had no idea that dragons were intelligent beings capable of conversation. Every tale he had ever heard of them cast them as feral, dangerous, man-eating monsters that only existed to destroy. "How did you get here?"

The dragon sighed. "I was captured on the mainland, about two centuries ago. They drugged a cow until it died, and I took the bait. By the time I woke, I was being dragged across a desert with these damnable chains on me. They loaded me on a boat, and brought me here." Tapping his talons against the ground, the dragon mused. "Though this cave is getting a bit cramped, it's better than being in the hold of that stinking ship. I'd much rather have flown."

"You would fly for an entire month? You can do that?"

Sargoth chuckled. "No. I've been down here for two hundred years. I doubt I could properly raid a cow field now. I'm hardly the dragon I once was. No, I would likely have to sell half my scales to have a ship built to carry me, and hope I wasn't chained again."

Elias gestured to the chains. "These chains can hold you?"

The dragon tut-tutted at Elias. "So many questions. Is that why you are really here, to just keep asking questions until the mountains are ground to dust and the islands sink under the waves?"

Elias looked down, embarrassed. "Apologies, Sargoth. I have never met a dragon before."

"And I've never met a mountain elf that doesn't recognize magical chains when he sees them."

Elias held his hands up. "May I approach?"

Sargoth laid his claws flat on the ground. "You may."

Elias approached the dragon and looked over the manacles. They were solid, as if they had been forged onto his arms, with no visible seams. He reached out to touch them, and found that they were cool to the touch, cooler than the air surrounding them. The links that were connected to the manacles ran down into the lava, but never seemed to take the heat.

"Do you know how they come off? How we can remove these chains?"

Sargoth sighed. "The only way to remove these chains is to use an amulet forged in the Abyss. It resembles an eight-pointed star in a ring, made of black iron. Like this." He tapped the emblem on his forehead with one talon, before laying his clawed hand back down on the glass floor. "They are rather common on the mainland, especially if the Felle are nearby, but out here on the islands, not as much." He inclined his forehead to Elias, letting him get a closer look at the emblem that was held onto his forehead with fine chains. "Press the amulet here, and chains will fall off." He lifted his head back up to look at Elias again. "I'd imagine that the only place you'd find a medallion like that is either on the mainland or on the island that they refer to as the Fortress."

Elias furrowed his brow. "The Fortress?"

One of the elves, who had retreated around the corner when the dragon showed himself, called forward. "The Hollow Island, Kaiwhakaora."

Elias considered the situation for a moment. "We do have three of those amulets. They were worn by assassins that tried to kill me a year ago... I kept one of them. It is with my things on my ship, the Leviathan. The other two are on Greenreef."

Sargoth leaned back, his serpentine neck coiling into an 's' shape. "Your ship is nearby?"

Elias nodded. "It is."

The dragon narrowed his eyes. "Why would you release me?"

"Because nobody deserves to live their lives in chains."

"Even though I could swallow you whole and not even have to chew?"

"You could have done so already. You haven't."

Sargoth moved his head down closer, right in front of Elias. "If you release me, what do you ask in return?"

Elias shook his head. "Nothing in return for releasing you. But if you help me destroy the pirates, and rid the island of their influence, then I will sail you back to the mainland."

Sargoth settled back, considering. "Done. I agree. Go, then, and fetch your medallion. I'll wait here." The dragon let a shadow of a smirk cross his features at the little joke, and sank back into the lava. As Elias and his companions left the cavern, all that could be seen of the dragon were his bright blue eyes, watching them disappear around the bend in the tunnel.

~   ~   ~

The light of the day hurt his eyes as Elias stepped out of the cavern. He had been underground for maybe half an hour, but his eyes had already accustomed to the torchlight. The sun was well over the horizon, and he knew that he had overstayed his time limit. He should have been sailing back to Port Greenreef and the friendly islands well before now.

There was a shout from up ahead, and one of the warriors pointed to the north. A fleet of eight ships were sailing fast towards the Leviathan and the Iron Oar. Three were ahead of the pack, bearing down on the anchored vessels.

As he ran down the hill towards the beach, he saw the two ships from his armada draw anchor and turn towards the pirates. Delain meant to attack!

The three leading ships veered hard to port, cutting around and away from the Leviathan, which was ahead of the Iron Oar. As they turned, he could see blue skinned mariners on the deck. Those three ships were sailed by Jonas and his men! He must have captured the pirate vessels on the western coast of the island!

His heart was in his throat as he turned towards the path that led from the cliffs to the beach. There was no way he could get there in time, and the landing boat would be destroyed as soon as it came within range of the warring ships. This was a naval battle he would have to observe from the shore, as much as it killed him inside to do so.

The captured ships ran abreast of the pursuing pirate vessels, and though they were nearly a mile distant, Elias could swear he saw arrows flying back and forth between the ships. Jonas must have had those ships packed to the brim with warriors!

The Leviathan was turning towards the rising sun, making to flee, while the Iron Oar was entering the fight. As it drew close to the nearest ship, there was a flash, and splintered wood flew from the Oar; a sound like thunder was audible immediately thereafter.

The main mast of the Iron Oar fell to the side, crashing into the ship they had been engaging. Elias ran into the waves, dragging a landing boat with him. He could no longer sit on the shore and watch as his comrades were killed. He had to get out there and do something. He was vaguely aware of many hands grabbing his shoulders and armor, hauling him back towards the shore.

"Elias! No! You'll be killed!"

He shook them off like birds from a tree branch. "Our warriors are being killed right now! I have to help them!"

One of the warriors leapt out in front of him, holding his arms out wide. "No! Our warriors are slaying pirates! Our warriors are battling for their lives right now! If they fall, what honor do you do them in joining them before you avenge them?" He placed his hands on the landing ship and hauled it back towards the shore. "You must live to rally against those who would destroy our brothers!"

The waves shoved at Elias as he fought a battle with himself. The Iron Oar was settling lower in the waves as blue-skinned warriors swarmed over onto the other ship. The three ships that Jonas had captured were veering about to make another pass at the other five pirate vessels.

"What can we do? Those are our warriors out there!"

The warrior that had stopped him in the waves turned towards the mounting battle at sea. "Now we trust in the gods, Elias. Now we trust in our brothers."

~   ~   ~

The sun was high in the sky, beating down on Elias and the ten elves who sat on the beach with him in silence. There was no trace of the Leviathan; she had sailed east while the battle had raged between the pirates and the ships captured by Jonas and his elves. The Iron Oar had sunk, having been blasted by cannons mounted on one of the pursuing ships from the Hollow Island.

Of the three ships that had turned to fight the oncoming pirates, two had been scuttled and sank. The other one had turned and fled around the north end of Ahi Maunga, due northeast. Three of the pirate ships chased it, while the other two turned around and sailed back northwest, around the Cursed Island. They hadn't even brought one ship down.

As far as he knew, Delain had gone down with the Iron Oar. Geoff would have taken command of the Leviathan in his absence. Jonas would have been on one of the ships that engaged the pirates... whether or not he was on the ship that escaped, Elias did not know.

There was no hope for a rescue; the Leviathan was too slow, and a single ship would be far too easy to pick off while they boarded. Their only hope at this point was to wait until nightfall, row towards Ahi Maunga, the Fire Mountain, and try to capture a proper sailing vessel. This is the haphazard plan that he had come up with, and he didn't like it at all.

The sky was turning red as the sun settled behind the low mountain on the Cursed Island. It had been at least half a day since they had seen a ship. They hauled the landing boat into the surf, and started the arduous task of rowing for the nearest island. Nearly twenty miles over rough water, it would not be an easy task, but it was their only chance.

No sooner had they broken past the waves of the surf than a ship rounded the southern point of the island, then another, and another, and another. They redoubled their efforts, until one of the warriors stood up, peering towards the ships.

"Those are our ships! From the south village!"

Elias himself stood, setting the ship to rocking. In the light of the setting sun, identifying the ships by design was difficult, and neither he nor the pirates flew any standard. It wasn't until he saw the blue skinned passengers gathered at the rail of the forecastle that he allowed himself to believe they were friendly.

As the ships came closer, Elias and his warriors started shouting and waving their arms. One of the vessels came closer and circled around towards them, while the other three continued east. Refugees crowded the rail, along with a fair number of painted warriors. Among them, one face Elias recognized immediately.

"Martin! Martin, thank the gods! Hurry, throw a rope down!"

Martin started shouting orders, directing the freed slaves back from the rail, while the warriors and sailors went about helping Elias and his men board the ship.

As soon as he was aboard, Martin pulled him to the side. "Elias! What happened? Why aren't you on your way back to Greenreef?"

Elias sat on a barrel, and started stripping off his armor. He had been in it for most of a day, and it was starting to wear on him. "That great power that Marl told us about, the sea elves confirmed it was still here. We searched for it and found it... it was a dragon under the mountain of the Cursed Island."

Martin passed him a waterskin, and Elias drank deeply. "When we came out of the cave after striking a deal with the dragon, the Leviathan and the Oar were under attack. We couldn't row out to fight them, we'd have been destroyed before we ever got there. The Iron Oar... she was..."

He lowered his head, for a moment, seeing the splintered wood being blasted off of the oldest ship in their fleet, hearing the thunderous explosions that marked her death. "She was destroyed. Sank by one of the pirate ships. Two of the ships that Jonas captured were sunk as well. One other fled north around Ahi Maunga. We haven't seen her since."

Martin sank down, sitting on a crate. "By all the gods and all the hells... What of Jonas? What of Delain and Geoff?"

Elias shook his head and looked up. "I do not know. The Leviathan escaped, as far as I can tell, and if Geoff captained it, then he lived. I don't know which ship Jonas sailed. He may have lived, he may have died." He looked up at Martin. "How was it that you were still here? Why weren't you already half a day's sailing away?"

Martin rested his elbows on his knees. "We ran into some trouble after Jonas had left. Nothing we couldn't handle, but a ship sailed south down the western coast. We had moored our ships in the hollow of a dead volcano just offshore. With our forces, we could have taken it, but we would have lost too many men. We had all of the slaves loaded onto our ships, but we had to wait until after the pirates made landfall, searched the village, and sailed back north. I wanted to make sure they weren't going to come back around the island, and I wanted to accompany Jonas when he sailed through with the supply ships."

Martin was silent again. "When he never came, by late afternoon, I made the decision to sail back. We came up from the south and saw debris in the water, then spotted you." With that, he stood and marched towards the helm. Pushing the helmsman off of it, he brought the ship about and turned it east. Elias climbed up the ladder to the helm on top of the aftcastle.

"Where are you taking us, Martin?"

"Greenreef. Our mission is not complete until we get these elves home." He set his jaw. "It's what Jonas would have done. Complete the mission."

Elias watched the man for a moment, then nodded. "I agree. Let's bring these elves home. We can regroup at the Port."

~   ~   ~

They sailed east, the four ships ranging out in a line, single file. On the second day, they caught up to the Leviathan. The enormous ship had a much deeper draft than the smaller ships, and sailed much slower.

Elias boarded a landing boat and transferred to the Leviathan, his armor in tow. Geoff was captaining it, as he had assumed, and was overjoyed to see him. He rushed up to Elias and took his giant hand in both of his own.

"Elias! Thank the gods, I thought you were slain!"

Elias shook his hand. "No... not me. Have you seen any of the other ships?"

Geoff led the way to Elias's chambers. "Not since nightfall last night. They were sailing fast, and rightly so. After the attack in front of the Cursed Island, I was afraid that they would come after us. We've got enough warriors to defend ourselves if we were boarded by one ship, but not two or three, and if they turned their cannons on us, then we'd all be on the bottom of the sea right now."

"But nobody followed?"

Geoff shook his head. "Nobody but you." He opened the door for Elias, and followed him in. Three blue skinned elves, refugees from the slave villages, followed them in, carrying Elias's armor. They set it on the floor in front of his armor stand, and left, closing the door behind them.

Awkwardly, Geoff stood near the table. "Elias... I have to ask... Delain?"

"He was on the Iron Oar?"

Geoff looked down at the man, nodding.

"Then he is dead. The Iron Oar was sank covering the retreat of the Leviathan."

Geoff nodded again. "And Jonas?"

"I would expect the same. Two of the captured supply ships were sunk. I don't know which one he sailed on, but one of them escaped. It was being pursued by two other vessels when we last saw it disappear north around Ahi Maunga, the Fire Mountain."

Geoff sat down in one of the chairs, his face pale. "So Jonas and Delain are lost. Many warriors are lost. Most of the supplies are lost." He looked up at Elias. "How can we win this war?"

Elias drew back his chair and sat down himself. "We must regroup at the Port. We've more than enough ships to sail immediately upon the Hollow Island, and the Cursed Island no longer produces supplies for the pirates. Within two weeks, they'll be eating each other behind their walls. It will take that long to resupply and recover from this strike. In a month, this war will be over."

Geoff clasped his hands together, looking at the marks on the map, where their plan had been laid out. "How can you be sure?"

Elias looked down at the black iron medallion in his hand, turning it so that the red gem in the center caught the light. "Because now, we have a dragon on our side."

~　　~　　~

1ˢᵗ Waning Summer Moon, Year 4369

The choppy water of the straight between the western islands and Greenreef herself was a welcome sight. After four days of sailing, Elias was ready to set his feet on the sands of the Seagate and put the fighting behind himself for a moment. He needed to see if Jonas had survived; a part of him refused to believe he wasn't on the third ship. He would either be at Seagate, waiting for him, at the northern village being set up for the refugees, or in Port Greenreef, overseeing the aftermath of the voyage.

The four ships had accompanied the Leviathan since they had met up two days ago, and they had made good time despite the slower speed of the giant ship. It took them four hours to sail across the straight, but they were at Greenreef at last. The familiar sight of the western coast was a relief to Elias. Soon, he would be home, and would see Coral again.

Home, he thought to himself. His heart ached from the last time he had seen her. He hoped that she could forgive him for his actions that night, when his hurt overcame his heart.

The ridge that protected Seagate from the brunt of the sea came into view, and his heart skipped a beat in his chest. Black plumes of smoke rose over the arm of the volcanic mountain. While he had been away fighting the pirates, Greenreef had been attacked.

Chapter Twenty-Two

1ˢᵗ Waning Summer Moon, Year 4369

Wreckage floated in the sheltered lagoon at Seagate, and around the steep stone cliffs that dropped into the sea. The tide had pushed it in through the archway, and the stone ridges had kept it there, floating and bobbing about until it found the shore. The landing boat Elias was on rocked and bumped about as splintered wood and debris were pushed out of the way. He recognized it as fragments of the ship that had been set outside of the Seagate to guard it while he was away.

Whatever had happened here had been explosive, violent, and no more than a day ago. Most of the huts on the beach were reduced to cinders, burned or torn to the ground. The carefully spaced and cared for palm trees that had once offered shade now lay on the ground, either charred or hacked down. The entire village was reduced to rubble.

Farther up the beach, the lodge was a smoking, gutted ruin. The front half had collapsed, leaving only most of the rear section standing, its skeletal support beams like blackened ribs jutting out of the sand. Fires still burned on the slope of the mountain behind the village, pushing the jungle back even farther and leaving nothing but ashes in its wake.

The shore was littered with bodies as Elias and his crew ran the boat into the sand. He jumped out at a full run, leaving the other elves to pull the boat out of the waves. Seawater splashed up to his waist unheeded as he forged towards the scene of the battle. Warriors and villagers lay slain on the sand and in the surf, some of the bodies floating in the waves. Elias could see no survivors.

"Coral!" he cried, running towards the lodge. "Coral!" As he approached, one of the supporting timbers collapsed, dropping a significant portion of the rear of the building. Ash, smoke, and sparks billowed upwards as the flames crackled back to life. He reached the front steps to find an elf curled up, face down on the stone, blood pooling in front of him. Gently, he rolled the elf over, to find that it was Marl.

The older elf was breathing shallowly, his eyes closed, when Elias moved him. He winced in pain, catching his breath, and his eyes flickered open.

"Elias... Thank the gods you're here!"

Elias lifted the seer, causing him to cry out, and carried him away from the burning ruins of the lodge. When they were safely away, he set him down under one of the few palm trees still standing.

"What happened here?"

Marl struggled into a different position, gasping from the pain. He had a large, ragged wound on his stomach and a broad cut along his face, running from his forehead, across his nose, and onto his cheek. "It wasn't the pirates. They were men, from the mainland. These were dressed entirely in black, like the assassins you killed last year."

Marl paused, catching his breath. "Orcs and men, and an ogre. They landed just northwest of here in the night, and struck while the village slept."

Elias did his best to remain calm, but panic was gripping him. "Marl, where's Coral? Where did Coral go?"

"I sent Jayd to get her from your hut. The attackers were closing on the lodge, and they needed to escape. I haven't seen her since. They were supposed to go to the temple on the mountain..." He looked up the slope. The fires that had burned the jungle were almost two-thirds of the way up the mountain. If they hadn't made it to the temple, they would have been burned over.

Elias called over one of the warriors, who was looking for more survivors. He instructed him to stay with Marl until Geoff could arrive to treat the seer's wounds. Once he was sure Marl would be cared for, he sprinted across the beach towards the site of the hut he had shared with Coral. Smoke and wreckage obscured his path, but it didn't take him long to find it amongst the ruins.

It was destroyed. The platform that the three-sided structure had been built on was nothing more than a few charred posts barely sticking out of a bed of embers and burned wood. On the sand, half burned, was Coral's embroidered skirt of white leather, and the silver and pearl necklace that Jayd was fond of wearing.

Elias's mind raced. There were no bodies nearby, none that looked like Jayd or Coral in view. There were definitely signs of a struggle, as the sand was tossed and turned by footprints, some of them enormous. Those would be the orcs or the ogre, more than likely, but the dry sand was a horrible medium to preserve tracks. Searching over the area for a moment, he was able to find a pair of smaller tracks, barefoot, that led southeast through the village, towards the ridge that separated Seagate from Port Greenreef, and the pens where the sea elves kept their herds of swine.

The larger tracks followed them.

Elias broke off at a dead run, leaping over burned wood, fallen trees, bodies – whatever got in his way. He thought his heart would explode in his chest. The sound around him felt like it was dimming; all he could hear was his own ragged breath and thundering pulse in his ears.

He crested the low sand dune that separated the animal pens from the rest of the village and froze in his tracks.

Tied to each one of the tall, thick posts that made up the enclosure was an elf. From what he could see, they were all females, at least a hundred of them. Stripped naked and tied by the wrists to the posts, some had their arms high, facing away from the fence, while others were tied low, curled into fetal positions.

Two warriors crested the hill beside him, and let out a cry. Elias ran down the hill, followed and then passed by the faster elves, drawing a dagger from his waistband to cut the captives loose. By the time he got there, though, he saw that most of the women had been killed, their throats cut, or run through the heart or stomach. He started searching, frantically, for survivors.

Every elven maiden he reached was carefully cut free and laid on the ground. His heart pounded every time he approached one of the bloody bodies, praying that it wouldn't be Coral.

The fifth elf he came to was Jayd. Her wrists had been tied high over her head, and her ankles spread apart. Blood ran down her legs, and hundreds of cuts covered her stomach, chest, and neck. He went to cut her wrists free when her eyes snapped open and she gasped.

"Elias! Elias, they came for us! They came for you!"

He lowered her to the ground, laying her on her back. She started struggling. "No! No, Elias, Coral! You have to save her! You have to stop them!"

"Jayd! Jayd, calm down! They're gone! They've been gone!"

"Where is Coral!? She was tied next to me! Where is she!?" She looked back at the fence and froze, then let out a single, loud wail. Jayd's screams pierced Elias's ears, bringing his panic back. He looked back at the fence, where Jayd was looking, and his heart shattered.

There was Coral, her leather halter cut loose and hanging askew, stained red with her blood. She had been tied with her wrists and legs spread on the fence next to Jayd, and like her mother, blood ran down her legs. Her face was bruised and beaten, her fair blue skin was covered in cuts and abrasions. One of her arms was twisted at a strange angle, obviously broken.

Through her stomach was a long sword; not a cutlass or saber, but a straight, double-edged weapon favored by soldiers. It had been driven into her just below her breasts and out her back. A black medallion, the same eight-pointed star with a red stone set into the center, hung from the handle.

Numbly, Elias approached her body. "No... no... no no no no no no no..." he whispered, taking her face in his hands, lifting it gently. "No, you can't be dead, no..." Her half-lidded eyes were unfocused and no breath came from her lips.

Carefully, slowly, he drew the sword from her stomach with one hand, cradling her head with the other. "Shh, shh, it'll be okay, don't worry, Geoff will be here soon." Turning to face the village, he screamed. "Geoff! Geoff, I need you!" His throat hurt from the effort. He was vaguely aware of Jayd's continued screaming, as well as the cries of some of the other women who had survived the assault and were being cut down.

Elias dropped the sword and medallion into the sand and cut Coral's bonds. He cradled her in his arms as he sank to the sand. "Geoff!" he screamed again, as the man crested the hill. "Get over here now, she needs you! I need you!"

The young man sprinted up, carrying his bag of healing supplies, but stopped short. He dropped the bag and took a few steps closer. He saw Elias cradling Coral's body, tears streaming down his face, and fell to his knees in front of the giant elf.

"Elias... she's gone. I can't bring her back from the dead."

Elias wept, burying his face in the crook of her neck, next to her head and shoulder. Throwing his head back, a wordless, keening cry tore out of his throat, loud enough to be heard throughout the whole of Seagate and beyond. It continued until his breath ran out and the sound strangled itself in his lungs, then he took a deep breath and did it again.

His last word to her had been goodbye. The last thing she had seen was him walking away from her. He had never told her he loved her, he had never told her he was sorry, and now he never could.

~　　~　　~

2nd Waning Summer Moon, Year 4369

Elias stood on the beach, looking out through the Scagate. Marl stood next to him, his stomach wrapped in linen bandages, a strip of gauze across his face. There had been only a handful of survivors, mostly the women who had been tied to the fences and left for dead. Marl was the only male who had survived.

Elias, along with the rest of the crew of his ship, had lain the bodies of all of the fallen on the beach in preparation for their burials at sea. In some situations, they would have instead held a funeral pyre, but there were far too many dead, and most of the wood had already been burned.

An envoy had been sent to Port Greenreef, to see if they had been attacked. As far as Elias could tell, Seagate was the only target. From what he had been able to gather from Marl and Jayd, as incoherent as her words were, it hadn't been a pirate envoy as they understood it; it had been a detachment of the Felle Army. The medallion left on the handle of the sword that had pierced Coral was proof of that, as well as the presence of ogres and orcs. Where they had gone, nobody could say. No ships had been seen leaving the island, but it was a big island. There was no telling from where they came or where they went.

Elias stared to the south, watching the waves rolling across the decimated beach. What had once been a paradise was now a graveyard, spoiled by the slaughter that had taken place.

"I should have been here. I should never have sailed for the Cursed Island."

Marl leaned on his staff. "That may be true. Maybe if you and our warriors had been here, they would never have attacked. Perhaps they would have been repelled." He sighed and slouched. "Maybe they would have brought more men, more soldiers. Maybe you would have been killed too. Maybe I would have lost my wife as well as my daughter. Maybe I would have been killed."

He shook his head. "Fuck maybe." It was the first time he had ever heard Marl use that word. "Now all that remains is retribution. I know that you were successful in your attack against the Cursed Island. Tell me about it."

Elias recounted the battle on the island, as well as what he had learned of Jonas's efforts in the southern village. He told Marl about the dragon in the caves, and the naval combat where they lost the supply ships and the Iron Oar.

"All told," he said, "we lost about a third of our warriors. We rescued almost seven thousand slaves from that island."

Marl shook his head. "In the game of numbers, this is still a victory."

Looking down at Marl, Elias narrowed his eyes slightly. "How can you say that?"

Marl looked up at Elias, meeting his eyes. "Do you not think that every mother, every wife, every son or daughter, every father of every elf that has fallen during this war feels as you do? When they learn that their son, their brother or husband, their father will never come home? This village is not the only one to have been attacked in this last year, Elias."

"I know that."

"Then you know that the pain you feel now is the pain that my people have felt since the men from the mainland came here."

Elias turned back to the sea. "So. Now that we have taken as much of a blow as we have. What do you suggest we do now?"

"We destroy them. Every last one of them. Nobody survives. No prisoners. No bounties. No trades. No escapees. Everyone dies."

Elias nodded. "Those are my thoughts exactly."

There was a cry from behind them, and Elias and Marl turned to see what it was. A group of elves was clustered around Coral's body. Elias ran up the sloped sand, leaving Marl behind. He pushed through the crowd to see Jayd laying over Coral's body, a woven shawl over her shoulders. She cradled Coral's head in her hands and wept. Rising to her feet, she turned on Elias and Marl.

"This is your fault! You did this!" She drew a long obsidian knife and pointed it at Marl. "You convinced her to force the prophecy! You couldn't even wait for the very gods you serve to deliver us a warrior who would save us!" She turned to Elias, pointing the knife at him. "When she came to you to tell you the truth, you scorned her! You pushed her away and went away to fight your war! You used her body and broke her heart!"

Marl stepped forward, "Jayd, listen to yourself! You don't know what you're saying!"

Jayd brought the knife back to bear on Marl, making him stop short of her. "I know exactly what I'm saying. I would rather follow my daughter to the afterlife than live here in a world where people discard lives like pieces in a game!"

She turned the knife in her hand.

Marl rushed forward. "Jayd, no!" he screamed as she plunged the knife into her chest.

Elias stood, shocked, as Marl seized Jade's hands, pulling the knife from her chest. The seer caught Jayd's body as she fell, dropping to his knees and cradling her head in his right hand while he pressed his left over her wound, trying to staunch the flow of blood. When Jayd's breath finally went still, he did not wail or cry out, instead weeping quietly into the sand.

~   ~   ~

Elias and Marl sat side by side in front of the fire, Geoff across from them. The night was cold on the beach, with no huts to stop the wind and no trees to slow it as it blew west along the beach. The scouts they had sent to Port Greenreef had returned. The city had been attacked as well, but had fared much better. The security force there had been able to repel the attackers, and the ships of the Port Authority had joined in the battle with the ship Elias had left behind.

Jenna had taken command of the defense efforts and led the warriors at the port to victory. There were some minor repairs needed due to fire and arrows, and they had lost three score warriors, but they had made the Felle soldiers pay dearly for them.

There had been no sign of Jonas; he had not captained the ship that had escaped the battle. The elves on the north coast had started settling in, retreating from the coast and camping along a river where they could still reach the sea with their shallow canoes.

Marl had been right. Number for number, life for life, the operation had been a success.

The fire crackled in the darkness, the silence of the beach only broken by the sound of the waves. Jayd and Coral had been buried at sea at sunset. There were no flowers left to adorn their bodies, no wine or honey to anoint them with. Marl spoke the words that his people spoke, but Elias did not hear them. All he could see was Coral's face, shrouded as it was, sinking into the water. He memorized every curve, every line. The way her jet black hair framed her cheeks, her fine cheekbones, her delicate nose, large, doelike eyes.

It was Marl who broke the silence. "When will we strike the Hollow Island?"

Elias held his gaze in the flames. "As soon as we have enough blasting powder to fill a ship with. We need about three tons."

Marl nodded. "The alchemists have been working since you left, almost ten days ago. They have a good amount of it, but not that much. They need more time."

Geoff tossed a chunk of wood onto the fire. "Time enough to let the pirates starve a little more. They sank two-thirds of what they had stored up, and we took all of their slaves."

Elias nodded. "I have an idea that will make it easier to fill the barrels. We need fragments of obsidian, the size of a fist." He stirred the coals with a stick, causing sparks to roll into the night sky. "We break them into shards and mix them throughout the powder. When the barrels explode, it should throw the stone through the air. Anyone caught in the path will be cut."

Geoff looked up at Elias. "Bloody hell, Redwood. That... that would cause some devastation."

Elias nodded. "No survivors. No prisoners. No bounties. All of them die."

He turned to the side and took his bedroll, which he had brought from the Leviathan before he sent it on to rendezvous with the rest of the elves. "In the morning, I'm going to Port Greenreef. I assume the Slingstone is still moored there. It's our fastest ship now. I will sail to the Cursed Island, and free the dragon. I will return here with him... that should give the alchemists another week and some days to complete their task. I want as many assistants as they need to help them."

He lay the bedroll out near the fire. "I leave as soon as the sun clears the horizon in the morning. Who is coming with me?"

Geoff nodded. "I will."

Marl spun his staff in his hands. "I will, as well."

Elias looked over at him. "Are you sure? You're no warrior."

"Don't underestimate me, son. There are more ways to fight than with steel or stone if the gods allow it. Right at this moment, I do not care what the gods do and do not allow."

Elias nodded. "As you will, then."

Elias lay down, and pulled the blanket over himself. Sleep was faster in coming than he thought it would be; his body was exhausted, but his dreams gave him no rest that night.

~   ~   ~

The view of Port Greenreef from the ridge overlooking the city was a sorry sight indeed. Though the level of destruction was nowhere near the totality of what happened at the Seagate, smoke still rose from several piles of rubble that were once buildings. The tavern where Elias and Coral had stayed when she was not at Seagate had taken heavy damage, having been gutted by fire; the stone walls were still standing, but had been scorched and blackened by fire. One of the docks was broken and submerged in the bay, and several ships were moored to the remaining piers for repairs.

As he had hoped, the Slingstone was anchored out in the bay, seeming relatively untouched. Further out, past the boundaries of the harbor, the Leviathan was anchored, looking like the behemoth it was named after.

Men and elves were bustling about, cleaning up the damage and starting on repairs. As Elias, Marl, and Geoff approached the docks, they found Jenna and Martin supervising the efforts, directing the workers in the distribution of the scant remaining materials. They were in the process of sending a team of lumberjacks into the forest to hunt for trees that could be cut into beams for rebuilding when Jenna noticed Elias approaching.

She stopped midsentence, setting down the parchment she held. "Elias. Welcome back."

"I wish I could say that it is good to be back."

She nodded, looking down at the list in front of her. "I heard what happened in Seagate. By the time we were able to send anyone to check on the village, you were already there." She looked back at him, her face weary. "I am sorry, my lord. I couldn't save her while you were away."

He shook his head, setting a hand on her shoulder. "It is no fault of anyone here. All we can do now is finish our task."

She set her hand on top of his, squeezing it gently. "As you wish. What is our next move?"

Elias filled her in on the plan, the dragon, and his upcoming voyage. She listened in silence, taking notes with a quill and parchment. When he had finished, she looked over the new list.

"We have these resources to spare, enough food and water for the journey. How many men will you be taking with you?"

"Myself, Marl, and Geoff, and well as twenty-two volunteers."

"Twenty-one," Martin spoke up from the side, where he had been listening. "They killed Jonas. I'm going with you."

Jenna handed the list to a dock worker, and instructed him to start the preparations. "Twenty. I'm going with you as well. This lot here already know what they are to do, and the Port Authority here can supervise the rebuilding as well as I could. I'm tired of sitting here on land." She looked up. "Besides. I have a feeling that we'll find someone there that needs me."

Elias furrowed his brow. "What do you mean? We took every elf off of that island."

She shook her head. "I couldn't explain it if I tried. But this is a voyage I need to go on." She looked up at him again. "You and Jonas and the rest of the men left me behind on every single voyage you've gone on. All due respect, Elias, but it won't happen again. You're not going to leave me behind like some wilting flower."

Elias nodded. "As you will, milady."

She chuckled mirthlessly. "I'm not a lady."

"And I'm not a lord."

She smirked. "You are here. When will you accept that?"

Elias frowned. "When I am done with these pirates, I'm done here. I'm going back to the mainland. There's nothing left for me here. I need to go somewhere and be nothing for a while."

Jenna's halfhearted smirk softened, and she looked sad. "You will never be nothing, Elias. You've got too much greatness in you."

Elias shrugged. "Right now, I just want to kill pirates and Felle. I'll figure out the rest when I'm done."

She nodded again. "You'll have plenty of time for that on your trip to the mainland." She looked out to the sea, at the Slingstone. "Well, let's get everything loaded up. We're traveling fast and light, I take it?"

He nodded. "Very. How long until we're loaded, do you think?"

Martin turned from some dock workers. "Three hours to load the food and water we'll need. I figure you can drum up some volunteers in that time. Should be ready to cast off in four hours."

"Good. We'll meet on board then."

The five companions parted ways for the time being, going about their tasks. Their core circle was shrinking.

Chapter Twenty-Three

7th Waning Summer Moon, Year 4369

The Slingstone was not the most comfortable vessel for long voyages. It had no hold, no lower decks, no forecastle or aftcastle, just the cargo deck and oars. The wind was strong, blowing to the west, so they had no issues with speed, but the sun baked them as they skimmed over the water.

At the rate they traveled, the voyage only took three days. By the end of the first day, they passed the straight between Greenreef and the other islands. By the second day, they approached the end of the island chain before the second long straight. They sailed straight through the night, taking shifts at the helm, and by dusk on the third day, they saw the low mountain on the Cursed Island at the horizon.

The sun was well below the horizon and the moon was bright in the sky by the time they landed on the original beach where he had brought his army ashore a bit over a week before. The Slingstone was small enough that they didn't need a landing vessel, but still large enough that they couldn't run it right up to the beach. The waves were still up to Elias's thighs when he jumped over the edge and forged through the surf to the shore.

They followed the path to the top of the cliff immediately, wasting no time in waiting for the dawn. They each carried their own torch, but did not light them on the beach. Instead, they waited until they stood at the mouth of the cave. The hot air still came out of the opening like a dry wind; the twenty elven sailors milled about the opening, hesitant to enter the recesses of the earth.

Elias bid them to wait on the beach, but make no fires that could be seen by passing vessels. He lit five torches within the cave, one for himself and each of his companions that would accompany him down. Jenna, Geoff, Marl and Martin all took one.

"I've got a bad feeling about this," said Martin, looking pensively into the cave.

Geoff shrugged. "I've just got a bad feeling. I don't like being this close to the Fortress."

Jenna stepped past them. "Bad feelings or not, this is why we are here. This cave could hold the key to our victory. There is no time to waste."

Marl was quiet, holding his torch. He stood near Jenna, waiting and watching Elias.

Elias held his torch high. The flickering light illuminated the cave around them, reflecting off of the smooth obsidian walls. "I told the dragon, Sargoth, that I would free him. He will help us destroy our enemy here. Now that we know the Felle have a presence here, we'll need all the help we can get... and Sargoth could be that help." He turned to Martin and Geoff. "You can stay here on top if you like. I am going down below."

He started down the tunnel, Jenna and Marl falling in step behind him. Martin and Geoff weren't far behind, despite their initial misgivings.

The trip down seemed to be significantly faster than it had been the first time, at least to Elias. Perhaps the fact that he knew what was coming made it seem shorter. By the time the red glow of the lava pit was visible, they were all sweating from the heat. He paused at the entrance to the chamber. On the ground in front of the final turn were several charred skeletons, their flesh and clothing burned away to ashes. Several swords lay on the ground, melted against it as if they had been made of wet paper and dropped unceremoniously as their owners were slain. The weapons were all of the type favored by the pirates – basket-hilted, with single edged, slashing blades.

Elias looked back at his companions, nodding to them in reassurance before he entered the chamber. Jenna and Marl followed closely, Martin and Geoff trailing behind. Sargoth was lounging on the stone in front of the lava, his giant form sparkling in the light of their torches. He looked almost red in the darkness.

He rolled to his side, propping up his chin on his giant claws again. He moved in a very humanoid manner, Elias thought, marveling again at the sheer size of the dragon.

"So you have returned. I'll admit, I had started to wonder if you would. I suppose I just assumed that 'I'll be right back' meant the same thing, whether one was a dragon or an elf or a human."

"There were some complications... our fleet was under attack when we got outside, and the ship that held the pendant was fleeing. We didn't get back to our island for four days, and when we did, we had been attacked." He choked a bit, his memory of what he had found at the Seagate threatening to rise up, but he pushed it back down.

The dragon looked at him, tilting his head to the side. "I knew about the battle outside; I did not know about the battle at your home. I am sorry to hear that." He gestured one clawed hand towards the charred skeletons in tunnel that had entered through. "That lot chased someone in here, and threatened to kill us both. Such things don't sit well with me."

Elias looked aside at Jenna and Marl, who glanced back. There had been a survivor from the destruction of their fleet? Perhaps someone left behind on the island?

Sargoth smirked at their puzzlement. "He should be back soon. We've been helping each other out since he came here. He brings me pigs, I cook them for us. He is, apparently, about as fond of raw meat as the rest of you are." He looked up the tunnel past them, and sniffed twice. "He should be returning shortly. You may wish to step out of the tunnel... it's going to get rather hot there."

Behind them, they could hear the faint squealing of pigs, and a voice shouting at them to keep them moving. Elias stepped aside, allowing the other four to enter the chamber, and step to the side of the entrance. It wasn't long at all before several terrified pigs bolted down the tunnel towards them, hooves clattering on the smooth stone. The dragon inhaled slightly, then spat a ball of fire at the animals.

The pigs squealed in agony as the fire – then the dragon – consumed them. His head and neck moved like a snake, snapping forward and grabbing the pigs in single bites. One by one, the animals disappeared down his gullet, until just one animal lay twitching on the ground, smoldering. Sargoth reached forward and plucked off its legs, both front and back, then ate the torso and head. As he breathed searing hot breath on the remnants, they could smell the pork flash cooking.

Footsteps came up the tunnel, and the man who chased the pigs into the chamber came into view. A shade under six feet tall, he had black hair and a scruffy beard. His clothing was from the mainland, dirty and smudged with soot.

"Jonas!" Jenna cried, and ran out from behind the stone outcropping that had sheltered them from the worst of the heat. She threw her arms around the man, almost tackling him to the ground.

Jonas cursed in surprise, staggering to the side as he caught her in his arms. Elias stood in shock, watching as Jenna dragged Jonas's head down to hers for a deep kiss. Marl, Geoff, and Martin stood by, equally shocked.

Jonas finally extracted himself from Jenna's embrace. "By the gods, woman, what are you doing here?"

She shoved him, violently. "What am I doing here? What are *you* doing here? I've been going mad for a week! I thought you were dead!"

"*I* thought I was dead! I've been stuck on this island for a week and a half, feeding this dragon!"

Sargoth snorted, licking his claws clean, as Elias stepped forward. "Jonas."

Jonas turned and saw the four of them standing off to the side. "Elias! Martin, Geoff, what are you doing here? How did you get here?"

Elias filled Jonas in on the events that transpired after the battle, the journey home, and the attacks at Greenreef and the Seagate. In return, Jonas told them how he survived. After the Iron Oar was destroyed, he and the elves on his ship attacked the pirate vessels, allowing the Leviathan to escape along with the rest of the ships bearing the slaves. His ship was destroyed like the Iron Oar was, with the cannons that the pirate vessels had fitted into their ships. All hands were lost, except for him. He swam for shore, making it to the sandy beach before collapsing.

"High tide woke me up when it hit me, and I crawled farther up. I wasn't wounded, not really, except for some cuts and scrapes. There are sharks in these waters; I don't know how I survived. Maybe they were too busy feasting on our fallen..."

He shook his head. "The days here are hot. This island doesn't have the trees, nor the same size of mountain on it that Greenreef does, so it doesn't get the same rain. There's a spring not far from the mouth of the cave, and I used the cave for a shelter. Pirate ships have been circling this island for days, so I needed a place to hide. I guess they saw my campfire."

Sargoth chuckled. "I had smelled him for days. He didn't reek of fermented wheat or corn. When he came running through, I knew he wasn't with the ones who had me chained here." He held up his wrists. "Still chained here, to that point. In any case, when he saw me he ducked to the side, and I... greeted those who were chasing him in a fitting manner." The dragon inclined his head towards the charred remains at the entrance of the chamber. "I think they honestly thought I wouldn't burn them. No, I simply wouldn't eat them." He picked his dagger-like teeth with a claw. "I have standards, after all."

Jonas sat against the back wall, Jenna sitting close to him, his arm around her waist. "We had an arrangement, I bring him pigs, he cooks them for me. We keep each other company, and he doesn't eat me."

Sargoth snorted again, raising a horned eyebrow ridge. "I said I have standards. Some may say your kind taste like pork, but I disagree."

Jonas chuckled. "Aye, fair enough. Anyhow, he told me to sit tight, that he figured you would be back, and I sat tight. The pirates have more or less stopped patrolling this island... it no longer brings them food or repairs their vessels. However..." He looked over at Elias. "I have seen many ships sailing in from the south. It looks like they've called in their forces, one way or another. While I've been here, I've counted no less than ten ships come by, and that's just between here and the Fire Mountain. Who knows how many have come in from the west."

Sargoth drummed his claws against the obsidian floor, like knives tapping on glass. "Not to put too fine of a point on it, but I will say that being chained up in here for a century or two does sort of drag on, especially when the end is in sight." The dragon tapped the emblem on his forehead. "If you release me and take me to the mainland, as per our deal, I'll help you destroy the residents of the Fortress. That works for both of us."

Elias pushed off of the wall where he had been leaning, listening to Jonas. "Yes, of course. I should have done that right away. My apologies." He reached into a pouch hanging from his belt, and removed the medallion he had brought with him from the Leviathan. He held it out to Sargoth. "Here is what I promised."

Sargoth shook his head. "I cannot do it. You must release me." He lowered his head, setting his chin on the ground, his body sliding into the pit of lava. There was a hissing sound as he did so, and the smell of hot metal rose from the molten stone. "Press the medallion against the insignia on the lock between my eyes. Make sure the chain is coming from the point that you put towards the top."

Elias slowly approached the dragon, whose head was as tall as a horse, though it was sitting on the ground. The chains ran on either side of his eyes, and around behind his jaw, hooked behind his thorny spikes. The clasp between his eyes had the same eight-pointed star insignia, but upon closer inspection, it was indented in the same shape as the medallion, with a notch on top for the chain. Gently, he set his left hand on Sargoth's snout to steady himself, reached up, and pressed the medallion into the socket.

The medallion instantly grew hot, so hot that Elias could hear the sizzle as it scorched his fingers. He jerked his hand back, shaking the heat away, which was harder than it would seem, even in the heat of the room. The medallion flashed bright red, and melted, pouring out of the indentation. The red heat spread to the rest of the chains, and they too slowly started melting off, first at the indented clasp, and then spreading to the rest. It fell off like putty, liquefying on the ground. The manacles on the dragon's arms also started to glow red, melting off and sliding back into the lava. Sargoth pulled himself out of the pit and onto the stone floor entirely, and Elias could see truly how massive the dragon truly was. Not counting his tail, he was at least forty-five feet long, from his nose to his haunches, with his tail at least that long.

Sargoth's wings stayed tightly clenched to his back, making him rather slender and somewhat smaller than the circumference of the tunnel leading to the chamber they were in. "If you don't mind, it's been a long time since I've seen the sky. I'm going to step out for a moment." Slowly at first, then with an increasing speed and urgency, the dragon moved towards the tunnel and through it, his claws digging into the stone, leaving long, deep scratches in the volcanic glass.

Elias looked between the other occupants of the room, each of which was sitting back against the walls, having given the dragon all the space he needed to vacate the chamber. "I think we had better follow him."

They made their way up the tunnel to the surface, Elias and Marl leading the way, Jonas and Jenna behind, Martin and Geoff bringing up the rear. The night was still dark when they reached the cool open air, refreshing after the stifling heat of the volcanic caverns. Sargoth was perched on the cliffs by the sea, his nose up, his tail extended behind him. The small group walked down the path that had been freshly cleared by the dragon's passage.

As they approached, Sargoth spread his wings. Elias had never seen them completely unfurled, and was struck again by the sheer size of them. Easily a hundred feet from wingtip to wingtip, the span was incredible, almost half the length of the Leviathan itself. There was a sound like timbers snapping and groaning, and Elias realized it was the dragon's joints.

"Oh, I haven't been able to do that in so long..." Sargoth breathed, his words ending in a rumble of satisfaction. "I need to fly." With that, he pushed off of the cliff, his wings catching the air as he dropped.

Elias stood on the cliff as the rest of his group approached from behind. The dragon was a silhouette against the stars, the moonlight reflecting off of his silver scales as he wheeled and looped above the water.

"Someone is bound to see that," Martin said from Elias's left.

"Let them see. We're going to burn them all into the waves. When we're done, every single pirate in these islands will be dead or so afraid to come back, they will consider this place cursed." Elias set his jaw, watching Sargoth turn back and forth, gliding on the tropical air currents. Soon, very soon, this war would come to an end.

~   ~   ~

Sargoth kept pace with the Slingstone as they sailed, but the progress was slow going. Two hundred years underground hadn't kept the dragon in peak physical condition, but the winds were favorable. They had to stop at each island for him to rest, so the passage back to Port Greenreef took five days rather than the three it had taken before. They took this opportunity to notify the settlements on each island that they should relocate to the main island of Greenreef, Rapa Matomato. It was considered safer if they weren't spread out amongst the islands, as several other major settlements had been struck as well, and a few more ships had been lost.

They paused at Seagate for Sargoth to land; it had been decided that a nearly one hundred foot long dragon walking about Port Greenreef might not be the best idea for a population that had just been attacked. As Elias and his crew pulled away from the arch, Sargoth perched on the Seagate, watching them go. There were plenty of wild pigs running around, now that the herds kept by the sea elves there had been set loose during the raid, so Sargoth would have plenty to eat. Elias couldn't bring himself to disembark. He had made a decision to never return to the ruins of the village at Seagate; there was far too much pain there for him. He would keep his residence in the captain's quarters of the Leviathan.

It was four hours' sail from there to Port Greenreef. Elias spent the trip going over the plan. They would rally their forces from every island on the way. This battle was going to be held mostly at sea. The plan was to obliterate the Fortress in one strike with the explosive ship. It was the same tactic that the pirates had used against them when sinking the Papaya's Vengeance, Jonas's ship, during the battle where they scuttled the Leviathan. This time, however, it would be scaled up enough that the explosion should obliterate the structures that had been built in the inside the defunct volcano.

However, all of the ships that had been called in would be anchored around the island as a defense, so they would need to cut a pathway to their gigantic gates first. Luckily, if there was a strong westward wind, they should be able to tie the rudder into place and sail the ship directly into the gates, and hopefully through them before Sargoth set it on fire.

They had captured enough cannons that they could outfit each ship with ten of them, which wasn't much, but enough that they could cause significant damage while Sargoth caused chaos from the sky. A dragon turned the tide significantly in their favor, even with the added forces Jonas had seen sailing past the Cursed Island. Though, by all estimates, there could be as many as thirty ships waiting for them.

The forces of Greenreef had been significantly depleted during the raid on the Cursed Island... they had lost many warriors and a number of ships. Of the ten ships that had sailed east, nine came back, and one more had been captured. However, in the raids that had occurred while they were away, they had lost five more ships, one at each island. This brought their total down to thirteen.

Thirteen against as many as thirty. This battle was going to be bloody indeed, but they did have their secret weapons. The explosive ship should take out a good portion of the pirate fleet, as well as anything left inside the Hollow Island, but that lowered their active fighting vessels to twelve.

Elias stared out across the waves, consuming his mind with thoughts of the upcoming battle. Even seeing the vibrant green of the jungle split by the scorched remnants of the fire that had torn the foliage in half was enough to set his stomach into aching. Every time he had a quiet moment, she came into his mind. He couldn't even think her name without his throat closing up and his eyes burning.

She had opened her heart to him, had come clean to him, and he wasn't there to protect her. He wasn't an idiot; he knew what they had done to her first. Then they had driven a sword right through her stomach, killing her and their child. Maybe she had begged for mercy, maybe she had tried to tell them she was pregnant, so they would let her live. Instead, they butchered her like an animal.

He gritted his teeth, pushing the pain away and replacing it with fury. He would show no mercy when they attacked the Hollow Island. There would be no survivors. There would be no prisoners.

~　　~　　~

New Grain Moon, Year 4369

It had been two weeks since the attack on Seagate. The final preparations were being made, and almost every sea elf in the island chain was on Greenreef. The logistics of managing that many people boggled Elias's mind, but Marl had it mostly under control. There were several other village sites that had gone long unused on the biggest of the islands, but the influx of elves filled them beyond capacity. There were some squabbles, some disputes, but all of them were handled in a just and peaceable manner.

Marl set up a small council of elders, one from each island, that would govern if he was killed during the upcoming battle. Elias tried to insist that he should stay behind, but Marl would have nothing of it.

"There is nothing left here for me. I do not hear the whispers of the gods anymore, and none of my bloodline will take my place. I still feel them guiding me, but I do not hear them. I am no longer a speaker for the gods."

They stood on the end of a pier, looking out over the bay, which was filled to capacity with ships being readied for war. Elias looked down at Marl, who stood next to him. "Who will speak for the gods then?"

Marl shrugged. "That is not for me to say. Perhaps I have lost favor with them. Perhaps I have lost faith. Perhaps they speak to nobody now. I don't know."

Elias nodded. "Are you sure you wish to come with us?"

Marl gazed out to sea, not looking at Elias. "You couldn't keep me off of that ship. I will accompany you on the Leviathan. I will need two more days to prepare. You can pick me up outside of the Seagate as you pass."

Elias set his hand on Marl's shoulder. "You will have those two days." The preparations would be done the next day, but this was a concession he would make for the shaman, who seemed even older than he was as of late. Elias understood that feeling perfectly. "Perhaps we can both fill the holes within ourselves with the blood of our enemies."

Marl shook his head again. "Remember that you become whatever it is that you fill yourself with. If you fill yourself with death, you become death. If you fill yourself with love, you become love."

Elias stood quietly for a moment. "I never told her that I loved her."

"She knew."

"That makes it hurt even more."

"That's how you know it was real."

Marl set his hand on Elias's arm, patting him twice, before turning and walking back towards the shore. Elias stayed at the end of the pier, watching the landing boats load the ships with supplies; food and weapons, water and medical supplies. Barrels and barrels and barrels of blasting powder, more than he had ever seen.

He inhaled deeply, willing himself to keep standing. He hadn't slept a full night since Coral's death; he was exhausted, and every time his mind grew quiet, it was filled with her. It made him feel terrible that only now that she was gone, his heart and mind were filled with her. If only he had been there, if only he had been at the village to protect her.

He gripped the post at the end of the pier, and forced his pain away again.

Two days. In two days, he would be on his way to vengeance.

Chapter Twenty-Four

2ⁿᵈ Waxing Grain Moon, Year 4369

The Leviathan lay anchored outside the arch at Seagate, waiting for Marl to come out to them. They had arrived early in the morning, and it was nearing noon. Thankfully, the sea air was cool on this day, the sky overcast. Summer was beginning to release its grip on the islands, and the cooler air of autumn could be felt rolling over the waves – not cold by any means, but without the warm humidity of the summer.

In the year that he had been here, Elias had noted the consistency of the weather; they had a wet season and a wetter season, but it seldom got what he would consider cold. Snow would occasionally fall on top of the mountain, but the steam from the hot lake in the caldera kept it from sticking for too long.

The entirety of Elias's fleet of warships was anchored with him, all thirteen ships filled with warriors. Each ship had at least a dozen iron balls cast for each cannon, and was stocked with enough powder to fire them.

Elias was in his quarters, reviewing the battle map when there was a knock at the door. The doorknob turned, and Geoff stuck his head in. "Elias? There's a canoe coming in."

Elias stood, pushing away from the table. "Excellent. Is Marl on board?"

"I couldn't tell. There's five elves... one of them is dressed all in white, the others are warriors."

He accompanied Geoff to the rail, where Martin, Jenna, and Jonas stood, looking back to land. A large canoe made its way through the choppy water, with two blue-skinned warriors rowing in the front, and two more in the back, with a single white wrapped figure in the middle. The figure's head was covered in a white hood and mantle, and at this distance Elias could only just make out the blue and red embroidery on the leather, but not the design.

"I'm going to assume that is him. Prepare to take on passengers, and send the signal for the rest of the ships to set sail."

Martin pushed away from the rail, and headed to the aftcastle to sound the signal horn. Geoff threw the rope and plank ladder over the side as the canoe pulled up alongside the ship, and the occupants climbed up.

The white wrapped figure was the third up the ladder, after the warriors on either side. Its build and stature were the same as Marl's, but his skin was deep blue, whereas Marl always hid his skin from the sun, never letting it darken. Now that he was this close, Elias could see that the white wrappings were linen bandages, covering fresh cuts. They weren't bleeding through yet, but there was an orange tinge under them, in large, swirling patterns like the warriors painted on their skin before battle.

The figure drew back the hood, and it was indeed Marl, but not as he was when Elias last saw him. His skin was darkened to the same blue that Coral's had been, the same color the warriors had, but his face was covered in half-healed scars, intricate swirls and points that had been cut into his skin. His hair, once long and black, was chopped off roughly, and had turned pale gray.

It was his eyes that were the most shocking. Where they had once been the same emerald green that Coral and Jayd had, his irises were now stark white, shot through with red flecks. The whites of his eyes were tinged yellow, but not like jaundice or sickness, more like the yellow of a dandelion.

Elias looked him over, shocked at his change. Marl turned around, and caught his staff, which had been tossed up to him by one of the elves in the boat. His movements weren't smooth and gentle like they once were; he moved sharp, fast, like one of the warriors.

Tao was the next over the rail, quick and agile. He had captained the ship that had escaped from the Cursed Island.

Marl held a hand out towards him. "Tao will be accompanying us. I asked him to stay behind, but he steadfastly refused."

Elias never looked away from Marl. "That seems good. We can use every warrior that we can get."

Marl's eyes met Elias's, and the younger elf was completely unnerved. "My appearance shocks you."

Elias slowly nodded. "I would be lying if I said it didn't."

Marl started unwinding the bandages on his arms. As he did, he revealed his skin, unpainted, but colored nonetheless. The cuts on his arms were of the same fashion as the cuts on his face; swirls and triangles, patterns of dots, all mostly healed scars. "I may have lost the ability to hear the gods, but they still hear me." The cuts on his flesh were much more healed than they should have been, even if they were made just after Elias had last seen him. "I may have lost my faith in them, but apparently, they still have faith in me." He chuckled mirthlessly as he unwrapped his chest. "Or they at least still have a use for me."

Every inch of his skin was covered in the fresh scars, red designs tattooed into his flesh. Some of the cuts were still open, seeping slightly, but no blood.

Jenna stood aside, next to Jonas, staring at the shaman, wide-eyed and somewhat paler than her dusky skin normally allowed her to be. "By the gods, Marl, what happened to you?"

Marl turned towards her and smiled, bowing slightly. "Don't worry, madam. Nothing happened that was against my will."

Elias stepped towards him. "Marl... I know you want to fight, but can you?"

Marl's smile disappeared. "You may fight wearing steel and swinging a sword that has no right to be as large as it us, but I fight in other ways." Green electricity crackled from his hand along his staff, and a very slight hum grew, then faded as quickly. "Not everything that we learn while serving the gods is benign."

Elias looked him over again, nodding slightly. "I can believe that." He held out his hand. "I look forward to fighting alongside you."

Marl sidestepped Elias's hand, and embraced him instead. Elias leaned down to make it easier, and hugged him back.

"As do I, Kaiwhakaora. Let's shed some blood."

~   ~   ~

6th Waxing Moon, Year 4369

The Leviathan led the fleet as it crossed the final channel between Taonga Tama and Ahi Maunga, just before dawn. Each island had been deserted as they passed, all of the sea elves having convened at Rapa Matomato. It was somewhat surreal, knowing that each vibrant, green island they sailed past was completely deserted, even if it was temporary.

Twelve ships followed behind, eleven of them filled to capacity with warriors, as the Leviathan and the Iron Oar had been when they took the Cursed Island. The twelfth rode low in the water, sailing as slow as the Leviathan, loaded as heavy as it was with the powder barrels. The prow had been reinforced with more beams and iron plates, which made the ship heavier, but much better for ramming. The ram that had been affixed to the Slingstone had been reworked to fit the vessel, protruding from the front of the ship like a second nose.

Sargoth lounged on the upper deck of the Leviathan, curled up between the main mast and the aftcastle, taking up a less room than a dragon his size rightly should. He reminded Elias of a cat, the way he curled up and watched everything. Elias descended from the top of the forecastle, and sat on a crate near the dragon's head.

"Six hours, and we're at war."

Sargoth shifted in place. "You're already at war."

Elias nodded slightly. "That we are. But this is what will end it."

"You're right. One way or another, this war ends."

Elias looked over at the dragon. "Are you worried?"

Sargoth chuckled. "Me? No. There are no weapons you or the pirates possess that can pierce my hide. I may have to live on these islands, but I'll survive."

"What about the Felle? They chained you once, they could do so again, and we know they're here."

Sargoth rolled his head to the side to look at Elias with one enormous eye. "I suspect that they *do* have the power to kill me, and that is exactly what they would have to do if they decided to try to put chains on me again."

Elias nodded again. "That goes for both of us."

Sargoth rested his chin back on the deck. "Jonas told me of your time in chains, in the belly of the ship. He told me much of you, of your time on these islands. I had heard some of the pirates speak of you, some of the slaves as well."

Elias sighed. "I suppose they would. What did they say?"

"They say you cannot be stopped. They say you cannot be killed. They say that you will do many great things."

"Do you believe them?"

Sargoth smirked. "Do you?"

"It is the way of dragons to answer questions with questions?"

Sargoth chuckled, his motions vibrating the deck planks. "What else did you expect?"

Elias shook his head, smiling slightly. "Gods, save me from the wit of dragons."

Sargoth sighed, and pushed himself up on his elbows, reclining on the deck. "My first question was serious, Elias. Do you believe that you cannot be killed? Because you can. Do you believe that you cannot be stopped? Because I could, conceivably, stick my claws through your stomach right now, and you would be stopped. You could lose this battle here today. If you do, your warriors would keep fighting, but they could lose."

Sargoth rolled, settling on his back. "And if they did, all of the elves on the big island of Greenreef would die, or be enslaved, or worse. Every island here would be a cursed island. The pirates, though few in number, would have a vast base with lots and lots of manpower available to them." He rolled back to his front. "A veritable pirate kingdom."

Elias slapped his hands down on his knees. "Then I suppose we can't let that happen. What is your plan during the battle?"

Sargoth shrugged. "Fly around, breathe fire."

"And if the Felle are present, and use magic?"

"Kill them first." Sargoth moved his head closer, and whispered conspiratorially, holding one clawed hand up as if shielding his words. "I don't know if you know this or not, but it's not the first time I've had to fight. I've faced mages and priests before. They all smell the same as they burn."

Elias stood up, patting the dragon on the neck. "This is true." He moved towards the forecastle, stepping past Sargoth's head. "I'm going to start putting on my armor... it takes some time."

Sargoth smiled. "I'm already wearing mine."

Elias couldn't help but smile. "Alright, smartass. We'll see you in action in half a day." He bowed slightly to Sargoth. "I'm going to prepare. Do you need anything?"

Sargoth rose to his feet, stretching. "I could use something to eat. I'm going to hunt some pigs. I will meet you at the Hollow Island in six hours."

Elias shielded his eyes from the rush of wind as the dragon spread his wings and launched himself off the deck, winging to the southeast. Elias caught himself as the ship rocked from the dragon's takeoff. Elias certainly hoped that Sargoth would be as much help in the coming battle as he thought he would... otherwise, this war was as good as lost.

~　　~　　~

The sheer cliffs of the Hollow Island loomed in front of them as they sailed towards it at full speed. Having never seen it before, Elias hadn't appreciated the sheer scale of the gates that had been built over the breach in the cliffs. They towered at least a hundred feet over the waves, with hinges so enormous that it defied logic. The tops of buildings could be seen over the crest of the cliffs, wood shingled and worn, but it was the armada in front of Elias that brought him the most worry; thirty-five ships sat broadside to them, many with cannons at the ready.

Most of them flew the banners of various pirate captains, but the third of them that were in front of the gate flew red flags with black eight-pointed stars on them; the banner of the Felle's ships, Elias assumed. He had never come across one of their ships before, so was not familiar with them, but the insignia matched the ones found on the fallen soldiers at Seagate and Port Greenreef, as well as the assassins that had attacked him and Coral at the beach and the handful of Felle soldiers that were aboard some of the ships.

The ships were black hulled, matching the rest of their color scheme, but their sails were striped red and black. One of the ships, the largest, had four masts and was nearly as large as the Leviathan, but was shaped more like the Iron Oar had been, sleek and fast. On the prow was the figurehead of a giant horned skeleton; whether it was painted white or made of actual bone, Elias couldn't tell at this distance. Its arms were outstretched, gripping the bowsprit, which was made to look as if it jutted out of the skull's gaping maw.

Elias and the rest of his fleet veered to starboard, putting the gathered pirate and Felle vessels to their left. One ship, the ship full of blasting powder, kept sailing true towards the gate. As he watched, he could see the few remaining sailors diving off of the ship, abandoning it to its fate. One of the ships tailing him slowed to pick them up; this had all been planned out ahead of time. Tao had insisted on being on that ship, to make sure that everything went according to plan. As well as an able bodied warrior, he was an adept sailor and commander of warriors. Nothing could go wrong as long as he was in charge.

Except for the black ships; they had not counted on them. They sprang forward with an unnatural quickness, and closed on the ship sailing towards the gate. If they sank it before it collided, then their hopes of breaching the Fortress were lost.

Elias cursed. Where was that dragon? Had he abandoned them? Had he played them all for fools?

The Felle ship in the lead, the giant one with the skeletal figurehead, closed on the Leviathan, changing its course, aiming to come alongside them. As it drew closer, Elias could see the deck was swarming with black clothed humanoids; whether they were men or orcs, he could not say at this distance.

Cannon fire opened up behind him as the first strikes were made. If only they had captured these weapons earlier in their campaign against the pirates... they would have lost far fewer ships. He looked back to see several ships locked in combat. The powder filled ship was under heavy fire as it hurtled through the gathered forces in front of the gates of the Fortress. Bits and pieces of the hull rained down on the water as it was blasted by cannons.

As Elias watched, a bolt of black energy hurtled down from the top of the gates, and struck the ship on the deck, knocking down the mast. There was a slight delay, then a deafening explosion, the force of which Elias felt, even as far away as he was. Hot wind assaulted the ships, along with a shockwave through the ocean and air that caused even the Leviathan to buck and heave in the water.

In the split second before the blast hit and knocked him to the deck, Elias could see an expanding white wall of vapor, and it was with this wall the shockwave hit them. Shards of obsidian thudded into the Leviathan's thick hull and mast, slashing small holes in the sails. A few of the warriors on deck cried out, having been hit by pieces of stone or debris.

The ship had been destroyed well before it hit the gates; they still stood firm. The ships that had been near it, however, had been completely obliterated. There was no sign of them, except the churning, surging surface of the sea. He didn't have time to do an accurate count, but by his estimation, Elias figured that at least ten of the ships facing them were destroyed.

Elias scrambled to his feet, struggling to maintain his balance on the heaving deck. He saw Marl clinging to the rail on the side of the deck, his staff in one hand, the other gripping a rope and belaying pin. Water began to rain down on them from the sea, having been thrown into to air by the explosion.

The large enemy ship that had been coming towards them had survived the explosion in relatively the same shape as they had, shaken but undamaged. They were no longer sailing at the same extreme speed they had been, but were more coasting along towards them, carrying on their course. Elias could read the name of the ship carved into the side; the Risen Dead. As they drew up alongside the Leviathan, Elias gave the command.

"Fire!"

The Leviathan had been outfitted with twenty cannons alongside her port, and they were all pointed at the enemy ship now. There was a moment's hesitation, but then the shots started ringing out, one after the other, growing in tempo until all twenty had fired their shots.

Shattered wood and planks were blasted from the other ship's hull as the attack ran along her starboard side, causing the black ship to shudder and groan. The Risen Dead returned fire with upwards of twenty cannons of her own. The cannonballs slammed into the Leviathan's hull, smashing through the sturdy timbers in a few places; the Leviathan's timbers were almost two hands thick, enough to repel most attacks.

A green bolt of lightning slammed into the enemy ship, playing over the deck like an electric stream of light, igniting the wet timbers as if they were dried parchment. Elias looked over to see Marl back on his feet, hanging over the edge of the ship, clinging to the rigging with his left hand, his right outstretched, clasping his glowing staff. It was from the end of his staff that the lightning came, in one long, continuous stream.

Elias had never seen the like before, and was dumbfounded. Before he knew it, the Risen Dead was sinking below the waves, its deck on fire, the flames green and hungry. They consumed wood and flesh indiscriminately with the same unnatural speed. He sprinted towards the helm, ducking under arrow fire from some of the nearer enemy ships, his own warriors gathering at the railing to return fire.

A great roar sounded from behind him, and he turned towards this newest threat. Coming in low, a bright, shining figure winged over the water. It was Sargoth, approaching from the east instead of the south, towards the gathered ships ahead of the Leviathan. As he flew closer, Elias shouted orders from the helm, piling on sail and veering to port, turning back towards the gate. Another roar overwhelmed the sound of battle, and Sargoth was upon the pirate vessels. They tried to scatter in front of him, veering out of his path. He flew past the nearest vessel, strafing it with a long blast of fire from his mouth.

Elias almost lost himself watching the dragon attack; it was a thing of awe to see such a beast in full combat. Instead, he returned his focus to the task at hand, breaching the gates. His initial plan had failed, so now the only hope was to manually scale the gates and open them from the inside. This was about to get very bloody, especially with the four or five ships between him and the gate.

"Elias! The cannons are ready to fire again!" Geoff's voice caught his attention. Just in time, as well, seeing as how a ship that had been seeking to get on their starboard side was now approaching their port, on the left. As they drew up alongside, he signaled Geoff, who bellowed the command into the bowels of the ship. As they passed the enemy, the cannons fired in almost perfect rhythm, the shots colliding with the pirate vessel in nearly the same place, almost directly amidships.

The ship broke in half, capsizing almost immediately under the force of the onslaught. It had been a smaller vessel, similar to the Slingstone in that it had no lower decks and no hold. The pirate archers had barely had time to loose a volley before their ship sank out from under them.

Ahead of him, the battle raged between his ships and the forces of the Fortress. Most of his forces were engaged in active combat, boarding other vessels and fighting on the decks of their own ships, as well as those of the pirates. It looked as though all of his ships were currently still afloat, while more than a few pirate vessels had fallen below the waves.

Sargoth landed on a boat ahead of the Leviathan and ripped into it, his tail smashing into the hull like an enormous flail while his claws ripped off planks like so much kindling. As he spread his great wings and lifted into the air again, he blasted the deck with fire as arrows rained upon him, bouncing harmlessly off of his scales.

A bolt of black energy from the top of the gate struck the dragon, causing him to falter and almost fall into the sea. He regained his balance, and rose into the air quickly, pushing himself away from the island. Another bolt of energy narrowly missed him, and the dragon circled higher, into the clouds.

Elias looked to where the black bolts had come from, and saw a tall figure on top of the gates, a flowing black cloak or cape blowing out from its back. It was too far away to make out any identifying features, but he could tell that it had its hand outstretched towards the dragon. "Marl! Marl, the gate! There's someone up there!"

Marl was by his side in an instant. He looked to where Elias pointed, and unleashed a torrent of green lightning at the spot the black energy had come from. The lightning crackled along his legs and arms, searing his skin where it passed, leaving trails of smoking flesh where it passed.

The bolt struck the stone near one of the hinges, blasting a small section of the cliff away. As soon as the stone started to fall away, Sargoth dove towards the island, tucking his wings in for greater speed, falling like a stone from a great height. He kept his mouth tightly shut, smoke trailing from his nostrils. As he closed on the gate, he unfurled his wings and flipped around, slowing his descent and coming in hindquarters first. He collided with the gate at a great speed, causing them to shake as he climbed up them. When he reached the top, he blasted the inside of the fortress with built up flame.

Marl fired another bolt of green energy, a battle cry ripping forth from him as the energy poured forth. It struck the gates near where the left upper hinge was anchored to the cliff, causing it to shatter and break free.

The gates, which were still supporting Sargoth, shuddered and listed inwards. Like some sort of great lizard, Sargoth crawled along the barrier towards the shattered hinge, and braced himself between it and the stone. In one solid wrench, he tore it completely loose from its moorings, and cast it down, into the sea. The shattered gate fell into the water, and promptly sank.

Boarding hooks grappled onto the railing near Elias, but he ignored them. The Leviathan was aimed directly at the new opening, and was sailing towards it at full speed. Any pirates looking to board this vessel would have to do so while it was in motion.

What he saw through the gaping hole in the side of the island was staggering. The inside of the sunken volcano was entirely lined with buildings built over the water level on scaffolding, and dozens of smaller ships were inside. All of the buildings along the north face were burning from Sargoth's assault. The buildings that weren't on fire were lined with men and orcs, all brandishing weaponry. As soon as the Leviathan was inside, Elias's warriors would be sitting targets for the Felle and pirate archers who were currently focusing all their attention upon the great silver beast perched atop their walls.

There was the sound of cannons being fired, and the wheel was shattered in his hands. Elias was thrown backwards from the impact, and another cannonball bounced off of the deck in front of his head, barely missing him. The Leviathan was under concentrated fire from several ships as she plowed through the floating wreckage of battle towards the vulnerable front of the pirate stronghold.

Several smaller ships were trying to make their way out through the opening as the Leviathan passed through, the sinking gates scraping the bottom of the hull. The ship that had been roped to her side was dragged along with her and brushed off against the rocks, crushing it to splinters. The hooks held fast and tore off the railing of the Leviathan, but were eventually clear of the great ship, while the smaller vessels were crushed under her keel like so much driftwood. The leviathan was a veritable juggernaut, despite the damage she was taking.

Elias clambered to his feet, moving to take cover from the arrows that would inevitably come. The wreckage building up in front of the Leviathan was slowing her, and they would come to a stop near the center of the open water in the middle of the island. Sargoth stayed at the top of the cliffs, prowling about and setting fire to the dry wooden buildings with his fiery breath.

There was a single great building built into the eastern cliff face, reminiscent of the lodge at Seagate that had been burned to the ground. It stood at least five stories tall, and looked almost as if an entire ship had been lifted up onto the craggy wall and stuck there as a foundation to build from. The roof was ablaze, but the lower levels were relatively sheltered from the dragon's onslaught.

On a balcony about halfway up, a familiar figure stood, looking down at him. Tall, broad shouldered, and covered head to toe in black armor, an enormous knight with the black star insignia of the Felle on its breastplate looked town at him. An equally gigantic greatsword was held in one hand, resting on the figure's shoulder.

The figure gestured, dissolving into a black shadow. The shadow hurtled through the air almost too fast for Elias's eyes to follow, and impacted the deck near the Leviathan's bowsprit. The ship shuddered as the shadow formed back into the armored knight.

Even with the entire length of the ship between them, Elias knew it was the same knight he had encountered almost a year and a half ago on the road from the Northlands to the coast. He dropped the harness that held his sword to his back off his shoulder, drawing his greatsword from its sheath as he left the aftcastle and jumped down onto the main deck. The dark knight leapt down from the forecastle as well, causing the ship to shudder again.

Geoff darted towards the knight from where he had concealed himself in the forecastle, longsword in hand. He was about to drive his blade into the dark knight, but without even looking, the figure swept his hand at Geoff as one would swat away a gnat, and he was knocked backwards into the forecastle door. The knight may as well have not even seen Geoff for all the attention he paid him.

Elias squared off with the figure, keeping his sword between them. "You followed me from the mainland, now here I am. Who are you? Tell me your name before I kill you!"

The knight reached up and removed his helmet. Strong, familiar features topped by long silver hair looked back at him with eyes that resembled mercury. Pointed ears poked through the silver strands, and though his eyes and hair were both gray, his face was youthful.

Elias's jaw almost dropped. This knight looked exactly like him!

Chapter Twenty-Five

6th Waxing Grain Moon, Year 4369

Elias gripped his sword, standing his ground. "What sorcery is this? Why do you have my face?"

The knight stepped towards him, causing Elias to step back. "On the contrary, Elias. You have *my* face. I'm here to take it back."

Elias gritted his teeth, moving to a more aggressive stance. "You speak in riddles and nonsense! Tell me why you're following me before I separate your head from your shoulders!"

The knight took another step forward, his blade pointed at Elias's right eye. "You were never supposed to be. Your power was supposed to have been mine, before you were even born. I am here to take it back. You're just a vessel to be drained, Elias." He gripped his sword in both hands. "Go ahead and fight back, or do not. It makes no difference."

Elias sprinted forward as cinders began raining down on them from the burning buildings. He swung his sword in a hard downward arc, cutting across the knight's body. Stepping back, the knight threw a horizontal slash that Elias barely ducked under, following the momentum of his own strike. Lunging forward, he reversed the direction of his swing, wrenching it free of the deck. His blade encountered the knight's crossguard, and he rushed in to strike him with his pommel. The satisfying *crack* as he connected with the man's jaw sent his opponent reeling back, breaking their grapple.

The knight kept his blade pointed at Elias while rubbing his jaw. "You've gotten better. Good. A more powerful soul means more power to take." Shadow flames began to rise up around him like before, spreading from where he stood out across the deck and along his blade. "You keep asking my name, Elias of Stromgard? My name is Darius Tessermyre, for what good it will do you." He returned his hand to the hilt of his sword. "I have already taken everything you have ever loved. Now it's time to take you."

Elias spat at him. "You talk far too much."

Tessermyre grinned, a somewhat fearsome expression on his face. "But you'll listen nonetheless. It was I who caused your mother's death." He started circling to Elias's left, and Elias circled to the right, matching him step for step. "We came from the same womb, you and I. We were supposed to be one soul. When we were born, your mother couldn't understand that I wasn't hers. When my true mother took me away, it broke her heart, and she couldn't survive the loss. She withered away and left you alone."

Elias snarled and launched himself forward again, hammering blows down at the knight, each of which was parried. When he came in for a powerful lunge, Tessermyre turned it to the side, and slammed his pommel into Elias's breastplate, knocking him to the side. The knight was insanely strong, moreso than anything Elias had ever encountered before. The knight laughed as he circled back again, looking for an opening to strike.

"Even when you found happiness here, I took that from you. You should have seen your woman's face when I took off my helmet. I've never seen so much terror and confusion in the face of one of my victims before."

Elias narrowed his eyes, gritting his teeth. "You killed Coral!"

Tessermyre paused in his steps. "Yes, I killed her. I killed her and I enjoyed killing her. But know this. I did not dishonor her. She had been despoiled before I came upon her." He lowered his blade for a moment, looking directly into Elias's eyes. "I revel in killing; there is nothing in this world that gives me greater pleasure. What happened to her had no honor." He lifted his swordpoint, keeping it oriented on Elias's chest. "I may want to kill you, and I have no compunctions about killing anyone close to you, but I had no part in what happened to her." He frowned. "What I did was a mercy."

Elias was no longer listening. His vision was red, his sight tunneled onto Tessermyre. An inhuman howl tore from his throat as he lost all control and attacked Tessermyre with a savagery born from grief. He swung his sword with both hands, his muscles straining under the exertion. Sparks flew from the blades as they clashed, the ringing steel barely penetrating his senses.

Tessermyre's confident face slowly changed into a frown, then gained a furrowed brow as he fended off Elias's frenzied attack. He reached out with one hand to grab at Elias's sword, but Elias was quicker and grabbed his first. He wrenched with everything he had, and tore the greatsword out of the knight's grip, kicking him in the breastplate. He threw the knight's sword away behind him, and advanced on the prone figure, who was pushing himself up on his elbows.

Elias raised his sword to strike Tessermyre down, but a bolt of dark energy struck him in the chest, hurling him backwards against the second mast and knocking the wind out of him, even through his breastplate. He gasped, trying to regain his breath as Tessermyre slowly rose to his feet. He stretched his hand out and another bolt struck Elias, crushing him back against the mast again, feeling like he had just gotten kicked in the chest by a horse.

Tessermyre retrieved his sword as Elias gasped, slumping against the thick mast.

"I had wanted this to be cleaner, but if I must destroy you with the power of the Abyss, so be it." He raised his hand as if he was holding a sphere, and Elias was lifted off of the deck, a crushing grip tightening around his neck. "Either way, little brother, we'll be one once more." He stepped closer and knocked the sword out of Elias's nerveless hand. "Just let it happen, let go, and your suffering will end." Tessermyre's voice was deep, soft, not unlike his own. He could feel the edges of his vision start to fade as he struggled for breath.

There was a loud *zap*, a whooshing sound, and the smell of ozone. Elias dropped to the deck, able to breathe again as a green glow faded away. Tessermyre was staggering backwards, clutching his scorched breastplate, looking towards the aftcastle. He lifted his hand towards the new threat, black flame gathering around his gauntlet, but another bolt of green lightning struck him, spinning him to the side and knocking him to the deck. He lay there, motionless, his sword fallen to the ground a few feet from him.

Marl was at Elias's side as he regained his senses. His skin was scorched and charred, the blue skin burned deeper, almost black. He shook Elias, forcing eye contact.

"Elias! Elias, get it together! Get up!" The seer hauled on Elias, trying to lift the giant to his feet.

Elias clambered upright, steadying himself with a hand on the mast. He rolled his shoulders, his bruised chest and neck protesting the motion. His sword lay on the ground between him and the fallen knight, and he cautiously retrieved it while keeping an eye on Tessermyre.

Marl leaned heavily on Elias and approached the knight with caution. The magic the seer was using took an enormous toll on his body, and though he was strong, he was fading fast. Elias stood over the knight and lifted his sword to deliver the final blow.

Tessermyre rolled suddenly, blasting dark energy out of both hands, into both Elias and Marl, sending them staggering back. Elias's armor protected him, absorbing most of the shock, split between him and Marl as it was. He swung hard, whipping his sword upwards, and grazed Tessermyre's face with the point, tearing a gash across one of his eyes. The energy slacked off, and Tessermyre clapped a hand over his face, cursing in a language Elias had never heard before.

The ship shuddered as a great weight struck it. It was Sargoth, landing on the deck just behind Elias. He lunged in to snap at the dark knight, but struck only shadow and flame. The dragon cast about, looking for his quarry, and spotted him atop the eastern cliff face, looking down at them. Before he could take off to pursue him, Tessermyre vanished again, a burst of black fire spreading in a radius from where he had been standing, annihilating a small building that had been next to him.

Elias ran to Marl. He had landed on a pile of rigging next to the stairs that led to the top of the aftcastle. Geoff was crouched next to him, attending to him in earnest. A large, ragged hole in his side oozed dark blood where he had been hit by Tessermyre's shadowy assault, and a bloody belaying pin lay next to him. Elias could see Marl's innards through the wound, peeking out through the hole.

The old sea elf's breath came short and shallow, blood tingeing his lips. His eyes were closed, but his reactions to Geoff's ministrations showed that he was still very much conscious. Elias knelt down next to him across from Geoff.

"What can I do? How can I help?"

Geoff shook his head. "You can't. All I can do is try to stop the bleeding, but he glanced off of the rigging rail, and that pin punctured his lung."

Marl chuckled slightly, bloody spittle flecking his lips and chin. "It's fine, master Geoff. Don't waste those supplies on me. Even if you could heal these wounds, I would not live to see the morning." He looked up at Elias, his shockingly white eyes shot through with red. "The gods demand their price, and they will not be shorted their dues."

Elias cradled the shaman's head in his large hand. "Marl, I'm sorry. I tried to kill him, but he got away."

Marl shook his head weakly. "We knew he would. This way, at least, I can go to my girls. They wait for me in paradise, under the branches of the great tree of bounty." He closed his eyes again. "I just pray that they can forgive me for what I have done." His eyes opened again, dimmer than they were before. The red flecks were spreading, covering his irises. "You know what you must do now. Pursue him. Find the scourge that killed our women, and make him feel the pain they felt."

Marl took Geoff's hands in his, stopping the young medic from ministering to his wounds. "No, Geoff. Let me go."

Geoff looked up at Elias, and he nodded, letting Marl's head rest back against the pile of ropes. After a few more ragged breaths, Marl's chest stopped moving, and his wounds stopped bleeding as quickly. Geoff shook his head, cursing quietly as Elias set his hand over the shaman's eyes. Marl's line had been completely wiped out.

~   ~   ~

The city inside of the island was in complete ruins. All of it burned – Sargoth had seen to that. There had been stores of blasting powder near the docks inside the Fortress, and as the store rooms burned, they went off one at a time, bringing sections of the thin cliffs down into the water.

Some of the ships that remained at the eastern side of the island reported that they had seen a black ship with an enormous skeletal figurehead rise out of the water – tattered and beaten, but floating nonetheless – and flee to the east, faster than any of them could sail. Elias guessed this to be the Risen Dead; it was no doubt brought back to the surface by the dark magic that Tessermyre has used to escape.

The pirate vessels had been completely routed, either burned and gutted or ripped to shreds by the dragon and cannon fire. Elias's fleet had suffered significant losses, but emerged victorious with the help of the dragon and Marl's magic. They sailed around the island, battering the remaining cliffs with cannon fire while Sargoth breathed his dragon fire against the bases. By their third pass, the walls had begun to slump and drop into the ocean. By the fifth pass, only jagged remnants stuck up above the water, no more than twenty feet at the highest. Never again would this island be used for evil.

The sun was just beginning to set as Elias and his remaining eight ships set sail for the Cursed Island. Jenna and Jonas had remained on the cannon line during the fighting but now oversaw the makeshift repairs to the Leviathan. Other ships fared better or worse, but of those still afloat, none were in immediate danger of sinking.

Tao and Martin took charge of directing the remaining ships and overseeing their repairs. Tao, who already didn't speak much, hadn't said a word since he was told of Marl's death. His connection with his warriors seemed almost telepathic, with them approaching him, asking him questions, and interpreting his nods and pointing as directives.

The night on the beach was a cold one. The villages had all been burned to the ground, so there was no shelter on the north end of the island. They worked in shifts through the night to repair the vessels to the point where they could sail to Rapa Matomato, using what wreckage they could find to fix the damage. Throughout the night, debris from the battle washed up on the shore, providing plenty of wood, and each ship carried some material for repairs anyways, providing plenty of pitch and planks to repair their hulls.

The Leviathan had a wealth of such materials, as well as a few specialty parts. Her rudder had been damaged, as well as her helm, but there were the necessary materials to repair them in her hold. By the time they were done, they had emptied the third deck entirely, which made plenty of room for Sargoth to lay down in. He was slender enough to tuck in his wings and climb through the cargo bays; it would be a functional, if not terribly comfortable room for his usage on the voyage back to the mainland.

By noon the following day, they were ready to sail again. Bodies had started washing up on the shore along with the wreckage; they had to depart before the decay set in, and disease started to spread. Each ship was captained by the most experienced sailors the sea elves had to offer, except for the Leviathan. Jonas took her helm, with Elias, Jenna, Martin, and Geoff on board. Elias maintained command, but Jonas wanted to be the one to pilot the ship.

Elias sat at the head of the large table in his quarters, Jenna to his right, Geoff and Martin to his left.

They sat in silence while they sailed, the sounds of the mariners on deck barely audible through the open windows at the aft of the ship.

Jenna leaned back in her chair. "So you've defeated the pirates."

Elias shook his head. "I didn't defeat them. I didn't defeat anyone. Not a single person. The warriors of the islands defeated them. You defeated them. *We* defeated them. I did not do this alone."

Geoff rested his elbows against the table. "When they write songs about this battle, Elias, whose names will be in them? Who will the stories be about for generations to come? You're so damn hung up on the semantics."

Elias shook his head. "I know that they will be about me, but I'm not the one who did it. I was just the figurehead. And if it was all my doing, then I am also the reason why thousands of elves died. I am the reason that Coral and Marl and Jayd are dead. I'm the reason Delain died."

Martin swallowed the bite of bread he was chewing. "Bullshit."

Elias quirked a brow. "Excuse me?"

Martin shook his head, and took a swig from a flagon of ale. That man always seemed to be eating or drinking something. "Bullshit. You didn't hold a knife to our throats. You didn't order us to do anything. You didn't force any of us to sail or fight with you. You showed us all what the right thing to do was, and because you showed us, we did it."

Jenna nodded. "If you hadn't forced everyone to stop sitting on their asses, then yeah, many would have lived. Many would not have died." She kicked her boots up on the table. "Many of those who would have lived would have been pirates. Many who died would have done so under the lash, instead of with a bow or a spear in their hands."

Elias nodded. "This is very true. I couldn't just sit idly by and let that happen."

Geoff drank from his own cup of wine. "Well, four centuries of elves did just that. That in and of itself means that you're a cut above. You did what tens of thousands of warriors and a dozen chieftains before you couldn't do... you united the islands and drove off the pirates for good."

They were silent again for a while before Jenna spoke up again.

"So what now?"

Elias lifted his mug of wine to his mouth and drained it. "Now, we sail to Port Greenreef, and finish the repairs to this ship and the others. I'll be taking the Leviathan back to Jetty, along with anyone who wants to come with me. Once there, I'm going to hunt down Darius Tessermyre and put his head on a pike."

Martin nodded appreciatively. "Seems fair."

Geoff nodded as well. "Aye, that's about right."

Jenna sighed. "You realize that he's probably joining up with his Felle army buddies, and will not be alone, right?"

Elias shrugged. "We just fought one army on boats. I can't imagine it would be any harder to fight another on land. Plus, we wouldn't be alone either."

She lifted an eyebrow. "Oh really?"

Elias shook his head. "No, we wouldn't. There's more than a few warriors on these islands that have no reason to stay, especially with their villages burnt. Some may wish to stay and rebuild, and I wish them nothing but the best. But there are some who want to leave and never come back. I'll offer them passage with me, a place in my camp, and Felle soldiers to rest their spears in."

He set his mug down gently on the table. "The Lonwick army should still be fighting the Felle, if they're still battling, and the men of the North know me. They seldom turn down a good fight, especially if there are spoils in it for them."

Jenna furrowed her brow. "What spoils?"

Elias gestured towards a chest near his bed. "That chest and four or five others are filled with gold. Just like you, I've gotten my share of the take from the pirates, as well as the bounties. I've had little reason to spend it, so it just kept piling up." He shrugged, pouring more wine from a carafe. "To be honest, it's been an irritation to keep storing it and moving it. I'll give it all to them if they fight for me, as well as anything they capture from the Felle. Steel, horses, whatever."

Martin drained his mug of ale. "And just like that, they'll fight, like mercenaries?"

Elias shook his head. "No. Not just like that. I'll have to convince an old friend, but I think he'll come around to it."

He stood, pouring a large flagon of ale. "I'm going to see how Jonas is holding up." He picked up the flagon and his own cup, and walked out of his quarters, headed for the helm. Jenna rose to go with him, but he held up his hand. "I want to talk to him alone."

She paused, then slowly sat back down as he closed the door. The stairs leading to the top of the aftcastle were steep, but traversable even with both hands full. The helm was situated just to the left of center on the ship, so as to keep the way forward visible to the helmsman. Jonas stood at the wheel, stoic and silent, one hand resting on the wheel and the other on his hip. His black hair, streaked with more gray than it had been upon their meeting, blew slightly in the sea wind as they sailed, the setting sun at their back.

Elias handed Jonas his flagon of ale without a word. Jonas took a long, slow drink, keeping his eyes on the sea ahead of them. Smacking his lips appreciatively, he nodded his thanks. "That was a good brew, it was."

Elias sipped from his cup of wine. "How goes the voyage?"

"We're making excellent progress. The wind is strong and at our backs, the sea is calm. It's almost like those gods you spoke with are speeding our voyage."

"Well, that wouldn't surprise me."

Jonas nodded again. "Nor I."

They stood in silence for a moment, Elias looking out over the ships in his small fleet. They had lost a large number of ships in the last month, more than half, and all hands with them. What was left was a very small remnant of what had once been a powerful force. The population of the islands had been severely depleted.

"Once the Leviathan is repaired fully, I'm sailing for Lonwick."

"I know."

"I'm going to hunt Darius Tessermyre down and kill him."

"I know."

Elias turned his head to look over at Jonas. "I'd be honored if you would come with me."

Jonas grimaced, and drained his flagon. "What the hell do you mean by that? Of course I'm coming with you. You think you could get rid of me that easily?"

Elias shook his head, smiling slightly. "I'd never dream of it, my friend."

Jonas held out his flagon towards Elias. "You'd better not, and if you do, you'd better wake up and apologize. You're stuck with me for a bit."

Elias chuckled and took the vessel from Jonas. "More ale?"

"Nah, lad. I remember one smart-mouthed little whelp of an elf that once told me I drink too much."

Elias looked down into his cup. "Whatever happened to that elf?"

Jonas was quiet for a moment. "I hear he died, not long ago, on a beach, near a woman he loved." He set his cup down on the base of the helm. "You're not the same lad that I met on the road to Fairhaven."

Elias leaned against the railing, and watched as they passed by Ahi Maunga. "So," he said, changing the subject. "You and Jenna. How long?"

Jonas rubbed the back of his neck ruefully. "I honestly don't know. Women have a different way of measuring these sorts of things than men do." He dropped his hand back to the wheel. "I figured it to be a two or three months. That was when she bruised my jaw for looking at a sea elf lass."

Elias laughed. "Then I'd figure it to be at least six."

"Aye, seems about right." He sighed. "I'm a bit long in the tooth to be starting a family. Never figured I'd live long enough to do it."

Elias looked down into his mug. "I'm going to be honest, Jonas, none of us have that guarantee. Where I'm going, I expect to see a lot more death."

Without looking, Jonas reached out and patted Elias on the shoulder. "Don't worry. I'll be there to pull your bacon out of the fire before it burns."

Elias set his hand on the man's shoulder as well. "I know you will." He reached out and took the wheel. "Go ahead, go inside and get something to eat, warm up. I'll steer for a while. Get some rest."

Jonas took his flagon from Elias and headed down the stairs from the aftcastle. The giant elf stood at the helm, steering the giant ship across a giant ocean. In the far distance, dark clouds gathered at the horizon. With the wind at their backs, the storm would most likely be pushed away as they sailed towards it. It wasn't enormous, but if they did happen to sail too close to it, they would have to anchor near one of the islands.

Lightning flashed from the clouds to the water, barely visible. Elias counted off the seconds as he waited to hear the thunderclap. Almost half a minute later, the faint rumbling could be heard. Yes, there was definitely a storm brewing, in more ways than one.

ABOUT THE AUTHOR

A father, husband, writer, and gamer, Brandon Cornwell resides with his family in the magical Pacific Northwest. Majestic redwoods, breathtaking mountains, and pristine beaches lend themselves to his creative process to bring his writing to life.

Always passionate about reading and learning, Brandon started collecting books at a young age. Among them were the works of Jules Verne, Charles Dickens, and more, but it was the work of J.R.R. Tolkien that really captivated his imagination. As he grew older, his collection became dominated by works of fantasy, and by the age of eleven, he had decided that his dream was to become a published author.

Now, more than twenty years later, he is pursuing his dream in earnest with the release of the first trilogy in the series Dynasty of Storms. See more of his work or dive into his world at his website, www.brandoncornwell.com

Did you like what you read? Please, leave a review on Amazon! Stories are written to be shared, so tell your friends!

www.ingramcontent.com/pod-product-compliance
Lightning Source LLC
Chambersburg PA
CBHW030902060726
47591CB00005B/1378